YANKEE DOODLE'S COUSINS

YANKEE DOODLE'S COUSINS

ANNE Burnett MALCOLMSON

Illustrated by

Robert McCloskey

Houghton Mifflin Company · Boston

The Riverside Press Cambridge

'72 1 0 2 6 4

2-80

The Riverside Press
CAMBRIDGE · MASSACHUSETTS
PRINTED IN THE U.S.A.

main rep.

For E. L. B.

Preface

TO many of us who teach school the recent upsurge in national feeling has posed a problem. This new consciousness of the goodness of life in America is inevitable and healthy. Never has there been so much need for an awareness of democracy and its blessings as in these tragic days. But how can we help our beloved ten-year-olds to an affectionate pride in their country?

To a youngster who, for his own good, must live under an authoritarian government-by-decree, whether of parent or teacher, 'democracy' is very difficult to understand. To a child whose personal geography is limited to a countryside or a city neighborhood, America as a nation is something incomprehensible.

The English youngsters are lucky in their national heroes. They have King Arthur and Beowulf and Robin Hood to fight for, each in his own way outrageously congenial to the ten-year-old world. Our children have George Washington and Abraham Lincoln, whose heroic qualities, magnificent as they are, are essentially adult qualities. The Lone Ranger is more at home in the imagination of a fifth-grader than is either of these more worthy gentlemen.

Fortunately there is no need for frantic invention on our part. We have a tremendous fund of American tradition and folk literature on which to draw, but until recently it has been denied its proper place in the cultural sun. We teachers who have been educated in the East are too much in the habit of looking to England and Europe as the source of all literary merit, and have snubbed American folk literature as 'rough-neck,' or at best given it the doubtful honor of being considered 'interesting local color.'

The few stories which have risen above the snubs to become American classics are grand to read aloud to children. Unfortunately, because of rhetorical style and 'literary' vocabulary, most of these make 'tough going' for the child who tries to read them to himself. Even the Uncle Remus stories, told in dialect, demand a mature reading skill.

Within the past twenty years the American scene and the American idiom have come into their own in literature for adults. There have been a number of excellent books and plays about our national folk heroes. Older boys and girls have been introduced to the giants of the New World. But for younger children there is still a lamentable lack of reading matter that presents traditional American lore without apology or condescension.

The yarns that have grown out of young America belong to children, as much by right of sympathy as by right of heritage. Paul Bunyan and Pecos Bill are ten years old at heart. Their humor, their wildly romantic exaggerations, their quixotic naïveté, their lack of self-consciousness, and their hard-headed adaptability to circumstances — all these are qualities of the average fifth-grader.

When Mike Fink yells, 'I'm a Salt River roarer! I'm a ring-tailed squealer!', he's a blood brother of the bantam-weight quarterback who warbles, 'C'mon, men, let's mow 'em down.' He's the blood brother also of one Robin Hood who invited the Bishop of Hereford to dine on the king's venison and made him dance for his dinner.

But to get back to the problem of making America and the things it stands for come alive to the fifth grade, I can't help thinking that one way of going about it is to introduce a few of our Yankee heroes to their descendants. Paul Bunyan's Real Americans can help our children identify themselves with the working, democratic, industrial civilization that is America.

This collection of stories is by no means an answer to the problem. The only virtue it may have is that it's an attempt to present a scattering of Real American heroes in a book which younger children can read to themselves. Instead of collecting material at first hand throughout the country, I've done most of my research in the files of the Library of Congress, picking other people's brains. So far as possible, I've tried to acknowledge my debts. And these are legion.

I should like to make grateful acknowledgment —

To Paul R. Beath for permission to use material from 'Febold Feboldson';

To Josef Berger for permission to use the story of 'Ichabod Paddock' from his book 'Cape Cod Pilot,' published by the Modern Pilgrim Press, Provincetown;

To C. E. Brown for permission to use material from his book 'Paul Bunyan and Tony Beaver Tales,' Madison, Wisconsin;

For the story of 'The Golden Cities of Cibola,' which is adapted from the original in Hallenbeck's 'Legends of the Spanish Southwest,' by permission of the publishers, The Arthur H. Clark Company;

To Mr. J. Frank Dobie, of the University of Texas, for permission to use his material about the 'White Mustang,' and for permission to use material from the article 'Jean Lafitte,' by E. G. Littlejohn, published in The Texas Folk Lore Society Publication, No. III;

To Doubleday, Doran & Company, Inc., for permission to reprint the first and last stanzas of the 'Stormalong' ballad from 'Iron Men and Wooden Ships,' by Frank Shay;

For the use of material from 'The Hurricane's Children,' by Carl Carmer, copyright, 1937, adapted by permission of Farrar & Rinehart, Inc., publishers;

To the Nebraska Writers' Project for permission to use material about Antoine Barada and The Gran Quivira from 'Nebraska Folklore';

For the quotation, 'Sunrise in His Pocket,' reprinted from 'Davy Crockett,' by Constance Rourke, by permission of Harcourt, Brace & Company, publishers;

To Mr. Lucien Harris for permission to use material contained in the stories of 'The Tar Baby' and 'The Deluge,' from 'Uncle Remus, His Songs and Sayings,' by Joel Chandler Harris;

To Henry Holt & Company, Inc., for permission to use material from 'Mike Fink,' by Blair and Meine;

For material which has been adapted from 'Paul Bunyan,' by James Stevens, by permission and special arrangement with Alfred A. Knopf, Inc., authorized publishers;

To J. B. Lippincott Company, of East Washington Square, Philadelphia, Pennsylvania, for permission to use the stories of 'The Gift of Saint Nicholas,' adapted from 'American Myths and Legends,' by Charles M. Skinner, and 'Why the Negro Works Harder than the White Man,' from 'Mules and Men,' by Zora N. Hurston;

To Longmans, Green & Company, Inc., for permission to retell the story of 'The Mule Humans,' from 'Tall Tales of the Kentucky Mountains,' by Percy MacKaye;

Preface

To the University of North Carolina Press for permission to use material from 'John Henry,' by Guy Johnson;

To the University of Pennsylvania for permission to use material from 'Minstrels of the Mine Patch,' by George Korson;

To Albert Whitman & Company, of Chicago, Illinois, for permission to use material from 'Pecos Bill,' by James Cloyd Bowman;

For permission to retell the stories of Stormalong and Kemp Morgan from 'Here's Audacity,' by Frank Shay; copyright, 1930, by him;

To Miss Margaret Gaskill, for her generous advice on problems of reading level and vocabulary;

And, of course, to my husband, for his patience during dull winter evenings when his wife was trying to be an 'author.'

Contents

THE EAST

THE SOUTH

THE MISSISSIPPI VALLEY

Contents

THE WEST

The East

John Darling

I

MANY, many stories have been told about the Erie Canal. Of them all, the one I like the most is the story of John Augustus Caesar Darling. John Darling probably had many other impressive names. But his friends called him John for short.

He wasn't much as a little boy. He lived on a farm in upper New York State. He helped his father feed the pig and milk the cow. In the spring he went into the maple woods and helped hang the sugar buckets on their hooks. He pitched hay in the summer and gathered apples in the fall. That is about all we know about him then.

But as he grew older he became more interesting. He was about eleven years old when he first became important. His father sent him out to the field. He hitched the team of steers to the old wooden plow. As he moved up and down the furrow, he sang himself a song — a song that he loved dearly

'I've got a mule and her name is Sal,
Fifteen miles on the Erie Canal.
She's a good old worker and a good old pal,
Fifteen miles on the Erie Canal.'

It was a long song, with more verses than you can count on the fingers of your right hand. Sometimes the verses changed. Sal wasn't always a mule. She was occasionally a cook, 'the very best cook on the Erie Canal.'

As he sang to himself and to the steers, young John Augustus Caesar dreamed of the future. Some day he would own a boat. He would ride up and down the Erie Canal, like a king on his barge.

All of a sudden, John woke up from his dream. He stopped singing. Right ahead of him loomed a big stump, at least six feet high. It was too late to turn away. Already the oxen had passed it, one on each side. Here were John and his plow, about to be stuck on the stump.

John Darling shut his eyes. He whipped his oxen and they pushed ahead. The old plow went right through the stump, with John after it. Yes, the stump split in two as clean as a whistle. John could hardly believe his eyes. He turned around to take another look at the stump. Just as he did so, the two halves rose up from the ground and fitted themselves together.

Now, things like that don't happen to a plain ordinary farm boy. John Augustus Caesar Darling rubbed his eyes. He went back and felt the stump to make sure. There it was, as solid as a brick wall. Only magic could have done such a thing.

His family laughed at him when he told them what had happened. They didn't believe it at all. John himself, however, knew that he had had a sign. Some day he would be an important man. There was no doubt in his mind about that.

The following summer his remarkable powers were proved to his family. Mr. Darling, his father, noticed that the roof was leaking. He put the boys to work whittling shingles

2

John Darling

from pine boards. Then he propped a ladder against the side of the house. It was John's job to nail the shingles to the roof.

Unhappily, the weather was bad. A fog had rolled over the whole of upper New York State from Lake Ontario, as thick as pea soup. Even so, John put on his raincoat and climbed the ladder. He climbed to the very top and carried his shingles with him. One by one he fitted them in place and nailed them together.

All day long he worked. Shingle upon shingle, he hammered until the roof was finished. He had, in fact, made a whole new roof. He couldn't see it all at once to admire it because the fog was so thick.

When he climbed down again the sun came out and chased away the fog. Then John discovered his wonderful mistake. He had hammered the shingles together twenty feet above the ridge-pole of the house. There hung his roof in mid-air. He had laid it on top of the fog.

As a grown man, John Darling first went to work as a 'sugarbush' man. In other words, he had a stand of maple-sugar trees. He loved to go out into the woods and to tap the trees when the sap began to run. Into each he inserted a short pipe, and under each pipe he hung a bucket. Then, when the sap had collected in the buckets, he took them home. He boiled and boiled until his kettles were sticky with delicious maple syrup.

He was particularly fond of maple syrup on buckwheat cakes. All winter long he had his favorite dish for breakfast. In the spring he cut off his long beard. His first wife used to collect his whiskers and boil them down in the big kettle Usually she boiled out several gallons of syrup that had stuck to the beard during John's breakfasts.

3

The thing that finally discouraged him from the maple-sugar business was the mosquito. As you know, mosquitoes love sweets. They used to hover around Darling's maple trees. They were as large as airplanes. Their buzz-buzz-buzz sounded as loud as the hum of a sawmill. They stung the farm hands when they came to collect the sap. They stung even John himself.

At last John thought of a way to be rid of them. His sap pans were large iron kettles. Into one of these he put some pure maple sugar. Then he turned it upside down under one of his trees. He hid himself inside, his big hammer in his hand. Sure enough! The mosquitoes smelled it. They came from miles around to nibble at the sugar. But the iron kettle was in their way. Buzz-buzz-buzz! They put their stingers to work. They bored through the iron of the kettle until they reached the soft sweet sugar beneath it.

John was too smart for them. As each stinger bored through the iron, John came up with his hammer. He flattened the mosquito's bill against the inside of the kettle.

Within an hour all the mosquitoes were safely fastened to the sap pan. They were so angry they buzzed like a hangar full of planes. But there was nothing they could do about it. At last they lifted their wings and off they flew. They took John Darling's sap pan with them, firmly fixed to their bills.

Before long, John Augustus Caesar Darling tired of farming. The 'Erie Canal' song ran through his head until it nearly drove him mad.

> 'Low bridge, everybody down!
> Low bridge, for we're going through a town,
> And you'll always know your neighbor,
> You'll always know your pal,
> If you ever navigated on the Erie Canal.'

John Darling

You can see for yourself how John must have felt. As he followed the plow he couldn't help singing, 'Low bridge.' Even the steers thought he was a little silly. There wasn't a bridge anywhere near the cornfield.

At last he couldn't stand it any longer. He sold his farm and his sugar trees and went to Albany. There he bought himself a canal boat, a beautiful boat. He painted it white and named it the *Erie Queen*. He fitted up the captain's cabin with his favorite possessions. This was a home after his own heart.

John filled up the hold of the *Erie Queen* with shoes and watches and plows and started off for Buffalo. His old horse plodded along the tow-path, pulling the boat. Sometimes John walked beside the horse smoking his pipe. Sometimes he sat on deck in the sun, his big face shining with pleasure.

It was perfectly all right for him to sing the Canal song now. After all, you don't feel silly bawling out, 'Low bridge, everybody down,' when there is a low bridge ahead of you.

Up and down the Canal slid the *Erie Queen*. When she reached Buffalo, John unloaded his watches and shoes and plows. He sold them to the pioneers who were moving west into Ohio and Indiana. Sometimes he sold them to the captains of the Lake ships. They took them even farther west, up through the Great Lakes to Wisconsin and Minnesota to the Swedes and Norwegians.

When John had sold his wares, he bought others. From the Lake captains and Western farmers he bought lumber and coal and hay. Then he and the *Erie Queen* headed back to Buffalo. Here he sold his cargo to the Eastern merchants.

Back and forth, back and forth, from Albany to Buffalo, back and forth moved John Darling, as happy as a king. He

stopped at the locks to chat with the lock-keepers while they raised his boat into a higher level, or lowered it into a lower one. He knew all the other boatmen by name. He swapped stories with them.

One of the stories was about a boatman who had taken his barge down to New York Harbor. There in the harbor he had found a dead whale. He mounted the whale on his barge and scooped out the inside. He cut windows through the ribs and propped the mouth open to make a door. The whale's interior was fixed up as a cabin. People came flocking to see the boatman's prize. He charged them two pennies apiece to look around inside. Soon he was very rich.

To cook his meals John Darling hired a young woman named Sal. He claimed she was the original 'Sal' of the song, 'the very best cook on the Erie Canal.' She made buckwheat cakes that were as light as goose down.

She was more than a good cook, however. She was a remarkable woman. Sal was over six feet tall, freckled, cross-eyed, and twenty-three years old. She was indeed a daisy. Furthermore, she had red hair, so red it outshone the glory of the sunsets. It glowed like a whole cluster of fireflies. In fact, on dark nights, John had Sal sit in the bow of the boat. He used her for a headlight.

Before long, John Darling was completely in love. The only thing he needed to make his happiness perfect was Sal. Sal, however, had many other beaux. Every boatman, every lock-keeper was in love with her, too. Whenever John asked her to marry him, she said, 'No!'

At last he persuaded her to give him a chance. She arranged to hold a contest. All the Canalmen were great fishermen. On quiet afternoons they liked to trail their fishing lines over the sides of their boats. Often they caught enough pickerel or perch for their suppers. Sal agreed that she would marry the man who caught the most fish on a certain day.

All her other suitors, of course, were told about the contest. They fixed up their fishing tackle. They brushed their beards and combed their mustaches, and put on their best store clothes. On the proper day they came together at the meeting place.

The contest began at midnight and lasted until the following midnight. Twenty-four hours in which to catch a bride!

John Augustus Caesar Darling, handsome in his new suit, sat at the bow of the *Erie Queen*. Up and down the Canal, as far as one could see, were the boats of his rivals. Each of the men held a fishing line in his hand.

Unfortunately, the other suitors had good luck. They reeled in their lines, one after another, until their decks were piled with fish. Poor old John had not a nibble. He jiggled his fishing pole, but nothing happened. He sat perfectly still. Nothing happened. By noon he had not a fish to his name.

By sundown the other suitors were growing tired. They had been hauling in bass and perch all day long, and were ready to quit. Most of them gave up and started to count their catch. But not John. He sat on the deck of the *Erie Queen*, sadly holding his fishing pole. His big tank was still empty. Not a fish.

Meanwhile, Sal had been watching the contest from the bank. She saw John and his empty tank. She felt sorry for him, because she really wanted him to win.

As soon as it was dark she climbed aboard his barge. John was surprised to see her. Her beautiful red hair shone like the tail of a comet. It lit up the whole Canal.

This gave John an idea. 'Put your head over the side,' he

8

John Darling

said softly to Sal. She did as he told her. The light from her hair gleamed out across the black water to the other bank. In its path swam a school of fat black bass.

The fish were attracted by the light. They acted like moths around the flame of a candle. One by one they jumped into John's boat. They didn't wait for him to catch them on his line.

'Now put your head over the other side,' John whispered to Sal. He was afraid to startle the fish. There, in the path of the light, swam a school of pickerel. One by one they, too, jumped out of the water onto the deck of the *Erie Queen*. They didn't even wait to be invited.

With Sal's help, John Darling soon had his hold full of squirming, fine fish. The decks also were piled high with them. When at last the village clock sounded midnight, he and Sal were knee deep in perch and bass and bullheads.

The judging took place in the courthouse. The other Canalmen swaggered in with their catches. Each was sure that he had won Sal's hand. Imagine the dismay when John came in. The judges counted his fish. Without any question at all, they had to admit that he had won the contest. Sal tried to look surprised when he claimed her. But everyone could see that she was more pleased than surprised.

They were soon married. John Darling took his bride to Niagara Falls for their honeymoon. When they returned to the *Erie Queen*, the neighbors gathered and gave them a big party. They had songs and dancing and a fish fry and maple syrup and buckwheat cakes. It was a great success.

From then on, John's happiness was complete. He used to sing out his favorite song at the top of his lungs. People two miles away could tell he was coming when they heard him shout, 'Low bridge, everybody down.'

Yankee Doodle's Cousins

He changed the verse a little, though. Instead of singing,
'I've got a mule, and her name is Sal,' he sang,

> 'I've got a wife, and her name is Sal,
> Fifteen miles on the Erie Canal.
> She's a good old worker and a good old pal,
> The very best cook on the Erie Canal.'

The Gift of Saint Nicholas

2

THREE hundred years ago in the little city of New Amsterdam lived a young cobbler named Claas. A fortunate young fellow indeed was Claas. He had a lovely brick house with a garden, a big pond full of fat white geese, a thriving trade, and a pretty wife whose name was Anitje. He had worked hard for these blessings from the first bleak day when he landed on the shores of the New World, an orphan boy from Holland. He now was a rich man, rich enough to ~~wear~~ own eight pairs of breeches at once.

The only dark cloud in his sky was Roeloffsen, the burgomaster, an old miser who had long been in love with Anitje. As the richest old bachelor in the town, he had expected her to marry him without any question. When she married the poor cobbler boy, the burgomaster's pride was hurt. He swore that he should have his revenge. Whenever Claas and Anitje walked out in their Sunday clothes, with their family of fat Dutch children toddling behind them, he hid behind the heavy curtains of his house and said terrible things.

At last his ugly thoughts were put into deeds. He taught the village blacksmith to make hobnails for the townspeople's boots. These nails made a dreadful racket as they clattered over the brick streets. But they kept the boots from wearing out. The boots wore so long that poor Claas had very little business as a cobbler. He had a very hard time of it to make ends meet.

This was not enough for the black-hearted burgomaster, however. Claas and his Anitje still lived in their fine brick house and walked out on Sundays in their handsome clothes. Roeloffsen had to think of something else.

Soon he knew what to do. As an officer of the city he ordered a new street to be built. This street ran right through the middle of Claas's pond. The city builders came and drained the pond. Poor Claas had to sell his beloved geese. This was a great blow to him, because the eggs he sold at the marketplace helped make up for the boots he was unable to sell.

But this was not the worst of it. As Claas sat by his fire sorrowing for the loss of his geese, he had visitors. These were men from the city council. Since the road ran through his land, they said, he should pay for its building. They demanded fifty pieces of gold for this purpose. Fifty pieces of gold! That was all Claas had tucked away in his teapot.

Claas and Anitje had to work harder than ever to keep their family fed and clothed. They sold vegetables from their little garden and managed to make themselves a fair living. Then came the jealous burgomaster. He built another road, through the middle of Claas's garden patch this time. Once again the poor cobbler had to rob his teapot of the vegetable money in order to pay for this road.

And so it went. Every time Claas made a little money, the

burgomaster built a new road and made him pay for it. Before long, he had to sell his fine house. No longer could he afford to wear eight pairs of breeches, nor Anitje her twelve petticoats. The little family was poor. They had sold all their belongings except a bare few. They lived in a miserable little cottage with only a dirt floor.

The wicked old burgomaster at last was satisfied. He danced with joy when he saw how low the cobbler had fallen. This would show the people of New Amsterdam that no orphan boy could outdo the wealthy Heer Roeloffsen!

On Christmas Eve, as the burgomaster was enjoying his fine dinner, Claas and Anitje and their children sat huddled before the fireplace in their little cottage. The very last log burned on the hearth and gave out little heat at best. Their cupboard, like Old Mother Hubbard's, was bare. After their supper of bread and cheese, not a crumb remained. A poor Christmas this would be. No presents, no blazing fire, not even a dinner!

Of all their possessions, only two treasures remained. One was the Bible which Claas's mother had given him long ago. It was bound in beautiful leather and held shut with silver clasps. Claas was tempted to take off these clasps and sell them. They might bring him enough money to provide a Christmas for his children.

No! said Anitje. To sell the clasps from a Bible would be wicked. He should never think of doing such a thing. Better it would be to starve than to feast on the sale of holy things.

The other treasure which remained was a pipe. This was a special, lovely pure meerschaum pipe which to Claas had a magic meaning. As a little boy, leaving his home for the New World, he had found the pipe in his stocking. Where it had come from he could not tell. He was sure it was a present from the good Saint Nicholas himself.

The thought of selling this treasure nearly broke his heart. Even so, it was better than the thought of selling his mother's silver clasps. He reached down into the family chest and took out his beloved meerschaum. Sadly he rubbed it against his trousers and watched it gleam in the firelight.

As he rubbed it the cottage door swung open and a blast of cold air filled the room. There before the fire stood a fat little stranger, about three feet tall. He was dripping with snow, and icicles hung from his shaggy eyebrows and his long white beard.

'Br-r-r!' muttered the stranger crossly. 'It's a wonder you wouldn't answer the door when a traveler knocks. Fine manners, I must say, on a night like this!'

All thoughts of the pipe were forgotten as Claas and Anitje stared at their visitor. The children scrambled to hide under the bed. Only their bright blue eyes shone out from behind the curtains.

'Well, come along! Come along!' went on the visitor, growing more angry every minute. 'Don't stand there! The least you can do is to put another log on the fire so that I can warm myself. Can't you see I'm half frozen?'

'I-I-I-I'm very sorry, sir,' admitted Claas, finding his tongue at last, 'but there is no other log to put on the fire. You're very welcome to warm yourself at our poor hearth.'

'Well, then,' snapped the stranger, 'send one of those ragamuffins out to the woodshed. I'm freezing, I tell you!' He glared at the children, who pushed themselves farther back under the bed hangings.

'Oh, sir!' cried Anitje, 'if only we had more wood in the

shed we would gladly fetch it for you. But, alas, this is our last stick. We have no more to keep ourselves warm.'

'Humph!' snorted the little fellow. 'That's very careless of you. But what must be, must be.' With that he cracked the fine cane he carried over his knee. It broke into several pieces. These he tossed onto the coals. As they struck the fire, something wonderful happened. Each of the pieces of the cane changed into a big birch log. The dark coals blazed up and soon the room was dancing with the light of a huge fire.

'That's better,' muttered the stranger. 'Upon my life, I thought I should turn to an icicle for all you cared.'

The children crept out from their hiding place to gape at the magic blaze. Claas and Anitje rubbed their eyes.

'And now, I suppose, you're going to let me starve to death, too!' sneered the visitor, looking in the direction of the cupboard. 'It's a wonder you wouldn't invite me to have some supper. I haven't eaten since this morning.'

Tears came to Anitje's eyes. 'Oh, sir, whoever you may be, we should indeed be happy to give you our last crumb. But,' she sobbed, 'we have nothing to eat in the house. We ate our last scrap of cheese for our evening meal.'

'That was certainly rude of you,' barked the funny little man. 'Here I come, after a hard day's tramp over the mountains, through wind and rain and snow! You say you have no fire to warm me! You say you have no bread to feed me! My dear lady, I know better. Your shelves are heaped with cakes and apples. And if that's not roast goose I smell cooking, I'll eat my beard!'

Without thinking, the whole family stopped to sniff. Why, they did smell roast goose! And cabbage and onion and mince pie and pumpkin! These delicious smells were fairly bursting from the oven door. They looked quickly at the cupboard. Its shelves were groaning under bowls of apples and pears and platters of cakes and cookies. The water jug was filled to the brim with sweet cider.

'Don't stand there, don't stand there like a forest of trees!' shouted the stranger. 'Can't you see I'm dying of hunger? Get me something to eat and be quick about it. No food, indeed! Why, there's a whole feast in that oven. Put it on the table.'

Not knowing whether to be overjoyed or frightened, Claas and Anitje set the table and drew it before the fire. They opened the wide door of the oven. There indeed were the goose and the vegetables and the pies they smelled.

At the sight of the richly spread table, the children forgot their shyness. Hungrily they feasted. But none of them ate so much as did their visitor. Time and again he passed back his plate for another drumstick. An ordinary goose has only two legs, but this one sprouted a new one whenever the little man passed his plate.

When at last the fat little stranger had had enough and the buttons had begun to burst from Claas's coat, the table was cleared away. No longer did the visitor snap angrily at his hosts. He leaned back in his chair and lit his pipe. A twinkle appeared in his eye and he patted the children's blond heads. For an hour he sat talking pleasantly with the happy family, telling strange and marvelous stories of distant lands. But not once did he tell them who he was.

At the stroke of midnight he got up from his chair. 'I must be off!' he exclaimed. 'Thank you indeed for a pleasant evening and a delicious dinner.' He turned to Claas. 'Don't ever sell that pipe!' he shouted.

With that, a gust of wind down the chimney filled the

whole room with smoke. Before the family could open their smarting eyes again, the stranger was gone without so much as a good-bye.

In the morning Claas was awakened by a great hammering at his door. There was Burgomaster Roeloffsen and a party of soldiers. 'We have come to arrest you!' they screamed. 'You are a wizard, a witch, a magician. You are a disgrace to the city of New Amsterdam.'

Poor Claas didn't know what to make of it. Why should anyone call him a wizard? He was nothing but a poor cobbler who had had a lovely dream.

'Come!' roared the burgomaster. 'Open the door and let us in. We shall have no wizards in our city!'

As he slowly awakened, Claas looked about him. The wretched little cottage had disappeared. He was standing in the hall of a great house. The walls were hung with silks, and from the cupboards shone silver platters and copper bowls. He looked timidly out of the window. Around him spread wide lawns and gardens and in the distance glimmered the ice of a huge pond.

'Open up, I say,' bellowed the burgomaster. 'Open up in the name of the law. We have come to take you to jail as you deserve.' Claas opened the door. In poured the soldiers.

'Aha!' screamed Heer Roeloffsen, his face red with anger. 'Seize him! Seize the witch! He has not only changed his cottage to a fine estate. He has filled his chests with gold.'

Before the astonished Claas the burgomaster lifted the lid of a chest. The great box was full to the top with pieces of money.

'You thief! You robber! I'll...' But before he could finish his sentence, a pair of invisible hands clapped themselves over his mouth. More hands which could not be seen grabbed

The Gift of Saint Nicholas

the soldiers. Then came an awful whacking and thrashing as the unseen arms paddled the burgomaster and his party with unseen switches.

'Ouch! Help! Stop it!' yelled Roeloffsen. But the paddling went on. The soldiers ran down the path to the main road and headed away from town, crying and yelling and trying to defend themselves from the blows of the unseen paddlers.

That was the last ever seen of the jealous burgomaster. Claas and his family lived on in their fine new home, never wanting for food or warmth. How their good fortune had come they did not know. The only clue they had was a piece of paper slipped under the door. It said simply, 'Don't ever sell that pipe.'

Captain Kidd

3

FAR out on the ocean wanders a ghostly ship, its sails shimmering in the dark of night. Sailors have seen it often, and have heard the sad howling of the wind through its rigging. Sometimes when the wind is right they can hear the mournful song of its unhappy captain, who paces the deck bemoaning his fate.

> 'Oh, my name was William Kidd, when I sailed, when I sailed,
> My name was William Kidd, when I sailed.
> My name was William Kidd,
> God's laws I did forbid,
> And so wickedly I did, when I sailed.'

On and on he sings, verse after verse, telling the whole grim story of his life.

In 1695 Lord Bellomont called Captain William Kidd into his office in London. Shortly before the noble lord had received the King's message. He was to be the new governor of the colonies of New York and New England. It was his job to rid the seas of pirates and French privateers who

preyed on the trade between the New World and the Old.
He needed able men, of course, to help him carry out his
orders. Who was more able to do this than the famous Captain Kidd?

For many years Kidd had sailed the seas in His Majesty's
service. He was known as one of the best shipmasters on the
Atlantic. Furthermore, he had already captured a number of
privateers in the French wars. Lord Bellomont was certain
that he had made a good choice.

But the captain hemmed and hawed. After all, fighting
pirates was a dangerous thing to do for a living, and he had
his wife and children to think about. They were waiting for
him in his fine home in New York. How he longed to see
them! Captain Kidd was no ordinary buccaneer; he was a
peaceful, home-loving citizen.

Lord Bellomont tried everything he could think of to persuade the captain. He mentioned the honor and the glory
that would be his. He begged him to think of his duty to his
king. Still the sailor said, 'No.'

At last the new governor, who had made up his mind to
have Kidd, called in the Lords of the Admiralty. They had
the final say. Unless the captain would agree to fight the
pirates, his ship would be taken from him and he would be in
disgrace. This was too much for William Kidd. He had to
say 'Yes.'

When Kidd arrived once more in New York Harbor in a
fine new ship *Adventure*, the whole town turned out to meet
him. Lord Bellomont, who had crossed the ocean before
him, was there to welcome him as a hero. The people
shouted and waved flags in his honor. On the dock stood his
wife and children, proud of their husband and father.

The glory could not last, however. As soon as he had

Captain Kidd

fitted his ship with supplies for a long voyage and had signed on an extra crew, Captain Kidd had to set about his business. Up and down the coast he sailed, looking for his enemies. The pirates, who had heard of his coming, had all run for cover. Not a buccaneer could he find!

He set his sails for the West Indies and prowled in and out among the islands, still looking in vain for pirates. Back and forth across the Caribbean, along the Spanish Main where they liked to prey on treasure ships, he hunted them. But the unhappy captain was out of luck. No pirates!

He became homesick, thinking about his family in New York. The crew became bored, thinking of the buccaneers that didn't show up. Tempers began to snap on board the *Adventure*. To keep his men from quarreling, Kidd sailed across the Atlantic and around Africa to the Indian Ocean. This was another favorite place for the Jolly Roger, the black flag of the ocean robbers.

But in the Indian Ocean he couldn't find what he was looking for. Kidd had permission from the British Government to attack the French, because the two countries were at war. Not even a French ship sailed across his path.

At last a caravel showed itself across the horizon. Without waiting for their captain's permission, Kidd's crew got ready for battle. They were tired of sailing without capturing anything. Here came a fleet of ships, full of treasure from the Indies, waiting to be captured. Poor Captain! It was the British East Indian fleet, bringing gold from the colonies to the mother country. He had no right to attack his own country's navy.

Nevertheless the crew opened fire. They had no chance against so many ships, but all they cared about was a chance to fight someone. Before nightfall they had to run for their lives. They had captured none of the treasure. All they had gotten was the bad name of 'Pirate.'

From then on, things went from bad to worse. Here was Kidd made a pirate against his will!

Some weeks later the *Adventure* met the *Royal Captain*, another British ship. Captain Kidd knew that word of his attack on the gold fleet would soon reach England. He had to do something to clear his name. So he invited the officers of the *Royal Captain* on board his ship and entertained them with a fine feast. He was going to explain to them what had happened.

But while the officers of the two ships were dining together in a friendly manner, the crew of the *Adventure* once more rose against their master. They tried to capture the *Royal Captain*. In his anger Kidd threw a bucket at William Moore, the ringleader of the mutineers. It struck him on the head and the surly sailor fell to the deck, dead.

The other ship got away, but even so Kidd was in a pickle. He was not only a pirate, he was a murderer.

Instead of giving himself up to the British Navy and explaining what had happened, Captain Kidd ran away to Madagascar. This great island off the coast of Africa was a hotbed of piracy. In her ports lay the very ships Kidd had started out to catch. From their masts floated shamelessly the Jolly Roger. Swarthy, cruel-faced men with gay clothes and gold ear-rings swaggered through the streets. They boasted openly of the prizes they had taken, and no one paid any attention to them.

What a pleasant life these bandits seemed to lead! They had money in their pockets, and chests full of silks and jewels in their cabins. They feasted like kings on foods and wines brought from the four corners of the earth.

Captain Kidd

Culliford, the worst robber of the oceans, was in port when Kidd arrived. He was the very one Lord Bellomont had been most anxious to capture. Many a British man-o'-war had he sent to Davy Jones's Locker. But Kidd did not arrest him. He had dinner with him, instead. When the party was over, unhappy Captain Kidd hauled down the red, white, and blue flag of Great Britain and hoisted the black skull-and-bones of the pirate. He had become Culliford's partner.

For several years the new sea-robber roamed the Indian Ocean. He captured a large Armenian trader, the *Quedagh Merchant*. She was much larger than the *Adventure*, with more room for loot in her hold; so he sent her crew to the bottom, moved his crew and his treasure aboard, and set fire to his own ship.

To all outward appearances, Kidd was now a true pirate. He preyed on any ship that crossed his path, regardless of her flag. Proudly he flew the Jolly Roger, and ran into port in Madagascar to feast and swagger with his new friend Culliford. But at heart he was sad. He longed to see his wife and his children. He thought often of the sorrow he had caused them, of the shame they must feel for his disgrace.

His crew, too, bloodthirsty as they were, were growing tired of the pirate's trade. The *Merchant's* hold was full of gold. Why shouldn't they return to their homes? Each of them had money enough to live in luxury for years to come.

So Kidd started home. He sailed first to the West Indies. Here he planned to send a message to Lord Bellomont, explaining his misfortune and begging the governor's forgiveness. He thought he could say that the ships he had captured were French, and everything would be all right.

Little did he know what lay in store for him! No sooner had he reached the West Indies than he learned the truth.

The British Government had set a price on his head. He was not only a pirate, he was a murderer in their eyes. He could hope for no forgiveness from Bellomont or from anyone else.

In spite of this turn of affairs, he decided to take a chance. He bought a little sloop, the *Antonia*, and put aboard her a small part of his treasure. The remainder he left on the *Quedagh Merchant*, in charge of his chief officer, and ordered her into a secret cove to hide out until his return. Then he took the *Antonia* north.

He stopped first in Delaware Bay. This seemed to be a safe harbor in which to bury some of his treasure. Hardly had he placed a chest in the ground, however, before a party of passers-by noticed him. They recognized him at once. They set off for Philadelphia to warn the colonies that Kidd had returned.

He dared stay at anchor no longer. He moved to Long Island Sound. Here the *Antonia* hid each night in a different cove, while Kidd tried to reach Lord Bellomont. He managed to have his wife brought to him under the cover of night. She was broken-hearted by the notices which proclaimed her husband an outlaw. She was sure he was an honest man and promised to help him return to the governor's favor.

Nevertheless Lord Bellomont refused to see him and to listen to his story. If Kidd set foot on American soil, he should be arrested as a common thief. This was all the governor would promise.

Then the captain tried a different line. He picked out the finest silks and jewels in his chest and sent them to Lady Bellomont. Perhaps they would soften her heart and she would plead for him with her husband. Alas for Kidd! Lady Bellomont kept the jewels, but she refused to help him.

Captain Kidd

After many weeks, word came that the governor would see him. Bellomont had gone to Boston. If Kidd would come to him there, he would listen to the pirate's tale.

Light-hearted, Captain Kidd sailed to Boston. Dressed in his finest he walked up Beacon Street to the governor's offices. Alas! He never reached them. The message had been a trap. Before he knew it, he was in chains, bound for London and the Execution Dock.

The Lords of the Admiralty gave him no mercy. Like any common outlaw he was sentenced to death. Up over the Thames River, from which he had sailed proudly six years before, swung his body — a warning to would-be pirates.

Very little of his treasure was ever found. Some people believed for a time that he had buried it in the sands of Long Island and Cape Cod. But all the hardy souls who tried to dig it up were frightened away by strange ghosts who screeched and moaned and flapped their pale arms at the diggers. Strange Money-Lights, little balls of fire which rose from the earth, kept away others.

All that was left of the unhappy captain was his ghostly ship and his song.

> 'Farewell, the raging main, I must die, I must die,
> Farewell, the raging main, I must die.
> Farewell, the raging main,
> To Turkey, France and Spain,
> I shall ne'er see you again, I must die.'

Joe Magarac

4

STEVE MESTROVICH worked at the open hearth in the Hunkietown steel mill. For an old man he was very strong. He boasted that in his youth he had been the strongest worker in the steel counties.

The pride of his life, however, was his daughter Mary. Mary's eyes were as blue as cornflowers. Her hair was as blonde as molasses taffy. On Sunday afternoons, all the young men of Hunkietown came to call on her.

As her friends knew well, Mary was in love with Pete Pussick. But in the custom of Slovakia, from which Steve had come, a girl had nothing to say about her marriage. Her father decided that for her. It had always been that way.

Steve, of course, wanted Mary to be happy. But it never occurred to him that she might wish to pick out her own husband. Furthermore, he had once sworn a solemn vow that his son-in-law would have to prove himself the strongest young man in the Allegheny Valley.

On Mary's seventeenth birthday, her parents decided it

was time for her to have a husband. Steve made his plans. He invited the steel workers from all the Pennsylvania mills to come to a party. He sent his invitations to Homestead and to Bethlehem and to Johnstown, as well as to Hunkietown.

He sent to Pittsburgh for the refreshments, for soda pop and ice cream. Mrs. Mestrovich baked pies and cakes until her kitchen was full. Steve collected the materials for the contest. The prize, of course, was Mary.

The party took place on Sunday afternoon. All the Hunkies came dressed in their best clothes. But none of them compared with Mary Mestrovich. She looked like a queen. She sat on a raised platform. She wore a beautiful red-and-green silk dress bought in the store. Over her head was draped a lace scarf brought from the Old Country by her Slovak grandmother. Her dainty brown fingers sparkled with glass rings.

At the stroke of two, Steve announced the contest. There were to be three rounds. In each round the suitors were to take turns lifting a dolly bar. A dolly bar is a long heavy bar of metal. Anyone who failed to lift the dolly off the ground had to drop out.

The guests cheered their favorites. The young Hunkies rolled up their sleeves. Steve blew the whistle.

One by one the lads bent over the heavy dolly and tugged. The Hunkietown boys raised it easily enough. But one of the Johnstowners and a couple of Homesteaders had to drop out.

'Go sit with the women,' sneered the boastful winners at the unhappy losers.

The second dolly was much heavier than the first. Only three men were able to lift it — Pete Pussick, Eli Stanoski, and a man from Johnstown.

These three had still to lift the third dolly, which was much heavier than either of the others.

First the Johnstown fellow tried — in vain. Eli took his place. He pulled and pulled, but for all his straining he couldn't lift the bar. Then came Pete. The crowd cheered and cheered. It was obvious that he was going to be the victor. Mary blushed with pleasure.

Pete puffed and struggled in vain. He managed to get one end of the dolly about an inch off the ground. Try as he might, he couldn't lift it up all at once.

Poor Pete! No prize for him! Poor Mary! No husband for her! And poor Steve! No son-in-law for him, after all his planning and boasting!

Someone in the back of the crowd began to laugh. It wasn't a sneering laugh at all. It sounded like the deep, quiet bubbling of molten steel in the furnaces.

To the astonishment of all, there stood a giant. None of the Hunkies had seen the like of him before. He was seven feet tall if he was an inch. His blue eyes were as clear as a baby's. They twinkled as he grinned at the gaping people. If he hadn't been so large, he would have been a very pleasant-looking fellow.

The crowd parted as he stepped forward. He stooped over the third dolly bar and, with one hand, lifted it over his head and twirled it around as though it were a light cane.

'Hurrah!'

'The winner!'

'He's won!'

Everyone shouted as the big fellow flipped the dolly into the air and caught it behind his back. Steve rushed forward to congratulate him and to find out who he was and where he came from. The giant stood there grinning until the noise died down. Then he told his story. His name was Joe Magarac, he said.

'Joe Magarac!' The Hunkies began to snicker. In the language of the Old Country, 'magarac' means jackass.

'Sure, Magarac, Jackass, that's me,' Joe said. Once again he laughed his deep, bubbling laugh. 'Eat like a mule and work like a mule. That's Magarac.' The Hunkies knew then and there that they were going to love this big fellow, whoever he was.

To their surprise he opened his shirt and invited the men to tap his chest. One by one they cracked their knuckles on his skin and winced with pain. The giant was all steel, not flesh and blood like other men — just hard, cold steel.

He was born in the heart of the iron-ore mountains down in the core of the earth. He had lain there for centuries until a miner stumbled on him and told him about the great world outside. Then he had come down from the hills to work in the steel mills.

While he was telling his tale, Mary sat shuddering. The thought of being married to a steel monster frightened her. When her father explained to the newcomer that he had won himself a wife, she nearly fainted.

But Joe Magarac set her at ease. 'A wife?' he asked. 'What can Magarac do with a wife? Eat like a mule and work like a mule, that's all I want. Let me work in your mill, and let Miss Mestrovich marry Pete, who is the strongest man here except me.'

So Mary and Pete were married with everyone's blessing. Joe was given a job tending open hearth Number Seven in the Hunkietown mill.

What a steel worker he turned out to be! He stayed on the job day and night. He lived, if you could call it that, at the

Joe Magarac

Hunkietown boarding-house. The landlady said he was certainly right about his name. He had five meals a day, and at each of them he ate more than any mule she ever saw.

The bosses agreed that he worked like a mule, too! Men came from steel mills all over the country to see him — from Gary and Pittsburgh and Birmingham and Youngstown. It was a pleasure to watch him. He was a whole crew in himself.

First he gathered the raw materials, heavy chunks of ore, pieces of scrap iron, great blocks of limestone, and dumped them into the furnace. Then down on hands and knees, he blew steadily on the fire until it had been fanned to white heat. He didn't bother with the big bellows the ordinary Hunkies used.

When the mass inside had melted down, Joe would sit in the door of Number Seven and with his long steel arm he would stir the mixture round and round and round. Not even the best of the regular workers could stand the fierce blast from the open hearth. But Joe liked it. He sat there stirring for hours without even perspiring.

As soon as the steel had cooked, he poured it into the ingot mould. Then came the part he liked most of all. As the golden mass cooled, Joe grabbed it in his hands as you might take a piece of hot candy at a taffy pull. Handful by handful, he squeezed it between his fingers. Through each slit oozed out a perfect steel rail.

Magarac enjoyed squeezing out rails, eight at a time, so much that soon the mill yard was stacked with them. He was like a baby with a new toy. The foreman suggested that he take a rest now and then. But Joe grinned and shook his head and kept on squeezing. Soon the piles of rails stood so high the mill itself was hidden from view. The company couldn't sell rails as fast as Joe Magarac made them.

Yankee Doodle's Cousins

The bosses met and sighed over their problem. They decided to close the mill for a week. They didn't like to do it, but there seemed no other way to clear the yard of all Joe's rails.

So the foreman came to Number Seven and told Joe about it. He explained that the fire was to be checked and stoked to burn at low heat. Thus it could be rekindled easily when the mill opened again. The steel giant said nothing, but tears of disappointment gathered in his eyes. He sat down in front of his hearth and shook his head sadly.

The following Monday the mill reopened. The salesmen had been busy. Most of Joe's rails had been sold and shipped away. Only a few small piles were left in the yard. The other firemen poked their fires and fanned their flames. But no one tended Number Seven.

Where was Joe Magarac? They looked high. They looked low. They sent search parties all over Hunkietown. But no trace of the giant could they find.

In the midst of their search, a low bubbly laugh rang out from Joe's old furnace. It grew louder and louder. It sounded as though the furnace was having a good joke all to itself.

The startled Hunkies rushed to Number Seven and looked in. There in the center of a pool of molten steel as golden as sunlight was the grinning head of Joe Magarac. His eyes snapped and twinkled as he called for the foreman and the bosses.

When they came running, Joe explained what he had done. He said he was broken-hearted when the mill shut down. Work like a mule! That was all he knew how to do. And if he couldn't work — well, an empty mill was no place for him!

So, after he stoked his fire, he crawled in on top and melted himself down. All week long as he was cooking, he was thinking. A great thought had come to him.

He asked them to do as he told them. As soon as he was cooked through, they were to mould him into great beams and girders, which would be the purest steel in all the world. Then they were to tear down the old building and around Number Seven they were to build a new one out of these new steel beams. He told them where each rivet was to be placed. This new mill, he said, would be the showplace of the steel industry. There would never be a finer one.

As he finished speaking, his head sank below the surface and all that was left of the great steel giant was the sound of his bubbling laugh.

His instructions were followed to the letter. By spring the new mill was finished. The company declared a holiday and a big party was arranged for the dedication.

As part of the ceremony, they had a contest of strength for the young men. Pete Pussick won. But this time the prize was not Mary Mestrovich. It was the honor of tending open hearth Number Seven in the Joe Magarac mill in Hunkietown.

The Ghost of Dark Hollow Run

5

MAYBE you don't believe in ghosts. Hans didn't either. But it was a ghost that caused his sad adventure in Dark Hollow Run.

Hans was a poor orphan who lived in Holland almost two hundred years ago. He used to watch the big sailing ships in the harbor at Amsterdam. They came from the English colonies in America. The one thing he wanted more than anything else was to go there.

He had a dream in his head. If only he could get across the ocean, he'd have a fine farm and pretty wife and a family of fat blond children. What more could anybody want? But Hans was poor, too poor to pay for his passage.

One day the captain of a sailing vessel came to him. He said he knew a Dutch farmer in the colony of Penn's Woods. The farmer was rich, but he needed help. If Hans would promise to work for him for seven years, the farmer would pay for his passage to the New World.

Hans almost cried for joy. He signed the papers promising to do anything the farmer asked. Almost before he knew it, he was on the ocean.

On board ship was a pretty Dutch girl named Neltje. Neltje, too, was an orphan. Like Hans she had promised to work for her passage. By the time he reached Philadelphia, Hans was head over heels in love. Of course he was happy when he found out that Neltje was going to work for the wife of his own master. He made up his mind that as soon as their seven years were up, he'd marry Neltje. His dream would come true.

It wasn't long before Hans had learned all about his new job. Farmer Klaus was a kind man, but he worked his servants as hard as he worked himself. Hans had to milk the cows and paint the big red barn and thresh the wheat and carry the water. Although he had been born in the city, he soon knew all the tricks of a big Pennsylvania Dutch farm.

He learned other things, too. The farm servants told him stories about the countryside. One of their favorites was the story of the haunted schoolhouse.

Not far from Farmer Klaus's acres ran a brook which was called Dark Hollow Run. For about a mile it ran through a little ravine, where the trees formed an arch overhead. In the summertime the ravine was very dark.

Here in Dark Hollow stood a crumbled ruin that had once been a village school. Only the walls were standing. Grass grew up where the children used to sit.

Many years before, the farmers had hired a young schoolmaster from Connecticut. He was a stern young man. He sat at his big high desk and scowled at the pupils over the

The Ghost of Dark Hollow Run

rims of his spectacles. When anything went wrong, he had only one cure. This was a stout birch rod.

He whipped the boys for teasing the girls. He whipped the girls for teasing the boys. He whipped them all for not knowing their lessons. He whipped them for asking too many questions. Sometimes they thought he whipped them to amuse himself.

One warm spring afternoon as the schoolmaster sat scowling at his desk, a bird flew in the open window and perched on his head. He looked so funny that all the children laughed. They giggled and snickered and laughed out loud. They knew the master would be angry. But they just couldn't help it.

They were right, of course. The master was very angry. He picked up his birch rod and whipped all the students. But when he came to the biggest boy, his rod wore out. It had been used so often it broke in half.

This made the schoolmaster more angry than ever.

'Stay in your seats,' he raged. 'I shall cut myself a new rod, and then we'll start at the beginning again. Wicked children! To laugh at your schoolmaster! I see I shall have to beat some sense into your stupid heads.'

With that he strode out the door to the woods to cut himself another birch.

But when he had left, the children left, too. They formed themselves into a double line, led by the biggest boy. They walked out the door and never were seen again.

The schoolmaster returned with his new birch to find an empty schoolhouse. He ran about the county looking for his pupils. The farmers ran after him, blaming him for the disappearance of their sons and daughters.

Of course, no one wanted to use the school building after

that had happened. So a new house was built nearer the village, and the old one fell into disuse. On stormy nights, ever after, the stern schoolmaster returned to walk up and down the Dark Hollow, his birch in his hand, waiting for the children to come back.

But to get back to Hans! When he heard the story he only laughed. Some of his fellow servants believed it. Wild horses couldn't drag them into the ravine on a dark, stormy night. As we said before, however, Hans didn't believe in ghosts.

Neltje heard the story. She was a little frightened. When Hans laughed at her and said he would protect her, she felt better. They often used to walk through the Hollow when their chores were done. Hans would joke about the ghost, and dream about the farm he and Neltje would have some day.

All the farmhands liked Neltje, however. By the time six of his years were over, Hans began to be worried. He had to admit that he had too many rivals.

One morning Farmer Klaus called Hans to him. He had grown very fond of his big Dutch servant. He trusted him completely. He said he was sorry that Hans would soon be leaving him to make his own fortune. As a gift, Farmer Klaus promised to give him fifty acres of good river-bottom land to farm as soon as the year was over.

But since Hans was still his servant he asked him to take the wheat to the mill and to be back by suppertime with the flour.

Hans's hopes and dreams flew sky high! Fifty acres of good black land — all his own! He must tell Neltje of his good fortune. When she heard about it, she would surely pay no attention to the other fellows. She would have eyes only for him.

But the mill was a long ride and he had to be off. He had no chance to talk to her before he left. So he stopped only to ask her to meet him in the ravine at sunset.

He set off for the mill with the bags of wheat in front of him. His old mare plodded along happily in spite of his clucking and kicking. Hans whistled and sang. His heart was as light as a feather pillow.

As he rode down the Hollow, he looked lovingly at every stone and every tree. He tried to imagine how Neltje's eyes would shine when he asked her to marry him and share his fifty acres. He tried to picture her sitting beside the schoolhouse in the late afternoon sun, waiting for him.

He laughed as the horse splashed through the water when they forded the brook. By the time he reached the mill his face was as flushed and shiny as an apple.

The miller was a jolly old man. But he was slow. He didn't like to hurry. He liked to sit at his door and smoke his pipe and talk with the farmers who brought corn to be ground. There were several farmers at the mill when Hans arrived. Since he was only a servant, he had to wait his turn.

It seemed to be hours before the miller got around to him. By the time his grist was ground, and the bags of white flour had been sewed up and tied securely to the saddle, the afternoon sun had nearly sunk behind a bank of black clouds.

As the clouds crept higher, Hans grew more nervous. He thought of Neltje waiting beside the schoolhouse. He kicked his heels into the old mare's sides, but Molly wouldn't trot.

Still the sky grew darker and darker. Hans could see the

tops of the trees bending in the distance as the storm moved closer. Finally, just as he reached the ford across the Run and entered Dark Hollow, the storm broke.

The wind whipped through the ravine like a tornado. Poor old Molly, who had refused to trot before, took to her heels and galloped down the road. Hans lost his hat. His long blond hair streamed out behind him.

Then came a flash of lightning and a clap of thunder. It sounded as though it had struck right under Molly's feet. The mare shied and Hans had to throw his arms around her neck to hang on for dear life. The flour bags broke open. Soon Hans and Molly were covered from head to foot with the white powder. Then came the rain.

Meanwhile, Neltje was waiting in the schoolhouse. At first she was only impatient when her beau didn't come on time. Then the black clouds closed in over the Hollow and she became frightened. The old ruin was no place to seek shelter in a storm.

As she sat there shivering, she thought of the schoolmaster and his ghost. She heard the wind z-zinging through the branches. It was only the wind. But to Neltje it sounded like the schoolmaster swinging his birch rod. She heard the first big raindrops falling on the leaves. They were only the raindrops, but to her they sounded like the slow footsteps of the schoolmaster's spirit.

Then came the storm. Neltje sat huddled in a corner, soaking wet, and crying as though her heart would break. She was angry at Hans. She was afraid her mistress would scold her. She was wet and cold and miserable.

And now, above the noise of the storm, she heard something else. A horse's hooves were rushing up the Hollow road. It was Hans, of course!

The Ghost of Dark Hollow Run

She ran to the door of the schoolhouse to meet him. She swore she would forgive him for everything if he would only take her home.

But what did she see? Instead of Hans and lame old Molly, here came a terrible monster. It was galloping toward her like a ghost on horseback. It was white, all white and scary. The awful creature on the horse's back was waving its wild white arms at her.

She couldn't hear what it was yelling. She didn't stop to listen. All she could think of was the ghost of the schoolmaster, riding a horse, and coming to get her.

She took to her heels and ran as fast as she could back to Farmer Klaus's home. Several times she stumbled. She couldn't help looking back. There was the wild white monster riding after her. The faster she ran, the faster it followed and the louder it yelled.

She reached the farmhouse just as the ghost clattered into the barnyard. With a frightened shriek she fell into the kitchen and fainted.

When she came to her senses, Farmer Klaus was laughing. He was laughing so hard his eyes were full of tears. He was holding his sides to keep from splitting.

And on the porch stood Hans, her fellow servant, looking mournfully into the kitchen. His face and clothes were streaked with white flour paste. In his hands he held two empty flour sacks. He was trying to explain that what she had seen was not the schoolmaster's ghost, but him and old Molly.

Farmer Klaus thought the joke so good that he forgave his servant for losing the grist of flour. At the end of the year he kept his promise and made Hans the present of the fifty acres.

But not so Neltje. She didn't think the adventure funny at all. When her year was up she married the village carpenter. And poor Hans spent the rest of his days as a love-sick bachelor on his river-bottom farm.

King Coal

6

'I am a donkey driver,
    The best on the line.
There is no donkey on the road
    That can come up to mine.

'Then shout, boys, hurray,
    My troubles they're but few.
No other donkey on the road
    Can beat Jerusalem Cuckoo.'

SO SANG the mule-drivers, the young boys of fourteen
or fifteen who used to work for King Coal. Day after day
they worked in the mines. They hauled loads from the min
ing chambers to the foot of the shaft. Old King Coal himself
was the merry old soul who lived deep in the heart of the
Pennsylvania mountains. He was the spirit of anthracite,
the hard coal that heats our houses and apartment buildings.

You might expect the mule-boys to be unhappy, living most
of their lives underground. As little fellows of eight or nine
they were put to work sorting out the good coal from slate

and stone. As they grew older they went into the dark shafts to look after the donkeys and later to become full-fledged miners.

Nevertheless, the mule-boys had their fun. They made pets of their donkeys and raced them up and down the mine passages. Or they played tricks on each other and on the grown-up miners. But on Saturday nights they had the best time of all. Then all the people of the mine-patch gathered on the village green for a party. The fiddlers played while the townsfolk danced. The minstrels told their stories and sang their songs, while the boys listened to their tales of the old days in the mines of King Coal.

Many of the stories were about ghosts and fairies who lived in the mines. The miners were superstitious people. They heard the ghostly hammers of the Tommy-knockers. These were strange, gray little gnomes who lived in the tunnels. Of all the weird noises that were heard under the earth, the most familiar was the tap-tap-tapping of these Tommies. Some persons claimed that the noise was made by water seeping through layers of rock and dripping on the floors beneath. But the miners knew this wasn't so. They knew that the Tommy-knockers were going about with their hammers, testing the walls to make sure that all was safe for the humans under their care.

Then there were the ghosts of dead miners who came back to finish their work or to help their fellows. And sometimes the stories had to do with fake ghosts. Once a pair of mule-boys found an old goat. On his horns they fastened a miner's lamp. The poor old beast ran bleating up and down the tunnels in the darkness. He scared the wits out of the miners who saw him and thought he was a spirit. The mule-boys, who were afraid of a thrashing, never told the truth about

their 'spirit,' and for many years the mine was thought to be haunted.

But all the stories the minstrels told were not about the dark life underground. Some of them, like the story of Bachelor John, had to do with the gossip of the mine-patches. Bachelor John was an old peddler. He was truly an ugly old man, with a long scraggly beard and a ragged suit of clothes. On pay-days he came around to sell his shoe-laces and glass jewelry to the miners' wives.

Poor old Bachelor John wanted a wife more than anything in this world. One by one he courted all the widows in the Pennsylvania towns. None of them would marry him. No one would agree to cook his supper and mend his clothes.

One pay-day night Bachelor John stopped at Number Six. He had had a busy day, and at night he curled up in his pack to sleep. The people of the mine-patch, however, gathered at the village tavern for a party. The noise of their dancing and singing made him feel more lonely than ever. At last the keeper of the tavern took pity on the lonesome peddler. He invited him to come to the party and to warm himself at the stove.

As Bachelor John sat on the side-lines watching the fun, a young woman entered the room. She sat down beside him. She was dressed all in black, with a heavy black veil over her face to show that she was a widow. Old John had never seen her before, and soon the thought struck him that she was the only widow in Pennsylvania to whom he had not proposed. Perhaps she would marry him!

He lost no time. Before two dances were over he popped his question. To his amazement the pretty young widow said, 'Yes!' John was so happy he could hardly stand still. He wanted to be married at once. The innkeeper learned of the peddler's good fortune and sent for the squire. The squire came and performed the marriage. The blushing bride kept her veil over her face, but that did not matter to Bachelor John. He was so happy to be married that he danced with every woman at the party. At last, worn out by his joy, he fell asleep on the tavern bench.

In the morning Peddler John awoke. His bride was nowhere to be seen. She had run away.

When the sleepy bridegroom looked for her, all the miners shook their heads. They knew nothing about any wedding, they said. Why! John must have been dreaming! There wasn't any marriage, there wasn't any bride! But as they said this they had to work hard to keep from laughing.

At last the innkeeper told John the joke. The 'bride' had been one of the mule-drivers, dressed up in his sister's clothes. The whole patch had played a trick on the peddler. He wasn't married, after all. Poor old Bachelor John was still Bachelor John!

One of the favorite stories told by the minstrels on the Saturday night sprees was about the Burning Mine. This was a remarkable tale.

Many years before in the Heckscherville Valley a crew of miners had stumbled upon a wonderful cave. Its walls and ceilings were of pure black coal. Unfortunately, however, water had seeped down from springs overhead and in the bitter cold had frozen into icicles. The whole roof of the cave was covered with the green ice. This, of course, made their work harder. They had to chip away the glassy stuff before they could reach the fine coal which they were after.

One of the miners had what he thought was a good idea. He built a fire in the cave on a Saturday afternoon. The heat from the fire would melt the ice, and by Monday, when the mine opened again, the coal would be free of its covering. His fellows agreed that this was the thing to do. They put away their picks and shovels and waited for the fire to do its work.

When they returned to the mine on Monday they found that a terrible thing had happened. The heat had indeed melted the ice. But more than that, it had set fire to the coal. As soon as the men reached the shaft on Monday morning they could smell the thick smoke from the huge furnace underground. This was a terrible disaster.

The mine, of course, was useless. The company closed down its Heckscherville plant, because no one dared to work near the awful heat. One by one the miners drifted away from the patch and went to work in other places. Before long, the mountain was left to burn by itself.

The vein of coal inside it, however, was so thick that the fire smoldered on for many years. Under its heat the stone cracked and broke. Gashes appeared in the sides of the hill from which poured out thick black smoke. The ground itself was warm to the touch. The brooks which tumbled down the hillsides boiled as they ran.

With the coming of winter an even stranger thing happened to the burning mountain. All around it the country was covered with ice and snow, the trees were bare, and the grass was brown and dead. But here the grass stayed green, the trees kept their leaves and blossomed, flowers dotted the meadows. Any snow that fell from the sky melted and ran off into the hot-water streams. Birds flying south for the season saw this summery paradise and settled in its forests, thinking they had reached South America. It was summer all year around.

At first the superstitious mining folk were afraid of the

miracle in their midst. To them the whole mountain was bewitched, and although they liked to look at its pleasant greenness from a distance, they refused to go near it.

After some years a brave miner decided that something should be done about the Burning Mine. Underneath the smoldering vein, he knew, ran another vein of coal. It was a shame for this to be wasted. The people who had lived at the Heckscherville patch tried to make him change his mind when they heard about his plans to open up a new shaft. The fairies would surely bring down a curse on the head of anyone who touched the ground, they said.

In spite of their fears he bought the mountain, hired a crew of brave men, and sunk his new shaft. He dug it deep into the earth, far below the one which burned near the surface. Even so, he had trouble. As they chipped out their first passage, the miners ran into a puddle. Its water was so hot it scalded the soles off their boots. They were forced to give up and return to the top to ease their blistered feet.

Marvel of marvels! When they took off their socks they found no marks of the scalding. Instead, all their corns and bunions had been washed away. The skin was perfectly clear and smooth. One of them who had had a scar on his hand had accidentally put his hand in the water. The scar was gone, and instead of the rough, chapped, wrinkled paw of an old man he had the soft smooth hand of a child.

To make sure they weren't dreaming, they ran back to the patch and gathered up all the sick old people. One by one they carried them down into the hot puddle. After a soaking each returned to the surface healthy and young. They had discovered the Fountain of Youth.

When the news got out, all thoughts of coal were forgotten. Who wanted to bother with coal when he heard about the healing waters of the Burning Mine? No one, of course! The new owner changed his plans. Instead of a mine he built a large hotel, with wide porches looking out over the hillside, and pipes running down into the magic well.

In almost no time people began to come from New York and Philadelphia. They came on crutches, on stretchers, and in wheel chairs. After a bath in the healing spring, or a cupful of its water, they danced like children, completely well. Old men who had come to the Burning Mine through the bitter storms of January were soon playing tennis on the hotel courts and dancing in its ballrooms. What a gay place it was!

When the Irish miners saw what was going on, they still shook their heads. No good would come of this, they knew! The fairies would never stand for it.

At last the owner went too far. If the mine water would cure ills in Heckscherville, why wouldn't it do the same everywhere? He put the wonderful water into bottles and kegs and shipped it all over the United States. People who were unable to come to the Mine ordered it by the case. But this time the Irish were right. King Coal himself had been offended.

Suddenly the mine stopped burning. The mountain grew cold, the trees drooped, and the brooks choked with ice. By morning the hotel was covered with icicles and its lovely lawns were knee-deep with snow. Even worse, the Fountain of Youth was gone. No longer did its waters cure the ills of mankind.

The poor hotel-keeper had to give up his new business. Once again the mountain rang with the picks of the miners and the saucy songs of the mule-boys.

Ichabod Paddock

7

IN the old days Nantucket was a noisy, busy place. Weather-beaten sailors with rings in their ears worked on the docks. They climbed the rigging of whaling ships that came into port from the seven seas. Many of them stomped about the town on wooden legs. Their faces and hands were striped with scars. They were a tough lot.

The toughest of them all was old Captain Ichabod Paddock. He had been the master of a whaling ship for as long as anyone on the island could remember. On his ship his word was law. He roared like a lion above the ocean storms.

But once inside the gate of Mrs. Paddock's kitchen garden he was as meek as a lamb. He couldn't call his soul his own. Frail little Mrs. Paddock had him under her thumb. It was, 'Ichabod, wear your boots.' It was, 'Ichabod, don't trail dirt into the parlor.' It was, 'Ichabod, do this; Ichabod, do that,' from morning until night.

Now, Ichabod loved his wife. He brought her presents from whaling stations all over the world. He brought her rugs from Persia, porcelain from China, and ivory from Africa. But as you can see, he didn't have much fun at home.

Some of the islanders said that was why he spent so much time chasing Crooked Jaw. Crooked Jaw was a mean old whale who was known from Hong Kong to Halifax. They had all tried to get him. But none had ever sunk a harpoon into his tough old hide.

A prize was offered to the whaler who could bring him in. Ichabod heard about it one morning as he was doing an errand for his bossy wife. Right away he straightened his shoulders and wiped the hen-pecked look off his face. 'Here's my chance,' he said. So he jumped over the garden fence, picked up his sea chest, kissed Mrs. P. good-bye, and ran to the harbor.

He lost no time fitting out his ship. He rounded up the biggest, strongest, meanest crew on the island. The sailmakers mended the sails. The blacksmiths sharpened the harpoons and the lances. The merchants filled the hold with supplies for a ten-year cruise. By the first running of the tide the sturdy little whaling ship was ready to ride out of the cove.

When he felt the swell of the ocean under him, Ichabod made a solemn vow. He wouldn't come back to Nantucket until he had Crooked Jaw's oil in his barrels.

It was a year before he and his crew caught up with the big old whale. They were dodging icebergs off the coast of Greenland when the lookout yelled, 'Thar she blows!'

Sure enough! Off to the north they saw a little white feather of steam. It had a funny twist in the middle that meant only one thing. Crooked Jaw! They lowered the boat. Captain Ichabod himself took the harpoon and stood in the bow. The men pulled on their oars for all they were worth. Soon they were almost on top of their prize.

Crooked Jaw was an ugly beast. He had a hump on his back. His big lopsided head looked like a cliff rising out of the water. The flukes of his tail were as wide as the whaleboat was long. His little pig eyes glared red as he caught sight of the captain. Even Ichabod, the master whaler, felt his knees shake as he came face to face with his sworn enemy.

With a powerful thrust he threw the harpoon at the hump on the whale's back. It struck the leathery hide and slid off into the water without catching hold. Crooked Jaw winked his little red eye as much as to say, 'Thought you had me, didn't you?' With a flip of his flukes that sent Ichabod sprawling flat on his back, the whale dove to the bottom of the sea.

The next year they caught up with him near Australia. Meanwhile Captain Ichabod had made himself a new harpoon, twice as heavy and twice as sharp as the first. He spent five hours a day practicing with it to be ready for his enemy.

But this time the same thing happened. Crooked Jaw shrugged his skin, winked his eye, and dove to the bottom, unscratched.

Once a year for the following eight years the captain and the whale exchanged courtesies. The more they met, the madder Ichabod became. Every year he made himself a new harpoon. The last two or three were so heavy that he could hardly lift them. He practiced until the muscles of his right arm were too big for his coat-sleeve. And still he couldn't pierce Crooked Jaw's hide.

The last time they met, Ichabod lost his temper. 'I'll fix

that whale,' he muttered to himself. 'If iron won't get him from the outside, it'll get him from the inside.'

So he tucked a dagger in his belt before he took his stand at the bow of the whaleboat. He lifted the harpoon as if he were going to strike. This time he didn't throw it. To Crooked Jaw's surprise he simply dropped it overboard and jumped in after it. As the giant beast opened his mouth in amazement, Captain Ichabod swam down his throat.

Such a coughing and spluttering as took place then has never been heard or seen since! The brave captain was tossed this way and that. He was shaken up and shaken down. He felt himself being sucked through a whirlpool into the whale's stomach. He grabbed right and left to find something to hang onto. Before he could right himself he was dumped, 'bang,' onto a hard rocky floor.

He lay there awhile, too worn out to move. At first he could see nothing. But as his eyes grew accustomed to the blackness he saw a little light flickering in the distance. He rubbed his bruises and dragged himself toward it.

You can imagine his surprise when he reached the place it came from. There was a stout oaken door with a shiny brass knocker. Over the door hung a trim little lantern. In front of the stoop lay a mat with 'Welcome' written on it.

He didn't really believe what he saw. But he lifted the knocker and let it fall. It rang with a sweet note. From inside the door came a lovely woman's voice, 'Come in, Captain Paddock.'

Ichabod's hair stood straight up on end. His teeth chattered. His knees knocked together like shutters in a high wind.

Because he couldn't help himself, he lifted the knocker again and let it fall. This time it rang with a heavy iron

clang. A deep bass voice called: 'Come right in, Paddock. We've been waiting for you for ten years.'

At that, the captain opened the door. There, in as pretty a ship's cabin as any he'd ever seen on a Yankee clipper, sat two people playing cards. One was a beautiful mermaid with eyes as green as seaweed and hair as red as the sunset. The other was a cross-looking man in a red suit, with crooked horns and a long red forked tail. Ichabod knew well enough who this was — none but the Devil himself.

The mermaid smiled and asked him to sit down. 'We'll be through in a minute,' she explained.

'You see, we're in the middle of a game of rummy. We're playing for a valuable prize.'

'Wh-wh-what is the prize?' stammered the whaler, trying to be polite.

The Devil scowled. He lifted his tail and pointed its fork at Ichabod. 'You!' he snarled.

'And stop that racket,' he added, as Captain Paddock's teeth began to chatter like castanets.

The game was soon over. After a couple of plays the lovely mermaid laid down her last card and said, 'Rummy!' She had won.

The Devil screamed with anger. 'You've tricked me!' he shrieked. 'You've tricked me! But I'll get the best of you yet.' With a flash of sulphur and brimstone he disappeared.

The next thing Ichabod knew he was lying on the floor. The mermaid was holding a bottle of smelling salts under his nose.

'I'm sorry he frightened you,' she was saying. 'He can be very rude sometimes. I hope you'll forgive us.' With that she placed a hand under his shoulders and helped the captain sit up. The smell of sulphur was gone and in its place was another smell, warm and delicious. It made his mouth water.

As he sat up blinking he saw that the table on which the cards had been spread was set for dinner. At each of the two places was a steaming bowl of good New England clam chowder. Beside it was a plate of johnnycake, and from the little cookstove oven came still more delightful odors.

'You must be very hungry after all you've been through,' said the mermaid in her soothing voice. 'Do join me in a simple little supper.'

Now, you must remember that the captain had been at sea for ten years. For breakfast, dinner, and supper, dried beef and hardtack were all he had had to eat. No man in his shoes could resist her invitation.

After the chowder came roast turkey with stuffing and baked squash and pumpkin pie and gingerbread and all the good things he'd remembered from his days on land.

When the mermaid finally cleared the table, Ichabod, who was feeling much better by this time, pulled out his pipe and began to tell stories about his adventures. He was so happy smoking his pipe and bragging to his pretty new friend that he forgot all about his plan to kill the whale.

When it was time for him to stop bragging and return to his ship, he bowed his most courtly bow and promised to come back for supper on Tuesday.

His men didn't know what to make of it. They thought he was dead. They were kneeling on the deck, saying prayers for his departed soul, when he climbed over the railing soaking wet. Of course, they were glad to see him alive. But from the strange gleam in his eye they knew he was bewitched. They tried once or twice to ask what had happened. But after he had beaten up the first mate and the cook, they went about their business with no more questions. Bewitched or not, Captain Paddock was still the toughest skipper in the whale trade.

Crooked Jaw, their former enemy, no longer tried to avoid them. The big whale had had a change of heart. He romped and played in front of the ship like a St. Bernard puppy. And everywhere he went, Ichabod followed. The pilot was ordered never to let the whale out of his sight.

It was a good thing, too. Crooked Jaw led them from one school of fish to another. Before long the hold was chuck full of whale oil. The deck was piled high with whalebone. Every man on board knew that he'd be rich when he got back to Nantucket.

The only thing that worried the crew was their poor bewitched captain. Every Tuesday and every Friday he spent the day in his cabin. He polished his boots. He brushed his best Sunday uniform. He starched his lace cuffs. He combed his beard and waxed his mustache. At suppertime, in all his finery, he jumped overboard and swam boldly into Crooked Jaw's open mouth.

Strange to tell, Captain Paddock got fatter and fatter. His men, after ten years of hardtack and dried beef, were growing thinner and thinner. One Friday night, after the skipper had come back to his ship, the cabin boy hung up his clothes to dry. He noticed something sticky in one of the coat pockets. When he put in his hand he pulled out a soaking blob of what smelled and tasted like gingerbread.

The captain had forgotten all about his wife. He'd forgotten all about his solemn vow. And worst of all, he'd forgotten about his first meeting with the mermaid and about the Devil's part in the picture. So it never occurred to him as he followed Crooked Jaw over the ocean and enjoyed his

Ichabod Paddock

pleasant Tuesday and Friday suppers, that he was being led into trouble.

He didn't pay any attention to directions. He didn't see that the Devil was leading the whale. And he didn't see that the whale was leading him back to Nantucket. He was too bewitched to see that he'd sailed right up in front of Mrs. Paddock's kitchen garden.

Mrs. Paddock was in her garden. She was overjoyed to see her husband's ship sail into view. She ran into the house for her spy-glass. When she looked through it, she saw her husband standing on the deck, fat and healthy and dressed up in his Sunday best.

Then she saw something that changed her joy to sorrow. The captain jumped overboard and swam right into the jaws of a giant whale. She cried aloud as though her heart would break.

The men on the ship heard her cries. When they recognized the village of Nantucket in the distance, they didn't know what to do. They couldn't go ashore without the skipper. And he was in the middle of the whale.

They held a meeting on the deck. After a long discussion they decided to send the cabin boy ashore to tell the captain's wife about his tragedy. Maybe she would be able to help them all.

When she first heard the story she sobbed louder than ever. Her neighbors came to comfort her. They began to sob. The poor little cabin boy howled along with the rest of them. The racket made Crooked Jaw lift his head out of the water.

As he did so, Mrs. Paddock looked up. Being a clever woman, she saw at once that there was a witch inside the whale. She knew what to do about that.

She wiped her eyes and sent her neighbors home. She built

a big fire in the stove. She collected all her silver, her great-aunt's tea set, her grandmother's spoons, and her own best thimble. She put them in a kettle and melted them down. From the melted silver she made a fine little harpoon, just big enough to fit her frail hand.

When the skipper climbed over the railing that night, shaking the water out of his eyes and licking the last crumb of gingerbread off his mustache, there stood his loving wife.

She wasted no time for foolishness. 'Ichabod,' she said, holding her silver harpoon in one hand and grabbing her husband's ear in the other, 'you and I are going whaling.' With that she marched him off to the smallest whaleboat. The men lowered the boat into the water.

'Now, Ichabod, start rowing,' ordered Mrs. Paddock as she took her place in the bow and lifted her silver harpoon.

As soon as Crooked Jaw saw her coming, he had the fright of his life. The old whale knew only too well that silver will always kill a witch. And, of course, a mermaid is a witch of the sea. He tried to dive to the bottom. But Mrs. P. was too quick for him. The harpoon held fast. The terrified whale dashed back and forth, carrying the captain and his wife on the wildest Nantucket sleigh-ride of all time.

When at last the monster was worn out and brought in to the harbor, the captain tried to tell his strange story. Most of the townsfolk raised their eyebrows and tapped their foreheads. They thought he was touched. Mrs. Paddock said simply, 'Ichabod, don't talk such nonsense.'

But when Crooked Jaw was cut up for oil, inside his stomach was found a long piece of seaweed shaped something like a mermaid. And where her hair should have been, the weed was as red as the sunset.

Stormalong

8

Stormy's gone, that good old man,
To my way, hay, storm along, John!
Stormy's gone, that good old man,
To my aye, aye, aye, Mister Stormalong.'

STORMY'S gone, of course. He died before the last
Yankee clipper furled her silver sails. But stories about
'that good old man' are told still wherever old sailors
gather. Just where Old Stormalong was born isn't important. He first appeared on a wharf in Boston Harbor. The
captain of the *Lady of the Sea*, the largest clipper ship in the
China trade, was signing on men. Stormy gave his full name,
Alfred Bullrod Stormalong. Without looking up from his
ledger, the captain wrote down the initials, 'A. B.'

A. B. Stormalong stood five fathoms tall, which is the
same as thirty feet. The captain glanced up at his new man.
He whistled with surprise. 'Phew!' he said. 'There's an
able-bodied seaman for you, boys.'

Someone noticed that the giant's initials stood for just

that. From that day to this sailors have tacked A. B. after their names. This shows that they are able-bodied seamen like Stormy.

Old Stormalong's size and strength helped him a lot on the sea. He didn't have to climb the rigging to furl the topsails. He just reached up from the deck and did it. He could hold the pilot's wheel with his little finger even in the worst weather. In less than a week he'd been promoted from common sailor to bos'n.

The cook didn't care much for his company, however. He made too much work in the galley. He had a weakness for food. He knew a good deal about cooking and wanted everything prepared just so. Besides, he wanted lots of it.

He liked a couple of ostrich eggs fried sunny-side-up for breakfast. For lunch he expected a dory full of soup. After his meals he used to lie out on deck in the sun and pick his teeth with an oar.

But Old Stormy was too valuable a man to dismiss because of the cook's grumbling. There were many occasions on which the *Lady of the Sea* would have become the *Lady on the Bottom of the Sea*, had it not been for her bos'n.

Once, for instance, in the warm waters of the tropical Atlantic, the captain gave orders to hoist sail and weigh anchor after a morning of deep-sea fishing. The crew heaved and strained at the capstan bars. The anchor refused to budge. Something was holding it fast to the bottom. Not even when Stormalong heaved along with the crew would the heavy iron stir.

So Old Stormy stuck a knife into his belt and dove overboard to have a 'look-see.' Hand over hand he climbed down the anchor chain. Suddenly great waves arose. A commotion began on the ocean floor. The surface frothed and

64

churned. From below came sounds of battle. The crew could see dimly two dark forms struggling in the water's depths. Then the long, black, slimy arm of a giant octopus slapped into the air.

At the sight of it the crew gave up their bos'n for lost. No human being could possibly fight single-handed one of those great devils of the sea and come out alive. But before they had a chance to arrange a funeral service for him, Old Stormalong climbed slowly up the chain and pulled himself on deck.

'Phew!' he sighed. 'That old squid was a tough one. Had hold of the anchor with fifty arms and grabbed the bottom with the other fifty. He won't trouble us now, though. Tied him tighter than a schoolboy's shoe-lace. Tied every one of his arms in a double knot.'

A year or so after this adventure Old Stormy lost his taste for the sailor's life. He said it was the food. He was tired of hardtack and dried fish. He had a hankering for some tender, fresh green vegetables.

His shipmates, however, guessed that the real trouble was lack of space. The *Lady of the Sea* was the biggest clipper afloat, but even so she cramped her bos'n. He couldn't sleep stretched out anywhere on board.

After a last voyage around Cape Horn, Stormalong left the wharf at Boston with his pay in his pocket and an eighteen-foot oar over his shoulder. He bade his friends good-bye. He said he was going to walk west, due west. He would stop and settle down as soon as someone asked what the long pole might be. He figured that any county whose inhabitants didn't recognize an oar was far enough from the coast for him.

The *Lady's* crew heard nothing from their shipmate for several years. Then in the San Francisco gold rush the mate had news. Stormy had bought a township and was one of

Stormalong

the best farmers in the whole U.S.A. Stormy a farmer? The mate couldn't believe his ears. But when he was told of Farmer Stormalong's miracles, he knew it was his man, without a doubt!

Stormalong specialized in potatoes. During his first growing season the whole countryside dried up. It didn't rain for six weeks. The little spring that fed the horse trough gave only enough water for the stock. There was not an extra drop with which to irrigate the crops.

Then Old Stormalong went to work. He labored over those drooping, dying plants until the perspiration ran from him in rivers. He sprinkled those potatoes with the sweat of his brow. At the end of the season, when other farmers were moaning over their burnt acres, he drove to market with a bumper crop of the largest, tastiest spuds ever to be mashed with cream and butter.

In spite of this success, Stormy wearied of farm life. He was a restless fellow. Often at night when he had milked the cows and locked the hen roost, he sat in front of his stove and dreamed about the old days on the ocean. At last he couldn't deny to himself that the sea was calling him back.

Word spread through the countryside about a new ship, the *Courser*. It was so huge that it couldn't enter Boston Harbor. The inlanders thought it was just another Yankee yarn. They laughed about it as they sat on the front porch of the country store. But to Stormalong the *Courser* was more than a fable. It was a dream come true.

He sold his farm and returned to the East. For several days he hung around the waterfront, looking like the ghost of his former self. His ruddy salt-sea color was gone, his eyes had lost their shine, and the 'shellbacks,' or sailors, who had known him in the old days realized that he was a sick man, yearning for the feel of the spray.

They couldn't tell him much about the whereabouts of the big ship he was seeking. It was a real boat, all right. It had anchored outside of Cape Cod some time before with a cargo of elephants for Mr. Barnum's circus. The *Lady of the Sea* had been pressed into service as a tender to bring the freight to shore.

The more the old bos'n heard about the *Courser* the more his mouth watered to see her and join her crew. At last, when a whaler brought word that she was cruising along the Grand Banks off Nova Scotia, Stormy couldn't stand it any longer. He dove off T Wharf and swam out to sea.

The next time his old friends saw him, he was the captain of the big vessel. The old fire was back in his eyes, his cheeks were brown as mahogany, and his spirit was dancing. For the *Courser* was the only ship in all the world which suited him. He was the only skipper in all the world to do her justice.

She was so long from stem to stern that it took a man on horseback a good twenty-four hours to make the trip. A string of Arab ponies were stabled in front of the fore-bitts for the use of the officers on duty. The masts were hinged to let the sun and moon go by. The mainsail had been cut and hemmed in the Sahara Desert, the only expanse of land large enough for the operation. When a storm blew up from the horizon, the skipper had to give the order to man the top-sails a good week in advance. It took the men that long to climb the rigging.

This last fact had its disadvantages, of course. Until the United States Weather Bureau caught on to the trick of sending out weather reports in advance, the *Courser* was often caught in a hurricane without notice enough to furl in her cloth. She was large enough to ride out any storm, even in full sail, without much damage. But there was no way of telling how far off her course she'd be blown in the process.

One time, for instance, during a North Atlantic winter gale, the *Courser* was pushed this way and that until she ended up in the North Sea. As you know, the North Sea is just a little sea, and not in the same class with an honest-to-goodness ocean. In fact, it was so small and crowded with islands that the *Courser* couldn't turn around.

There to port lay Norway and Denmark. Straight ahead lay the continent of Europe, and to starboard the British Isles. Stormy roared with anguish. He feared lest his clipper, his lovely queen of the five oceans, would have to join the lowly North Sea fishing fleet for the rest of time.

There was a way out, however. When Stormalong and the mate measured the English Channel they found that at high tide it was an inch or two wider than the *Courser*. With luck they might squeeze through it and out into the Atlantic again.

So the skipper sent the officers to Holland to buy up all the soap in sight. Then he put his crew to work, soaping the sides of the big boat. They slapped the greasy stuff on thick until the *Courser* was as slippery as an eel.

Captain A. B. Stormalong himself took the pilot's wheel and steered. Just at the turn of tide, with her full sails set, the *Courser* glided through into the broad Atlantic Ocean. But she had a close call. The headlands on the English coast scraped most of the soap off the starboard side of the vessel. To this day the cliffs at Dover have been white.

After this adventure Old Stormy was talked about in every port in the world. No sailor could deny that his highest ambition was to ship on the *Courser* under 'that good old man.'

Great was the mourning from Portsmouth to Hongkong when news of Stormalong's death finally came. Several reports of it were spread around. One version had it that he was drowned in a storm off Cape Hope. But most of the tales agreed that he died of indigestion. His magnificent appetite had finished him.

His old shipmates gathered for the funeral. They made him a shroud of the finest China silk. They dug his grave with a silver spade. They lowered his coffin into the ground with a silver chain, the color of his sails. And the tears that fell from the eyes of those hard old salts drenched the earth like the rain of a nor'easter.

> 'Old Stormy has heard an angel call,
> To my way, hay, storm along, John.
> So sing his dirge now, one and all,
> To my aye, aye, aye, Mister Stormalong.'

The South

Ole Massa and His Chillun

9

I. THE FLOOD

UNLIKE the other chapters of this book, this tells three stories, not one. These tales are very, very old, so old that no one knows where they came from. The negro slaves told them in the cotton fields of Georgia and Alabama, in the tobacco fields of the Carolinas, and in the rice fields of Louisiana. Some persons think they were brought from Africa when the negroes were taken from their homes to serve the colonial planters. Others think that they were first told by the Indians.

In the very beginning of the world, before man was created, the animals were the important creatures. They carried on all the business and ran the government, as human beings do today. The lion was their king. Every year they met in a big assembly to talk things over.

One year the assembly met as usual. The elephants, the giraffes, the zebras, the dogs, the cats, the hummingbirds, the pigeons, the dragonflies, the spiders, the lobsters, the crawfish, the earthworms — they all packed up their lunches, put on their Sunday clothes, and went to the meeting.

Mr. Lion sat upon his throne and tried to call the crowd to order. He had a hard time of it. Everyone wanted to talk at once. The mule brayed and the cow mooed and the pig squealed. The tiger growled and the coyote howled and the panther snarled. Every one of the big important animals made a speech. The confusion, of course, was awful. No one could hear himself think.

The elephant became excited. He stomped up and down trying to make himself heard. Without knowing it, he trampled on one of the crawfish and smashed him into the mud. That was the end of Mr. Crawfish.

The other crawfish were worried. They were little creatures and certainly no match for the elephant. While they were worrying, the big beast put his foot down again. Squash! Another crawfish was ground into the mud!

This made the tiny animals angry. They gathered together all their cousins and uncles and aunts and went to King Lion. They drew up a long speech, complaining about the elephant's carelessness. But with all the noise going on, King Lion couldn't hear them. He paid them no attention at all.

The crawfish ran up and down through the crowd, trying to find someone who would listen to their complaint. The mule kept on braying, the cow kept on mooing, and the pig kept right on squealing. Only the mud turtle and the spring lizard would pay them any attention.

At last they lost their patience. They were so frightened and so angry they decided to quit the assembly, for good and all. With their friends, the turtle and the lizard, they took the shortest way out. They bored holes into the ground and disappeared. Down, down, down they bored until they reached the springs under the earth. They were at last safe from the elephant's clumsy feet.

But what about the other animals? When the crawfish hit the hidden springs, water began to spout up from their holes. It gushed up and up until it covered the whole world with a great flood. All the other animals, who were too busy and too big and too important to look out for their small friends, were carried away by the waters and drowned.

II. WHY THE NEGRO WORKS SO HARD

Up in the sky above the troubles of the earth sat Ole Massa. He was a kindly old man with a white beard and a black frock coat, who looked after his 'chillun' down below. When the waters of the flood had gone down, he took the world away from the animals and gave it to men.

At first all men were alike. Large and small, weak and strong, white and black, they lived together as brothers. None of them had to work. Ole Massa gave them pork chops to eat and store clothes to wear. It was a happy time, indeed.

At last Ole Massa saw that man was becoming very lazy. His 'chillun' expected him to do all the work. All they wanted to do was to lie out under the trees and sing and laugh and eat fruit. He decided that something would have to be done about this sad state of affairs.

One day he sent down two bundles tied up with fancy ribbons. One was a big bundle with curious bumps and bulges that looked interesting. The other was a little one, a poor thing at best. Ole Massa himself came down and made an announcement.

These two bundles were prizes, he said. All the men in the world were to run a footrace. The winner of the race should have the big prize, the loser the little one. This aroused his lazy 'chillun.' Each of them wanted to win the big, bumpy parcel.

At last the day of the race dawned. Ole Massa sat in the judges' stand, very handsome in his silk hat and his black coat. The women and children cheered from the side. The men danced up and down at the starting point. Then they were off!

At first the white man ran ahead, but before the race was over, the black man was in the lead. His long legs carried him to the victory. The white man was left far behind, gasping for breath.

Proudly the winner stepped up to the stand to receive his prize. Behind him stood the unhappy loser. Ole Massa brought out the two bundles. Before he presented them, he made a speech.

'Oh, my chillun,' he said, 'for a long time you have been lazy and good-for-nothing. Now you must work. Each of these prizes contains tools. Take them and use them!'

With that he wrapped himself up in a cloud and vanished.

The white man opened his prize first. There lay a pen and a bottle of ink. He knew well enough what to do with them. Without any further ado he pulled down a big piece of paper and began to write. He wrote figures, accounts, letters, stories, books, orders, laws, and anything that could be written with pen and ink.

Then the black man opened his big prize. He wept when he saw what it contained. Inside lay a plow and a hoe and a sickle and a pick and a shovel and an axe. These were the tools of the hard work. He knew well enough what to do with them.

Ever since that day the white man has been figuring with

his pen, sitting in an office in his store clothes; and the negro has been bending his back and straining his muscles, hoeing the corn and chopping the wood and picking the cotton and plowing the field.

This is why, said the slaves, the negro has to work so hard.

III. BRER RABBIT AND THE TAR BABY

The hero of most of the old negro stories was neither a giant nor a wise man. He was Brer Rabbit, as sly and mischievous a creature as has ever been seen. He spent his time playing tricks on the other animals, especially on Brer Fox.

Time after time Brer Fox thought he had Brer Rabbit under his thumb. He licked his chops and filled his kettle, expecting to dine off rabbit. But time after time the cottontail made a fool out of the greedy fox.

The most famous of his pranks concerns the tar baby. The fox was tired of being tricked by his long-eared friend. His mouth watered for a steaming plate of stew, rabbit stew. What's more, he thought he knew how he could solve both problems at once.

Brer Fox fancied himself an artist. Some careless person had left a bucket of tar about, and this was exactly what he wanted. With great pains he went to work and modeled a little man from the sticky black stuff. It was a fine statue, life-sized and for all the world like a pickaninny. On its head Master Fox placed an old straw hat. It certainly looked real.

With this manikin he planned to catch his old enemy. He placed the little tar fellow beside the road and hid himself in the bushes to see the fun.

Soon, clippety-clop, down the road came Brer Rabbit.

Ole Massa and His Chillun

Being a friendly soul, Master Rabbit stopped to say 'Howdy!' to the little black stranger. The tar baby, of course, said nothing.

'Good morning,' said the rabbit, a little louder, and he tipped his hat. The tar baby said nothing at all.

This seemed rude to Brer Rabbit. All the animals, even the fox and the wolf, said 'Howdy' to one another.

Brer Rabbit walked up closer and yelled, 'Nice weather we're having' at the black figure. Still the tar baby said nothing.

'Well,' snorted the rabbit, 'you're stuck-up, aren't you? Don't you know enough to speak when you're spoken to? If you don't, I'll slap your sassy face.'

The tar baby, of course, said nothing. The rabbit was as good as his word. He slapped the black creature with his right paw. This was what the fox had planned all along. The paw stuck fast in the sticky tar.

Brer Rabbit was becoming angry. 'Let me go!' he raged. 'You're not only stuck-up, you're mean. If you don't let me go I'll slap you with my other hand.'

When the tar baby paid no attention to his raving, Brer Rabbit reached out and slapped him again with his left paw. It stuck, too. The fox, hiding in the underbrush, had to hold his sides to keep from laughing out loud.

Then the rabbit began to kick. First he kicked with his right foot, which stuck fast in the tar, then with his left. He was furious.

'If you don't let me go,' he yelled, 'I'll butt you with my head, you low-down, mean, stuck-up thing, you!' The tar baby sat as still as a lump on a log, and Brer Rabbit butted. Here he was, completely stuck up in the ball of tar! He couldn't budge.

The fox came out from his hiding place with tears of laughter falling down his cheeks. His little joke had worked perfectly. No more would he have to suffer the insults of the saucy cottontail. He and Mrs. Fox and all the little foxes would have themselves a feast.

Immediately Brer Rabbit saw that he had fallen into a trap. For all his slyness, he had been caught. But he didn't turn a hair when he saw Mr. Fox. His mind began to work faster than it had ever worked before. He had to get himself out of the pickle he was in.

Turning to his captor he put on his saddest expression. Crocodile tears came to his eyes. 'You've finally caught me, Mr. Fox,' he sniffed. 'Yes, I know I've been mean to you in my day and I deserve anything and everything you will do to me ... (sniff!) ... I'm sorry for all the trouble I've caused you. Really, I am, dear Mr. Fox ... (sniff!) ... I've been a selfish, mischievous, horrid rabbit ... Do with me what you like.'

Brer Fox was pleased with himself. He let the rabbit go on with his humble apologies.

'Do anything you wish, dear Mr. Fox,' sobbed Brer Rabbit, looking up quickly to see how his enemy was taking his talk, 'anything at all ... but please, kind Mr. Fox, don't throw me in the briar patch. Roast me alive! I deserve that.'

The fox scratched his head. 'It's too much trouble to build a fire,' he said. 'I think I'll hang you instead.'

'Oh, hang me, please, hang me,' begged the rabbit, looking very humble. 'Hang me from the highest tree in the forest. But don't throw me in the briar patch.'

'I haven't any string,' said the fox. 'I'll have to drown you.'

'Drown me, then,' murmured the rabbit, pretending to be

faint with fear. 'I don't care any more. Drown me, if you wish, but please, oh, please, *don't* throw me in the *briar patch*.'

This time Brer Fox lost his head. He said to himself: 'If he's so afraid of the briar patch, that's the very thing. I'll throw him in right away.'

Without any more conversation, the fox picked up the rabbit by the leg. He swung him around his head and threw him as hard as he could into the middle of the briar bushes. This, of course, was exactly what Brer Rabbit wanted him to do. The thorns scratched the tar from his hands and feet and head. In a flash he had scrambled free and was off up the hill.

The next thing Brer Fox knew, his rabbit stew was sitting at the top of the hill as saucily as ever. He had been fooled again!

'I was born and bred in a briar patch,' sang the rabbit mischievously, as he disappeared over the hilltop, 'born and bred in a briar patch.'

Mule Humans

10

THE mountain people of Kentucky are very careful of their speech on Amber Days. These are the days which Old Horny, the Devil, has planted among the others in the calendar in order to trap weak humans. If anyone makes a false wish on one of these days, it will come true. You may laugh and say this is just a foolish superstition, but the Kentucky people know better. They saw what happened to Godsey Scrorse and his wife Mondie.

Mr. and Mrs. Scrorse lived in a tumble-down cabin halfway up the mountain. They had an old sow and some little pigs, a few chickens, and a patch of corn. Godsey was a clumsy, lazy old fellow who spent most of his time just 'a-settin'.' And Mondie was as impatient and as cross as her man was lazy.

One afternoon, as Mondie was sweeping the cabin floor, Godsey kept getting in her way. He lay sprawled out just where she wanted to sweep. When he moved, he tripped over the broom. Mondie began to scold. Godsey scolded back. Soon they were quarreling, yelling, and calling names at each other, like a pair of jay-birds.

'You're a fine one,' Mondie stormed. 'Always in the way. Clumping on everyone's feet. Just like a mule. The fact is, you're nothing but a mule from the waist down.'

'Oh, stop your chattering,' Godsey retorted. 'You're always braying at people. In fact, you're nothing but a mule from the neck up.'

'Is that so?' Mondie tried to say. Instead of the words, however, all that came out was the high, shrill bray of a donkey, 'Eee-yaw!'

Poor Godsey! He looked at his wife and saw that her head had suddenly turned into the long bony head of a mule. He was so frightened he jumped up and tried to run out of the cabin door.

His own head hit the ceiling. He looked down. Instead of his two legs, he had the four long legs of a jackass.

They stared at each other with horror. Then they saw the calendar. It was an Amber Day!

Mondie began to sob, 'We're bewitched!' But not a word came out, nothing but 'Eee-yaw! Eee-yaw!' Godsey tried to put his arms around her to comfort her, but his four long legs were hard to manage. One of his heavy, horny hoofs came down 'plunk' on her foot! She brayed louder than ever.

At last Godsey decided to ask Solomon Shell what to do. Solomon was a wise man, a story-teller, who lived in the valley. He was a famous old fellow, with long hair hanging over his shoulders, and a beard 'as wild as a stubble-patch.' His neighbors believed he was a devil-charmer. If anyone knew how to cure an Amber Day enchantment, Solomon Shell certainly did.

So Godsey left Mondie rocking sadly by the fire, with her

Mule Humans

big donkey head in her hands. He scrunched himself through the low doorway and galloped down the valley road.

Old Solomon was surprised to see his friend peering in at him through the top of the window. He thought Godsey must be standing on a chair.

'Come in, neighbor Scrorse,' he called. 'Sit down by the fire.'

Godsey shook his head. 'Can't come in,' he answered sadly. 'Can't sit down, either.'

'What's the matter, Godsey?'

'You'll have to come and see for yourself,' was the mournful reply.

So Solomon knocked out his pipe and went to his door. There, of course, was Godsey, with his long mule legs. He wasn't standing on any chair, after all. His empty trousers flapped in front of his powerful forelegs.

'Whew!' whistled the wise man in astonishment. At his whistle, the mule's hind legs began to prance and his tail switched.

'Whoa, boy! Whoa, Godsey!' called the unhappy Mr. Scrorse to his donkey half. Then he explained what had happened. He told the old story-teller how he and Mondie had quarreled, how they had forgotten about Amber Day, and how they had been changed into Mule Humans. He had come to ask Solomon to help them.

'Well,' said the wise fellow, stroking his wild beard, 'I don't know exactly what I can do for you. Amber Day poison is mighty strong poison. It's hard to cure.'

Godsey's hopes began to fade as Old Sol shook his head. He could make only one suggestion himself.

'I thought you could take the mule out of us and swap your shoats for it. It's a powerful beast,' he said. He whacked himself on the haunch to show Solomon how sturdy the donkey was.

'Yes,' agreed Solomon, 'maybe I could at that. But before I swap my pigs for any four-legged beast, I want to have a look at the whole beast.'

'Climb up!' cried Godsey, pointing to the mule's back. 'Climb up and come have a look at Mondie.'

So Solomon pulled himself up on Godsey's donkey-back. He took one of the empty trouser-legs in each hand as reins. He dug his heels into the creature's sides. The hind legs danced and bounced for a moment.

'Gee-up!' yelled Godsey. And off they went!

What a ride they had! Old Sol declared later he expected to be shaken plumb to pieces. The closer they got to the Scrorse cabin, the more anxious Godsey became to have the enchantment cured. The faster he galloped.

A mule's back is not the most comfortable seat in the world. And Godsey had got himself changed into one of the toughest, boniest critters that ever lived. His backbone stuck up like the ridgepole of a barn. It wasn't long before Solomon had to let go of the trousers and clasp his arms around Godsey's waist in order to hang on.

They raced up the valley road, whooping and hollering, scaring pigs and chickens out of their path. Solomon hung on for dear life. His long hair and his scraggly beard flapped behind him like clothes on a washline. The sweat poured down Godsey's neck and off his flanks. His tongue hung out.

On the way they passed Preacher Charlie's cabin. Preacher Charlie was just returning from the well with a bucket of cold water in each hand.

Godsey paused to ask him for a drink. But when Preacher Charlie saw him, his hair stood up on end.

Mule Humans

'Heavens above us!' he shrieked. 'The Devil is among us!' And with that he jumped over his gate and lit out for his porch. The buckets flew out of his hands. The cold spring water spilled all over the ground.

Next they came to Fiddler John's. The fiddler was sitting in his yard practicing for the square-dance on Saturday. Godsey slowed down again to ask him for a drink.

'It's a horse critter of the Revelation!' John shouted, thinking he'd seen a ghost. And instead of giving them a drink, he fiddled a mad new tune, faster and wilder than anything he'd ever done for a mountain square-dance.

The fast jiggy music from his fiddle got into the mule creature's feet. Godsey pranced off, half galloping, half dancing. He kept on high-stepping it until he reached the door of his own cabin, halfway up the mountain.

When Solomon Shell had caught his breath, they went inside to see Mondie. She, poor woman, was so ashamed to see company coming that she had hidden her head under her apron. There she sat, rocking back and forth in her rocking-chair, sobbing her queer donkey sobs as though her heart would break.

Both Godsey and the wise man had to plead with her before she would take down her apron. When she did at last, Old Sol shook his head. He looked first at the husband and then at the wife, and he shook his head again.

'Tsk! Tsk! Tsk!' he chuckled. 'I'm afraid I can't swap you my shoats after all. There isn't a whole critter between you.'

Sure enough! Godsey had the body and the legs of a mule. Mondie had the head. But there was no neck to connect them!

Now they were in a pickle! The two Scrorses looked at each other hopelessly. They almost cried from disappoint-

89

ment. Were they going to spend the rest of their days as Mule Humans?

'Wait a minute,' said Solomon Shell, stroking his beard and thinking hard. 'There's one last chance. Amber Day poison is devil poison. And there's a cure for almost every devil poison in the Scripture. Let's see what it says about this one.'

So they got the big family Bible down from the mantelpiece. Solomon took it in his lap. He started reading in the first chapter of Genesis. He read through the story of Creation, and the story of Cain and Abel. Then he read through the tales of Joseph in Egypt, and of Moses and the Israelites in the desert. And at last he came to the story of Balaam and the Ass, in the Book of Numbers. Then he stopped.

'Here's your dose of Scripture, all right,' he told them. He read aloud, Numbers XXII, Verse 28: 'And the Lord opened the mouth of the ass, and she said unto Balaam, "What have I done that thou hast smitten me these three times?"'

With that Solomon Shell went out into the woods and cut down a stout oak branch. He stripped it of leaves and twigs. He told the Scrorses to stand quietly. Mondie was frightened and started to blubber again. But he paid no attention.

'It's Scripture, isn't it?' he demanded. 'It's the only cure for Amber Day poison, isn't it?'

Then he took his oaken stick and hit them each three blows. Each time they yelled from the pain. But the third time their mule parts left them.

Yes, Mondie's head and Godsey's legs flew off at the third blow of Solomon's stick. They flew out the door. Somehow or other they melted together as they flew and with one big leap they jumped over the moon. Anyone standing near by could see that that strange mule had cloven hoofs, just like Old Horny's.

When the mule parts had left them, Godsey and Mondie were once again their normal selves. He had his own two legs back in the trousers of his overalls. She had her own head, with her hair pulled tight into a knot.

'Well,' said Solomon Shell, 'I guess that's that. You're all whole again. Now be careful.'

The Scrorses couldn't thank him enough. They begged him to stay for dinner.

'Please stay,' pleaded Mondie. 'You've been to so much trouble on our account. It wouldn't have happened if God- sey hadn't been such an old ——'

But before she could get out the word 'mule' to finish her sentence, both Godsey and Solomon clapped their hands over her mouth. The clock had still another hour to run before the end of Amber Day. They weren't taking any more chances.

Since that time, Godsey and Mondie and all the good folk of the Kentucky mountains have been especially careful of their speech on Amber Day.

Blackbeard

11

UNLIKE most men, who make themselves as handsome as they can, Captain Edward Teach made himself frightful. For Captain Teach was a pirate, and he wanted to look the part. His long, silky dark beard, braided into pigtails and tied with little bows, was looped around his ears. Because of it he was known on the high seas as Blackbeard.

His clothes were brightly colored. At his waist he wore a gay sash, stuck through with three pairs of old pistols. Under the broad brim of his pirate hat he wore a row of matches. Whenever he met an enemy, he lit them. In their dancing light, his black eyes snapped horribly and his ugly grin made fearful patterns of shadow. He looked like something out of a nightmare.

Blackbeard liked to play jokes and then to sit back and laugh until he cried. In his own eyes he was very funny. No one else thought so, however, not even his own wild crew. Although they laughed when he did, they didn't care much for his sense of humor. They recalled too well the

time he shot his bos'n, Israel Hands, in the knee. The poor
bos'n, who had to spend the rest of his life hobbling around
on a wooden leg, didn't see the joke. Teach, however, considered it extremely funny. 'I'm not a bad fellow, after all,
boys. What's a little prank between friends?' he roared,
holding his sides as Israel stumbled away.

The people of the Southern colonies didn't care for his
sense of humor, either. When he swooped down on a seaside
farm, stole the cattle, and burned the barn, it was hard for
the farmer to see the joke. When his crew roared into a village, shooting their pistols into the air and frightening the
villagers out of their wits, the villagers didn't think they
were funny at all. From Georgia to Virginia Blackbeard's
'little jokes' were feared and hated.

At last the people of the colonies had enough. They wrote
a long letter to the King, telling him of their troubles with
the pirates. The King promised to do what he could. Unfortunately, the Royal Navy was weak. England and France
had just finished fighting a war, and the King had few ships
left with which to punish the sea-robbers. They were almost
as strong as the Navy.

Instead of sending out a fleet of ships to wipe the pirates
off the seas, the King sent out a warning. He said he would
forgive the sea-robbers, if each and every one of them would
promise to be good. They could not all, of course, come to
London to take the oath to the King in person. They could
make their promises to the royal governors of the royal
colonies.

Blackbeard saw the notice and sailed up the coast to North
Carolina. Here he got down on his knees before his old
friend, Governor Eden. He placed his hand over his heart
and swore that he would become an honest man. Governor

Eden gave him a big sheet of paper with the royal seal on it.
It told the world that Blackbeard had been pardoned for his
crimes. Then the two men shook hands. History doesn't
say so, but they must have winked at each other as they did
it.

All the people of the colonies cheered when they heard
that Teach would stop playing his jokes on them. But they
cheered too soon. As he left the governor, Blackbeard met a
merchantman, the *Great Allen*. She was bringing supplies
badly needed in the colonies. 'Ah-ha!' roared Teach, lighting the matches under his hat. 'Let's have some fun, boys!
Here we go!' With that his ship, *Queen Anne's Revenge*, opened
fire. The next thing anyone heard of the *Great Allen* was the
story of its wretched crew. Teach had marooned them on a
rocky island and burned their ship. He was up to his old
tricks again.

Before long Blackbeard had gathered a regular fleet of
ships. Beside the *Queen Anne's Revenge*, he had the *Adventure*.
This was a smaller ship he captured from an English captain.
It was a fast, sturdy little boat. He took its captain prisoner
and put Israel Hands in charge of it. Perhaps he felt sorry for
his joke on the bos'n.

In the Bahamas he met another pirate, Major Bonnet.
Bonnet was a weak man, as pirates go. He was no match for
the mighty Captain Teach. When Teach offered to make him
his partner, he was delighted. There was a catch in the offer,
however. Poor Major Bonnet spent the rest of his career
moping in his cabin and walking the deck unhappily, doing
nothing. Blackbeard put another man in charge of his ship
and made Bonnet practically a prisoner.

With his three ships, Blackbeard felt perfectly safe to play
jokes whenever he pleased. The Royal Navy could do no-

thing about it. Once a man-o'-war was sent after him. The pirate only laughed, lit the matches under his hat, drew up his ships for battle, and scared the man-o'-war back into harbor.

His pranks became worse and worse. There was nothing he didn't dare to do. Once, after a battle with other pirates, he needed medicine to heal his men's wounds. His ships were full of gold and booty with which he might have bought what he wanted. But that wouldn't have been much fun for him.

He sailed up the coast until he reached the harbor of Charleston in South Carolina, the richest city in the Southern colonies. Governor Johnson was the bitterest of Teach's enemies. Even so, the pirate sent him a message demanding supplies.

Governor Johnson sputtered. Send supplies to Blackbeard? Certainly not! Right now in the harbor, a ship was making ready to sail for England. On board was a member of the City Council. He carried the governor's message, asking for more help from the King to wipe the pirates off the face of the earth. Send supplies to Blackbeard? Indeed not! Arrest him instead!

When Captain Teach learned that the governor wouldn't give him what he wanted, he only laughed. He thought of a good prank he could play this time.

The Charleston harbor was big and broad, but it had only one narrow opening into the sea. Through this had to pass all the ships coming from and going into the city. Blackbeard drew up his little fleet outside this gateway. One by one the English ships sailed out of the harbor. One by one Blackbeard captured them all. He made prisoners of the passengers and the crews and placed his own men in charge of the ships.

Blackbeard

Among the prisoners was the member of the Council with his message to the King. When Teach saw the message he was tickled even more. He threw back his head and roared. He clapped the poor councilor on the back with a clap that sent him sprawling.

As soon as the Charleston harbor was empty and all the ships were tied up outside, Teach sent his men into the town. They shot their pistols into the air and kicked the people on the shins. They swaggered through the streets up to the governor's palace, where once again they gave the governor Blackbeard's message. 'Medicine and supplies, and be quick about it.'

Governor Johnson did more than sputter this time. He called a meeting of the Council. They sent messengers into the countryside to beg for help against the pirates. But they got little help. Most of the colony's soldiers were off fighting Indians. They sent to North Carolina for help. Here they got none at all. Governor Eden was Teach's old friend. He alone thought his friend's joke was funny.

At last Governor Johnson and the Council had to admit that they were licked. They had no ships nor men with which to fight. Furthermore, they knew that they were in danger. If they didn't give up the supplies, the pirates would turn their guns on the city and send their prisoners to Davy Jones's locker. With heavy hearts the councilors handed over their chests of medicine.

Blackbeard's eyes sparkled with joy when he saw his men returning with the chests. He didn't care much about the medicine, but he thought this the best joke he had ever played.

As soon as the supplies had been put aboard, Teach set his prisoners free. First he kissed all the ladies, and robbed all the men of their money. He nearly split with laughter when he took the governor's letter to the King from the angry councilor. Then he sent the captured ships and their passengers back into Charleston Harbor and sailed away.

All the years that Blackbeard had been sailing the seas he had had no home. Now that he was a very rich man, he began to think that it would be fun to have a fine house and to go about in society. He knew that Governor Eden was his friend, so he went to North Carolina to settle down.

His men weren't very pleased at the idea. When they complained that they had no wish to settle down with him, he played another of his tricks. He landed them on an island in Topsail Inlet. Then with a few of his favorites he slipped back aboard the *Queen Anne's Revenge*. 'Boom!' roared his cannon as it fired into one of the empty ships. 'Boom! Boom!' Again and again it roared until all his fleet, except the *Revenge*, had sunk to the bottom of the inlet. The men rushed to the shore to see what was going on. They could hardly believe their eyes when they saw their captain sailing out into the ocean, leaving them behind. They were marooned with no food; Teach was gone with all their riches.

With his favorites he found a hiding place in another inlet, Ocacroke by name. Here he built himself a fine estate. He bought himself fashionable clothes and a handsome carriage. He trimmed his beard and learned to dance. From the looks of him, as smooth as any dandy, no one would have known that he was the same wild sea-robber who lit matches under his hat to frighten his enemies.

The governor's plantation was not far away. Before long the pirate was an important man in the colony. The other colonists hated him, but the governor was his friend. The two men gave each other rich presents. Soon Blackbeard was invited to the governor's balls. All the pretty ladies had to dance with him. If they refused the governor became angry.

You might think that he would have been satisfied with his fine new life. But not Teach! He still liked to play jokes. Now and then he put on his old pirate's dress, gathered his crew, and slipped out to sea. He was still the robber, looking for treasure and sending ships to the bottom. But now he shared his sense of humor with the governor. Whenever an angry shipowner complained and tried to have Teach brought to the law, Governor Eden pardoned the pirate. Blackbeard was grateful and made Governor Eden still more presents.

At last the colonists could stand it no longer. They knew that their own governor would never help them. He was almost as bad as Blackbeard. So they wrote a letter to Governor Spotswood of Virginia, who agreed to help them.

First Governor Spotswood offered a big reward. To anyone who could capture Blackbeard himself, he promised five hundred pounds of gold. For each of the pirate's officers, he promised fifteen pounds, and for each of the men, ten pounds.

This was not all he did, however. Secretly he fitted up two men-o'-war, the *Lyne* and the *Pearl*. He called together his bravest officers and from them picked two, Captain Brand and Lieutenant Maynard, to take charge of the ships. They picked their crews from the best men in the colony.

Silently the two Virginia ships slipped into Ocacroke Inlet. The officers hoped to take Blackbeard by surprise. When they reached the pirate's fine plantation, however, he was waiting for them. His friend, Governor Eden, had sent him warning. From the walls of the little fortress Blackbeard's cannon looked them in the face. Blackbeard himself was standing on the dock, his hands on his hips, enjoying his new joke. To show the Virginians that he had no hard feelings, he invited them to dinner. He had a grand feast prepared for them. When the meal was over he held up his wineglass and offered a toast to their health and good luck.

No sooner had the Virginia officers returned to their ship than Teach's cannon roared and the fight was on. But this time the joke was on Blackbeard. He had not counted on their courage. The battle raged for hours. The pirates on the shore and the Virginians on their ships gave each other shot for shot.

When at last the smoke was cleared away, Blackbeard was dead. All his pirates had been killed except poor old Israel Hands. The Virginians gathered up the treasure which the robbers had hidden away. They loaded it into the holds of the *Pearl* and the *Lyne*, to take it back to their governor, who had promised to return it to the real owners. They took with them Blackbeard's body, to prove that he was really dead. Poor old Bos'n Hands was allowed to go free. He had had enough punishment from the pirate himself.

When Governor Spotswood announced Blackbeard's capture, all the colonists except Governor Eden rejoiced. This time they knew that they were rid of Captain Edward Teach and his sense of humor for good and all.

John Henry

12

OL' JOHN HENRY, the steel-drivin' man, was as big as
an oak, as strong as a bull, and as black as a skillet.
Some people say that he was a roustabout on the Mississippi,
others that he was a fireman on a Mississippi steamboat.
But the real John Henry was a railroad man. His story has
been told over and over in ballads sung by negroes and railroad men from Roanoke to Altoona.

As a pickaninny, he sat on his old pappy's knee in East
Virginny. And his old pappy said to him, 'John Henry, son,
yo're gonna be a steel-drivin' man.'

The little black boy smiled up into his pappy's eyes and
nodded. Then he looked ahead into the Years to Come and
said, 'The Big Ben' Tunnel on the C. & O. Road gonna be
the end o' me.'

The Civil War was fought. The slaves were set free. The
United States began to grow, spreading from the Atlantic to
the Pacific. Everywhere men were chopping down trees,
clearing farms, digging ditches, blasting tunnels, and build-

ing — houses, farms, factories, bridges, railroads — trying to make room for themselves.

In spite of the prophecy, John Henry went to work for the railroads when he grew up. On one of his early jobs he belonged to a crew which laid the track. They had still a hundred yards to finish when the foreman looked into the valley and saw the 5.15 express heading for them sixty miles an hour. The sun was shining in the engineer's eyes. He failed to see the flags signaling him to stop. In another ten minutes that express train would hit the unfinished track. There was going to be an awful wreck. The foreman waved his arms and yelled. But the 5.15 kept on coming lickety-split.

Then John Henry came to the rescue. He told the other workmen to stand back out of his way. He wrapped the hundred yards of steel track into a coil. Once, twice, he swung it around his head. On the third swing he let go. As straight as an arrow the track shot out into the air and fell to earth right in its proper place.

There was still no time to lose. John Henry grabbed a mouthful of spikes and picked up a heavy hammer in each hand. He ran down the ties as fast as he could go, spitting out the spikes through his teeth and smashing them into place. As he drove in the last spike and jumped aside, the 5.15 rushed past without so much as a jolt. Until he got back to the roundhouse and heard the story, the engineer didn't even know what danger his train had escaped.

As a reward for John Henry's heroism the railroad made him a steel-drivin' man on the Big Ben' Tunnel. The steel-drivin' men were the brave fellows who blasted the tunnels through the mountains. They drove long rods of steel into the heart of the rock to make holes for the dynamite. The holes had to be deep. It took a strong man to hammer a

steel bar into a granite boulder. These tunnelmen were the biggest, toughest, strongest workmen in the world.

Of them all, John Henry proved to be the biggest, toughest, and strongest. With each hammer stroke he could drive the steel twice as far into the rock as the next man. He could strike twice as fast, too. He worked so fast that his helper, Li'l Bill, had to have a bucket of ice water on hand to keep the handles of his sledges from catching fire. Even so, the big steel-driver burned up two hammers a day. Cap'n Tommy, his boss, said proudly that John Henry did the work of four men. He loved him as he loved his own son.

One day a stranger came to the tunnel selling a new-fangled gadget. It was a steam drill. He said it could drill holes faster than three men working together.

'That's nothing,' said Cap'n Tommy. 'You can take your engine and get out. I've a steel-drivin' man, name of John Henry, who can drill holes faster than four men working together.'

The salesman, who didn't know any better, laughed politely.

'Don't waste your time and mine, sir,' added Cap'n Tommy. 'My man can beat your drill to the bottom of a spike any day in the week. Good day, sir.'

The salesman didn't leave. He tried a new approach. 'I'll tell you what I'll do, Cap'n,' he said. 'I'll make a little bet with you. If your man can beat my drill, you may have the drill free, absolutely free. If he can't do it, you buy two drills from me. That ought to be fair enough.'

That touched the Cap'n's pride. He went around to see John Henry.

'There's a man in town who says his steam drill can beat you driving steel, son. That isn't so, is it?' he asked.

John Henry

"'Course not,' laughed John Henry. 'You bring that thing around here and I'll show him.'

Polly Ann, John Henry's pretty yaller-girl wife, overheard the conversation. She remembered the prophecy John Henry had spoken when he was a baby on his pappy's knee. 'Big Ben' Tunnel on the C. & O. Road gonna be the end o' me.' She begged him not to try.

John Henry only laughed at her and said that prophecy was just woman's talk. 'Besides,' he added, 'I'm a steel-drivin' man and I'll beat this steam drill if I lay down my hammer and die doin' it.'

Cap'n Tommy slapped John Henry on the back for joy. The bet was made. The tunnel crew prepared for the contest. John Henry bought a fine new hammer with a twelve-pound head and a four-foot handle. He named it Polly Ann for good luck.

At last the great morning arrived. People came from the mountains of Pennsylvania and Virginia and Kentucky to see the negro race the drill. Polly Ann, in her best blue dress, brought her little pickaninny baby and laid him in the grass where he could see his pappy. John Henry took up his position. Li'l Bill brought the bucket of ice water and stood ready to hold the spike in place.

Cap'n Tommy, in his high silk hat, made a speech to the crowd. At its end he turned to John Henry. 'Son,' he said, 'if you beat that contraption, I'll love you as I never loved my own child. I'll give you fifty dollars and a new suit.'

The onlookers shouted, 'John Henry, you can't beat that drill.'

'Who says I can't?' called back the giant, rubbing his hands together. 'Why, I'll drive my steel into the rock before it gets started.'

105

Then the timekeeper fired his gun and the race began. Slowly at first, then more quickly the heavy sledges fell. *Chug-chug-chug*, the steam drill drove its spike inch by inch into the rock. *Bom-bom-bom*, John Henry drove his. The only sound in all the mountains was the rhythm of the blows.

The water in Li'l Bill's bucket was soon hissing with steam. The steady thunder of the hammers made some of the country people fear that the mountains themselves were falling down. At the end of the first hour the steam drill was forging ahead. For every *bom-bom*, there came a *chug-chug-chug*.

'Pour some water over me,' called John Henry. So Polly Ann poured cold spring water over his back to wash off the dust. All the while she was doing it he kept on driving, faster, faster, faster.

At the end of the second hour the *bom-chug*, *bom-chug*, *bom-chug* sounded like a hurricane. John Henry had caught up with the drill. The muscles rippled under his black skin. The sweat ran in rivers off his nose and his back.

'Li'l Bill, sing to me — and sing fast,' said John Henry. So Li'l Bill sang his favorite hammer song. John Henry kept time.

Now, in the third hour, he pulled ahead. For every two *chugs* came three *boms*. His spike was going deeper than the drill's. The veins stood out on his temples. His blue dungarees were drenched black with sweat. Bill kept on singing and John Henry kept swinging.

And then the crowd began to cheer. John Henry had six inches more to go, the steam drill had a foot. *Bom-bom-bom!* Three inches! *Bom-bom-bom!* Two inches, one inch!

Cap'n Tommy clapped his hands. Polly Ann cried. The mountains echoed with the cheering of the onlookers. John

John Henry

Henry had won! The steam drill had still eight inches to go. Like a great shrieking tornado, the crowd rushed forward to clasp the hero's hand. But it stopped suddenly, in silence.

For there beside his spike lay John Henry, gasping for breath. He'd won, all right. He'd beaten the drill. But with his last powerful stroke, his great heart had burst within him. Polly Ann knelt beside him and placed his little pickaninny in the palm of his hand.

John Henry looked down at the baby, just as his own pappy had looked down at him. John Henry said: 'Son, yo're gonna be a steel-drivin' man. But the Big Ben' Tunnel is the end o' me.'

And with that he laid down his hammer and he died.

Tony Beaver

13

TONY BEAVER, the great lumberjack of the South, lived 'up Eel River.' You won't find Eel River on any maps. The geographers haven't decided where to put it. The people of Louisiana and Arkansas are sure that it's in the cypress swamps. Georgians are just as sure that it's in the turpentine hills. North Carolinians insist that it's in the Smoky Mountains. But West Virginians, who know most about Tony, say that Eel River is high up in their own Alleghenies.

It's not hard to visit the camp, however, if you really wish to see it. Just send word to the lumberjack himself by the next jay bird you see, and Tony will send his path after you.

By the way, this path has an interesting story. One autumn day long ago, as Tony Beaver walked through the woods, something tickled his legs. It felt smooth and ribbony, like a snake. He tried to brush it off, but it clung to his boots and licked at his laces. Glancing down, he saw a baby path, dancing, frisking, romping around him. Tony searched the bushes, expecting to find a mother road near-by. But the path was all alone.

From the way the little fellow wagged its tail and jumped up and down, Tony guessed that it must be lonely. From the looks of its stones and weeds, which hadn't been brushed in a long time, he knew it lacked a mother's care. It was obviously an orphan, just a poor little orphan path that led from Somewhere to Nowhere.

Tony took a fancy to it and carried it gently back to Eel River. Here he gave it food and brushed the cockle-burrs out of its grasses. He let it sleep in front of the fire. In time it became the camp pet. The boys were fond of the clever little thing and taught it a number of tricks. When it became old enough and strong enough, Tony made it his special messenger.

The path still has one bad habit which Tony has never been able to cure. It likes speed. It skims over the hills and down the valleys like a runaway roller-coaster. Some timid people who have visited Eel River say they'd rather spend the rest of their lives at camp than ride home on that streak of greased lightning.

If you aren't too shaken up when you get there, you will find Eel River an unusual logging camp. It's very large, in the first place. After all, Tony and his jacks are big men. In the second place, the bunkhouses look like overgrown watermelons. Instead of the square log buildings you find in Minnesota and Maine, these are shaped like footballs. Their outer walls are smooth and green, their inner walls soft and pink. The bunks and chairs are carved from the same hard black stone as the fireplaces. In case you think your eyes are spoofing you, the bunkhouses really are watermelons.

Before Tony became interested in logging, he had a melon

Tony Beaver

farm. He grew fruit so huge that the hands had to use buck-saws to cut them from the vines. The only trouble with them was they were too big to haul to market. Tony had to think about that problem for several days. While he was thinking he sat by his fire and smoked his pipe. The clouds of black smoke rising from his corncob made the people of Arkansas hide in their cellars. They thought a tornado was blowing up.

Finally Tony figured it out. He built a railroad right up to the melon patch. Three flatcars were hitched together. The smallest melon was rolled aboard. The engine chugged off with Tony Beaver sitting on top of his prize, as proud as you please.

Unfortunately, the tracks ran up a steep grade and down again in a hairpin turn. The engineer, who wasn't used to hauling a load of one watermelon, forgot to be careful. The cars lurched against the hillside. The cargo wobbled unsteadily. Then, whang! The melon, Tony and all, rolled off the flatcars, down the hill, and splashed into Eel River with a kerplunk that caused a flood as far away as New Orleans.

The force with which it hit the water broke the melon into a thousand pieces. For hours the river churned red. It looked as though Farmer Beaver had been drowned. But, no! He simply pulled himself up on one of the seeds and paddled ashore.

As the other seeds floated downstream they caught against the dam by the sawmill. The jam there gave Tony an idea. He made a bargain with the miller, who cut them up into planks and sold them for hardwood. Thus Tony Beaver became interested in the logging business.

He didn't want to waste the rest of those melons. He had his boys roll them to the edge of the field. They dug out the red meat, cut doors and windows, and put in chimneys. Then they built fireplaces of some seeds and carved others into furniture. Lo and behold! There stood as fine a set of bunk-houses as ever was!

The most interesting person at the Eel River Camp is, of course, Tony Beaver himself. He's too great a person to describe. You'll have to see him for yourselves. And until you do, you'll have to be satisfied with stories of some of the wonderful things he's done.

Some years after he'd given up farming and gone into the lumber business, Tony was brought again into the public eye. He still kept a small garden of a few thousand acres on which he raised peanuts. His 'goobers,' as he called them, were sold at circuses and baseball games all over the United States. He had also a stand of molasses maple trees, which produced the sweetest, most delicious syrup you ever poured over a flapjack. They say Paul Bunyan used to send for a small ocean of it every year.

Tony Beaver never could learn to do things in a small way. One season he produced so many goobers and so much mo-lasses that even he was swamped. The circus people com-plained that peanut shells were heaped so high in the tents the audiences couldn't see the rings. Negro mammies from Richmond to New Orleans moaned that they couldn't fry cakes fast enough to sop up the 'lasses. Even so, the Eel River warehouses were bursting with unsold goods.

To add to Tony's troubles it began to rain. It rained for days and nights without stopping, until the hill country above Tony's private town of Eel River Landing was flooded. At first the townsfolk didn't mind. They found it entertaining to be able to sit on their own front porches and watch hen-houses and church steeples sweeping past them downstream.

Tony Beaver

Still it poured. They began to be alarmed. Their own levees were about to break. It looked as though Eel River Landing itself might be washed out into the Gulf of Mexico.

A committee was elected and sent to ask Tony if he could do something to stop the flood. He shook hands with all the members and sat down in front of the bunkhouse fire to smoke his pipe and think. Soon a Big Idea came to him.

The members were sent home to collect all their friends and relations at the peanut warehouses. The loggers were sent to the molasses stores. Big Henry and Sawdust Sam, his foreman, hitched the big oxen to the vinegar cruet and the salt box, and drove them to the riverside. The big logger himself borrowed a wooden spoon from the cookhouse and followed after.

As soon as everyone had met, Tony gave his directions. The townsfolk shelled the peanuts as fast as they could and tossed the nuts into the river. The lumberjacks emptied the molasses barrels into the water from the other side. Sam dumped in the salt. Big Henry poured in the vinegar. Great Tony Beaver straddled the flood, one foot on one side, one on the other, and stirred that river for all he was worth.

The goobers and 'lasses stuck to the reeds. They clogged the river bed. The current began to slacken. Eel River was oozing, not racing, toward the town.

Then the sun came out, the hot noonday sun. A sweet-smelling mist arose as its rays heated the mixture. Still Tony swished his spoon from bank to bank. Bubbles appeared gradually along the shores, little pearl bubbles at first, then big balloon bubbles. Finally the whole river boiled up. The steam rose higher than the mountains. The odor was delicious!

Tony's spoon churned faster and faster. As the river bub-

113

bled and hissed and spouted, its brown speckled waters thickened. From time to time the big lumberjack lifted his ladle and let it drip. Each time the drops fell more slowly, until at last one spun out into a fine hard thread.

With that, Tony Beaver tossed the spoon aside and jumped to the bank. With a jerk he yanked a cloud across the sun. Immediately the river cooled. The thick, sticky mass stopped seething and began to harden. The current had stopped completely. There above Eel River Landing stretched a dam and a broad lake, as brown and quiet and hard as a rock. Except for the white pebbly specks made by the goobers, it was as smooth as a skating rink.

The townsfolk cheered. A holiday was declared and the committee gave Tony a vote of thanks for saving the village. The kids ran home for their ice skates. Soon everyone was gliding in and out among the peanut bumps. People for miles around came to help celebrate.

It was the best party West Virginia ever had, except that there were no refreshments. These were easily supplied, however.

'Break yourself off a piece of the dam,' Tony suggested to a hungry-looking youngster. 'It tastes mighty good.'

The boy thought Tony was joking. But when the big logger reached down and broke off a hunk, he agreed to try it. M-m-m-m! It certainly did taste good. One or two other brave fellows tried it. Soon there was a scramble for the sweet nutty stuff.

Tony had not only saved the town. He had invented peanut brittle.

The Mississippi Valley

Johnny Appleseed

14

THIS is the story of Johnny Appleseed, as strange and lovable a man as ever lived in the American wilderness. Some say that his ghost still lingers in the apple orchards of Ohio and Indiana.

Appleseed, of course, wasn't his real name. His parents proudly named him Jonathan — Jonathan Chapman. Young Johnny Chapman spent his boyhood playing in the woods and on the farms near his Boston home.

As he grew sturdy and brown, two things became clear to all who knew him. First, he was a born orchardman. He understood trees, especially fruit trees. Second, he was going West. He had heard tales of the wonderful rich country behind the Pennsylvania mountains, the country of Daniel Boone and the pioneers. He was going to see it. As a young man he went to Pittsburgh, bought himself a little farm, and planted an orchard.

At that time Pittsburgh was West. Nevertheless it wasn't far enough West for Johnny. Day after day, people passed his farm. They came on foot, on horseback, in rickety farm wagons, in handsome coaches — all bound for the wilderness of the Ohio Valley. Some of them stopped at his door to ask for water, or food, or a night's lodging. To all of them Johnny gave what he could.

Johnny felt sorry for these people. He knew how lonely they were going to be without the towns and pleasant farmlands they had left behind. He wanted to help them. But how could he, a poor nurseryman, do it? Sometimes he had hardly enough to eat himself.

One night his question answered itself. He'd give them all apple orchards. So he did. To every traveler who stopped at his cabin, he gave a bag of apple seeds. The pioneers were nearly always grateful. They wrote home to their friends about the generous man near Pittsburgh. Soon Johnny had given away all the seeds he could spare. He started bothering his neighbors. Most of them were gruff Pennsylvania Dutchmen. They thought their young friend was a little crazy. But they were glad enough to give him the mash that was left in their cider presses, if he could use that.

Patiently he worked all winter, picking out the seeds from the sticky mess. He dried them with care, and sewed them into little deerskin pouches, to be ready for the rush of spring travelers. When spring came, he left his own farm and went to the waterfront with his treasures. Here, where two rivers meet to form the great Ohio, came the travelers from the East. Some came to ferry across to the dark opposite shore, others to pile their belongings on flatboats which would carry them down to the unknown West. And here Johnny stayed, giving away his 'orchards.' People soon forgot that his name was Chapman. Along the levees and highroads they called him Appleseed.

Johnny Appleseed

Soon Johnny began to worry. If these orchards were really going to grow, they needed a trained orchardman to take care of them — someone who knew how to plant and prune. Who could do that? The answer was simple — Johnny himself. He sold his farm and bought a couple of flimsy canoes. He heaped them full with the cider mash, tied them together with a piece of rope, and went West.

For the next forty years until he died, Johnny had no home of his own. He paddled his little canoes up the creeks and backwaters. Wherever he found a likely spot he stopped. He cleared away the underbrush and planted the seeds from small deerskin pouches. Then he built a fence around his plot, to keep the deer from nibbling the first tender shoots — and off he went again. Several times he ran out of seeds. He had to go back to Pennsylvania for more cider mash, to be dried and sorted and packed in pouches for more orchards.

Now and then when new settlers moved into the countryside, Johnny 'sold' them the saplings from his forest plots. If they had money he charged 'a fib-penny bit' for each tree. But more often than not he took old clothes as a swap, or let the pioneers 'buy' the orchards with promises to pay him later.

As you can see, he didn't make much money this way. That didn't worry him. He didn't need much money. He liked sleeping out in the open. He never wore shoes, even in the worst blizzards. At first he wore the cast-off clothes he received for his young trees. After a while, even these became too civilized. So he begged an old coffee sack from a storekeeper, cut a hole for his head and two for his arms, and let it go at that. Hats were a nuisance, too. Since he had to carry a kettle to cook his cornmeal in, he solved the problem by wearing the kettle.

Yankee Doodle's Cousins

He had no gun and no hunting knife. Not even the Indians, those master woodsmen, could understand this fact. Johnny, however, lived well on berries and apples and roots and the cornmeal mush he stirred up in his hat. As for shelter? Many an old settler will tell you that when Johnny was invited to spend the winter night in front of his cabin fire, he shook his head politely. He said he'd rather sleep out in the open with his friends the animals.

This strange little man with the odd outfit and the scraggly beard was a welcome guest in all the tepees, lean-tos, and cabins in the Ohio Territory. Wherever he went, he managed to carry little presents for the settlers. These were usually trees and 'yarbs' for the grown-ups, bits of calico for the little girls, and odd pebbles and shells for the boys.

But best of all he had a stock of stories. In the wilderness, news was scarce. The pioneers rarely had news of the neighbors who lived five miles away, news from back home, or news of what was happening in the world. Johnny talked and listened to everyone he met. In time he became a sort of living newspaper and postman for the people in the wilderness.

But the news he liked best to tell was his news 'fresh from heaven.' After he had shared a supper with a family in some lonely clearing, he sat before the hearth and read aloud from his Bible. Sometimes, in his own strange Biblical language, he told about his visions. One granny who listened to him when she was a little girl said he used to make the cabin 'blossom with the roses of Galilee.'

The boys, of course, liked most to hear him tell about his life with the Indians. The Shawnees, a fierce tribe, were still the terror of the Ohio country. Not many of the white settlers had much to do with them. But Johnny really lived with them. It is hard to understand how he escaped harm at

their hands, going about unprotected as he did through the forest. But when you understand the Indians, you can readily see why. The Shawnees thought he was a medicine man. Woe to any brave who touched a hair on the head of a holy person! Once, while camping in the forest, Johnny had met an Indian who was suffering from a fever. Johnny knew well what plants could be used to cure illnesses. In a day or so he had cured the brave. From that time on, the Indian was his devoted friend. He even asked the white man to visit him in his camp.

At first the other Indians were suspicious. They made Johnny prove his worthiness. His body had been so toughened by his life in the woods that he was as strong and courageous as a red man. He stuck pins through his flesh without flinching. He walked barefoot through the snow in the bitter cold weather. He could tell direction by instinct, and he knew as much wood-lore as his hosts. In fact, he knew more than they did. He knew ways of planting corn to make it grow better. He knew how to cure sicknesses and wounds. The red men were amazed when they saw him take a red-hot iron and burn the ragged edges of a gash he had received from a sharp stone. Everyone knew that this was a good way to keep out infection. But how many had the courage to do it?

Johnny was as good an Indian as any of them. So he was made a member of the Shawnee tribe. Throughout the whole West he was known as the Indian's friend.

Many of the stories he told the settlers were about his adventures with animals. He dearly loved all living things. He considered it a sin to kill or to harm any of them. The animals seemed to understand this, and some people thought he understood animal-talk.

Johnny Appleseed

One chilly night he was walking through the woods when he began to feel sleepy. He picked out a hollow log and started to crawl in. Unfortunately, a honey bear had had the same idea. All at once, Johnny touched something soft and furry. He heard an angry growl only a foot from his head. You and I might have been frightened. But not Mr. Appleseed. He apologized politely to the bear, backed out of the log, and found himself another shelter in the crook of a tree.

Another evening he sat down beside a little stream and built a fire to cook his cornmeal. As the sun sank and darkness fell, he noticed that hordes of tiny gnats were being attracted by the light. Worse than that, they were being burned in the flames. Johnny was hungry, but he couldn't stand the thought that his fire was taking the lives of his insect friends. 'God forbid,' he said, 'that I should build a fire for my comfort that should be the means of destroying any of God's creatures.' So he put it out and hunted for berries to give him strength until morning.

For several years Johnny had a pet wolf who followed him wherever he went. This was a strange pet indeed, especially in the frontier country. Wolves were hated and feared almost as much as were the Indians. But this wolf was different. Johnny had found him caught in a trap. Its heavy iron jaw had cut his leg. There he lay waiting for an angry frontiersman to come with his rifle.

Johnny Appleseed, however, had no rifle. He walked fearlessly up to the snarling beast and soothed him. Unafraid he pried open the jaws of the trap and set the animal free. Carefully he bound up the wounded leg. He brought water from a near-by spring and gave the wolf a drink from his old mush-kettle hat. He treated him as though he were a sick baby. As the sore healed, the wolf attached himself to Johnny. He padded behind him in the woods and watched over him at night. He was the orchardman's friend and favorite until an angry farmer, mistaking him for the thief in his chicken yard, shot him.

Perhaps the most dramatic of all Johnny Appleseed's adventures was his saving of the fort at Mansfield. In 1812 the new United States and the British went back to war. It was a foolish war, but the two nations felt bitterly toward one another. To help themselves, the British got the support of the Indians in the Territories. They felt that the white men had treated them unfairly. They were eager for the chance to fight. Johnny did what he could to persuade the Shawnees, his adopted brothers, to be peaceful. But as much as they loved him, they voted for war.

Johnny himself refused to fight the Indians. He thought of them as foolish children. He knew they couldn't understand what they were doing. Even so, he felt it his duty to help the American settlers. When he heard that the Indians were going on the warpath, he got busy. He traveled night and day through the wilderness. At each frontier cabin he paused only long enough to give his warning. 'Rise up,' he called. 'Take your family to the fort at Mansfield.' Then he quoted from the Bible, '"For behold, the tribes of the heathen are round about your doors, and a devouring flame followeth after them." '

One by one the settlers left their cabin clearings. Some of them fled in their nightshirts, leaving behind all their belongings. They could see the red skies in the north, where the Shawnees were burning farms and towns.

How safe the fort at Mansfield, Ohio, looked to them as they ran out of the forest! Its big blockhouses loomed up at the corners. Its cannon threatened from the walls.

Johnny Appleseed

Unfortunately, however, there was little food inside the stockade. Even worse, there was little water. The village spring was outside the fort. People from miles around had come to seek shelter. When at last all the pioneers had gathered, it was clear that the fort could not hold out for very long. Unless word could be sent to the American garrison at Mount Vernon, thirty miles away, Mansfield was lost.

The captain called a meeting of all the men. He explained how much they needed help. He called for a volunteer to run through the woods to Mount Vernon to ask for help. But the pioneers stood there, silently. The trip to Mount Vernon meant almost certain death. The woods were full of enemies. And even without these, it was a dangerous trip.

Then came a clear, calm voice from the back of the crowd. 'I will go,' it called. It was Johnny. He had already done his part. For days and nights without sleep he had been hurrying through the countryside carrying his warning. He must have been very tired. But here he was again, offering to make the long dangerous journey to Mount Vernon.

The men protested. 'I know the trail,' he said, 'and I shall be safe in the forest. My brothers will not harm me.' Without further ado he was off.

All night he sped on his errand. Worn out, he stumbled into Mount Vernon and aroused the captain of the garrison. Then without rest or refreshment he led the soldiers back. Shortly before he reached the fort, he stopped. He had done his duty, but he refused to take part in the fight. He would curl up in a log and sleep, he said. He was tired. And besides, there was an orchard near-by that needed his attention in the morning.

The soldiers reached Mansfield in the nick of time. The Shawnees had already made an attack. But, sandwiched between the fresh army and the fort, they were soon beaten off.

As the years went by, the Ohio Territories were left in peace. Johnny's saplings grew into large trees. New settlers moved in and cleared the land. The wilderness became a rich farming country, crossed with roads and dotted with villages. Things became too civilized for the strange little man. So he moved West with the frontier into Indiana and Michigan and Illinois. In his coffee-sack shirt and his mush-kettle hat, he planted his seeds in the forests and carried his 'news fresh from heaven.'

One day many years later a farmer found his worn-out old body lying beside a little orchard in the woods near Fort Wayne, Indiana. Johnny Appleseed had died looking after his beloved trees.

Mike Fink

15

I'M a Salt River roarer! I'm a ring-tailed squealer! Whoop! I'm half wild horse and half alligator and the rest of me is crooked snags an' red-hot snappin' turtle... I can out-run, out-jump, out-shoot, out-brag... ary man on both sides the river from Pittsburgh to New Orleans and back again to St. Louee! Cock-a-doodle-doo!'

Mike Fink, the bad man of the Ohio River, was not at all modest when he made this famous boast. Whether or not he was as bad as he liked to think remains to be seen.

Mike started out as a keel-boatman. In his day there were no steamboats to carry people and goods up and down the rivers. Instead there were long flat boats, like barges, which drifted downstream with the current and had to be pushed upstream by poles and oars. The men who worked on these keel-boats were very strong. In order to get his job, Mike had to beat up the rest of the crew. When Baptiste, the French boss, saw him handing out black eyes and broken noses, he knew that Mike was the man for him.

Yankee Doodle's Cousins

Mike was as clever as he was wild. He could steer a boat in and out of the snags; he could make her dance over a falls like a lady at a ball. Before long, he was his own master and could lick any other captain between Pittsburgh and New Orleans, as he boasted. He became very famous.

One of the things for which he was best known was his skill with a rifle. With his long-barreled gun, Bang-All, he could shoot the wings off a hummingbird. He proved his skill once and for all when he was a young boy.

Farmer Neal, his friend, had a shooting match. As a prize he offered his best steer, a fat animal which would keep a family in food for several weeks. Anyone could come and shoot for twenty-five cents a chance. All the woodsmen from the countryside came to try their luck. Little Mike came, too, in spite of the laughter of the men. 'What? Let a baby shoot with us?' they sneered. 'You go back home to your mother and make mud-pies.'

This made the youngster angry. All the money he had was one dollar and twenty-five cents. 'I'll take five chances,' he roared at the top of his voice. 'I can shoot better than any of you. You'll see!'

The others laughed all the harder. He seemed to be a brave lad, however, so they agreed to let him take his turn at the end of the contest. One after another the grown men aimed their rifles at the target. By the time they had finished, it was chewed to pieces by bullet holes. Only a diamond-shaped hole showed where the bull's-eye had been.

Then up stepped young Fink. Slowly he raised Bang-All to his shoulder for the first of his five shots. He looked down the barrel at the target, taking his time. After what seemed to be an hour he pulled the trigger. Zing! Right through the center of the diamond flew his bullet.

Mike Fink

The crowd roared. 'That was only luck! You can't do that again! Move the target!'

'All right!' yelled back Mike. 'Move the target. You haven't seen anything yet.'

The target was nailed to another tree farther away. Again Mike took up Bang-All, looked down the barrel, and pulled the trigger. Once more the bullet cut clean through the center of the diamond. The crowd said that the target should be moved even farther away.

After the fourth shot Farmer Neal himself bet that Mike couldn't do it again. 'Leave the target where it is, this time, and let us see if you can hit it,' he shouted. The boy grinned and lifted his gun. He didn't bother to take a careful aim. He banged away.

'Hooray!' yelled the judges as they looked over the target. 'You missed it, sonny. You didn't even touch the paper. Who says you can shoot?'

'Missed it, indeed!' sneered Mike. 'I'll show you if I missed it.' With that he took his knife and dug into the bark of the tree. Out came two flat bits of lead, one on top of the other. The fifth bullet had hit the fourth and driven it into the wood. The young marksman turned around to glare at the crowd. 'Cock-a-doodle-doo!' he roared, beating his chest and flapping his arms. And before the astonished crowd he walked off with the prize steer.

From that day on Mike and Bang-All were the champions. Not many rivermen tried to beat him. Once Davy Crockett challenged Fink to a contest. Davy and Mike had long been friendly enemies; neither would admit that the other was better than *he* was! First Mike aimed Bang-All at a family of little pigs in a near-by pen. One after the other he shot off their tails. 'Pooh!' sneered Davy, 'you left them each a half-inch of tail. I'll finish the job.' So he shot off the stubs as clean as a whistle.

Mike began to worry a little. He couldn't let the hunter from the Shakes of Tennessee win at his own game. Then the boatman saw his chance. Mrs. Fink, a patient woman, walked to the well. As she stood quietly drawing a pail of water, her husband raised his rifle. Bang! The pretty shell comb she wore in her hair broke into two perfect halves. One of them fell to the ground. Mrs. Fink didn't feel a thing.

'Let's see you knock the other half out!' Mike cried.

This was too much for Davy Crockett. No gentleman would shoot at a lady, no matter how well he handled a gun. 'Consider it a draw, Mike,' he said politely. 'I won't try to beat that shot.'

Not only was Mike famous for his shooting; he was famous for his mischief as well. When he saw something he wanted, he didn't bother to buy it properly. Neither would he stoop to stealing like a common thief. He usually got his way through trickery.

The keel-boat was drifting down the Ohio River when Mike saw a flock of fat sheep grazing on the bank. He and his crew hadn't tasted fresh meat for a long time. The sight made him hungry. 'Well, boys,' he roared, 'it looks as though we'll be having a leg of lamb for dinner tonight. Tie the boat in to the shore.'

It so happened that the keel-boat was loaded with barrels of snuff bound for Natchez. Mike filled a bucket with the horrid brown stuff and carried it ashore. He picked out six of the best-looking animals and rubbed their faces in the bucket. Of course, the snuff made the sheep sneeze. Their eyes watered and grew red, and the unhappy beasts ran bleat-

ing around the pasture frightening the others. Then Mike called the farmer.

'Look here, friend,' he said sadly, 'your sheep are sick. They have the Black Murrain. It's a terrible disease. If you don't shoot them right away the whole flock will catch it and die. Why! I've seen thousands of sheep die of this very thing! I do feel sorry for you. To think of losing such fine fat animals!' With that he shed a crocodile tear, and the poor farmer looked worried. He had heard about the dreadful disease that killed whole flocks overnight.

'You'd better shoot them now,' went on the boatman, 'before they give it to the others. And be sure to throw their bodies into the river.'

'Alas! Alas!' cried the farmer. 'What shall I do? I could never shoot the sick ones without hitting the healthy ones. I'm not smart enough with a gun. Won't you shoot them for me?'

Mike pretended to feel badly about the whole thing. He shook his head until the farmer got down on his knees and begged. 'If you'll do this for me,' he sobbed, 'I'll give you two jugs of my best peach brandy.'

At last Mike Fink agreed. He shot the unfortunate sheep and dumped them into the river. The grateful farmer brought the jugs of brandy and said good night. As soon as it was dark, the boatmen fished up the bodies of the sheep, had themselves a fine dinner, and went on their way.

They thought they were safe. A little farther down the river they tried the trick over again. It worked, too. But before long the news got back to the first farmer. He saw that he had been robbed, and he went to the judge at Louisville.

When Mike and his gang returned from their trip downriver, they found that they were under arrest for stealing sheep. Every officer in the country was looking for them. For a long time they were able to hide in a cave beside the river. At last the governor offered a big reward for their capture. The poor sheriff, who needed the money, was a friend of Mike's. He knew where the boatmen were hiding, too, and he went to call on them in a friendly way.

After a long conversation he got Mike to give himself up and to come into court. 'On one condition,' said the boat-man. 'I'm not at home on dry land. I have to have my boat under me to feel right. If I can come to court in my keel-boat I'll be very glad to come. And you can have the reward money.'

The sheriff, of course, thought that this was another of Mike's strange jokes. 'Don't look so worried,' snapped the boatman. 'I'll fix it.'

On the day of the trial, the judge and the townsfolk met in the courthouse on the top of the hill. Everyone wondered how Mike would come 'in his boat.' And then they all saw! The big flat-bottomed keel-boat was mounted on wheels and hitched to a team of oxen. All the boatmen stood in their places on the deck with their big poles in their hands. As the oxen puffed up the hill, Mike called out to the sheriff, 'Is everything ready? I can't stay long.'

The sheriff knew that the judge was angry. He tried to tell his friend about the judge's anger. But for all the faces he made Mike and his boys rode merrily on into the courthouse square. What a sight they made as they jumped down from the boat and marched into the room in their red shirts, all shouting 'Cock-a-doodle-doo!'

The boatmen sat down in the front row. The judge scowled at them over his glasses and began to read. 'I charge you, Michael Fink, keel-boatman, with stealing sheep,' he read. All the people in the room scowled at the thieves. It was perfectly clear that Mike and his boys were going to be put into jail for their tricks.

All of a sudden, before the judge could catch his breath to say anything else, Mike jumped up from his chair. He blew a terrible blast on his horn. 'To your places, boys,' he yelled. 'We're leaving.' And with that the boatmen jumped out the window, took their oars in their hands, and pushed the boat, wheels and oxen and all, down into the water of the Ohio River. 'We had a pleasant time,' Mike called up to the judge and the worried sheriff. 'We'll call on you again some day!'

That was the last time that anyone tried to arrest Mike Fink.

Once, it's true, Mike Fink bit off more than he could chew. He was so pleased with himself after his escape from the law that he thought he could do anything. At a river inn he met his old friend and enemy, Davy Crockett. Davy had been boasting about his wife, who wasn't afraid of anything under the sun.

'I'll scare her!' roared Fink. 'I'll bet my Bang-All against your Betsey that I can scare the daylights out of Mrs. Crockett.' The bet was made, and Mike crowed his old crow, 'Cock-a-doodle-doo!' to settle the matter.

He searched through the swamps until he found an old alligator with a horrible face. He dressed himself up in the 'gator's skin and lay beside the road until Mrs. Crockett set out for her evening walk.

As she walked up to him, Mike opened the huge jaws of the 'gator right in her path. She stepped quietly aside as though he were nothing but an old stump. He swished his

136

tail back and forth and crawled up beside her. She paid no attention at all. She certainly didn't look frightened.

This made Mike angry. He rose up on the 'gator's back legs and tried to give Mrs. Crockett an alligator hug. It didn't frighten her at all. Instead it made her angry. She turned around and looked at him with her worst look. Lightning flashed from her eyes. She was awfully mad!

Mike tried once more. He moved closer and tried to hug her again. 'That's enough, you lowly worm!' she screamed. 'Take that!' And with her toothpick she cut off the 'gator's head. Then, of course, she saw Mike inside the beast's skin.

'So that's your trick, is it?' cried Mrs. Davy Crockett, rolling up her sleeves. 'I'll teach you to bother respectable women on their evening walks. Come out and fight like a man!'

Without another word she lit into the bad man. She swung her handbag and kicked and bit and pulled and punched. When the battle was over, she rolled down her sleeves again and went on her way. Poor Mike Fink! He lay there in the swamp, bleeding and sore. 'I'm a Salt River roarer,' he whispered to himself as he counted stars. 'I'm half wild horse and half cock-eyed alligator ...' But the word 'alligator' in his boast sounded feeble. The great Mike Fink, who could crow like a rooster and fight like a wildcat, had been licked. Worse than that, he had been licked by a woman!

Dan'l Boone

16

DURING the French and Indian Wars, General Braddock and his red-coated soldiers marched into the wilderness of western Pennsylvania. General Braddock knew very little about Indians and about the wilderness. As a result his trip was a failure. In his train were two men, however, who could have helped him had he asked their advice. These were two young men, hardly more than boys, who well knew the ways of the wild frontier.

The first of these was a young surveyor; his name was George Washington. The second was a lad from North Carolina who drove a supply wagon; his name was Daniel Boone.

At night around the campfire young Dan'l listened to the stories told by an old scout. John Finley, the scout, had wonderful tales to tell. He had hunted bear and buffalo beyond the Appalachian Mountains. He had dodged Indians on their forest trail, the 'Eskippakithiki,' the 'Warrior's Path.' He had seen the 'dark and bloody ground,' Kaintuck.

Yankee Doodle's Cousins

Although Kaintuck was a wonderful country with rich plains and tall woods, no Indians lived there. It was their battle-ground. There the tribes from the North met the tribes from the South. Neither would allow the other to settle in the lovely country. From their struggles the land took its name.

As young Dan'l listened to John Finley's tales he wanted more than anything in the world to see Kaintuck for himself. Day after day he teased the old scout until the latter gave his promise that some day he would take the boy across the mountains into the 'dark and bloody ground.' Twelve years later the promise was kept.

The rest of the story is well known. Young Dan'l saw Kaintuck and loved it. He led his family and his friends into its great forests. They cleared the woods and planted farms; they built little towns and forts and called the country Kentucky.

Boone did more than explore Kentucky. When people from the Eastern States moved in to share his new land, he felt crowded. His nearest neighbors lived within ten miles of his farm! A man didn't have room to breathe! So Dan'l moved his family again, farther west this time, into the wilderness west of the Mississippi. Here he had all the room he liked. He explored the great plains and the Missouri River Valley. As a very old man he went hunting all alone as far as the Rocky Mountains.

There are many stories, however, that the history books don't tell about Dan'l. There is, for instance, the story of his meeting with his wife.

Dan'l was a great hand with a rifle. Had he lived some years later, he could have taught Mike Fink and Davy Crockett a few tricks. While they were babies in their cradles, he was shooting the pin feathers off the eagles who soared above the Smoky Mountains. Once, so they say, he saw a wildcat leap upon a frontier baby. The wildcat thought he was going to have a tender bit of meat for his dinner. But Dan'l drew his gun to his shoulder, pulled the trigger, and Mr. Wildcat fell dead. The baby wasn't even scratched.

This adventure made Dan'l dislike wildcats intensely. Whenever he had the chance, he did his best to rid the woods of the mean beasts. One winter evening, as he returned to his father's home from a hunting trip, he saw two bright green eyes shining at him from the forest. They were wildcat eyes, he was sure, so he dropped to his knee, drew his gun to his shoulder, and sighted down the barrel. The green eyes shone brighter than ever. But something made Dan'l hold his fire. Those bright green eyes were different from the others that had stared at him. Instead of shooting, he walked bravely up to the beast to have a closer look.

Imagine his surprise! The eyes weren't wildcat eyes after all. They belonged to the most beautiful girl Dan'l had ever seen. There she sat crouching in the bushes. She was perfectly calm and not at all afraid, even though Dan'l had started to shoot her. By the time he had taken a second look at his 'wildcat,' Boone was head over heels in love. He took the girl back to the settlement, and soon they were married.

Dan'l wasn't very good at book learning. His spelling was hardly of the best. For many years a sample of it could be seen in the bark of a tree. Here he had carved this message, 'D. Boon cilled a bar,' as a record of his bear-hunting. He could read his own messages, however. Most of them were notches carved into trees.

As a young hunter he made three notches in the bark of an ash sapling to show where he had spent the night on a hunting trip. Then he went his way and forgot all about them. Twenty years later, after he had explored the whole state of Kentucky, a group of men came to him. They were having a great deal of trouble over a piece of land. The deed to the land said that its boundary began 'at an ash marked by three distinct notches of the tomahawk of a white man.' But no one could find the ash tree.

The men knew that Dan'l had been hunting in the country and thought he might have put the marks on the tree. They asked him to help them find it. Dan'l, of course, had marked hundreds of trees in the twenty years that had gone by. He scratched his head and tried to recall which tree this could be. At last he remembered.

The country had changed greatly since Boone's hunt. Where once had been wild forest, now were farms and fields. Nevertheless, Dan'l took the men to the spot at which he had started his trip. Through woods and over streams he led them until they reached a large ash tree. Not a sign of a notch could be seen on its bark. The men shook their heads; they thought that Boone had made a mistake. But Dan'l knew better. He walked around the tree until he found the right spot, took his hunting knife and cut away the bark. There, right under his cut, were the three notches that had been made when the tree was a slender young sapling.

The most exciting stories about Dan'l Boone have to do with his escapes from the Indians. Although the latter were his enemies, they admired him and thought that he had magic powers. On his first trip into Kaintuck he was surrounded by a party of braves on the Warrior's Path. They were out to kill anyone who dared get in their way. Boone had nothing but a knife with which to defend himself; the braves had guns. He started to run away from them through the forest, dodging this way and that, trying to cover his tracks. They followed him. Suddenly he disappeared. His tracks disappeared, too. Not a sign of the hunter could they find. They decided that it must be one of the spirits who had led them on this merry chase. As they turned back to their war party, Dan'l laughed to himself in the top of a tree. He hadn't vanished at all; he had saved himself by swinging up into the air on a wild grapevine.

Another time he was crossing a grassy meadow when a shot rang out above his head. An Indian had fired at him from the woods. Dan'l had no way of hiding himself. It was too far to run to the cover of the forest. 'Bang!' spoke the Indian's gun, again and again. Dan'l could hear the bullets zing past his ear, but none of them touched him. How did he save himself? As he told the story, he waited for the brave to fire. When he saw the flash from the gun, he knew just where the bullet would go; he was able to duck out of its way.

His luck was not always good, however. Once in a while he was caught by his enemies. Even then he managed to get away from them. At times he talked the Indians into letting him go. Once he pretended to swallow his hunting knife and made the braves believe that he had magic powers. That time they set him free as fast as they could. No Indian wanted to make a magician angry!

Before many years were over, Dan'l had met and escaped from so many Indians that he knew most of them by name. He enjoyed matching his wits with theirs. He liked to tease them about his escapes. A group of Shawnees made up their minds to capture him once and for all. They crept up to the edge of his farm clearing and waited for a chance to catch him. Soon they had their chance.

On his farm Dan'l grew tobacco. When the leaves had

reached the right size, they had to be hung in a shed to dry. Farmer Boone chose this very day to untie the bunches of dry, brown tobacco leaves that hung from the rafters of his barn. The braves saw him leave his house, and knew that their time had come. He had no gun with which to defend himself.

As he worked high up in the rafters, the Indians entered the barn and demanded that he give himself up. Dan'l saw that they had him where they wanted him, but he refused to surrender. He pretended to be very humble. He greeted the braves in a friendly way and asked them for one last favor. Before they took him away, he wanted to finish untying the tobacco. When this was done, his family could sell the leaves and have a little money with which to live when he was gone. The braves, who admired his coolness, agreed to this. They settled themselves on the floor of the barn and Dan'l went on working above their heads. From time to time he asked about their wives and families, told them bits of gossip about other Indians he had seen, and soon had them chatting pleasantly.

All at once, before they could see what had happened, Dan'l dropped an armful of the brown tobacco into their up-turned faces. The leaves broke into bits as they fell; the dust filled the whole barn. The Indians coughed and spluttered, their eyes watered, and they gagged on the stinging brown dust. Quickly Dan'l jumped down from his perch and ran to his house. Here he could defend himself. Once again he had tricked his friendly enemies; the poor braves had nothing for their trouble but red eyes and raw throats.

These Shawnees were the very ones who had captured him years before during the Revolutionary War. At that time, the settlements in Kentucky were no more than little forts.

Dan'l Boone

Dan'l's own village of Boonesborough had only a handful of men with which to defend itself. Its few log cabins were built inside a stockade. The settlers depended on the hunters to supply their food.

Boone knew that the woods were full of Shawnees who were working for the British. Even so, the fort needed food and he agreed to get it. As luck would have it, he ran into a party of braves who took him captive and marched him through miles and miles of wilderness along the Warrior's Path to their home in northern Ohio. Dan'l knew that he was in great danger. The British had set a price on his head because of his help to the American colonists. He had little chance of escaping from the war party, which guarded him carefully day and night. His only chance was to make friends with his captors.

Dan'l behaved like a perfect prisoner. He showed the Shawnees as many tricks as he knew. He gave them his word that he would not try to escape. Soon they trusted him so much that they allowed him to walk freely without thongs to bind his hands. By the time they reached their village, they wanted to make him a member of their tribe.

First Dan'l had to undergo many tortures. He had to run through a line of braves, each of whom slashed at him with a whip. His bravery and his strength were enough for them. He was as good an Indian as any of them. So he was taken into the tribe and the Shawnees called him their brother.

Before they had captured him, however, the Shawnees had promised to turn him over to the British commander in Detroit. Whatever else might be said against them, the Indians kept their promises. Therefore Dan'l's new brothers took him to the British headquarters. The commander was well pleased, for he knew that Boone was his most dangerous enemy in the West. He put him in irons as a prisoner of war.

The Indians had come to be so fond of their new tribesman that they hated to see him taken prisoner by the British. With their reward money they paid his ransom, and once again he was free.

He was not really free, however. During his stay in Detroit he had heard plans for an attack on the settlements of Kentucky and Western Virginia. All the tribes from Ohio and Indiana were to gather together to make one huge war party. The British were to give them guns and bullets. Then they would attack the little frontier forts and give the settlers no mercy. The Shawnees knew that Boone had heard of these plans and that he would try to warn his friends.

Therefore they kept a sharp lookout whenever Dan'l went hunting. They still treated him as a brother, but they made him stay within their sight. Whenever he was given powder and shot for the hunt, he had to return what was left to the tribe. They took no chances on his having powder with which to shoot his way out of camp.

Nevertheless Dan'l was too smart for them. He managed to steal powder for himself. Instead of using a full portion of it for each shot on the hunt, he used a half portion and hid the rest. Soon he had enough for his purpose. On a dark night he sneaked away from the camp, ran silently through the forest, and headed for Kentucky.

The journey was long and hard. He had to cut through bramble patches and swamps to avoid Indian trails and the braves who were looking for him. He did not dare to shoot game for food. The sound of his gun would tell the Indians where he was.

After days of hardship he reached Boonesborough. How he longed to see his wife and children! Poor Dan'l! When he reached the settlement, they were not there. Thinking he was dead, they had returned to their old home in North Carolina!

He had little time to think about this misfortune, however. He had work to do. The fort had to be gotten ready for a long battle. Other settlers had to be warned. Food had to be collected. Men had to be sent for help.

Almost immediately the Shawnees appeared. The battle was fierce. Weak and weary as he was, Dan'l Boone fought with the others until he was wounded. Then from his bed he directed the battle.

At length the noise of the battle stopped. Boonesborough had been saved, and Dan'l was able to take his well-earned rest. The war party's plans had failed. Kaintuck, the 'dark and bloody ground,' was saved for the United States. Some day it would become Kentucky, the peaceful country of rich towns and grassy meadows.

Davy Crockett

17

WHEN Davy Crockett went to Congress, he didn't waste his time making dull speeches. He told stories. He had a great many stories to tell, too — stories of his life as a hunter, a backwoodsman, and an Indian fighter. Sometimes he was carried away by his stories. People began to expect almost anything from him.

His fame spread far and wide. During his second term in Washington, it was feared that the world was coming to an end. Halley's Comet shone in the sky. This was a particularly bright comet with a long tail. It came fearfully close to the earth. Bits of burning metal flew off and showered fields and forests. The sky was streaked with shooting stars.

This comet had appeared before. Whenever it came close to our planet something dreadful happened. People feared it meant disaster again. But with Davy in Congress they thought they might be safe. They sent a committee to him, just as people send committees to Washington today. They asked him to help them. At last he agreed. If the comet came any closer, said he, he would climb to the top of the Appalachian Mountains. There he would stand until he could catch the old comet and wring off its tail. This made the committee feel better and they went home satisfied.

Davy Crockett was born in the Tennessee hills. As a tiny baby, he was cradled in the shell of a snapping turtle. His crib cover was a panther's skin. A crocodile curled itself up into a ball for his pillow. From the very beginning he was a remarkable person.

As a young man he fought in the Indian Wars. All over the Tennessee and Arkansas country he hunted coon and bear. He even tried his hand at farming. Everything he saw and did gave him a new story to tell.

Throughout the Shakes, as his part of Tennessee was called, Davy was famous for his grin. It spread from ear to ear. No one could look at it without smiling back. People thought that it had strange powers, and told how Davy had once grinned a coon out of a tree.

On the top branch of a pine sat the fat little coon, grinning like a Cheshire cat. Davy needed a new cap. He liked the markings on the little creature's tail. But he had left Betsey, his long rifle, at home. All he could do was to stand there and grin. He stretched his lips as far as they would go and fixed his snapping eyes on the coon. After an hour the animal gave up. The glare from Crockett's smile was too much. Down fell the raccoon. He had been out-grinned by the hunter.

On another occasion in the Shakes, Davy saw another coon. This time he decided to grin him down for the fun of it. Davy grinned and grinned, but nothing happened. He stood there all night long, grinning. Rattler, his hunting dog, who usually went wild with excitement when his master hunted a coon, acted very strangely. He paid no attention, but curled up at the foot of the tree and slept soundly.

In the morning, Hunter Crockett saw his mistake. What he thought was a coon was only a big knot on the branch. What a fool he had been, grinning at a tree all night long! His grin had not been wasted, however. It had burned all the bark off the tree.

Beside Rattler and Betsey, Crockett had two unusual hunting companions. His favorite was his old bear, Death Hug. Davy had brought him up from a tiny cub. He had a saddle and bridle made for the old creature and often rode him around the wilderness. Death Hug saved his life on one occasion. Davy was surrounded by angry Indians, who were out for his scalp. As soon as the bear saw the danger he leapt into a tree with his master on his back. From branch to branch he swung, faster than the Indians could follow. He crossed the whole forest this way and came down in friendly country.

The second was an alligator whom he called Mississippi. Davy and Death Hug were skating on the frozen Niagara River, above the falls. It was getting on toward spring. Without any warning, their piece of ice broke off from the rest and headed for the falls. They were indeed in a pickle! But Death Hug saved the day. Davy locked his arms around Death Hug's waist. He guided the chunk of ice over the great waterfall and they landed safely at the bottom, without even a ducking. The trip had been such great fun, Davy wanted to do it again. So he called Mississippi and jumped on the alligator's back. The powerful 'gator took a long running start and hopped right up over Niagara.

Davy loved animals and the animals all loved him. They even elected him to Congress. His rival was a very rich man who lived on a big plantation. He had been to college and knew how to make long important speeches. He used big words and impressed the voters. He dressed in a long frock coat and a big silk stovepipe hat. Crockett was only a poor hunter from the Shakes. He had nothing but his buckskin hunting dress and his coonskin cap. The voters all flocked around the rich man.

The animals felt sorry for their friend. They went to work for him and told him not to worry. Whenever the rich planter got upon a platform, guinea hens and bullfrogs gathered at the foot of the stand. Wild turtle doves and pigeons collected in the trees overhead.

As soon as he opened his mouth to speak, up went a chorus. 'Cr-ck-tt! Cr-ck-tt! Cr-ck-tt!' croaked the frogs. 'Cr-ck-tt! Cr-ck-tt! Cr-ck-tt!' clucked the hens. 'Cr-ck-tt! Cr-ck-tt! Cr-ck-tt!' cooed the doves and pigeons.

Davy stood on the side-lines and grinned. The voters were charmed. They stopped listening to the speaker on the platform and went off to vote for the backwoodsman.

Davy once gave a party for the birds and animals on a Fourth of July. He gathered them together under the Liberty Tree. In a long, flowery speech he thanked them for their help and told them how much he loved his country. He wound up with twenty-six big cheers for Uncle Sam and the states. There were twenty-five states in those days. Then he added two little cheers for Texas and Oregon, which were almost states, but not quite.

The birds and animals listened quietly. They paid more attention than did the members of Congress in Washington.

After the speech, Davy taught them all to dance. Death Hug and Mississippi moved among the party dancing with all the guests. Ben Hardin, **Davy's friend**, whistled **all the** dance tunes he knew.

This Ben Hardin **was Davy's** best friend in Congress. They had known each other for a long time. They first met on the Mississippi River. Davy was paddling his log canoe when he spotted a strange craft, floating toward him. It was a raft with several kegs nailed together on top. Sitting on the kegs was a little fellow in a sailor's dress, with a sailor's pigtail hanging down his back.

It looked as though the two crafts were going to crash, but neither Davy nor the stranger would give way. Each began to swear at the other and to tell all the awful things he would do to him. They became so mad at one another that there was nothing to do but to fight it out.

They paddled to the shore and went to it. After the battle they shook hands and became friends. The stranger said his name was Ben Hardin. He was so wild that when he wanted a rest, he leaned against a cyclone.

Soon after this a Western cyclone hit the river. It roared along the bank and made straight for the two new friends. Poor old Ben! For all his bragging, he was scared. Davy laughed, however. He grabbed a piece of lightning as it went by, greased it with rattlesnake oil, and jumped on its back with Ben hanging to his coat-tails. Off they flew across the cyclone and landed in the Shakes near Davy's home.

Ben and Davy lived together for a long time. Sally Ann Thunder Ann Whirlwind Crockett, Davy's beautiful young daughter, kept house for them. Then Ben fell in love with an Indian girl. He loved to dance. The Indian was the only girl in the world who danced well enough for him.

Davy didn't like the match. Nevertheless, he made an offer to his friend. If Ben could dance longer than the

Indian, she could be his bride. The old sailor agreed at once.

Davy invited his neighbors to the contest, which was held on Asphaltum Flats. These flats were so hard that lightning split into bits when it hit them. The fiddlers went to work. They played polkas and jigs and hornpipes and reels. They played everything from 'Weevily Wheat' to 'Pop Goes the Weasel.' Ben and the Indian girl whirled around and around so fast they soon became invisible. Even the Flats began to smoke from the beating of their feet. At last Ben had to give up. His pigtail wilted, and he fell in a heap, coiled up like an anchor chain.

Remarkable as all these stories are, they are commonplace compared to Davy's stories about the sun. His best adventure took place during the Winter of the Big Snow, shortly before Davy Crockett was killed fighting the Mexicans at the Alamo. The weather became frightfully cold. Everything in the world was frozen fast. When Davy tried to strike a fire, the sparks froze. Even the daybreak froze solid. Davy tried to keep warm by racing up and down the hills and singing himself a song about 'Fire in the Mountains.'

This is his own story of what happened. 'Well, after I had walked about a hundred miles up Daybreak Hill I reached Peak o' Day, and there I discovered what was the matter. The earth had actually frozen fast on her axis and couldn't turn around, and the sun had got jammed between two cakes of ice under the wheels, and there he had been shining and working to get loose till he was frozen fast in his cold sweat.

'"C–R–E–A–T–I–O–N!" thought I. "This is the toughest sort of suspension, and it mustn't be endured — something must be done or human creation is done for." It was so cold

Davy Crockett

on top of Peak o' Day that my upper and lower teeth were all collapsed together as tight as a frozen oyster. So I took a big bear off my back, that I'd picked up on my road, and threw him down on the ice, and soon there was hot sweet bear oil on all sides. I took and squeezed him over the earth's axis until I'd thawed it loose, and I poured about a ton of sweet bear oil over the sun's face. Then I gave the earth's cogwheel one kick backward till I got the sun free, and whistled, "Push Along, Keep Moving." In about fifteen seconds the earth gave a grunt and began to roll around easy, and the sun walked up most beautiful, saluting me with such a wind of gratitude it made me sneeze.

'I lit my pipe by the blaze of his topknot and walked home, introducing people to the fresh daylight with a piece of sunrise in my pocket.'

The Big Bear of Arkansas

18

THE big steamboat *Invincible* pushed up the Mississippi
River from New Orleans. Its back paddle churned
around and around, sending out a wake of white bubbles.
On deck stood a traveling man and a hunter. The hunter
was a famous man along the River. He was called the Big
Bear of Arkansas. No one remembered his real name.

The hunter was pointing out a certain spot to the traveling
man. He called it the Forks of Cypress. 'Right there,' he
said, 'right there I had my best adventure. Right there I shot
a creation bear.' Whenever a pioneer tried to describe something that was too big for his imagination, he called it a
'creation' creature.

That evening the Big Bear of Arkansas told his story.

When he first came to 'Arkansaw' he was a green young
boy. He knew very little about hunting and tracking. He
soon learned a lot, however. He discovered the tracks of
deer and panther and bear. In the fall, when the animals are
getting their new coats, their hides itch. The bears have the

worst time of it. They rub themselves against the wild sassafras trees, trying to ease the awful itch. Bunches of their hair are caught in the bark. A good hunter can tell the size of a bear by the height of these bunches.

One day, the hunter explained, he was walking through the forest, looking for bear, when he came to a sassafras tree. High above his head, at least eight feet above the ground, was a bunch of black hair. 'Creation!' he yelled. 'No bear could have scratched his back up there. It's either a joke or the biggest bear in all the world.'

He thought no more about it until he found another such mark, deep in the forest. This time he could hardly believe his eyes. 'If there is such a bear,' he said to himself, 'I'm going to hunt him. I'd certainly like to have his skin to make myself a blanket.'

He found no other trace of the big beast, however, and after a few days' hunting he returned to his farm. Here he found things in a sad state. Buzzards were circling about the sky over his cornfield. His pigs were squealing their little heads off. His biggest sow was missing.

In the field he saw the remains of his sow. All about the place where she lay were tracks, bear tracks, the biggest bear tracks he had ever seen.

At once he knew who had stolen his sow. It must have been the big bear, the one whose marks he had seen in the forest. No other animal could leave such tracks. He vowed that he would kill that critter. If he didn't do it, he swore by creation itself that he would die in his own tracks or go to Texas. He didn't know which.

The first time he chased the bear, he had no luck. All he found were tracks and bunches of hair high up on the sassafras trunks. Not even Bowie Knife, the leader of his hounds, was able to follow the big animal to its den. When the hunter returned to his farm, his big hog had been killed. There were the bear's big tracks.

'I'll get you yet,' muttered the hunter. He renewed his vow to catch the 'varmint' or go to Texas or die.

Three times he hunted the big animal without any luck. The bear became so bold that he came to the pigpen and stole his dinner, even when the hunter was at home. He ran away so fast that the hounds couldn't catch him.

This made the hunter furious. He thought so much about the big bear that he couldn't eat. He wasted away to skin and bones. He couldn't sleep. His hair began to turn gray. Still the big bear robbed his pigpen.

At last the hunter could stand it no longer. He picked up his gun. He called his hounds. He started out into the woods and swore he would never come back until he got his bear. His neighbors said 'Good-bye,' all except one. The one was a greenhorn named Bill, who had lately moved to Arkansas. He knew almost nothing about hunting and thought he might help.

The hunting party started out at sunrise. Very soon Bowie Knife was on the scent. He snuffed along the ground with the other hounds after him. Before long they were deep in the forest.

At last they found the bear. There he sat in the crotch of a tree, about six feet above the ground. The dogs raced to the foot and barked up at him. He sat there as quiet as a pond in low water.

The hunter and his friend took aim. The greenhorn shot first. His bullet struck the bear in the forehead. This was a foolish thing to do. It made the animal angry. His skull was so thick it didn't hurt him much. He climbed down from his crotch, snarling and growling. All but one of the dogs backed away and waited in a wide circle. That one was a young pup. The bear lifted his paw and batted him out of sight.

Then the hunter took perfect aim. He had to do something quickly to keep the angry beast from charging him and his hounds. He fired his gun, but nothing happened. Click! Click! The gun snapped. It had no cap to fire the powder. The hunter felt through all his pockets, but not a cap did he find. He was worried for fear the bear would attack his dogs.

Instead of turning on the dogs, however, the bear jumped over them and ran away. After him went the hunting party. As they ran the hunter felt something bobbing against him. It was the box of caps which had slipped into the lining of his coat through a hole in his pocket.

On and on ran the bear until he reached a little lake. Splash! In went the dogs after him. They raced to an island in the center. The two hunters looked about for means of crossing the water. At last they found a log and paddled themselves over. This time the greenhorn let his friend fire first.

Bang! The hunter pulled his trigger. Again the bear was merely wounded. He rushed out of the thicket with Bowie Knife hanging on to his fur. He tried to swim back to the mainland, but the dog held him fast.

At last the hunter shot him through the heart and the beast sank to the bottom of the lake. The two men rigged up a grapevine as a rope and hauled the carcass to the shore. They had killed the wrong bear! This critter was a big she-bear. It wasn't the 'creation' bear at all!

As usual, when the party reached home, the buzzards were circling over the cornfield. A pig was missing from the pen.

The Big Bear of Arkansas

Worse still, the neighbors had gathered at the cabin to laugh at the mistake. They made jokes about a hunter who couldn't tell a big bruin from a little she-bear. They offered to buy him glasses. They told the greenhorn to give his friend a couple of lessons.

This made the hunter angrier than ever. In front of all the people from the country he repeated his vow — to kill the creation bear or die or go to Texas.

He spent a long time making ready for his next hunt. He rested his hounds. He cleaned and oiled his rifle and made sure that he had plenty of caps and that the holes in all his pockets were sewed up. On Monday morning he started out. He left a note on his cabin door, telling his neighbors that he had gone. If he hadn't returned by sundown, they could have his farm, he said. He would never come back without the bear.

And then a strange thing happened. The creation bear climbed over the cornfield fence not a hundred yards away. He ambled as slowly and carelessly as though no one were around. Right for the pigpen he headed.

The hunter took aim and fired. His shot struck its mark. The critter wheeled and tore away. He didn't jump over the fence, he ran right through it. Into the woods he crashed with the hounds after him.

By the time the Arkansaw hunter reached him, the big creation bear was dead. It was the right bear this time. He lay there like a mountain. It took five men and a mule to carry him back to the clearing. His skin was so large it covered the bed, with several feet left over on each side to tuck under the mattress.

When he finished his story, the hunter sat quietly for a moment staring at his pipe. 'He was a beautiful critter,' he went on. 'Yes, sir, I reckon he was a real creation b'ar. I never could understand why he gave up so easy at the end. My private opinion is that that b'ar was an unhuntable b'ar, and died when his time come. Or maybe,' he added with a twinkle in his eye, 'he knew when he'd met his match.'

Pirate Jean Laffite

19

BARATARIA sounds like a country in a comic opera. In the early 1800's there was really such a land. At the mouth of the Mississippi in Louisiana, the waters of the river and the Gulf of Mexico form a large swamp. It is full of hidden islands which in those days were full of pirates.

The pirates of Barataria were a gay lot. They captured ships from Spain and South America, made their crews walk the plank, and brought the fine silks and wines and jewels to their kingdom of Barataria. Then they sent notices to the people of New Orleans. 'Come buy our fine wares. Cheap.' The people, who always liked to find a good bargain, flocked out to the market places in the swamp, bought up the stolen goods, and went back home feeling pleased with themselves. They thought the pirates were good fellows.

The boldest of the buccaneers was Jean Laffite. His brother had a blacksmith shop in New Orleans. He became very rich at his evil trade, and rode about the city in a fine coach. He wore beautiful expensive clothes, and danced at all the finest balls. Meeting him, you would never suspect that he was the leader of a rabble gang of cut-throats.

He was a tyrant, in spite of his dainty manners. Two things he insisted upon. The first was perfect obedience. None of his pirates dared to question any order given by the fearful Laffite. Secondly, he could not stand being called a pirate. He preferred the name of privateer. There isn't much difference between the two. A pirate attacks anyone he wants to. A privateer pretends that he is attacking an enemy of his country. Jean Laffite had a letter from the little country of Cartagena. This said that all Spaniards were enemies, and that it was all right for him to attack them. This made him a privateer.

Unfortunately Jean sometimes forgot to stick to Spanish ships. Once in a while he captured a prize that was flying the American flag. He claimed that he loved the United States and that his mistakes made him terribly unhappy. His unhappiness, however, didn't prevent his kidnapping the crew and stealing the cargo.

At last the American Government grew tired of Laffite's antics. The governor of Louisiana offered a big reward for his capture. This didn't bother Jean. He put on his best brocaded vest and his finest lace shirt and swaggered into the city. He even leaned against a wall on the main street, right under a placard that said, 'Five hundred dollars reward! Jean Laffite, dead or alive!'

'Pooh!' he sneered. 'The governor insults me. So I'm worth only five hundred dollars, am I? I'll show him what a real gentleman can do. I hereby offer fifteen thousand dollars for the capture of the governor.' He flashed his white teeth in a disarming smile and bowed politely.

The governor heard about it and choked with rage. He

called in the United States Navy and sent them to blow up the kingdom of Barataria. They had no luck, however. Their boats stuck in the swamp. They lost their way in the bayous. Laffite's men scattered into the wilderness and the Navy had to give up the search.

Then came the War of 1812. The English and the Americans fought up and down the Atlantic coastline, through the Great Lakes, and in the Gulf of Mexico. The English commander heard about Laffite. Because the American Government had put a price on the pirate's head, he supposed that the pirate would be only too glad to help the enemy. With great dignity, as though he were calling on a real king, the English commander put in to Barataria.

Jean received him royally. He gave a great feast for his guest. After dinner the two of them talked over the war. The Englishman told Jean of his plans to capture the city of New Orleans. He offered him thirty thousand dollars and the title of Captain if he and his gang would join the British forces.

Jean listened with attention. When the commander had said his say, his host thanked him for the offer and said that he would have to think it over. The commander went back to his ship sure that he had won a friend.

Meanwhile, Jean, who did love the United States in spite of his pirate's trade, wrote down all that the commander had said. He sent this in a message to General Andrew Jackson, who was defending the city. Furthermore, he offered to bring his cut-throat crew to help fight the British.

At first, Jackson was shocked by the message. Have a gang of pirates fighting for him? Not he! He'd rather go down to defeat than to have anything to do with a blackguard like Jean Laffite!

Pirate Jean Laffite

Later, however, when the British attacked, he felt differently about it. He sent for Laffite. The pirate gang came quickly to the aid of the city. The men fought bravely. No general could have asked for better, more loyal soldiers. In spite of the posters offering a reward for his capture, Jean Laffite was the hero of the day. His loyalty and courage had saved New Orleans from the British!

Jackson apologized to the king of Barataria. He wrote a long letter to President Madison, telling him of the privateer's heroism. The President replied by pardoning Laffite and all his men for all the crimes they had committed.

After this, you might suppose that Laffite would have given up his smuggling and his piracy. With a city at his feet he could have become very rich as an honest man. But not Jean! He soon fell back into his evil ways. Before long the Navy had to send another battleship to Barataria. The captain threatened to shell the pirates' lair, and Laffite was forced to move away.

No one heard of him for a while. But soon ships began again to be captured on the Gulf. Laffite had gathered together an even larger crew of cut-throats. He had built himself a little settlement at Campeachy, where the city of Galveston is today.

Here he was the absolute king. He lived in a large rambling palace called the Red House. This house had been built for Jean by the Devil himself. One dark night the pirate had looked up from his feasting to find the fiend standing beside him. The Devil made an offer. He would build a beautiful mansion for Jean, if Jean would sacrifice the very first living thing he saw in the morning.

Jean was delighted. He agreed to the bargain. The Devil went away to build the palace. Jean meanwhile made his own plans. There was a litter of ugly yellow pups in the yard. He called in his slave and had a pup brought to his bedside. When he awoke in the morning, there lay the puppy, a poor thing, but a living creature.

The Devil was furious when he saw how Jean had cheated him, and vowed that he would have his revenge. Laffite didn't care. He declared a feast in honor of his new home.

After many years of piracy Jean Laffite disappeared. No one knows truly what happened to him. Along the whole coast of the Gulf of Mexico, however, appeared stories of hidden treasure. People had seen mysterious figures walking up the shore carrying chests and spades. Others stubbed their toes against bricks of silver hidden in the beds of streams.

One old couple were having breakfast when three masked figures pushed through their door. The bandits sat down at the table and demanded food. The poor old woman had to serve them her last bit of bread and milk. Without a thank-you the three stalked off into the woods. An hour later as the goodwife and her husband sat shivering with fear, back came the tallest of the three. He drew his pistol and made the couple promise never to speak a word about their unwelcome guests. Then, flinging a dirty package to the floor, he strode away.

When the old people recovered enough to pick up the package, they found inside a thousand dollars in gold.

Even more amazing was the story told by an old soldier. On a grim, stormy night he rode along the gulf shore near the town of Laporte in Texas. It was cold and dark, and as he looked for a place to camp, he heard a thin piping cry. He followed the cry and came upon a deserted farm. In the barn were a herd of goats, huddled together to keep warm. In their misery they were trampling underfoot a tiny kid.

Pirate Jean Laffite

The old soldier picked up the kid and warmed it under his coat. He hitched his horse to a post and looked about for a place to sleep. The little kid bleated as though he were trying to give the old soldier a message. The man let him down and the kid led the way to a broken-down house.

Even in the gloom the soldier could see that this had once been a lovely mansion. He pushed open the door and lit a match. There, under the cobwebs and piles of dust, he could see the outlines of fine pieces of furniture. A fireplace was piled with wood, ready to be lighted. This was indeed good fortune. The soldier made himself a good fire and soon fell asleep in front of it, wrapped in his greatcoat.

How long he slept he did not know. In the middle of the night he awoke to find a tall man standing over him staring into his eyes. He was dressed in a long dark cape which covered a beautiful old-fashioned suit, with brocaded vest and lace cuffs.

He motioned to the soldier to follow him. He led the way through the old mansion, through one room after another, until he came to a small cellar hidden away at the back. Here he stopped and bent over to the floor. He lifted a trapdoor by its heavy iron ring.

Suddenly a light shone from the hole. There beneath his feet the old soldier saw an open chest filled with magnificent jewels and old Spanish doubloons. Bolts of silk were piled against its sides. It was a treasure beyond belief.

The eyes of the strange visitor sparkled as he looked into the chest. Suddenly he began to speak.

'I am the spirit of Jean Laffite, the pirate,' he said in a hollow voice. 'This treasure and even more was mine. Now I can find no peace. For fifty years I have been wandering about the world trying to atone for my evil deeds.'

The poor soldier was frightened by the ghostly voice. He looked about for some means of escape, but the ghost barred his way. 'Do not be afraid,' went on the spirit. 'I want your help. I shall not harm a hair of your head. All this treasure is yours.'

'Mine?' cried the startled soldier.

'Yours indeed,' answered the hollow voice. 'But it is yours on one condition. You must take it out to the world and use it for the good of mankind. It must all be spent to help the poor and the sick and the helpless. Only when it has all gone for this purpose shall I find peace.'

Here the ghost's voice became sad. 'But if so much as one penny's worth is spent for selfish pleasure...' He did not finish the sentence. Instead he wept bitterly. The trap-door clanged shut. The poor old soldier had to pick his way back through the darkness to his fireside, wondering what had happened to him.

At first he thought he was dreaming. He lay down again and fell asleep. Once more he awoke to find the ghostly figure looking down upon him. 'Do not forget,' it moaned. 'Until the treasure has been spent for mankind, I can find no peace.' With this he wailed again and disappeared into the gloom.

In the morning the old soldier awoke and looked about the house. True enough! He soon found the cellar and the trap-door with the heavy iron ring. The door was shut tight.

He mounted his horse and galloped into town. There he told his friends about his strange adventure. They were greedy. As soon as they heard the story of the treasure, they hurried out along the road he had taken. They found the house the soldier had described. But nowhere could they find a sign of the treasure. Instead, they were frightened away by the moaning of a ghost.

Over and over again the ghost groaned, 'Not a penny's worth must be spent for selfish pleasure... Not a penny's worth...'

And because he had betrayed the secret of the ghost, the old soldier was never able to find Laffite's treasure.

Febold Feboldson

20

THE state of Nebraska, for all its golden wheat, has had
its troubles. When it was first settled, the country
around Alkali Lake was upset by a mysterious sea serpent.
Giganticus Brutervious, as the monster was called, lived in
the bottom of the lake. Every day he rose to the surface and
ate twelve yearling calves from near-by farms.

Giganticus was a terrible creature. He had a head like an
oil barrel and great green eyes that flashed real fire. His face
was so frightful that the sun hid behind a cloud rather than
look upon it. Storms and tornadoes raged whenever he
flicked his ears. The mere flip of his tail made the farmers
for miles around horribly seasick.

A dude Yankee stopping at an Omaha hotel wouldn't believe the story. 'A sea serpent in this desert?' he roared.
'Oh! oh! oh! I can't stand it.'

The Nebraskans, being perfect hosts, decided to show him
They set up a fishing camp beside Alkali Lake and invited the
Yankee to spend the night there, free. Before morning, how-

ever, he staggered back to town, too frightened to speak. His hair had turned pure white. All he could do was to write on a slip of paper, 'It's perfectly true.' Then he fainted.

The Nebraskans stood for the monster as long as they could. He grew bolder and bolder. He swallowed an island from the middle of the lake. That was too much! The farmers elected a Committee to Investigate Giganticus Brutervious. They met and thought about the problem. They went out to the lake in the daytime and walked around stroking their chins. At night they raced back to Omaha to a safe spot in the courthouse.

It was decided that the lake should be drained. When the water was gone the monster had to go, too. The Committee offered one thousand dollars to anyone who would drain the lake. The Drainage Company asked four thousand dollars for the job. The Committee thought about it and said, 'Fifteen hundred dollars.' 'Not a penny less than thirty-five hundred,' said the Company.

While they were dickering, the monster disappeared. Giganticus Brutervious has never been seen since. The following winter the icehouse keeper found a mermaid frozen in a cake of ice. Perhaps she was the monster. Who knows?

Once rid of its sea serpent, Nebraska had other troubles ahead. For a while a bully named Antoine Barada ruled the Missouri River Valley. He was as kind-hearted as a baby, but as restless as a tiger. The worst thing about him was his temper. He lost it twenty times a day. For instance, he watched a pile-driver driving a forty-foot pile into the bed of the river to build a wharf. It was very slow work, of course. Suddenly Barada lost his temper. He picked up the big machine and threw it into the state of Iowa. With his fist he slammed down on the great pile. He slapped it down so far

Febold Feboldson

it hit an underground stream and made a well. The water spurted fifty feet into the air.

Barada's pranks, however, were nothing compared to the damage caused by Febold Feboldson. Poor old Febold! He was a kind-hearted, gentle fellow who meant well. But nothing ever turned out right for him. Every time he tried to do the right thing, he caused more trouble.

Originally Febold Feboldson had been a lumberjack for Paul Bunyan. He worked for Paul at the time the great lumber boss filled his camp with Swedes. Hels Helson, Anders Anderson, Lars Larsen — anyone with a name that ended in 'son' or 'sen' could get a job at his camp.

Soon Febold branched out for himself. He moved to Nebraska and started to work on his own. He did very well for a time, too, until his bad luck got the upper hand. The unfortunate fellow had a marvelous collection of animals. He would have been a great success in the circus business. The first of these strange beasts was the hide-behind. No one has ever seen one, not even Febold. It made a practice of hiding behind the loggers when they worked in the woods. No matter how quickly they turned around, the hide-behind turned just as quickly. There it was, hiding behind them and looking over their shoulders. This was annoying, to say the least. The only way that a logger could rid himself of the troublesome creature was to find a filla-ma-loo bird. This bird flew backwards over the logger's head. No hide-behind could stand to be seen by the filla-ma-loo bird, and so the logger could work in peace.

Then there was the hodag, sometimes called the huggag. Paul Bunyan had sent the first of these to Febold in the hope that it might help him get rid of the coyotes. This beast had been bred on Pinnacle Mountain, before Paul sold the mountain to Pecos Bill for the Perpetual Motion Ranch. In order to live on the mountain, the hodag had two short legs and two long ones. Out on the flat plains of Nebraska, the poor things were unable to stand up. There were no trees for them to lean against, so they proved to be entirely useless.

The coyotes finally met their match in the whimpering whingdings. The coyote, as you may know, is a sad creature. He sits on his haunches and bays at the moon as though his heart will break. Febold thought that the best way to get rid of them was to finish the job and break their hearts. The whingdings did it. Their whimper was heart-breaking, all right! It was a cross between the bellow of a spanked baby and the yip of a hurt puppy. The whingdings gathered beside the Dismal River and whimpered until the coyotes felt so bad they sneaked off into the Colorado Mountains and haven't been heard from since.

After the whimpering whingdings came the happy auger. A gay, light-hearted creature he was. He looked something like a kangaroo with a corkscrew for a tail. His job was to bore post holes. As you know, the ground in Nebraska is terribly hard. It's almost impossible to bore a hole for a fencepost. Febold bought some of the ready-made holes Kemp Morgan made out of his duster, but these didn't go very far. Then he tried the auger. The poor animal was gun-shy. Febold crept up behind him and fired his six-shooter into the air. The auger was so frightened he jumped up six feet and landed on his tail. The corkscrew bored into the earth and made a perfect post hole.

Alas! One of Feboldson's neighbors bought a machine gun in Kansas City. He fired it at the auger to see him jump. The *ra-ta-tat-tat* of the gun scared the wits out of the animal. He leapt into the air twenty feet at a leap until he disappeared over the Rockies. That was the last anyone ever saw of him.

The most useful animal Febold ever developed was the bee-line ox. He had been given the job of straightening the line between Kansas and Nebraska. At first he was stumped. He plowed a furrow with his oxen, but the furrow was crooked. Then he crossed the oxen with a bee. A bee always flies in a straight line. When he had produced a perfect bee-ox he hitched it to the plow and tried again. This time the furrow was straight, a real bee-line, as you can see on the map.

In spite of his success with birds and animals, poor Febold Feboldson was pretty much of a failure in other ways. After leaving Paul's camp, he bought a prairie wagon and a team of oxen and spent several years carrying pioneers across the Western wilderness to the gold rush of California. He did well at this until the year of the Petrified Snow.

The snow swept down and covered the whole state of Nebraska. Then it turned to stone. Traveling was impossible, and Febold, who made his living traveling, was having a very hard time of it. None of the pioneers would budge from the tavern stoves in Kansas City. Febold put his wagon on a sled, but still no one would hire him to make the trip West.

At last he thought of something. He drove out to the Arizona Desert and filled his wagon with its burning hot sand. This he carted back and poured on top of the stony snow. The heat from the sand melted the hard stuff and warmed the air. Soon Febold's customers got up from their firesides and agreed to hire him again. A great success, he thought.

He was wrong. When he returned from California he found that the sand had burned right through the snow to the ground. It had burned away all the trees and shrubs and plants in the whole state. Nothing would grow at all, and the heat was terrible.

When the kind-hearted soul saw what he had done to his dear Nebraska he was wretched. Instead of a rolling prairie, here was a barren desert where nothing bloomed. He swore that he would spend the rest of his life trying to right the wrong he had done.

He built himself a little sod shanty on the banks of the Dismal River. He tried to persuade the pioneers to stop and make their homes in Nebraska. If a few people would live in the state it might not be so bad. But the people wouldn't stop. They had their hearts set on the gold to be found in California.

Then Febold sent to Peru for a cargo of goldfish. He jumped these into the Dismal River one dark night. The next day he ran out to the rolling wagon trains. 'Stop! Stop!' he cried. 'I have found gold in the rushing streams of this beautiful state of Nebraska!'

The word 'Gold!' caught the pioneers' attention. They stopped their wagons and rushed to the riverbank. Eagerly they dipped their pans into the stream. The flashing of the fish looked like the gleam of a thousand gold flakes. But when the pans were lifted out of the water, there was no metal in them. Nothing but fish scales! The gold-crazy pioneers were furious and kicked Febold for all his pains. He couldn't understand why.

After his goldfish plan had failed, Febold tried to do something about the grasshoppers. Along with the burning sand from the Arizona Desert had come thousands of the insects. What the sands didn't burn, the grasshoppers ate. Perhaps people would stay if he could rid the state of these pests.

He heard that flying fish liked to eat them, so he brought

Febold Feboldson

in a school of the lovely silvery things. The fish ate the grasshoppers, but the fish were worse than the insects. The skies were full of them.

Now Febold had to do something about the fish. Every time he tried to make things better, he made them worse instead. He brought in timber wolves to eat the fish. The wolves did what they were meant to do. But without any timber around they became homesick. They spent their time howling. The noise drove people away. Then Febold planted cottonwood trees to make the wolves happy. The cottonwood trees bloomed cotton all over the state. Soon planters from the South heard about the crop and sent their negroes out to pick it.

At last it looked as though Nebraska was going to have some settlers. The negroes loved the easy pickings. The cotton grew so thick they didn't have to bend over to pluck it. When the lower branches had been stripped bare, Febold tried to please the pickers by bending down the top branches.

Unfortunately, those bent-over branches kept growing down into the ground. Only the trunks remained on the surface. The cotton pickers gave up and went back home to the South. The timber wolves hated to lose their trees and began to dig down into the earth to find them. Poor old Febold! He was right back where he started. The wolves dug holes all over the state and when they came up they had changed into prairie dogs. Grasshoppers or prairie dogs — what difference did it make?

At last he stopped trying to mend his mistakes. He went back to his shack on the Dismal River and sat down to think. If only he could find something, anything at all, that would bring back the green grass and waving grain to his dear Nebraska!

The next moment he had the right answer. Rain! Yes, that was it! If he could make it rain, the grass would grow green again, and people would come to live on the prairie. But how could he make it rain?

The Indians made a great noise, shaking rattles and beating drums, whenever they wanted to attract the rain. It nearly always worked. Febold had no rattle and no drum. He'd have to think of something else. Frogs, of course, made a big racket with their croaking.

The problem was solved. Febold Feboldson gathered together all the frogs from the dried-up Dismal River. They refused to croak at first. He had forgotten that they croak only when it is raining. But this didn't stop him. He put the frogs under a spell. Gently he stroked their heads and murmured into their ears, 'It's raining. It's raining. It's raining.' He said it slowly at first, then faster.

Before long the frogs believed him. They had fallen under his spell so completely that they thought it really was raining. One at a time they croaked, softly and timidly, then loudly and boldly. The noise grew and grew. And then came the miracle. The sky became gray with clouds. A low roll of thunder sounded and a wind blew up from nowhere. Splash! A few drops at a time, then a light shower, and finally in a cloudburst came the rain. Nebraska was saved!

Poor old Febold Feboldson stood out in the storm and clapped his hands for joy. At last his, and Nebraska's, luck had turned!

The West

Kemp Morgan

21

BULL COOK MORRISON kept a food stand in Snackover, Oklahoma. It was an ordinary little shack beside the highway. Most of his customers were 'boomers,' the tough fellows who worked in the oil-fields.

One afternoon his door opened with a bang. In came two boomers quarreling with one another. Each claimed that he was tougher than the other.

'You're not so bad,' sneered the first. 'Just watch me. I'll show you what it is to be tough... Oh, Bull,' he called, 'bring me a four-pound roast of beef, done rare.'

A four-pound roast is enough for any middle-sized family, with hash left over. But the second boomer wasn't impressed. 'That's nothing,' he snorted. 'Hey! Bull! Bring me that side of cow you've got hanging in the icebox. And don't bother cooking it. Just scorch the outside... Humph! I'm no sissy.'

Poor Bull hesitated to waste his good meat on these boasters. He was sure they couldn't eat all they'd ordered. But the boomers threatened to roast him instead of the meat if he didn't hurry.

Then the door opened again. In strode a giant as big as the Statue of Liberty. He was dressed in greasy overalls and his face and hands were smeared with oil.

'So you think you're tough, do you?' he roared at the two quarrelers. 'Say, Bull, bring me a live steer and a carving knife, will you? If there's one thing I can't stand it's cooked meat.'

He turned around and frowned at the boomers. 'Want to fight, either of you?' he asked politely. With that he rolled up his sleeves and showed a muscle as thick as a tree trunk.

'N-n-n-no, sir,' mumbled the frightened boomers. Their faces had turned whiter than Bull's tablecloths. In perfect step they climbed down off their stools and backed to the door. Once outside, they took to their heels and vanished in a cloud of dust.

As soon as they were gone, the giant called Bull aside. 'That about the live steer was just a joke,' he laughed. 'What I really want is a pair of T-bone steaks, well done.'

Poor Bull, who had been shaking in his boots ever since the giant entered, breathed a sigh of relief. He cooked the steaks perfectly, with exactly the proper amount of onion and gravy. The giant licked his lips when he finished his meal. 'Ah-h-h!' he sighed, wiping his mustache. 'That was really delicious. Permit me to introduce myself. My name is Morgan, Kemp Morgan. Could I interest you in taking a job as my personal cook?'

Kemp Morgan! Bull flushed at the very mention of the name. Why! Kemp Morgan was the most famous man in all Oklahoma. He was the man who had discovered oil. So many stories had been told about him that no one believed in him any more. He was like Santa Claus. And here he was in the flesh!

Poor Bull stuttered and stammered with pleasure. If the King of England had asked him to come to Buckingham Palace to cook the Royal Breakfast, he couldn't have been more flattered.

After a long conversation, Bull agreed to become Kemp's cook. First he protested that he wasn't good enough to cook for so great a man. Then he said he didn't know how to cook for a whole crew. All he knew was how to cook short-orders and sandwiches. When Kemp explained that there wasn't any crew, Bull felt better. Kemp himself did all the work. He was the only one to be pleased.

Kemp was as good as his word. He was the only member of his crew. Rather, he was a whole crew rolled into one person. As Bull got to know him better, he realized that the stories told about the giant were not half wonderful enough. He was a regular miracle of a man.

In those days, before better means were invented, men located oil by 'divining rods.' The oil, of course, was hidden in pools deep under the ground. People who thought they had special powers used to go about the oil-fields with forked sticks. When the stick turned in a certain direction, they marked the spot. Then they told the owners to drill their wells in these places. More often than not, these 'divining rods' were wrong. But it was the only way anyone knew to discover the oil.

Kemp Morgan had his own method. He walked across the fields with his nose bent down to the ground. Now and then he stopped in his tracks. He snuffed and snuffed like a hound on the scent of a rabbit. If the proper smell came to him, he knew that he had found an oil pool. He was always right.

Sometimes he bought up the land on which he had smelled oil. Sometimes he gave it away to other persons. He was a very generous man. Besides, he liked to go about smelling oil, for the very fun of it.

When he spotted a well for himself, however, he went to work. An oil well is not an easy thing to bring in. It takes a whole crew of trained men working together to drill the rock and manage the engine and build the derrick and the tanks. But Kemp needed no help. First of all he dug into the ground with a long-handled spade. When he had dug a narrow hole as far as the spade would reach, he took his sharpshooter and shot a further hole. This saved him a great deal of extra labor.

Into the bullet hole he placed his drill. Down, down, down through the rock he hammered the drill until he struck the pocket of oil. Then quickly he mounted his engine and built his derrick. An ordinary derrick was like a toy compared to his. These were as tall as the observation towers from which forest rangers watch for fires. One of them reached the sky. Like the mast of Stormalong's ship, it had to be hinged to let the sun and moon go by.

As soon as Kemp had finished his derrick he built tanks to hold the precious oil. Then, when a column of black liquid squirted up through the well, single-handed he put on the heavy metal cap and let the oil drain off into his tanks.

Bull Morrison used to stand on the side-lines and watch. His mouth hung open in admiration. Never had he seen anything like this. He almost always missed the capping of the gusher, however. As soon as Kemp was through with his morning's work, he wanted his dinner. Bull had to have it ready the minute the boss had washed the oil from his hands.

Some of the wells Bull watched Kemp bring in were indeed

wonderful. Some of them were strange. Only once did he bring in a 'duster.' A duster is a well that spouts gas instead of oil. It blows dry, hot fumes off into the sky, and then nothing happens. No oil follows the gas. The poor oil man has nothing to show for all his pains except a deep, empty hole in the ground.

Once Kemp brought in a duster. At first he was terribly disappointed. Kemp was never one to mope about his misfortune. He scratched his head and tried to think what he could do with the dry well. At last he had an idea. The farmers of Kansas were always complaining about their ground. It was so hard they couldn't dig holes in it for their fence posts. Without good, deep post-holes, of course, their fences were always blowing over in the wind.

The very thing! Kemp sawed up his well into lengths. He loaded these onto a train and sold them to the Kansas farmers as ready-made post-holes. They were delighted to have them and paid Kemp a very good price.

The following winter, Kemp brought in a gusher on the day of a big freeze. The air was so cold the oil froze as it spouted. There it was — a big, shiny black pillar rising out of Morgan's newest derrick. It was easy to handle. Kemp broke off a piece and smelled it. It was perfectly good oil.

Then he had an idea. Usually he sent his oil East in big tank cars. The freight charges for these were very high. Flatcars were much cheaper. But you certainly can't ship oil on a flatcar.

This was Kemp's chance. He sawed the pillar into lengths, just as he had sawed up his 'duster.' He loaded the cold, black bars onto flatcars and shipped them to the distillery. With that money he saved, he bought a whole packing-house full of T-bone steaks.

Kemp Morgan

The queerest well of all was an accident. The giant had to be careful not to hit his hammer too hard. Once in a while he forgot, and his drill went deep into the center of the earth. On one occasion he was swinging at his drill. He was day-dreaming at the same time. Harder, harder, harder he swung. At last one powerful stroke slammed the drill right through the center of the earth, like a needle through an apple-core. The other end came out in Brazil in the middle of a rubber plantation.

For days the new well gushed pure rubber. Men came from all over the United States to see the white milky stuff pouring into Morgan's tanks. At last a rubber man from Akron, Ohio, heard about it and made Kemp a handsome offer. Kemp, who liked a chance to turn loss into profit, was only too glad to sell.

Like many of his friends in Oklahoma, Kemp Morgan had several adventures that had nothing to do with his business. Often he had reason to make trips across the sandy plains and deserts. On one of these trips he made camp on the open prairie as the sun was setting. He hitched his mules to a sapling. He dug a little hollow in the sand near-by for himself. Soon he was fast asleep.

During the night a sandstorm blew out of the west. The wind howled about him. He had to cover his head with his saddle blanket to keep his face from being scratched by the flying sand. Throughout the storm he lay curled up as best he could. Finally he fell asleep.

In the morning the ground on which he was lying was full of holes. The sand dunes about him were gone. Further-more, his mules were gone. He thought he'd been carried off to a strange place. What on earth should he do next? He had no idea where he was.

Then, from above his head, he heard a familiar braying sound. Hanging from the top of the sapling by their halters, at least forty feet above him, were his mules. The storm had blown away forty feet of the topsoil. Kemp, resting on the ground, had sunk with the sand without knowing it.

He reached up with his powerful arms and bent the young tree over to the ground. The mules were a little weak in the knees at first, after their night of hanging in space. But soon they were able to walk and Kemp went on his way.

The tale which most Oklahomans enjoy telling about their hero is about the time he brought in the biggest gusher in the world. For years he had gone about the countryside smelling oil. Only once had he missed a gusher. Everyone in the state had faith in him. When he stopped and snuffed the ground, people rushed to the land offices to buy up the land. Or, if they owned it already, they rushed to the banks to borrow money for equipment.

In a little-known part of the state lay a wide prairie. Here Kemp stopped one night to make camp. As he bedded himself down, his nose began to twitch. There was the old smell of oil. Millions and millions of barrels of oil, right under him.

He had already as many wells as he wished. Instead of buying up the land he told his friends about it. Out they raced to the prairies. Each of them bought a section of ground and drilled in his well. They drilled down one hundred feet. No oil! They drilled down two hundred feet. No oil! They drilled down three, four, five hundred feet. Still no oil!

Some of them became cross with Kemp. They thought he had been joking. But when they complained to him, he shook his head. 'That's the biggest oil field in the whole world,' he insisted.

Kemp Morgan

Nevertheless, no matter where they drilled nor how far they drilled, they found no oil. Some of them had sold their homes to buy drills. They were hungry. Their children were going ragged. Kemp felt sorry for them, but still he insisted that this was the biggest oil field in the world.

At last the men became really angry. They marched to Kemp's house and threatened to have the law on him. They showed him their worn-out clothes and their hungry children. There was nothing for Kemp to do but to buy in their land. He paid each man enough money to pay for his equipment and to start life over again.

Then Kemp went to work. He had to prove to himself that he was right. He dug down with his long-handled spade. He shot his sharpshooter into the hole. He put in the drill and hammered as hard as he could. Bull Morrison kept count as he drilled deeper and deeper. He went down one mile. The smell grew stronger and stronger. He went down two miles. Three miles. Bull became discouraged. He begged Kemp to stop drilling. 'You'll wear yourself out,' he kept saying.

But Kemp paid no attention. He drilled down four miles, four and a quarter, four and a half, four and three quarters. Still no oil, but the smell grew strong and clear. 'It's coming! It's coming!' he yelled back at Bull. 'Get out of the way!'

Just as Kemp's drill marked the fifth mile, the rock broke under it. From the center of the earth came a loud rumbling and whishing! A cloud of gas and steam roared up through the narrow well. And then came the oil.

It spouted up to heaven. It drenched the whole state of Oklahoma. And all the men who had sold their land back to Kemp Morgan gazed in sorrow at the gusher that might have been theirs.

Kemp was so pleased he made no effort to cap the gusher. He just let it gush. He stood off to one side admiring it, and saying, 'I told you so ... I told you so.'

At last something had to be done about it, however. The angels complained that the floor of heaven was flooded with oil. The clouds were greased so that they slid and slipped around in the sky. There were thunderstorms and cloud-bursts all over the country.

Slowly and sadly, Kemp went to work again and fastened on the cap. He hated to do it. His gusher had been such a lovely gusher.

Then he felt more cheerful. He had made up his mind what to do with his oil. He loaded it into tank cars and sent it off to the East. He bought himself a new store suit and went to New York. When he received his money, he bought all the chewing tobacco he could find. He was going to give it as presents to his friends, the oil men of Oklahoma.

But on the train back Kemp Morgan fell to day-dreaming. By the time he reached Oklahoma he had chewed up all the tobacco himself.

The White Mustang

22

FOR over a hundred years, a wild white horse has roamed the Western plains. The Indians saw him before the White Men came. The Wild West cowboys and their brothers the Mexican *vaqueros* have been trying to catch him ever since. Some people think the Lone Ranger has tamed him and called him 'Silver.' But for all their 'Hi-yos!' I don't believe it.

Only one person has ever touched the white mustang. She was an old, old lady when she told the story to her grand-children.

Her family came to Texas in a covered wagon when Gretchen was a very little girl. With other pioneers they moved westward over the dusty plains, day after day. The oxen that pulled the wagons moved very slowly. There were no roads; the crude wooden wheels bumped over the hillocks and sank into the sand. The sun was hot. The dust and the sand covered everything in sight.

It was hardly a comfortable trip. For a tiny child of four

it was very tiresome indeed. No one could blame little Gretchen for whimpering and fretting. By the time the wagon train reached the *Llana Estacada*, which is the Spanish name for the Great Staked Plains, she had grown so restless that her mother lost patience.

The family had an old blind pack mare named Nelly. Nelly plodded along after the wagons, carrying sacks of cornmeal. She was a gentle animal with a slow gait.

One morning they let Gretchen ride on the meal bags on Nelly's back. To keep her from wiggling and falling off, they tied her securely to the pack. She thought it much more fun than riding in the wagon.

During the day one of the carts broke a wheel. While the men were repairing it, they turned the horses out to graze beside the river. Gretchen, tired out from her ride, soon fell asleep. She didn't awaken when Nelly wandered off from the others.

The hungry old mare followed a strip of green grass to the riverbank. The cool sandy riverbed soothed her tired feet. On up the stream she moved, munching the fresh grass.

Then Gretchen awoke with a start. From across the stream came a loud, proud whinny. Nelly lifted her head. Her ears pricked up. She sniffed the air and whinnied back.

Across the water stood a beautiful white stallion. His body was the color of fresh cream. His long white mane and tail shone like silver thread. He whinnied again and stamped his hoof, as much as to say, 'Come! Follow me! I am your king!'

Old Nelly pranced and capered like a baby colt. She plunged into the river and swam through the rushing current. Up she bounded onto the bank and galloped after the lovely horse. He paced across the prairie as though he were

on wings. After him flew the blind mare, with Gretchen
tied to her back.

The stallion led them on and on into a deep canyon.
Gretchen cried, but the wagon train had been left far behind
and there was no one to hear her. The two horses paid no
attention.

Finally they stopped in a grassy glen where hundreds of
mustangs were feeding. The wild horses caught sight of the
strange old mare and sniffed the cornmeal in the bags on her
back. Soon they were clustered around her, nipping the
sacks and trying to get at the grain. Poor little Gretchen's
legs were scratched and bitten by the hungry broncos.

The white stallion came to her rescue. He fought off the
others. With a couple of quick bites, he loosened the ropes
that tied Gretchen to the mare's back. He picked her up in
his strong teeth by the back of her dress and set her on the
ground beside a little spring. There the tired little girl fell
asleep.

In the morning, she was alone in the glen. Strangely
enough, she wasn't frightened. Everything seemed to be
quite all right. She heard a familiar whinny, and there stood
Nelly, but without the grain sacks. Gretchen clapped her
hands with joy. The mare rubbed her nose against the little
girl's neck.

Unfortunately the child was too small to climb up on the
mare's back. She tried once, twice, and three times. Her
arms weren't long enough to reach.

Without a warning hoof-beat, the white stallion appeared.
Again he picked her up by the back of her dress and set her
gently, oh, so gently, on Nelly's back. Before Gretchen
could reach out to pat him in thanks, he was gone.

That was the last she saw of him. The blind mare wan-

The White Mustang

dered safely back to the worried parents. Gretchen was very, very hungry, but otherwise none the worse for wear.

No one else was ever so lucky as to touch the white mustang. But everyone in the West, from the Rio Grande to Saskatchewan, knew about him and had a story to tell. A few, a very few, had seen him.

The Indians thought he was a spirit. Perhaps the Manitou, the greatest spirit of all, rode unseen on his back. Their arrows passed through him as easily as through air. He raced across the grass-fires in valley after valley. Always he came through without so much as a scorch. They called him the Ghost Horse of the Plains.

The cowboys and *vaqueros* had other names. To them he was the Phantom Horse or the White King of the Prairies. Often they saw him flying across the distance like a white bird. At night the ranchers heard his proud whinny outside their own corrals. Their range horses stomped and whinnied back, so they knew they weren't 'hearing things.' They could tell by his perfect hoof-prints when he had visited their watering troughs and salt licks.

They all wanted to rope him and to break him in. Many a young cowhand lay awake in his bunk, thinking of the mustang. He'd lie there thinking of how he'd throw the lasso, how he'd buy a saddle trimmed with silver and blue turquoise, and how the girls would stare when he rode the proud beauty into town. But that was as far as he ever got.

Perhaps it was cruel for men to dream of capturing the free King of the Prairies. But in those days men needed horses. They needed fast, tough ponies who could ride the open range after runaway cattle. Race horses were fast, but they were frail. And farm horses were tough, but they were slow. The wild mustangs who had lived on the prairies for three hundred years were just right. They had Arab blood in their veins. The white stallion, of course, was the best of the mustangs.

As years passed the white horse was seen more and more often. Perhaps he grew careless. A *vaquero* learned his favorite watering hole. Here he hid one spring night, waiting for his prize.

At dawn his hopes came true. The proud stallion picked his way to the edge of the brook and dipped his muzzle into the water. As quietly as a cat the Mexican poised his lasso. When the mustang raised his head, the noose slipped over his neck.

With a wild leap the mustang cleared the stream and yanked the rope out of the cowboy's hand. Once more he was free! But the noose remained around his throat. After that whenever he was seen the loose end of the lariat trailed behind him.

This taught him a lesson. He became more clever than ever at escaping his captors. It made the men of the West more anxious to capture him, however.

A group of Oklahoma cowboys thought they had him trapped in a large circular valley. At every mile they stationed a fresh rider on a swift race horse. Let the King try to run away from them this time!

But when the chase started, the mustang paced around the circle and out into the hills as calmly as a pony in a riding ring. The galloping race horses were unable to come near him.

At last a Canadian hunter heard the story of the white mustang. He had hunted wolf and deer and bear. He had never failed to catch his game. He boasted that he could take the King of the Prairies, too.

The White Mustang

He knew that mere speed and strength would never succeed. It took brains and patience. He boasted that he had brains and patience to spare.

He bought a ranch in the *Llana Estacada*. He knew the stallion was at home in this country. Out on the open range he built a box stall, as strong as a bank vault and large enough for two horses.

He lined the stall with the sweetest hay and clover he could find. He filled the feed trough with oats. He found the loveliest young mare in the whole country. She was a beautiful thing, slim and brown, with large deep blue eyes and a honey-colored mane. He led her into the stall and fastened her halter to an iron ring.

The door was fitted with a trap lock. Once the stallion stepped across the threshold, the heavy oaken gate would fall and the iron bolts would clamp shut.

His preparations complete, the hunter went back to his cabin to wait. He sat on his porch with a pair of powerful field glasses, watching the stall.

Sure enough! About sundown he heard the high, eager whinny of the mare. Another answered. The white stallion himself appeared on the horizon, pacing daintily toward the new corral. The mustang paused outside to sniff the air. He danced around the prairie, looking into clumps of sagebrush to make sure that no two-footed man was near. Then, when he was satisfied that all was well, he slipped into the stall.

Clang! The heavy gate fell. The bolts clamped shut. The Prairie King had been taken!

The hunter shouted for joy. He wanted to claim his prize then and there. But he decided to wait. It would be dangerous to face the angry stallion right now. Furthermore the stall was strong. In the morning the wild horse would still be there.

So the hunter went to bed and dreamed of the riches and the glory he would gain from his wonderful white steed.

In the morning, however, the hunter's dream turned to dust. Where the stall had been, there was now a heap of splintered wood. The iron bolts had been kicked into crumpled shapes. Not a single stout oaken beam remained.

And over the hill, pacing off toward the mountains, were the White Stallion and the lovely young mare.

The mysterious King of the Prairies and his brown companion were never seen again by human eye. Where they went, no one knows.

Some years later, cowhands noticed that the best mustangs taken in the roundups belonged to a new breed. These were faster and tougher than any captured before. When broken, they made wonderful ponies for the range and the rodeo. All of them were creamy white, with big patches of brown. Because of these spots the cattlemen called them *pintos*, or 'painted' ponies.

Of course, no one can prove it, but everyone knows that the *pintos* were the children of the White Stallion and his lovely brown mare.

The Golden Cities of Cibola

23

DON JUAN DE ESCOBAR and his pretty bride, Maria, rode with the gay company through the streets of Compostela. All the knights and noblemen of Mexico had gathered with their ladies. Some of them were riding north with Coronado to seek the gold of the wonderful cities of Cibola, in what is now New Mexico. Others had come to wish them luck.

What a sight it was! The three hundred Spanish knights rode in their finest armor, breastplates and lances flashing in the sun. On their helmets they wore the colors of their ladies. Don Juan's were silver and blue in honor of Maria.

'Farewell, my lovely one,' he whispered to her as the trumpet sounded. 'Within the year I shall return to lay at your feet such treasures as you have never dreamed. You shall have pearls and rubies to wear at your throat, and dresses of cloth of gold. Never doubt it. Remember the words of Da Vaca.'

Leaning down from his saddle, he kissed his young wife.

The trumpet sounded again, the leader Coronado lifted his sword. *'Dios y Santiago!'* he shouted. 'God and Saint James! He who lives, shall see!' Then off rode the procession, until it disappeared into the northern desert in a cloud of dust.

Back to Mexico City went Maria, to think happily of the day when her Juan should return, to lay his treasures at her feet. She had heard often enough of the riches promised by Da Vaca.

Two years ago a strange, weary creature had been brought to Mexico City by a party of soldiers. They had met him in the desert. He seemed at first to be an Indian, half dead with thirst. But he was no Indian. He was a Spaniard with a wonderful story to tell.

He said he had been shipwrecked off the coast of Florida, near the spot where Ponce de Leon had sought the Fountain of Youth. For years he had wandered through the wilds of America, sometimes cared for by the Indians. From them he had learned of a country so rich that its houses and walls were built of pure gold! No one could imagine the riches that were hidden there.

Then, miracles of miracles! On his wanderings through the desert he had seen it himself. From a hilltop he had seen shimmering in the distance the seven cities, the wonderful cities of Cibola. Every word he had heard was true. The walls gleamed in the setting sun, glittering with jewels.

When he had told his story, no one in Mexico could rest until the cities had been found. Francisco Coronado, then a favorite with the governor, had been given permission to ride north until he found them. He gathered three hundred of the bravest young knights, Juan de Escobar among them.

While Maria sat dreaming in her garden, Juan and his fel-

lows rode north. Over mountains and deserts they plodded, stopping at night to make camp beside a river or in a canyon. Coronado's party was like a small army. In addition to the knights, there were a thousand Indians to act as guides and servants and a thousand pack-horses to carry supplies.

As they moved slowly northward their fine silks faded in the hot sun, their plumes drooped, and their soft leather boots were scratched by thorns. Little they cared, however. Ahead of them lay the promised treasure house which they were to take for Spain.

Toward the end of the journey Marcos de Nizza, who had been sent ahead, raced back to the company. He, too, had seen the golden cities. In the rays of the rising sun their towers had glistened.

Without stopping to rest or to eat, the party pushed on. At the top of a hill they stopped. Before them lay the cities of Cibola. The golden cities of Cibola?

All their dreams and hopes were crushed. Under the bright light of noon huddled seven little mud pueblos. These were no golden cities. These were merely poor Indian villages.

Weary and disappointed as they were, the Spaniards rode down the valley to Hawikuh, the first of the pueblos. The Indians saw them coming and gathered to meet their visitors. Before the town they drew a line of cornmeal. This was a sign that they did not welcome the white man. If he chose to cross it, he must first conquer its defenders.

Coronado, angry at his failure to find gold, urged his men onward. Soon the weary Spaniards had a fight on their hands. This was what they had crossed the mountains and the deserts to find.

After the battle, the Mexican nobles had to decide what to

The Golden Cities of Cibola

do. They had conquered Cibola, but they did not dare to return to the governor without any treasure. They might be thrown into prison for their pains. Surely they would be the laughing-stock of all New Spain.

As they wondered what to do next, an Indian came into their camp. He told them of another country, the Gran Quivira, even richer than the cities they had hoped to find. Exactly where it was, he didn't know. Sometimes he pointed to the northwest, sometimes to the southwest. But he insisted that the Gran Quivira could be found.

No one could imagine the wealth of this magnificent place. It was like a second Garden of Eden. It lay on a broad river, six miles wide. The fish that swam here were as large as horses. Great canoes floated on the surface, each with its awning of cloth of gold. Golden eagles were carved on the prow. Forty slaves manned the oars of each canoe.

Tartarrax, the king of Gran Quivira, lived a life of royal ease. Each afternoon he took his nap on a bed of roses in a beautiful garden. He lay under a tree whose branches were hung with little golden bells. These jingled softly in the warm breeze and lulled him to sleep. Gold and silver dishes covered his table. When he prayed to the Queen of Heaven, he fingered a cross of gold and precious jewels.

All these wonders brought new hope to Juan de Escobar. He wrote a long letter to Maria, telling her of the uncounted wealth he would soon be bringing home with him.

For a year the Spanish soldiers explored the West. Coronado made a camp at the village of Tiguex. From this central point he sent out exploring parties, one in one direction, one in another.

Don Juan was sent first to the West. Through the painted desert and the petrified forest they made their way until they came to a great canyon, the Grand Canyon of the Colorado — but they found no sign of King Tartarrax and his tree with the golden bells. Other parties meanwhile had marched through the bare prairies of the Northeast, as far as Nebraska. These, too, returned without any gold.

Some of the men died of hunger and thirst, others were killed in battle with Indians. Of the brave three hundred, very few were left. Coronado knew that soon he would have to return to Mexico. As a last chance he picked twenty of his best men and sent them to explore the Rio Grande Valley. Perhaps here they would find their long-sought treasure.

Don Juan de Escobar was one of the twenty. Always in his thoughts was Maria, his bride, who waited in her garden at home. For her he should succeed. He knew it.

His party traveled south for several days. Soon they reached the fearful country which the Indians call 'the journey of death.' Rocky cliffs forced them to leave the river valley for the desert where sagebrush and cactus were the only living things.

As the little party slept in its camp the third night, three horses broke away from the others and wandered into the desert to find water. One of these belonged to Escobar. Without his horse an explorer was lost. So Escobar and his two companions set out to find their steeds. By nightfall of the next day they had not returned. The desert had swallowed them alive.

Sadly their fellows returned to Coronado. The great leader gathered together his followers and started back to Mexico. His trip had been a failure.

News of Coronado's return reached the capital of New Spain long before he did. Some Mexican Indians had seen his little army and raced to tell the governor of his coming.

The Golden Cities of Cibola

Not knowing that he was worn out and empty-handed, the gentlefolk of the city rode to Compostela to greet him. Their party was as gay as that which had cheered the explorers on their way.

Maria, of course, dressed in her prettiest gown, rode to Compostela to meet her husband. It had been more than two years since she had seen him. Little she cared whether or not he brought treasure. All she wanted to see was her Juan.

Eagerly she looked for him in the group of ragged, wretched soldiers. She called his name up and down their lines without an answer. No one dared to tell her what had happened. At last one of Escobar's friends, heart-broken to see Maria's disappointment, told her a lie.

'Don Juan is in another party,' he said. 'Some of the men rode south to Mexico City itself. You must have missed him.'

Maria hurried back to her home. But Juan, of course, was not there. A few of the explorers had reached the city ahead of her. They, too, were afraid to tell her the truth.

'Perhaps he has gone to your parents' home to find you,' they lied. 'Go there. He is surely waiting for you.'

Once again Maria raced off. But again she did not find her husband. Finally she learned the truth. Don Juan de Escobar had been lost in the desert. He had never returned. Heart-broken, Maria returned to Mexico City. She shut herself up in her home and refused to see anyone. Day after day she sat in her garden, thinking about her lost husband.

And then, in the fall of the year, soldiers appeared at her gate. Half carrying, half leading, they brought with them a thin, starving creature, too weak to walk by himself. Maria ordered her servant to feed the poor wretch. She herself could not bear to look upon him.

In a moment the servant returned to the garden. 'Come, Dona Maria, come at once,' he insisted. 'It is Don Juan.'

It was indeed Don Juan de Escobar. By a miracle he had kept himself alive in the desert, drinking the milk of the cactus. Indians had found him at a little spring and had taken him prisoner. Somehow or other he had escaped, and made his way home.

When he had been given food and rest and had told his story, he sat beside his happy wife in the garden. 'I have brought you no treasure,' he said sadly. 'The wealth of Cibola, the golden bells of Quivira — none of these can I lay at your feet, Maria.'

'What do I care about the golden bells of Quivira?' she laughed gaily. 'Come, see the treasure that I have for you. Perhaps you will think it even better than the gold of your seven cities.'

She ran into the house and soon returned. 'Here is our treasure,' she said. To Juan the treasure she brought was far greater than any he had hoped for. By the hand she led a tiny boy, the youngest Don Juan de Escobar.

Pecos Bill

24

GRANDY COYOTE was out for his afternoon run along the bank of the Pecos River. Grandy was the honored grandfather and chief wise man of all the coyotes of Texas. As he loped along, snuffing in the sagebrush, the sharp warning smell of human struck his nose. Ordinarily that was the signal for a smart coyote to head in the opposite direction. But Grandy didn't turn away. He had heard a baby cry from the direction of the smell. He went to see what was up.

In a clump of sagebrush lay a little boy about two years old. There were no grown-up humans near-by. The child must have fallen out of a prairie schooner as it jounced up the bank. The pioneers had families so large that one child could easily be lost without being missed for several days.

Grandy took a fancy to little Crop Ear, as he called the baby. He picked him up and trotted him home to the pack. He fed him and played with him until his foundling was as happy as any coyote cub.

As the years went on Grandy adopted Crop Ear as his own

and favorite son. He taught him all the tricks of the desert and the prairie. Crop Ear learned to sit on his haunches and bay at the moon. He ran on four legs as did the other cubs. He hunted with the pack. He learned the animal language and the bird language. He could speak with any living creature, except man, in his own tongue.

In order to protect his foster child, Grandy called a council of all the animals of the plains. From each one he asked a pledge that Crop Ear would not be injured. For he knew that the boy was at a disadvantage. All but the rattlesnake and the wowser agreed.

These two were the most bitter of all man's natural enemies. They were famous for their bad dispositions. The wowser was a cross between a mountain lion and a grizzly bear and had all the meanness and ill temper of both.

Fortunately Crop Ear soon learned to stay away from them. He listened for their warnings — the rattle of the snake and the snarl of the wowser — and so grew up to be a strong young coyote-man without mishap.

The only thing that Grandy refused to teach the boy was the fact that he was a human. No member of the tribe was allowed to tell Crop Ear the story of his adoption. So far as he knew, he was a coyote cub and had been born into the pack.

He might have gone through life without learning the truth if it hadn't been for a cowboy named Chuck. Chuck was riding the range when he saw a strange wild creature. It certainly looked like a man. But when it saw Chuck and his pony it slunk off into the bushes on all fours, just like a coyote. The cowpuncher tried to get a closer view. After a day of tempting it with bits of jerked beef from his lunch, he was able to pat its ugly matted hair.

He tried to talk to it in every language he could think of. He spoke in cowpuncher American, high-brow English, and *vaquero* Spanish. The creature sat on its haunches listening with interest. It seemed unable to understand. But Chuck could see that it was trying to recall something to mind. At last its face lit up with a smile. Out gushed a torrent of words such as 'Ga-ga. Ma-ma. Wa-wa.' Baby talk!

Yes, Crop Ear was talking baby talk. It was the only human speech he had known before his life with the coyotes. Naturally, when he started to speak like a human again, he started in where he had left off.

'Well, tan my hide!' exclaimed Chuck. He 'goo-gooed' back in great style. For several hours the two men stood there, gurgling and calling each other 'itsy-bitsy,' like babies in nursery school.

Then Chuck began to experiment. He branched out into kindergarten and first-grade language. Crop Ear had learned the secret of imitating from a mockingbird. He caught on quickly. By sundown he had mastered the art of speaking cultured English as well as any lecturer.

Then the real conversation began. Crop Ear told Chuck about his life with the coyotes. Chuck told him about the outside world. They talked for several days.

At noon on the fourth day, Chuck noticed that Crop Ear had a blue mark on his left arm. He looked at it carefully. It was a five-pointed star, just like the one on his own arm.

'Yippee, ti-yi!' he yelled. 'If you aren't my brother Bill, the one that fell out of the wagon on the Pecos bank! We always wondered what had become of you.'

Crop Ear asked Chuck to explain this outburst. Chuck then told him all about his family. Their mother had had trouble telling her children from the neighbors'. So she had them all tattooed with blue stars on their left arms. Whenever she saw a blue star, she knew the child was hers.

Although Bill, as he called himself now, hated to leave his dear friends the coyotes, he knew it was his duty to return to the human race. Chuck bought him an outfit of clothes and took him to his own ranch, the I.X.L.

The cow hands were amazed at their strange new mate. They were even more amazed at the things he could do. He never had to rope a cow. He talked to her politely in her own language. When the boys raced their ponies up and down the range, Bill took off his shoes and loped along on all fours. Even so he outran the fastest mustangs.

Soon he was elected the boss of the ranch. He took to the life as a duck takes to water. Before long he was making improvements.

Before Bill came to the I.X.L., a cowboy's life was very easy. The herds looked after themselves. Nobody cared whether or not they wandered off. All the hands had to do was to sit in the bunkhouse. They played cards and rolled cigarettes all day long. If they wanted exercise they raced their ponies. On Saturday nights they roared into the nearest village and shot it up.

Once in a long while a steer had to be roped and butchered for food. The method of roping was very poor. A cowboy laid out a loop of rope on the ground and hid behind a tree. When a steer stepped into the loop, the man pulled his end of the rope. Sometimes he had to stand all day before a steer would step in.

Bill changed all this. He invented the lasso. He practiced whirling it around his head and slinging the loop over the steers' necks. He became so clever at it he could lasso an owl out of the top of a tree while his broncho was galloping at full speed. Then he taught this trick to the I.X.L. boys.

He thought it was wasteful to allow the cattle to wander off into the hills without any mark of ownership. The star on his arm gave him an idea. He had Bean Hole, the cook, bend an iron into the shape of I.X.L. Then he heated it over the kitchen stove until it glowed like a ruby. He held it against the flank of a steer until the hair burned off. When the scar healed no one could mistake his animal. He had invented branding.

His next invention was the roundup. Every spring and every fall he had the boys ride out to the range and bring in all the cattle marked with his brand. It was simpler this way to keep track of the herd.

As you can see, the cowboys had no time left for their former lazy life. Bill kept them busy. Some of them resented all the work. They grew cross and tired and complained that they had no fun any more. So Bill had to scratch his head and think up another invention. This one was the rodeo. After every roundup he held a big party. Every hand in the outfit had a chance to show off. This made them all completely happy.

A few gangs of cowpunchers refused to take Bill's new method of cowpunching. They said the life was too hard. They much preferred their old lazy habits of playing cards and being tough and shooting up the towns on Saturday nights.

The worst of these gangs was the Devil's Cavalry. It had a hideout in a canyon called Hell's Gate Gulch. Old Satan was the name of the leader. He claimed that Bill was a sissy and that no coyote could tell him what to do. In defiance he rode into the town of Dallas and shot all the glass out of the windows. Furthermore he took to stealing cattle. He roped several of Bill's prize bulls and sold them to an Indian.

This made Bill mad. He vowed to make Old Satan listen to reason. He knew it would be a rough trip to Hell's Gate Gulch. He didn't want his boys to be hurt, so he went alone.

It was to be more of a trip than he bargained for. He had gone not more than a day's journey when he met his old enemy Granddaddy Rattler. The big old snake was coiled in the middle of his road. It sprang at his horse. The pony lunged aside and fell, breaking his leg. Immediately Bill was on his feet and grasped the snake.

The rattler was a strong fellow. But he was not strong enough for Pecos Bill. After an hour's terrible battle, the cowman had his enemy by the throat.

'Are you going to obey me?' roared Bill.

The snake gagged and struggled for breath. 'Y-yes, sir,' he said meekly.

'That's better,' said the cowpuncher, cooling off a little. 'Now wrap yourself around my arm and come along.'

With the snake coiled around his arm, Bill loped off down the road, on all fours this time. He'd had to shoot his horse.

At the end of the second day's journey Bill heard a snarl above his head. He looked up just in time to see the King of the Wowsers leaping down on top of him from an overhanging cliff. He jumped aside, but now he had another fight on his hands. Quickly the snake unwound itself and slid to the side of the road. The fight with the wowser was even worse than the fight with the snake. But at the end, Pecos Bill had his enemy's promise to come along meekly. Bill saddled him and bridled him. Then when the snake had coiled itself around his arm again, he set out riding the wowser.

At last the strange party came to Hell's Gate Gulch. Old

Yankee Doodle's Cousins

Satan and the Devil's Cavalry were having a merry time. They were sitting around their campfire roaring and bragging. They were telling all the terrible things they would do to Pecos Bill when they met him.

Bill moved up quietly behind them. With a terrible yell he stepped out. In that yell were all the animal and bird screams and roars and bellows he had learned as a cub among the coyotes. The wowser gave his own terrifying howl. The rattler shook his rattles.

The Devil's Cavalry were so frightened they couldn't move. They turned as white as a salt lick. Their knees shook so that their six-guns and cutlasses clinked like Christmas-tree ornaments in a strong wind.

· Bill strode into the midst of the party. 'Who's the boss of this outfit?' he growled.

Poor Old Satan fainted on the ground. When he came to he looked up timidly and murmured, 'I was, but you be now.'

That was all there was to it. Bill lassoed the gang together and carried them back to I.X.L., where he taught them to be good, modern cowpunchers. The rattler and the wowser came along too, as pets.

One summer, Bill had trouble with the weather. First came a drought. The range grass dried up and the cattle had nothing to eat. All the springs and rivers dried up. Bill dug a canal, hoping that this would solve his problem. It was a lovely canal, but no water flowed into it. Then Bill took his lasso and roped a ten-mile piece of the Rio Grande River. This was enough to last the ranch a day. Every morning before breakfast Bill had to rope himself another length.

As though this were not bad enough, the sky grew green. From the mountains came the wild roar of a tornado. The boys divided the cattle to keep them from stampeding. They did their best to keep them out of the hurricane's path. It wasn't any use. The tornado headed for them whichever way they went.

To save his ranch, Bill risked his own life. He swung his lasso around his head and let fly. The noose caught the tornado and Bill was yanked up, up, up into the middle of the ugly green cloud.

The thought that a human had roped it was unbearable to the cyclone. It whipped around and around, bucked up and down, tried side-kicking and sky-walking, all the tricks of a bucking steer. Bill held on for dear life. Over plains and mountains they raced. The cyclone tried to brush him off against the Rockies. It slapped him against the walls of the Grand Canyon. It bumped his head against the sky. Still Pecos Bill kept his seat.

At last, seeing that there was no other means of shaking off its rider, the tornado headed for the Pacific Ocean and tried to rain out from under him. Bill decided he had had enough. He picked out a pleasant spot in California and jumped. The force with which he landed dug a big hole. Today this is known as Death Valley.

One of the strange things the cyclone did was almost too much for Bill. Before he threw his lasso he put two things into his pocket, a twenty-dollar gold piece and a bowie knife. With these he knew he could get along wherever the tornado landed him. As soon as he hit the earth, he felt in his pocket. The twenty-dollar gold piece had been changed into a couple of half-dollars and a plugged nickel. The bowie knife had shrunk. It was changed into a lady's pearl-handled penknife.

Pecos Bill and His Bouncing Bride

25

THERE were two loves in the life of Pecos Bill. The first was his horse Widow-Maker, a beautiful creamy white mustang. The second, was a girl, a pretty, gay creature named Slue-Foot Sue.

Widow-Maker was the wildest pony in the West. He was the son of the White Mustang. Like his father he had a proud spirit which refused to be broken. For many years cowboys and *vaqueros* had tried to capture him. At last Pecos Bill succeeded. He had a terrible time of it. For a whole week he lay beside a water hole before he could lasso the white pony. For another week he had to ride across the prairies, in and out of canyons and briar patches, before he could bring the pony to a walk. It was a wild ride indeed. But after Bill's ride on the cyclone it was nothing.

At last the white stallion gave up the struggle. Pecos patted his neck gently and spoke to him in horse language.

'I hope you will not be offended,' he began as politely as possible, 'but beauty such as yours is rare, even in this glorious state of Texas. I have no wish to break your proud spirit. I feel that together you and I would make a perfect team. Will you not be my partner at the I.X.L. Ranch?'

The horse neighed sadly. 'It must be,' he sighed. 'I must give up my freedom. But since I must, I am glad that you are the man who has conquered me. Only Pecos Bill is worthy to fix a saddle upon the son of the great White Stallion, the Ghost King of the Prairie.'

'I am deeply honored,' said Pecos Bill, touched in his heart by the compliment.

'It is rather myself who am honored,' replied the mustang, taking a brighter view of the situation.

The two of them went on for several hours saying nice things to each other. Before they were through, the pony was begging Pecos to be his master. Pecos was weeping and saying he was not fit to ride so magnificent a beast. In the end, however, Pecos Bill made two solemn promises. He would never place a bit in the pony's mouth. No other human would ever sit in his saddle.

When Bill rode back to I.X.L. with his new mount, the second promise was broken. Old Satan, the former bad man, had not completely recovered from his badness. He was jealous of Bill. When he saw the beautiful white stallion he turned green and almost burst with jealousy. One night he stole out to the corral. Quietly he slipped up beside the horse and jumped into the saddle.

Pegasus, as the horse was called, knew right away that his rider was not Pecos Bill. He lifted his four feet off the ground and bent his back into a perfect semicircle. Old Satan flew off like an arrow from a bow. He flew up into the air, above the moon, and came down with a thud on top of Pike's Peak. There he sat howling with pain and fright until the boys at I.X.L. spotted him.

Bill was angry. He knew, however, that Old Satan had had enough punishment. In his kind heart he could not allow the villain to suffer any more than he had to. So he twirled his lasso around his head, let it fly, and roped Old Satan back to the Texas ranch. The former desperado never tried to be bad again.

The cowhands were so impressed by the pony's bucking they decided to change his name. From that time on they dropped the name of Pegasus and called him Widow-Maker. It suited him better.

The story of Bill's other love, Slue-Foot Sue, is a long one. It began with the tale of the Perpetual Motion Ranch. Bill had bought a mountain from Paul Bunyan. It looked to him like a perfect mountain for a ranch. It was shaped like a cone, with smooth sides covered with grassy meadows. At the top it was always winter. At the bottom it was always summer. In between it was always spring and fall. The sun always shone on one side; the other was always in shade. The cattle could have any climate they wished.

Bill had to breed a special kind of steer for his ranch. These had two short legs on one side and two long legs on the other. By traveling in one direction around the mountain, they were able to stand up straight on the steep sides.

The novelty wore off, however, and at last Bill sold the Perpetual Motion Ranch to an English duke. The day that the I.X.L. boys moved out, the lord moved in. He brougnt with him trainload after trainload of fancy English things. He had featherbeds and fine china and oil paintings and real silver and linen tablecloths and silk rugs. The cowboys laughed themselves almost sick when they saw these dude things being brought to a cattle ranch.

Pecos Bill didn't laugh. He didn't even notice the fancy things. All he could see was the English duke's beautiful daughter. She was as pretty as the sun and moon combined. Her hair was silky and red. Her eyes were blue. She wore a sweeping taffeta dress and a little poke bonnet with feathers on it. She was the loveliest creature Pecos Bill had ever seen.

She was as lively and gay as she was pretty. Bill soon discovered that Slue-Foot Sue was a girl of talent. Before anyone could say 'Jack Robinson,' she changed into a cowboy suit and danced a jig to the tune of 'Get Along, Little Dogies.'

Bill soon lost all his interest in cowpunching. He spent his afternoons at the Perpetual Motion Ranch, teaching Sue to ride a broncho. Sue could ride as well as anyone, but she pretended to let him teach her. After several months of Bill's lessons, she put on a show. She jumped onto the back of a huge catfish in the Rio Grande River and rode all the way to the Gulf of Mexico, bareback. Bill was proud of her. He thought she had learned her tricks all from him.

Sue's mother was terribly upset by her daughter's behavior. She didn't care much for Bill. She was very proper. It was her fondest hope that Sue would stop being a tomboy and marry an earl or a member of Parliament.

As soon as she realized that her daughter was falling in love with a cowboy, she was nearly heart-broken. There was nothing she could do about it, however. Slue-Foot Sue was a headstrong girl who always had her own way.

At last the duchess relented. She invited Bill to tea and began to lecture him on English manners. She taught him how to balance a teacup, how to bow from the waist, and how to eat scones and marmalade instead of beans and bacon. He learned quickly, and soon the duchess was pleased with him. She called him 'Colonel.'

When the boys from the I.X.L. Ranch saw what was going on they were disgusted. Here was their boss, their brave, big, cyclone-riding Pecos Bill, mooning around in love like a sick puppy. They laughed at his dude manners. They made fun of his dainty appetite. When he dressed up in his finery to call on his girl, they stood in the bunkhouse door. They simpered and raised their eyebrows and said to one another, 'La-dee-da, dearie, ain't we fine today!'

But for all their kidding they were broken-hearted. None of them had anything against Sue. They admired the way she rode a horse and played a guitar and danced a jig. But the thought of losing Bill to a woman was too much. Even worse was the thought that Bill might get married and bring a woman home to live with them. That was awful.

In spite of their teasing and the duchess's lessons, Bill asked Slue-Foot Sue to marry him. She accepted before he could back out. Her father, the lord, had always liked Bill and was terribly pleased at the match.

On his wedding day Pecos Bill shone like the sun in his new clothes. His boys were dressed in their finest chaps and boots for the occasion. Half of them were going to be grooms-men. The other half were going to be bridesmen. At first Bill asked them to be bridesmaids, but they refused. They said that was going too far.

They rode to the Perpetual Motion Ranch in a fine procession, Bill at the head on Widow-Maker. The white horse pranced and danced with excitement.

At the ranch house waited the rest of the wedding party.

The lord had sent back to England for a bishop to perform the ceremony. There stood His Eminence in his lace robes. On his one hand stood the duke in a cutaway coat. On his other hand stood the duchess in a stiff purple gown right from Paris.

Down the stairs came the bride. She was a vision of beauty. She wore a white satin dress cut in the latest fashion. It had a long lace train, but its chief glory was a bustle. A bustle was a wire contraption that fitted under the back of the dress. It made the skirt stand out and was considered very handsome in those days.

As Slue-Foot Sue danced down the steps even the cowhands forgot their sorrow. They jumped down from their horses and swept their sombreros from their heads. Pecos Bill lost his head. He leapt down from Widow-Maker and ran to meet her. 'You are lovely,' he murmured. 'I promise to grant you every wish you make.'

That was a mistake. A devilish gleam twinkled in Sue's eye. For months she had been begging Bill to let her ride Widow-Maker. Bill, of course, had always refused.

Now Sue saw her chance. Before she allowed the wedding to proceed, she demanded that Bill give her one ride on his white mustang.

'No, no!' cried Pecos Bill. Before he could stop her Sue dashed down the drive and placed her dainty foot into the stirrup. The duchess screamed. The bishop turned pale.

Widow-Maker gave an angry snort. This was the second time the promise to him had been broken. He lifted his four feet off the ground and arched his back. Up, up, up shot Slue-Foot Sue. She disappeared into the clouds.

'Catch her, catch her!' roared Bill at the boys. They spread themselves out into a wide circle. Then from the sky came a scream like a siren. Down, down, down fell Sue. She hit the earth with terrible force. She landed on her bustle. The wire acted as a spring. It bounced. Up again she flew.

Up and down, up and down between the earth and sky Sue bounced like a rubber ball. Every time she fell her bustle hit first. Back she bounced. This went on for a week. When at last she came back to earth to stay, she was completely changed. She no longer loved Pecos Bill.

The wedding was called off and the boys returned to the I.X.L. with their unhappy boss. For months he refused to eat. He lost interest in cowpunching. He was the unhappiest man Texas had ever seen.

At last he called his hands together and made a long speech. He told them that the days of real cowpunching were over. The prairie was being fenced off by farmers. These 'nesters,' as he called them, were ruining the land for the ranchers. He was going to sell his herd.

The I.X.L. had its last roundup. Bill gathered all the prime steers together and put them on the train for Kansas City. Then he divided the cows and calves among his boys. He himself mounted Widow-Maker and rode away.

The boys hated to see him go, but they knew how he felt. 'Nesters' or no 'nesters,' the real reason for his going was his broken heart.

None of them ever saw him again. Some of them thought he had gone back to the coyotes. Others had an idea that Slue-Foot Sue had changed her mind and that she and Bill were setting up housekeeping in some private canyon. But they never knew.

Some years later an old cowhand claimed that Bill had died. The great cowpuncher had met a dude rancher at a rodeo. The dude was dressed up in an outfit he had bought from a movie cowboy. The dude's chaps were made of doe-skin. His boots were painted with landscapes and had heels three inches high. The brim of his hat was broad enough to cover a small circus. Bill took a good look at him and died laughing.

Ol' Paul Bunyan

OL' PAUL BUNYAN, inventor, map-changer, scholar, giant, and hero — Ol' Paul Bunyan is the greatest of all Yankee Doodle's Cousins. Even Tony Beaver considered Paul his lord and master.

Most of the other heroes have disappeared. But not Paul Bunyan. He is an immortal. Like the old gods of the Greeks and the Norsemen, he lives forever. Wherever there are forests to be cut, rivers to be straightened, and lakes to be dug, there you will find his footprints and those of Babe, his big blue ox.

Although it's hard to believe, Paul Bunyan was not born in Real America, as he calls the United States. His name was at first Paul Bonjean. His father and mother were French Canadian fisherfolk from New Brunswick.

Nevertheless, Paul is the patron saint of the Real Americans. His people are lumberjacks and miners and engineers — all the people who do Big Things and have Big Thoughts. When they gather about their campfires and bunkhouse stoves, they swap stories and compare notes. Once in a while, some one of them will have a new story to tell. From the twinkle in his eye and the lilt in his voice, his listeners know that he is indeed a Real American. He has had a glimpse of Ol' Paul himself.

When cold winds blow down from Canada, when hot dust

storms sweep from the Western prairie, when the Northern Lights dance in the sky, when floods roar through the lowlands, then you know that Ol' Paul is up to his old tricks. doing Big Things in a Big Way.

How Paul Bonjean Became
Paul Bunyan

26

EVEN before he let out his first baby squall, it was obvious that Paul Bonjean was going to be a hero. He was a large baby, as babies go. Instead of the usual seven or eight pounds, *le petit* Paul weighed seventy or eighty. He was born with a long, glossy black beard and a pair of beautifully waxed and curled mustaches. Furthermore, you could see him grow.

Monsieur Bonjean, his father, nearly burst with pride. Before nightfall, however, he was worried. For the baby had drunk up all the milk that Marie, the cow, could give. The little clothes that Madame Bonjean had made were no longer of any use. The cabin bunk wouldn't hold him. Papa Bonjean wrung his hands in despair.

The neighbors did what they could to help. They gave the baby all the milk from their cows. They gave their sheets for diapers. They spread their blankets in the ox stall for him. Then they went home to bed.

In the morning the whole village gazed in awe at the new baby. He had grown so fast during the night that his chubby little feet and hands stuck out through the doors and windows of the ox shed. The big double sheets were stretched to the ripping point across his tummy. And he was as hungry as a bear. He doubled his little fist and banged it down on the ground, crushing to splinters several racks for drying codfish. He waved his little leg in the air, knocking down two pine trees and a retired sea captain. Something had to be done.

The first problem was food. All the cows in New Brunswick were herded together to give him milk. Several shiploads of cod-liver oil, meant for Boston, were put in storage for him. He had to have three barrels of it every day. The clothing problem was solved by a sailmaker from St. John. He cheerfully donated a pair of mainsails to be made into panties. The Ladies Aid Society offered to do the sewing. A wagon-maker gave a dozen cartwheels to be used for buttons.

Still there was no suitable place for the little fellow to sleep. No hayloft would hold him. Papa Bonjean tried to rent a field from a farmer. 'But,' objected the farmer, 'think of my crops. They will all be crushed and ruined.'

At last the problem was solved. A committee was sent to the shipyards in Maine. They found in one the half-built hull of a clipper ship. The ship was to be the largest in the China trade. As yet no decks nor masts had been put in. 'The very thing we want!' exclaimed the committee. So they bought it.

They asked the astonished shipwright to line the hold with featherbeds. Then they towed it up to the Bay of Fundy. With the aid of a large steam crane, they hoisted little Paul into his new cradle.

It was a perfect fit. The baby cooed and gurgled to show how happy he was, and soon fell asleep. The gentle rocking of the sea and the slap of waves against the shore were his lullabies. He slept soundly for two weeks, with his little pink thumb nestled against the glossy black of his beard and mustaches.

Unfortunately, when the time came to give him his bottle, he would not wake up. The fishermen rowed out to his cradle and yelled at him. He slept right on. The lighthouse keeper sounded the fog horn. Little Paul only sighed in his sleep. What to do next? Papa Bonjean went to the mayor. The mayor went to the Provincial Governor. The Provincial Governor went to the Governor General. He had a bright idea. He knew that part of the British Navy was stationed off the coast of Nova Scotia. So he wrote to the Admiral of the Fleet. The Admiral was very fond of children and agreed to help.

He ordered the fleet into the Bay of Fundy. He lined up the ships in battle formation opposite Paul's cradle. Then at a given signal they fired their cannon over the baby's head.

That woke him up! It frightened him, too! He opened his little mouth and screamed 'Maman!' which is French for 'Mama!' His scream was heard in Boston by the Coast Guard Listening Station. Thinking that the whole North Atlantic fishing fleet must be in trouble, the Coast Guard sent out all its ships to see what was wrong.

Furthermore, the child trembled so in his fright that his cradle rocked from side to side, kicking up waves seventy-five feet high. Even after all these years, the water has not calmed down completely. In some places in the Bay of Fundy the tides are still fifty feet or more.

In spite of difficulties which you can well imagine, little

How Paul Bonjean Became Paul Bunyan

Paul grew up. His childhood was a happy one. His parents adored him and he loved them in return. But something bothered him. His clear blue eyes grew dreamy. His thoughts wandered into far places. He seemed to know that some great task lay ahead of him. But what it was, he couldn't tell.

He went to school with other children. He was extremely bright for his age. Even so he had his troubles. In penmanship, for instance, he could write only one letter on a page. His geography book was so large it had to be carried by an ox team. Once in a careless moment he sat on his lunch box. When he opened it later, he found the first of his many inventions — hamburger!

He had soon learned all that school could teach him. Although he loved to read, he knew that he must learn other things. He had to find out what it was he had to do in life.

Papa Bonjean suggested that he try fishing. For a year young Paul worked with nets and ships. He was a great help to his father. Every morning at sunrise, he towed a pair of three-masted schooners out into the fishing banks of the Atlantic Ocean. Before breakfast he waded back to the docks, a schooner tucked under each arm. Their holds were jammed with cod and haddock. Fishing was easy, but it didn't satisfy him. It was too easy. Surely this was not the great work he had to do!

Next he tried hunting and trapping. He went up into the Canadian woods to learn from the Indian guides. They taught him to follow the tracks of animals, of moose and bear and caribou. He became so clever at this his teachers were amazed. Once he found the body of a dead moose. From the antlers he judged it to be fifteen years old. Nevertheless, he set out to follow the big fellow's tracks — just for fun. He traced them as they grew smaller and smaller, until they became the tiny hoof-prints of a faun. He didn't give up until he had reached the moose's birthplace.

The Indians taught Paul Bonjean other tricks, especially how to shoot. In time he became a crack shot. He invented a shotgun with seventy-six barrels to make shooting more interesting. At first it was impossible to sight down all the barrels at once. But Paul's inventive genius helped him out. He rigged up a system of mirrors. The first time he tried out the gun with the mirrors he brought down seventy-six duck.

On one occasion Paul Bonjean almost lost confidence in himself. He was traveling through the forest at twilight. Far up ahead he saw the head of a deer peek out from behind a thicket. Quickly Paul dropped to his knee and aimed his gun, a single-barreled rifle, between the deer's eyes. Bang! went the gun. Pouf! The deer vanished. Paul supposed that it had dropped dead out of sight.

But, no! As he straightened up, the little head popped back into sight from behind the thicket. It was very much alive. '*Parbleu!*' muttered Paul in French Canadian, '*ce n'est pas possible!* — It can't be true. I've never missed before.'

Again he dropped to his knee, drew his bead, and pulled the trigger. Bang! went the gun. Pouf! The deer vanished. 'Ha!' sighed Paul. He felt better for a moment. Then the deer's head popped back into place again, very much alive.

This time Paul lost his temper. He used all the French Canadian cuss words he knew. Once more he aimed and fired. For the third time the deer's head disappeared and popped back into place. Now Paul was really angry. He had missed three times in a row.

'*Nom d'un nom!*' he swore. 'I'll hit that deer yet.' And

How Paul Bonjean Became Paul Bunyan

with that he started firing one shot after another. His fire sounded like that of a machine gun.

At last he had used up all his ammunition save one shot. He had fired twenty-seven times. And twenty-seven times the little deer's head had popped back into view. He gritted his teeth, took careful aim, fired. The deer vanished. Paul held his breath.

The twenty-eighth shot had done the trick. Even so, that was a bad record. He decided to have his eyes examined.

When finally he reached the thicket where his game lay, Paul Bonjean slapped his thigh and roared with laughter. '*Ho! Ho! Ho!*' he shrieked, '*c'est à rire!*' For there, instead of one deer, lay twenty-eight, each of them shot squarely between the eyes.

As great a hunter as he was, Paul was not satisfied that hunting was to be his life-work. Something inside kept urging him on to different fields. He tried one thing after another. Nothing was right. At last the desire to find Something Big to do in a Big Way got to be too much. He became cross and sulky. He wouldn't eat his dinner, not even when his mother fixed his favorite dish — a roasted moose stuffed with wild boar and a dozen wild turkeys.

He had to get away from things. So with a pack of books and provisions on his back, his rifle over his shoulder, he trudged north into the wilderness of Labrador. He was so absent-minded he stepped across the St. Lawrence River without noticing. On and on he went. At last he found a cave big enough for him, on the coast. Here he settled for the winter.

All winter long he stayed there. He left the cave only to fish and to hunt for food. The rest of the time he lay by his fire, reading and dreaming and trying to figure out just what his life-work was meant to be. He became so interested in his problem that he didn't notice the strange and wonderful snow that was falling on the world. Outside everything was hushed. Forests and thickets, fields and trails, all were being covered with a bright blue blanket. It glistened and sparkled like ground sapphires. It was as blue as Paul's eyes.

Unaware of the miracle, Paul lay dreaming in his cave. Suddenly a great noise made him wake up. He heard the thunder of snow slipping off the roof of his cave. With a rumble and a splash a heavy object tumbled over the cliff and fell into the ocean. Paul rushed out to see what it could be.

Sticking up from the cold black water were the horns and the head of a baby ox. The newborn calf lay still among the icebergs. For a moment Paul thought it was frozen or drowned. He dashed into the sea to pull it out. But it was heavy, much heavier than an ordinary calf. He had to struggle before he could lug it onto the shore and into the warmth of his cave.

When he had finally laid it down before the fire and covered it with his blankets, he had a chance to admire it. The baby ox had bright blue hair the color of the strange snow. It was a big fellow, as big as Paul himself.

'*Ah, Bébé!*' he murmured as he stroked its baby head. At that it opened its big blue eyes, and feebly it licked his face with its big pink tongue. For days and nights Paul nursed the little calf back to health. What a remarkable beast he was! Paul himself had to go hungry, for *Bébé* ate everything in sight.

He was strong — fifty times as strong as any full-grown ox should be. He was playful. He loved to play hide and seek. He liked to lie down in the blue snow, which blended perfectly with his hide. His horns stuck up like black trees.

How Paul Bonjean Became Paul Bunyan

Then Paul would wander about calling, '*Bébé*, *Bébé*, where are you?' And at last *Bébé*, who had been lying in plain sight all the time, would jump up and charge at the big lumberjack.

When spring came, the lovely blue snow began to melt. As the sap began to stir in the trees, Paul's problem began to stir in his mind. Somehow or other, he began to feel that he was about to solve it. Night after night he dreamt the same dream. When he got up in the morning it was gone. All that he could remember was that it had something to do with Real America.

He decided to go to Real America. Perhaps he could find there the kind of work he was meant to do. One morning he packed a little lunch and called *Bébé*. Together they set out. By evening they had reached the border. Off ahead of them stretched the state of Maine, with its miles of pine woods. As far as the eye could see there were trees, nothing but trees.

Bébé romped on ahead. When a hundred-year-old pine got in his way, he kicked it impatiently with his foot. It snapped under the force of the blow and fell crashing to the forest floor.

And then Paul knew what it was he had to do in life. He had to go to Real America and invent logging. It was his job to cut down all those trees and to make room for all the Real Americans who were coming to plant farms and build cities.

He stepped proudly across the border. He started to call, '*Holà*, *Bébé!*' in French Canadian. But the words wouldn't come. Instead he heard himself shouting a new language — 'Hey, Babe!'

He stopped in amazement. He pinched himself all over. He discovered that he was a New Man.

'By the holy old mackinaw!' he said, and he slapped his knee. 'By the great horn spoon! I'm a Real American. And I'll be durned if I'm not goin' to log off this state before you can say "Jack Robinson."' With a whoop and a holler he started right in on his new job.

And that is how *Bébé* became Babe, the blue ox. And that is how *Paul Bonjean* became Yankee Doodle's greatest cousin — Paul Bunyan!

Ol' Paul's Camp on the Big Onion River

27

WHEN Paul Bonjean crossed the border into Maine and became Paul Bunyan, history was made. Together he and Babe moved into the great pine forests and started to work. Paul swung his axe and brought down the trees. He stripped the trunks of their branches and sawed them into logs. Meanwhile, Babe uprooted the stumps. The blue ox dragged his master's logs onto the ice of the frozen rivers. When the thaw came in the spring, Paul himself drove them to the sawmills and shipyards on the coast.

How the shipwrights loved to see him riding down the rapids! He spun the logs under his nimble feet, bringing masts and beams for the clippers. He was a fine figure of a man in those far-off days. His eyebrows and mustaches were as glossy and black as his beard. They ended in fine curls. To set off his natural beauty he liked to wear gay clothes. His hunting cap was wine red, his muffler as yellow as corn.

He wore a lumberjack coat with big orange and purple checks, and pants of tan with quiet gray stripes and a few crimson dots and crosses. Under his black boots he wore brilliant green woollen socks. He wore mittens of a plum-colored pattern on a background of white. No wonder he dazzled the villagers in the seacoast towns.

Before long Paul's business was too big for one man to handle. He had worked so hard that the forests of Maine had been cut over. He needed new helpers and new woods. So he invented loggers and logging camps.

Taking his loggers on his back, and hitching Babe to the bunkhouses of his new camps, he started west. He tried one place after another. First he put the camps down in one likely spot. The trees were tall. The snow was hard. Everything seemed perfect. By spring the river was piled high with logs. When the thaw came, the men started to drive the logs downstream. They drove and drove without getting anywhere. Three times they passed cut-over forests and well built logging camps. The third time one of the boys recognized his own bunkhouse. The camp was Paul's. It was then they discovered that the river ran in a perfect circle. They had driven past their own camp three times. With no outlet, they could never get their logs to the sea. So Paul had to try again.

He had trouble finding a good location. One river, which had a fine stand of trees, was full of boiling water. When the boys tried to spin the logs, the calks were scalded off their boats.

At last Paul found the right spot. It had its disadvantages, to be sure. But the great Bunyan could see that it might be made into an ideal camp. The river wound slowly through a rich valley. It was wide enough for two log drives at once.

Ol' Paul's Camp on the Big Onion River

The pine woods on either side were full of huge old trees. To make the boys happy, off to the north rose the Big Rock Candy Mountain. Its crystal sides shone in the sun. From its ravines gushed many lemonade springs and soda fountains. What a spot for a camp!

At first the only trouble seemed to be the smell of onion. The meadows were full of wild onions. The forests were full of them, too. When the boys started out to the woods, the biting odor made them cry. Blinded by his tears, one of them tried to chop down Paul's leg. He thought it was a giant tree.

This was discouraging. But Bunyan didn't give up. Word came that the garlic crop in Italy had failed. The Italian people were starving. Paul lost no time. He put the boys to work, harvested the onions, and sent them as a present to the King of Italy.

There were other disadvantages. The climate was bad for coughs and colds. The loggers sniffled and sneezed. However, Paul discovered that Lucy, the camp cow, liked to graze in the pine woods. Her milk was so strong of balsam that it tasted like cough syrup. He made the boys drink a glass each morning. Soon they were cured.

You can see that the great lumberjack was not easily discouraged. He was a tough one! Although the loggers were little men compared to him, they were tough, too! At first he hired only Scandinavians, Swedes and Norwegians. They were good workers. Paul liked the music of their names. They all had names like Lars Larsen, Pete Peterson, Jens Jensen, Eric Ericson, and Hans Hanson. One fine day, however, Paul hired a red-headed fellow who said his name was Murph Murphyson. He was a great woodsman. But in time the truth came out. His real name was Pat Murphy and he was Irish. The discovery nearly broke the heart of Paul Bunyan, who loved honesty above everything. He decided that it was better to have honest boys than to have all Swedes.

Among the most famous of his crew were Jim Liverpool and Shot Gunderson. Jim was an agile little Englishman. He could jump higher and farther than anyone his size. He could jump across the Mississippi in three jumps. Shot was an expert at spinning logs. He could walk out into the center of a running river on a log. Then he churned the water so fast that he could run ashore on the bubbles.

Big Ole was the blacksmith. It was his job to make shoes for Babe, the blue ox. When he carried a pair of these shoes in his hand, he sank two feet into solid rock at each step. The job for which he became most famous, however, was that of hole-puncher. After the doughnuts had been shaped out of sourdough, Big Ole placed them on his anvil and punched in the holes.

Another famous member of the crew was Brimstone Bill, who looked after Babe. No one was able to control the blue ox except Paul and Bill. It was Bill who hitched Babe to the crooked logging roads and straightened them out. His only fault was his language. He swore so much that one day he set the stables on fire. The other boys had to use a fire extinguisher to put out his cussing.

Feeding Paul's crew was no laughing matter. In the early years, the cookhouse was run by a master cook named Sourdough Sam. He took his name from the fact that he made everything of sourdough. This is exactly what it sounds like — sour dough. It rises as it becomes warm. As a matter of fact, it rises and rises and rises, and often explodes. Sam fed it to the loggers day and night. For breakfast he served it plain. For dessert he had Big Ole punch holes in it and called it doughnuts.

Poor old Sam! At last his weakness for sourdough got the better of him. The dough blew up. The old cook was in the kitchen at the time, and lost an arm and a leg in the tragedy.

Now that Sam was disabled, Paul had to get another cook. He sent to Quebec for his cousin, Joe Mufraw. He was a French Canadian. The *habitants* of Quebec live mostly on pea soup. So Joe threw out the left-over sourdough and fed the boys on his native dish. Once when Brimstone Bill and Babe were hauling a load of beans across the frozen lake, the ice broke under their great weight. Being a French Canadian, Joe Mufraw couldn't waste anything. He built a fire under the lake, and served the water as pea soup.

Unfortunately for Joe the boys grew tired of pea soup. You can see why. Paul sent south to Alabama for Hot Biscuit Slim. Slim was an artist. He took one look at the cookhouse and started to leave. Only when Paul promised to build a new one to suit him would he agree to stay. Slim's new building was a wonder. The dining hall was larger than Grand Central Station in New York. The tables were so long that a four-horse team was needed to haul the salt and pepper from shaker to shaker. Flunkies on roller skates dashed up and down filling the water glasses.

The kitchen was enormous. It was divided into departments. Overhead cranes carried the food from one section to the other. A special feature was the air-tight onion room, in which were stacked barrels and barrels of the fragrant vegetable.

Beyond the main kitchen stood a shack for the cooking of hotcakes or flapjacks. A small lake was dug to hold the batter. A second-hand steamboat was bought from a river captain to stir the ingredients. When the batter was properly mixed, it was poured on to the griddle. This was one of the marvels of the age. It was so large that at first there seemed to be no way of greasing it. Finally Slim hired an extra group of flunkies. He strapped sides of bacon to their feet and made them skate over the surface of the griddle.

With Hot Biscuit Slim in the kitchen, most of Paul's troubles were over. The food was so good that the men worked harder than ever. Paul himself had to spend all his time keeping books. He needed someone of his own stature who could boss the work in the woods. One fine day, almost in answer to prayer, a giant appeared at the camp. He was nearly, but not quite, as big as Paul. His name was Hels Helson, although he preferred to be called the Bull of the Woods. Some of the boys nicknamed him the Big Swede. The only Real American words he knew were 'Ay tank so!' When Paul offered him the job of foreman, he said simply 'Ay tank so!' And that was that.

At first Hels did a fine job. But, alas, his importance went to his head. He began to think he was as big as Paul. Meanwhile Paul Bunyan received an order to log off the Mountain That Stood on Its Head. He could see that the Big Swede's conceit was going to cause trouble. He decided to nip it in the bud.

Calling the Swede into his office, he explained the new job. The mountain really did stand on its head. The broad base was on top, the narrow peak at the bottom. All the trees grew straight down, with their roots above their heads. When Paul asked the Swede if he could manage the job, Hels said, 'Ay tank so,' and swaggered out of the office.

The next morning the new foreman sent the boys off to the job. They had a terrible time. They had to chop down the trees standing on their heads. They had to hang on to the ground for dear life, lest they fall into the valley below them. What a situation! The work went slowly and more slowly, until it was obvious that it would never be finished. At last Paul took over. He loaded his seventy-six-barrel shotgun with crosscut saws, aimed it at the mountain, and fired. Lo and behold! Seventy-six trees fell off into the valley, their stumps cut clean. Time and again he fired until the mountain was cleared of timber.

Meanwhile Hels Helson sat brooding on the side-lines. He wanted to be the boss. He resented Bunyan's interference. At last he could stand it no longer. With a flying leap he landed on top of the mountain.

Paul looked up. It made him angry to see the Swede showing off in front of his boys. 'Who do you think you are — the boss of this outfit?' he bellowed.

'Ay tank so,' roared back the Swede.

That was enough. No one had ever before dared to question Bunyan's authority. He rolled up his sleeves, and spat on his hands. With a running jump he landed on top of the mountain beside his mutinous foreman.

'We'll see about that,' muttered the great logger. He drew back his arm and placed his fist on the Swede's chin. The Bull of the Woods replied in kind. Soon the two giants were fighting, tooth and nail. Never before or since has there been such a battle.

The fight went on for weeks. When at last the dust and the noise died down, the mountain was gone. Instead of the upside-down miracle, there remained only a few jagged hills. The Big Swede lay unconscious in their midst. Paul, the hero, the giant, the demi-god, stood upright, wiping the dust out of his eyes. Never again did anyone question his right to be the Boss.

Yankee Doodle's Cousins

When the Swede recovered from his wounds, he apologized. Paul forgave him and made him his foreman for life.

About this time, the loggers came upon a new country which they called Pine Orchard. Here the trees grew straight and tall, without any branches or bark. Furthermore, they were spaced in straight rows. It would be as easy as eating pie to log it off. In fact, it was a lumberjack's dream. They lost no time in calling Paul. He whistled to Babe, and within an hour a temporary camp had been set up, and the loggers were hard at work.

The work went smoothly. In no time the logs had been stacked in neat piles and were floating down the river. Paul had spent a week in his office keeping books on the job. His eyes were tired and his whole vigorous spirit rebelled against figures and pens and ink. If only he had a bookkeeper!

He and Babe set out for a walk to rest his eyes. Suddenly he noticed a mountain where no mountain should have been. He heard a moaning sound he had never heard before. There, sitting on a cliff with his feet in the river, was another giant. He was no lumberjack like Paul or the Swede. That was easy to see from his store-bought clothes and his high white collar. He was groaning and running his hands through his hair in despair.

'My stakes!' he groaned. 'My beautiful, beautiful stakes.'

Paul was a tender-hearted soul, and the sight of this sad creature touched him. He asked what the trouble might be.

'Alas,' said the stranger, 'I am a surveyor. Ten years I have labored, all for naught. I surveyed this country and planted stakes at every section line. Now they are gone, and all my work is lost. Alas! Alackaday!' He groaned louder than ever.

248

Ol' Paul's Camp on the Big Onion River

Paul, of course, had no idea what he was talking about. But he knew how sad the other fellow must be if his work was lost. He wanted to help.

'What do you mean, your stakes?' he asked gently.

The mention of his stakes simply made the giant moan more than ever. It was an hour before he could speak clearly. 'My surveyor's stakes. I marked this country off into sections. Wherever two section lines crossed, I planted a stake. There were hundreds and hundreds of them, all my life's work. And now someone has cut them down.' He wiped a tear from his eye. 'They stretched out as far as the eye could see, like an orchard of straight pine trunks.'

An orchard of straight pine trunks? Pine Orchard! The two ideas crossed Paul's mind at once. Slowly a bright red blush spread up his neck and across his face. Even his glossy black beard turned fiery red in his embarrassment. Pine Orchard, of course! Those beautiful trees his boys had logged off had not been trees at all. They belonged to this giant.

It was hard for him to do it, but Paul admitted to the giant what he had done. The latter let out a howl of anguish, and again buried his face in his hands. He wailed and wept until a terrible thunderstorm swept the whole United States east of the Mississippi. The poor fellow was beside himself.

Paul felt very bad about the whole thing. There was little he could do to make amends. He could see that his stupid mistake had ruined the stranger's whole life. Gently he and Babe led the moaning giant back to camp and put him to bed in Paul's own bunk. They fed him all the best foods Slim knew how to make. They waited on him day and night. If only he would stop weeping and tell them how they could repay him!

Yankee Doodle's Cousins

Weeks later, the stranger recovered a little. He sat up in the bunk and smiled a faint wan smile. He said he was sorry for all the trouble he had caused his host. But he couldn't help himself. He had spent years working on that surveying, and his job depended on them. Now he had no job. There was nothing else for him to do in life. Then he introduced himself. He said his name was John Rogers Inkslinger, surveyor, inventor, and bookkeeper by profession.

'Bookkeeper?' roared Paul with delight. 'Bookkeeper? I am certainly pleased to meet you.' He wrung Mr. Inkslinger's hand until the poor creature winced from pain. 'I've been looking for a bookkeeper. Will you do me the honor of working for me?' he bellowed.

Poor Mr. Inkslinger was startled. But the offer of a job and the tenderness with which Paul had nursed him back to health made him forget his sorrow. The big logger led him to the office and showed him the stacks of books that needed keeping. The sight of pen and ink was too much for the invalid. He grinned. He dashed for the desk and started to work happily.

The work was all that he needed to make him completely well. He soon forgave Paul for the accident at Pine Orchard. Forever after he was the chief bookkeeper in Bunyan's camp. One summer, when the ink threatened to give out, he saved nine barrels of it, simply by leaving the dots off the i's and the crosses off the t's. He was, in fact, a man after Paul's own heart.

With Johnny Inkslinger in the office, the Big Swede in the woods, and Slim in the kitchen, Paul was at last free to enjoy himself. He was free to act the way a hero ought to act. And while he carried on his great business of logging, he did Big Things in a Big Way.

How Ol' Paul Changed the Map of America

28

THE map of Real America must have been very dull in the days before Paul Bunyan changed it. No mountains, no lakes, no rivers! Nothing but plain, flat land! You could roller skate from the Atlantic to the Pacific, if you wanted to do such a thing.

Whether or not Paul intended to make any changes, we don't know. Wherever he went, however, strange and wonderful things took place.

He had a remarkable effect on the weather. When Paul was around, the weatherman lost his head and the seasons turned somersaults. There was the Hot Hot Hot Summer, for instance. It happened soon after Hot Biscuit Slim came to Onion River.

Slim told Paul about the joys of eating corn-on-the-cob. He described it so well that Paul could feel the hot butter trickling down his chin. His mouth watered. He had to taste some. So he planted the whole state of Iowa with sweet corn and licked his chops.

Paul never had his corn-on-the-cob, however. The weather turned hot, hotter, hottest. The corn shot up out of the ground like smoke from a fire. The kernels burst from their ears and fell to the ground. Under the blazing sun, they popped as they fell. Soon Iowa was covered four feet deep with popcorn.

That wasn't the end of it, either. A big wind blew in from the northeast and carried the corn to Kansas. There it fell from the skies like a blizzard. Thousands of cattle, grazing on the Kansas fields, thought it was snow and promptly froze to death.

Then there was the spring the Rains Came Up From China. Paul and his boys were logging off the country around the Cascade Mountains in Oregon. They had only started the job when it began to rain. It didn't rain down from the skies. It rained up from the earth. For days on end, the ground oozed rain. Some drained off and formed the Cascade River with its lovely waterfalls. In other places it never stopped. It's still bubbling up in the hot springs and little geysers of Yosemite Park. Incidentally, it was from this season that Mount Rainier took its name.

Some years later, after Paul had returned to his Onion River Camp, he became restless. He'd heard about the cypress forests of Louisiana, and he wanted to see them. But before he reached them, it began to rain again. This time the rain fell down, all right, but it was all of a bright red color. For sixteen days and seventeen nights the Red Rain fell. Some of it is still running off in the Red River of Arkansas.

On this walk to Louisiana Paul got sand in his shoes. Of course, sand isn't comfortable to walk on. So he sat down

How Ol' Paul Changed the Map of America

on the Ozarks and poured out the sand into a ragged pile. This pile is known as the Kiamichi Mountains of Eastern Oklahoma.

I could go on all night telling you about Paul's special weather. There was the Year of the Hard Winter. The words froze in the air as soon as they were spoken. Several of the lumberjacks bumped into them in the dark and cut their foreheads. In the spring, when the conversations thawed out all at once, the noise was terrible.

Paul's most important work in changing the map, however, was done without any help from the weatherman. Just as in the case of the Kiamichi, he did it alone, sometimes by accident. Even Babe did some of it.

If you've ever been to North Dakota you know that there are huge tracks in the rocks. Scientists say that these are the tracks of dinosaurs. Dinosaurs were huge animals that lived in North America long before man became man. Of course, we know that they are Babe's hoof-prints.

There are many iron mines in Northern Michigan near Lake Superior. It was Paul who opened them in order to find metal for Babe's shoes. He opened a new one every time the ox needed to be shod.

You have read already about one of Paul's smaller feats. This took place when he fought the Big Swede on top of the Mountain That Stood on Its Head. After the battle, when the dust had cleared away, nothing remained of the strange mountain but a pile of broken earth. This is what we call the Bad Lands of the Dakotas.

Geography isn't a matter of maps alone. It takes in other things, such as businesses and farm products. Paul dabbled even in these. He went hunting in Canada one fine autumn morning. His little hunting dog Elmer suddenly found the track of a huge buck. Together Paul and Elmer trailed the buck down the St. Lawrence Valley, across Ontario. In Michigan Paul managed to shoot — but his shot merely wounded the animal. On and on raced the buck, the hunter after him. He plunged into the icy waters of Lake Michigan and struggled across. But the effort of swimming and the loss of blood were too much. The big buck fell dead on the opposite shore, right on the Chicago waterfront.

Paul didn't want the meat. He had a large dinner waiting for him back in Onion River. So he sold the carcass to a butcher, who cut it up and used it to start the meat-packing business, for which Chicago is famous.

The map of North America owes a great deal to a sad year in Paul's life. Babe became ill. His bright blue coat faded and grew dull. His lovely big eyes rolled unhappily. Paul and Johnny Inkslinger got down all their books on medicine and tried to cure him. Nothing did any good. At last Johnny suggested that a change in climate would help. Paul was only too glad to do anything that might cure his adored pet. Within an hour he had the bunkhouses packed and was off on his long trip west.

This time, of course, the procession moved slowly. Paul carried the bunkhouses on his shoulders and Brimstone Bill walked beside Babe, feeding him medicine and keeping cold packs on his head. It was a tiresome trip. In Colorado they stopped to rest. The Big Swede, in order to mark the trail, set up a pile of rocks. Paul helped him and stuck in a pike, or pole, in order to top it off. This has since become known as Pike's Peak.

From Colorado the party moved northwest. Paul had heard about the wonderful sulphur springs which cure all illnesses. In one corner of Wyoming he thought he heard one of these springs bubbling under ground. Here he stopped and started to dig a drinking hole for Babe. He'd gotten down about a hundred feet without striking water, when the hole dropped out from under. This surprised him so that he dropped his spade. Down, down, down it fell until it was completely lost from sight in the middle of the earth.

Paul was about to dig another hole with another spade, when he heard a rumbling and a hissing below. Whish! Like a shot out of a gun, his spade flew into the air. It was completely melted. It was carried up on a column of steam. High in the air it hung for a moment and then sank back into the hole.

Ever since that day, every hour on the hour, the spade has been shot up into the air and then has fallen back into the hole. Some years ago the Government named it Old Faithful and put Yellowstone Park around it.

The long trip over the Rockies was hard on the sick ox. By the time they reached Utah, he was unable to go any farther. His fever was high. He put out his pale tongue and feebly licked Paul's hand. His eyes looked up miserably as much as to say 'Good-bye.' Paul and Johnny were sure he was going to die.

The big lumberjack sadly dug a grave for his beloved Babe. As he dug he wept bitter salt tears. At last he was crying so hard he had to stop digging. He sat down beside the grave and let himself go. The tears gushed from his eyes.

Someone touched him on the shoulder. It was Brimstone Bill. Paul, of course, thought that Bill had come to tell him that Babe was dead. He wept more than ever. Not until a soft warm tongue licked his cheek did he realize that Babe was better. By some miracle the ox had lived through the crisis. He was still weak, but he was going to get well.

How Ol' Paul Changed the Map of America

Paul jumped up in joy. He hugged Babe and patted him and acted like a crazy man. He set off immediately for the pleasant climate of California, so that Babe could take it easy as he was growing stronger. But the grave full of salt tears was left behind. Great Salt Lake is there today, a monument to Paul's sorrow.

After a winter in California, Babe grew well and strong. Word came to Paul about the Stonewood Forests in Arizona. They were not far away, so he and Babe walked over one evening to see. The trees were as hard as rock. The wood was colored in lovely reds and yellows and browns. Altogether Paul thought it the most interesting logging country he had ever seen. He planned to bring his camp over and to start cutting right away.

Unfortunately, Babe's illness had left him with a bad case of hay fever. The dry, stone dust of the forest floor got up his nose. He sneezed. He sneezed again and again. His eyes began to run. Paul saw at once that this was no country for an animal with hay fever. So he gave up his plans and hurried back to California. Babe's sneezes had another effect, though. They raised the dust storms which blow across Oklahoma and Texas, burying farms and ranches under their white powder.

On the way back to California, Paul discovered a little river, shaded by walls of rock. The hot sandy floor of Arizona had burned his feet. The water looked cool and inviting. Paul pulled off his shoes and waded for a while. As he waded he let his pickaxe drag in the water behind him. To this day you can see the track it made. We call it the Grand Canyon of the Colorado River.

Paul Bunyan hated to hire himself out to another boss. He wanted to be the boss himself. Once, at least, he did agree to work for another man. The government needed a new bay, or sound. The President sent surveyors out to the West to find a good place. They suggested the coast of Washington. This sounded good to the President and he hired the Dan Puget Construction Company to do the work. Puget was a good man. But he was a little man, not used to doing things on Paul's scale. He worked and worked and worked. Alas, the job was too big for him.

He sent for Paul and begged him to come and help. Bunyan didn't like the idea of working for a man who couldn't do his own work properly. But he was kind-hearted. He felt sorry for Mr. Puget and agreed to his terms.

After one brief look around the country, Paul knew exactly what to do. Steam-shovels and pile-drivers were mere toys to him. He needed a glacier. He drove Babe up to Alaska, hitched him to a glacier with the sharp side down, and started back to the States.

They had hardly left Alaska before they had an accident. A pretty young schoolteacher with a pink parasol crossed the road. Most bulls go mad at the sight of the color red. Babe went mad when he saw pink. To make matters worse, the schoolmarm stopped in her tracks when she saw the enormous ox and his driver. In her surprise she twirled her parasol around and around, right under Babe's nose.

The big blue ox couldn't help it. He lowered his head, and pawed the ground angrily. Fire and smoke poured out from his nostrils. With a bellow of pain he rushed at the pink object and snatched it from the girl's hand. Then off he went like a tornado. He roared up and down the coast of British Columbia and the coast of Washington. The glacier dragged behind him like a driverless plow. It was several hours before they could calm him down. When at last they led him off to the stable, there lay a great gash in the earth. Puget Sound was dug. Not only Puget Sound, but the Hood Canal as well!

The biggest change Paul made in the map of North America was one of the first of all. It took place while he was building the Onion River Camp. He needed reservoirs for drinking water, both for his men and for the animals about the place. Babe, of course, drank a whole lake full every morning before breakfast. So the lumberjack dug the Great Lakes. He started with Lake Ontario. This proved to be too small to be practical. He moved a little farther west and dug Lake Erie, several sizes larger. These two little lakes did very well until his camp began to grow. When the Big Swede and Johnny Inkslinger joined his company he needed still larger reservoirs.

He dug Huron and Michigan, in the hope that they would prove to be enough. Not until he had finished the largest lake of all, Superior, did he have a really good water supply.

Babe and Brimstone Bill filled the lakes. They hauled water from the Atlantic Ocean on big sleds. Once Babe tripped over a small hill in the Huron Range. The sled turned over and spilled the big tank of water. Down to the south it poured in a rushing flood. Paul realized that the whole country would be flooded. Fields and towns and railroads would all be carried down to the Gulf of Mexico. To avoid disaster he grabbed up his spade. He ran ahead of the water, digging a channel for it to flow into. On either side of the ditch great spadefuls of earth were tossed into the air. They landed in long even piles, one to the east, one to the west. Paul Bunyan reached the Gulf just in time. The water spilled safely out into the ocean stream without doing any damage.

Yankee Doodle's Cousins

The ditch, as you may have guessed, is still filled with a great river, the Mississippi. The ridges of earth thrown up by Paul's spade are none other than the Rocky Mountains and the Appalachians. Wouldn't the map of North America be dull without these?

Glossary

A

Admiral: the chief officer of the navy.

Admiralty: the office in London that looks after the Royal Navy.

antics: pranks or tricks.

antlers: the horns of a stag.

artesian well: a deep well drilled straight down into the springs underground.

atone: to make up for something.

B

backwater: a small, shallow pond that flows into a stream or river.

balsam: a kind of evergreen tree.

Bang-All: the name of Mike Fink's rifle.

bass: a kind of fish.

bayou: a winding channel in the swamps of Louisiana.

Bébé: the French way of saying Babe.

Betsey: the name of Davy Crockett's rifle.

bit: a metal bar which, placed in the horse's mouth, connects the reins; part of the bridle.

blackguard: a wicked person.

blizzard: a very bad snowstorm.

block and tackle: a pulley; a system of ropes and pulleys which makes it possible to lift heavy things.

blockhouse: a log fortress.

bos'n: the boatswain; an officer on board ship.

bouquet: a bunch of flowers.

bowie knife: a long knife used by the pioneers, invented by Colonel James Bowie.

bronco: a small, wild horse of the Western plains; a mustang.

bruin: a bear.

buccaneer: a pirate; a sea robber.

bucksaw: a big saw attached to a wooden frame; used for sawing logs.

bullhead: a kind of fish.

bull's-eye: the center of a target.

bunkhouse: wooden house or shanty containing bunks for lumberjacks.

burgomaster: a high officer in a Dutch city; one of the important men in the town.

Glossary

C

calks: nails or bits of metal on the soles of boots to protect the leather and to prevent slipping.

canyon: a long, narrow gorge or ravine; the bed of a stream between high cliffs of rock.

cap (in *The Big Bear*): a small charge of powder or explosive which makes the gun fire.

cap (an oil well): to close an oil well with a heavy 'cap' of metal which prevents the oil from running off and being wasted.

capstan: a machine on shipboard which winds and unwinds the anchor chain.

caravel: a fleet of ships sailing together.

carcass: the body of an animal.

caribou: a large animal like a reindeer found in the Arctic regions of North America.

c'est-à-rire: French for 'What a joke!'

chaps: wide leather leggings the cowboys wear over their pants.

cider press: a machine that presses cider from apples.

cloven: split.

clue: a hint used in solving a mystery.

cobbler: a shoemaker.

comic opera: a funny play with music.

committee: a group of persons appointed to get something done.

Congress: the group of people who are elected by the citizens of the United States to go to Washington to make the laws.

corral: a pen for horses or cattle.

cotton batting: soft, thick rolls of cotton used in making quilts and stuffing for chairs, etc.

cove: a little bay or inlet.

coyote: a wild animal of the dog family, found on the Western prairies.

crest: the top, or peak, of a hill.

crisis: a turning point; usually a very serious time when things have to turn either for the better or for the worse.

critter: properly, a creature; a living thing.

crotch: a fork between two branches.

cruet: a bottle for holding vinegar or syrup.

curb: hold back.

cutaway coat: a formal coat for men.

cyclone: a very bad windstorm on the prairies.

cypress: an evergreen tree found in our Southern States.

D

Davy Jones's Locker: the bottom of the sea.

desperado: an outlaw; a bad-man.

distillery: a place where oil is made pure.

dory: a small rowboat.

doubloon: a Spanish gold coin.

Drainage Company: a company which

Glossary

makes a business of draining swamps.

draw: a tie.

drumstick: the leg of a chicken, or goose or turkey.

dude: a city fellow who tries to act like a cowboy; a greenhorn.

dungarees: work pants, usually made of blue denim.

dynamite: a high explosive.

E

Eminence (His): a title given to a bishop.

Execution Dock: a dock in London where pirates were hanged.

F

fang: a long sharp tooth of an animal.

fawn: a young deer.

fiend: a devil; a demon.

fire extinguisher: a machine for putting out fires.

fish fry: a party at which the refreshments are fried fish.

flanks: sides.

flats: a flat plain without grass or trees.

flinching: drawing away, as if in pain.

florist: a man who sells flowers.

flunkies: servants.

fore-bitts: the central part of a ship's deck, in front of the 'bitts,' posts for tying the cables; about the middle of the ship is what Stormalong means.

foreman: the boss of a group of workmen.

foundling: an orphan; a baby deserted by its parents and left for someone else to look after.

frontier: the last edge of settled country; the beginning of the wilderness.

frontlet: the forehead of a steer.

furl: wind up.

furrow: the track left by a plow.

G

gait: manner of walking.

galley: the kitchen on board ship.

geographers: men who write geographies; map-makers.

girders: steel beams.

glacier: big mass of ice; river of ice.

Governor General: the King's officer in Canada.

greenhorn: an ignorant fellow.

gun shy: afraid of the noise made by a gun.

gusher: an oil well from which the oil spouts into the air.

H

habitants: French-Canadian farmers.

hangar: a big shed for airplanes.

hard-tack: hard, dry crackers used on ships.

harpoon: a spear with a rope tied to one end; the rope is fastened to the whale-boat, and the spear is thrown into the whale.

'*harricane country*': part of Kentucky and Tennessee, sometimes swept by bad windstorms, or hurricanes.

high-brow: very dignified and learned; highly educated.

bobnail: heavy nail in the sole of a boot.

hoe-down: a square-dance party.

hoist sail: raise sail.

hold: space below the deck of a ship in which the cargo is stored.

hull: the outer walls of a ship without decks or masts or cabins, etc.

Hunkie: a person who works in the steel mills; most of the 'Hunkies' came to this country from southern Europe, and took their name from Hungary, one of the countries from which they came.

hurricane: a bad windstorm.

I

ingot mold: a hollow shape into which metal is poured; when the metal cools off and hardens it takes the shape of the mold.

inquisitive: curious; nosy.

instinct: a natural feeling or knowledge, like that of the animals.

interior: the inside.

irresistible: too strong to be resisted.

J

jerked beef: meat dried by hunters for their use on trips and during poor seasons.

johnny-cake: New England corn bread.

K

kid: a young goat.

L

lair: a den; home of a wild animal.

lariat: a cowboy's rope; a lasso.

lasso: a cowboy's rope; a lariat.

laughing-stock: a joke; someone who has been made to look foolish to his friends.

lean-to: a crude shanty or shelter, built of logs leaning against a ridgepole.

levee: a dike or bank to protect a town from floods.

liniment: ointment to cure aches and pains.

locks: the spaces between the gates of a canal; here boats are raised or lowered from one level to another.

log-drive: the job of floating the logs downstream to the sawmill.

logging: the business of cutting down trees.

long-barreled gun: a rifle with a very long barrel, used by the pioneers and explorers.

lumberjack: a man who works in the lumber camps cutting down trees.

Glossary

M

mainsail: the main sail of a sailing ship.

mansion: a large, grand house.

marksman: a man who is skilled at shooting a rifle.

maroon: to leave someone alone on a desert island.

mash: pulp; all that is left of apples after the cider has been pressed out.

maverick: a steer that has no brand; a wild outlaw.

medicine man: a person who is thought by the Indians to have magic powers.

meerschaum: a white clay from which pipes are made.

merchantman: a ship which carries merchandise; a freighter.

mine-patch: a little village around a coal mine.

minstrel: a singer or a poet; a man who tells stories in ballad form.

molten: melted.

mustang: a small half-wild horse of the Western prairies.

mutineer: a sailor who revolts against the officer of his ship.

N

Nantucket sleigh-ride: a wild ride in a whale-boat; after a whale has been harpooned, he swims madly away trying to shake off the harpoon and pulling the little whale-boat after him.

navigate: to sail.

new-fangled gadget: a new invention; some strange and new machine.

nugget: rough lump of ore containing gold.

O

open-hearth: a furnace for melting iron ore to make steel.

orator: a public speaker.

orchardman: a man who grows trees for a living.

P

parasol: a sunshade.

Parliament: the council of men who make the laws in England and Canada; very like our Congress in some ways.

passenger pigeon: a wild pigeon that once lived in the forests of North America.

patron saint: the saint who looks after a certain person or group of persons.

peddler: a man who sells things from door to door.

le petit: French for 'little one.'

Petrified Forest: a forest in Arizona; the trees are so old that they have turned to stone.

pickaninny: a Negro baby.

pile-driver: a machine which drives piles, or big posts, into the earth.

pioneer: an explorer or an early settler.

plot: a bit of ground.

Glossary

plugged nickel: a nickel that isn't worth anything as money.

poke bonnet: an old-fashioned lady's bonnet.

polka: a lively dance.

port: the left side of a ship.

possessions: belongings.

pounds of gold: English money, worth about five dollars.

prairie schooner: a covered wagon in which the pioneers traveled to the West.

privateer: a pirate; a man who attacks the ships of his country's enemies and keeps their cargoes.

prize: a ship captured by a pirate.

prophecy: telling what will happen in the future.

Provincial Governor: the governor of a Canadian province.

prow: the front or beak of a ship.

prune: to trim a tree, to take off its dead branches.

pueblo: a Southwestern Indian village of mud huts.

R

ragamuffin: a ragged, dirty child.

range: grazing lands.

reply in kind: to give someone the same treatment he gives you.

resent: to feel angry about something.

rickety: shaky, weak in the joints.

ridgepole: the pole that runs along the top of a roof, where the two sides join.

rigging: the ropes and masts of a ship.

ring-tailed squealer: an imaginary animal that sounded fierce to Mike Fink.

rivet: a nail or bolt that holds metal plates together.

rodeo: a cowboys' circus; a Wild West show.

round-up: gathering in the cattle from the range to brand them, etc.

roustabout: a man who works on the wharves and levees of the Mississippi River.

S

sacrifice: give up, or offer to a god.

sagebrush: a desert plant.

Saint Nicholas: the patron saint of Dutch children; like our Santa Claus he brings presents at Christmas time.

salt lick: a place where animals come to lick salt from rocks.

'Salt River roarer': another of Mike Fink's imaginary wild animals.

sapling: a young tree.

schooner: a sailing ship with two or more masts.

Scripture: the Bible.

scrub: low bushes in a thicket.

semicircle: a half circle.

settlement: a newly started town.

shaft: a tunnel, generally up and down, that leads to a mine.

'Shakes': the Western part of Tennessee and Kentucky.

Glossary

sheriff: an officer of the law.

shied (of a horse): bucked or reared.

short order: food that can be fixed quickly and easily, like hamburger and sandwiches.

shroud: a burial garment.

side-kicking: a cowboy term for a horse's bucking.

sign on: to hire a crew for a ship.

six-shooter: a gun that shoots six times between loadings.

skillet: an iron frying pan.

sky-walking: another cowboy term for a horse's bucking.

sledge: a heavy hammer.

sloop: a small sailing ship with one mast.

smuggling: bringing things into the country without paying the proper tax on them.

snags: rocks and tree stumps hidden under the surface of a river.

snuff: powdered tobacco.

sod shanty: a crude hut built of blocks of earth, sometimes with grass still growing from the blocks.

sombrero: a cowboy hat with a broad brim.

squid: a small octopus.

squire: the most important man in the county.

starboard: the right side of a ship.

steam crane: a large machine, operated by steam, for lifting heavy objects.

steam shovel: a big machine for digging, operated by steam.

stoke: to fill with coal.

store clothes: clothes bought at a store and worn on special occasions.

sugarbush man: a man who lives in the maple-sugar country.

sulphur springs: springs of water which contain sulphur.

superstition: a belief in something that you can't understand.

surveyor: a man who makes maps and works out the boundary lines between pieces of land.

T

tattoo: a picture or design marked on a person's skin.

'taxes and politics': things Congressmen usually talk about.

tender: a small boat that carries things between a large ship and the shore.

tepee: an Indian's tent or wigwam.

thaw: melting of the ice in the spring.

thresh: separate the kernel of grain from the straw.

tidal wave: a huge wave, so big that people think it must be caused by an earthquake under the sea.

timber: trees or lumber.

toreador: a bullfighter.

tornado: a bad windstorm.

train: a group of followers.

turpentine hills: hills covered with

Glossary

pine trees, from whose sap the turpentine is made.

turquoise: a stone found in the South-west.

V

vaquero: a Mexican cowboy.

varmint: pioneer slang for any low form of animal, generally a snake.

vein: a long layer of coal or metal in the rock.

vision: wonderful idea, or dream.

volunteer: a person who offers to do something.

W

wake: the waves that spread out behind a boat.

weigh anchor: pull up the anchor.

whaling station: ports from which whaling ships sail.

Y

Yankee clipper: a fast sailing ship that sailed from New England in the old days.

yarbs: herbs, plants used for medicine.

Life is hard. But a pouf? That should be easy.

Her first night out in Seaside Heights, New Jersey, Gia wanted to present the best version of herself. Hundreds of guys would get a look at her, and she'd be searching among them for her near future fling(s).

Her cousin Isabella poked her head into Gia's bedroom. "What the hell?" she said, clearly annoyed. "You're not done yet? It's been, like, an hour already."

Gia said, "The club will not run out of tequila before I get my hair right. So shut the fuck up."

Bella flopped onto Gia's bed. Nothing on her body bounced, including her new boobs. Tonight, she wore her "club" bikini top, two silver lamé triangles the size of Doritos connected by a couple of strings.

If there was one rule about how to dress on the Jersey Shore: less was more.

Fist pumps for SNOOKI!

"DRAWS OUR ATTENTION LIKE A BERSERK
WINDUP TOY."
—*The New York Times*

"INCOMPARABLE."
—*New York* Magazine

"AMERICA HAS GONE NUTS FOR SNOOKI."
—FoxNews.com

This title is also available as an eBook

A Shore Thing

A Novel

Nicole **"Snooki"** Polizzi

POCKET STAR BOOKS

New York   London   Toronto   Sydney   New Delhi

Pocket Star Books
A Division of Simon & Schuster, Inc.
1230 Avenue of the Americas
New York, NY 10020

First Pocket Star Books paperback edition January 2012

POCKET STAR BOOKS and colophon are registered trademarks of Simon & Schuster, Inc.

For information about special discounts for bulk purchases, please contact Simon & Schuster Special Sales at 1-866-506-1949 or business@simonandschuster.com.

The Simon & Schuster Speakers Bureau can bring authors to your live event. For more information or to book an event, contact the Simon & Schuster Speakers Bureau at 1-866-248-3049 or visit our website at www.simonspeakers.com.

Cover design by Michael Nagin.
Cover photography by Scott McDermott.

Manufactured in the United States of America

10 9 8 7 6 5 4 3 2 1

ISBN 978-1-4516-6672-4
ISBN 978-1-4516-2376-5 (ebook)

Dedicated to all my Guidos and Guidettes.
Thanks for loving the Jersey Shore
as much as I do.
Fist Pump!

Acknowledgments

I would like to thank all the people who helped make this book possible, starting with my amazing family. Thanks, Mom and Dad! You have been so loving and supportive. I wouldn't be here if it wasn't for you.

Thanks to my grandparents, Uncle Ben, Uncle Charlie, and Uncle Danny, who are no longer with us but I know are looking down on me.

My amazing pets—Rocky, Tommy, Vito, and Gia—are my best friends. Mew, Roof! That's "Thank you!" in animal speak.

Thanks to my cast mates and family from *Jersey Shore*. I love you, bitches!

Bryan Monti, you are my greatest bitch ever. Seriously, thanks for taking care of me.

Huge thanks to my caring managers, Scott Talarico and Danny Mackey at Neon Entertainment, aka Team Snooki. You helped bring me to where I am now, and where I may end up. You've been so wonderful for putting up with my phone calls at all hours of the day—and night!

Thanks to my literary agent, Scott Miller at Trident, for all your hard work, and to Jeremie Ruby-Strauss for getting the ball rolling.

I'm so grateful to Lauren McKenna at Gallery Books for your fabulous work, and being so understanding about my busy schedule and deadlines.

Lastly, thank you so much to Valerie Frankel, my collaborator, who helped translate my ideas onto the page. You rock, Val!

A Shore Thing

Chapter One

Karma's a Bitch, Bitch

Life was hard. But a pouf? That should be easy.

Giovanna "Gia" Spumanti was a hair-raising pro. She'd been banging out poufs since age eleven, or as soon as her fingers were long enough to hold a bottle of Deluxe Aqua Net. After ten years of trial and error to find the right combination of spray, twisting, and shine serum, Gia could add four inches to her overall height—which, at five feet flat, she could use. Gia's pouf defied the laws of gravity. It was her crowning glory. Although she'd love to wear an actual crown or a rhinestone tiara whenever she left the house, it just wasn't practical. It could fly off on the dance floor and take out an eye. The pouf, however, wasn't going anywhere (but up).

Tonight, humidity was a bitch. Her thick black mane refused to cooperate. Gia brushed it out to start over—again—feeling discouraged. Her first night out in Seaside Heights, New Jersey, she wanted to present the best version of herself. Hundreds of guys would get a look at her, and she'd be searching among them for her near future fling(s). After the year she had back home in Brooklyn—landing and losing a couple of jobs and boyfriends—she deserved the sexiest summer ever.

Gia hoisted the front section of her hair, holding it high over her head with one hand. With her other hand, she gave it a blast of spray. Then she twisted the clump into a bubble and fastened it in the back with a butterfly clip, aka a tramp clamp. Her tried-and-true technique should have worked. But her bump fell to one side like a deflated tire.

"Waa!" she whined at her reflection, but just for a second. Complaining wouldn't fix her pouf. It wouldn't make her tall and skinny. Or turn her rented Seaside Heights beach house/dump into a palace.

Dump was a slight exaggeration. But only slight. From the outside, the two-story, two-bedroom bungalow looked like an aging Atlantic City hooker. For a month, this hooker would be home. The photos on the real estate website that convinced Gia to rent the place sight unseen had been taken a few thousand years ago. Since then, sand and salt had ravaged the gray shingles and warped the shutters. The vibe inside, though? Much better. The kitchen was old, but clean (for now). The big and plushly furnished living room was painted berry pink, like a cranberry vodka cocktail. The couch—red velvet, supersoft—reminded

Gia of giant lips. She dubbed it the official Make Out Zone.

With any luck, hot guidos would kiss her on it.

Gia chose the smaller of the two bedrooms. The cozy room instantly charmed her with round porthole windows facing the ocean. The bed sagged in the middle, and the closet was the size of a Barbie Dream House. But the wall paintings of shells and seagulls and the sand-pink paint job were comforting. Gia brought her leopard-print bedspread from home, for that touch of the familiar. She could already picture herself and a yummy juicehead rolling around on top of it.

Her cousin Isabella "Bella," "Bells," and "Hell's Bells" Rizzoli poked her head into Gia's bedroom. "What the hell?" she said, clearly annoyed. "You're not done yet? It's been, like, an hour already."

Gia said, "The club will not run out of tequila before I get my hair right. So shut the fuck up."

Bells flopped onto Gia's bed. Nothing on her body bounced, including her new boobs. They were Bella's birthday gift to herself when she turned twenty-one a few months ago. She'd waited her whole life for tits to grow and finally gave up on Mother Nature and turned to Dr. Rosenberg. He boosted her from a 32B to a 34D. Not a major change. As a karate brown belt and runner, Bella couldn't haul around a pair of watermelons. Gia suspected the inflated boobs were a part (parts?) of Bella's overall life-reboot plan. After *six years* with Bobby Bonehead, Bells was single, willing and eager to make up for lost time. She must have packed two dozen bikinis for their month down the Shore. Tonight, Bells wore her "club" bikini top, two silver lamé triangles the size of Doritos connected by a couple of strings.

"What do you call those?" asked Gia, looking at her cousin's bottoms. "Denim panties?"

"Too much?" asked Bella, who rolled over to check if her short shorts showed crack and/or cheek.

"I can practically see what you had for lunch," said Gia. "Daisy Duke would be embarrassed to wear those."

"Good," said Bella, laughing.

If there was one rule about how to dress on the Jersey Shore: less was more.

Gia said, "If I could trade bodies with anyone, Bells, it'd so be you." Anyone would agree. Bells had long, smooth, tan legs, a luscious ass, tiny waist, and iron-flat belly, as well as the finest set money could buy.

Bella said, "What about you? *Real* boobs, great legs. Fun-sized and adorable. Seriously. Every guy you meet wants to tuck you into his back pocket and take you home."

If only it were true, thought Gia. Bella was a nine. Gia was, maybe, a seven . . . point nine. She'd put on some weight since her cheerleader days in high school. On her petite frame, one extra pound made her muffin top. Two pounds? It was a dough explosion. Gia tried not to stress about it. She could starve, not drink, and be skinny. Or she could have a good time and be curvy. Gia chose curvy. Any sane person would. But, when it came to weight, most girls were crazy.

"Just give me two minutes to fix this," she said, twisting her hair again.

"Go flat tonight," said Bella.

"I love my pouf," said Gia. "But maybe my hair is trying to tell me something. You have to know when to stop fighting a losing battle."

Bella frowned for a second, and Gia figured she was thinking about Bobby. Unlike Gia's relationships—her longest lasted about four hours—Bella and Bobby had stayed together *way* too long. He wouldn't let her go. At the end, he turned into a third-degree stalker, showing up at their apartment building, the family-run Italian deli where Bella worked, and all her favorite spots around the nabe. Carroll Gardens, Brooklyn, became a war zone for Bella. Bobby the land mine blew up all over the place.

"Brooklyn might as well be a million miles away," said Gia gently. "No one knows us here. We can be whoever we want." Giving up on the pouf, Gia moved on to the next step—unwrapping not one, not two, but *three* sets of false eyelashes. She bought lashes in bulk, a hundred sets at a time. She had to bring a separate suitcase just for her lashes, clips, makeup, hair products, and tan-in-a-can spray.

After using the brush-on adhesive, Gia pressed two rows of lush lashes to her upper lids. Then she fixed on the bottom rows. Batting her eyes at her reflection, she said, "Right this way, boys."

"Superhot," said Bella, saying the right thing, as always.

"Your turn," said Gia, calling her over.

Bella rolled off the bed and knelt in front of her cousin—which put them face-to-face. She closed her eyes. Gia put the lashes on Bella's lids.

"There," said Gia. "Now you'll kill the boys with one look."

"Not if you kill them first," said Bella, smiling.

———

Karma, the biggest and best club in Seaside Heights, was only a few blocks from their bungalow on Kearney Avenue. The cousins walked in their heels. Gia wore heels almost constantly. When she wasn't in her fuzzy pink slippers, she teetered in platforms, or, like tonight, six-inch stilettos.

A two-story structure, Karma had an open-air bar on its top floor, perfect for chilling on hot summer nights, taking a break from dancing, or catching an ocean breeze. The downstairs was divided into two parts. The first, a dark inside room that, even from the outside, smelled like mung beer, Axe body spray, and sweat. The other half of the ground floor was a palazzo bar, with a DJ riser and a dance floor. Through the windows from the street, Gia spotted five hot guys at the outdoor bar. Honestly? She'd get with any of them. Her heart started beating in time with the techno music. This was it! The first night!

Two doors to choose from to get into the club. One said GENERAL and had a long line of kids in front of it. The other—VIP—no line at all. Bella said, "This one," and pushed through the VIP door.

The bouncer sat just inside on a stool. "Hold up," he said. "IDs?"

They showed their driver's licenses. Both girls were twenty-one, legal anywhere in America to drink until they puked. The bouncer looked at them and said, "This entrance is for table service only."

Same annoying rule as New York City clubs. Table service meant you had to buy, say, a $400 bottle of vodka that cost $40 at a liquor store. Friggin' rip-off.

"But we're hot girls," Gia pointed out. "We don't need to pay for anything."

The bouncer sized her up. Which didn't take long. "You girls from out of town?"

"We're here for the whole month," said Gia. "If we like it, we might move here permanently, so you should be nice to us."

Gia didn't know if she should credit her sass or her ass, but he said, "Okay. Have a good night, ladies."

Once inside, she looked around. "Oh my God. He's here."

"Who?" Bella asked.

"My new boyfriend. I haven't met him yet, but I'm sure he's here somewhere."

"Let's go find him."

Gia felt eyes on her as she and Bella walked across the room. Alone, each cousin got her share of attention. Together? They couldn't miss. Gia in six-inch stilettos and a skintight leopard-print mini-dress that clung to every inch. Bella in a bikini top, teeny shorts, motorcycle boots, brown hair in a high ponytail to show off the angel-wing tattoos blazed across her back. Gia imaged the moment in slo-mo, the music falling silent, guys turning to watch them walk, her hair swinging with each step. And then, the scene returned to normal speed. They'd made an entrance.

Bella said, "Bar," and pointed toward the neon-lit tiers of bottles in the center of the dark room. At least six bartenders ran around inside the round bar, mixing and filling pitchers with beer. The crowd around it had to be three deep.

"We'll have to kick our way in," said Bella.

"Not necessary." A tiny dynamo, Gia cleared a path like a plow straight to the bar. Bella followed in her wake.

A bartender appeared to take her order. "Slippery Nipple," she said. "Extra slippery." Baileys and butterscotch schnapps. Yummy.

Two guys to her right slapped twenties on the bar to pay for it.

Bella said, "Tequila shot."

The bartender asked, "Lime?"

"Do I look like I want fruit?"

Two guys to her left slapped hundreds on the bar and offered to pay for her drinks for the rest of her life.

Of course, they accepted the kind offers. Drinks weren't cheap, and they had limited funds. After paying for the rental, new clothes, and repairs on Bella's 1995 Honda Accord, the cousins could barely afford to feed themselves. They both had to get jobs ASAP. In the meantime, they'd let willing donors buy their drinks.

"Hey," said one guy, after he'd nudged his way over to them. "I couldn't help noticing you when you came in."

Gia checked him out. Cute, in a puppy-dog way. Scrawny and scruffy, the Disney version of a heart-throb. He wore bangs in his eyes, cargo pants, high-tops, and a stretched-out white T-shirt with the words MR. PINK on the front. So *not* Gia's type. She preferred her men big, ripped, tan, and gorilla. This kid? He didn't even look Italian.

Bella, however, thought Zac Efron was a hottie. She introduced herself.

"I'm Benjamin," he said, holding out his hand to shake. Now Gia knew he was from up north. Shore guys didn't shake hands. They came in for a kiss on the cheek when they met a hot girl for the first time.

Gia could (and *should,* really) write a book about the difference between Shore and city boys. She knew both types well. Before her parents split three years ago, she lived in Toms River, five miles from Seaside Heights. Gia graduated from Toms River High School. Two days later, her mom, Alicia, moved to Brooklyn and into Aunt Marissa and Uncle Charlie's brownstone building. Gia was dragged along. She loved her family and couldn't part with her mom. Living in the same building with Bella was a dream come true, like finally having a sister.

But Gia missed her life down the Shore. Uprooting so quickly, she didn't get a "senior summer" between high school and college. She lost touch with most of her classmates as they went their separate ways, to college (like Gia, for a couple of years anyway), jobs, or on road trips that kept on tripping. Weird, how you could be so tight with someone, then drift apart so quickly and easily. In a way, returning to Jersey this summer was a homecoming for Gia. She hoped to reclaim that sense of belonging she never quite felt in Brooklyn, despite living with her extended family.

Bella and Benjamin ("Call me Bender," he said) seemed to hit it off. Gia half listened to their conversation, sipped her drink, and glanced around. One guy, a preppy with a sweater tied around his neck (barf), was looking at her, not in a nice way.

"What're you looking at?" she asked.

"Nothing much," he replied.

Shithead! She would have slapped him or thrown a drink or stamped on his foot, *something*. But another guy diverted Gia's attention. A hot guido was staring at her—in a nice way—from across the room.

Gia smiled at him. His back against the wall, he stood just off the dance floor, thumb in a belt loop. His chest muscles strained the fabric of his black tank top. It fit across a tummy that was hard and flat enough to cut salami on. No tattoos, which meant plenty of empty space on his arms to ink PROPERTY OF

GIA. He stared as if he could see through her dress, right down to the zebra-print bra and thong set underneath.

"I found him," Gia said to Bella, draining her Slippery Nipple in one long suck.

"Who . . . oh," Bella replied.

"You okay here with your boy?"

Bender said, "I'm your boy? Is that good?"

Bella laughed. God help her, she loved preppies.

Gia took that as permission to leave her cousin at the bar. Right at that moment, a Deadmau5 mix came on. He was her fave; it was a sign. She stepped onto the dance floor. The music took her over. Dancing had to be Gia's second favorite way to work up a sweat. It definitely beat going to the gym. For exercise, Gia cranked house music in her bedroom and danced until her legs felt numb. She loved dancing and was talented, too. Gia won a contest while in high school for shaking it the longest and hardest without spilling a single drop of her vodka tonic.

Tonight, she aimed her gyrating hips straight at Salami Boy. The guy could take a hint. In two seconds, he crept over to her. In five seconds, they were grinding, her butt pressed against his thighs.

She turned around to introduce herself. "I'm Gia," she screamed in his ear above the music.

"Rocky," he said, putting a bear paw on her waist and holding her against him.

Rocky in his jeans, thought Gia.

Even in the dark room, his blue eyes dazzled Gia. Ice blue. Something about light eyes on dark skin always made Gia's body temperature rise. The music was too loud to talk, not that it mattered. Gia wasn't interested in making a deep soul connection. Tonight was all about the three D's: Drinking, Dancing, and *Duh.*

"Are you from around here?" she yelled.

"You got a nice rack," screamed Rocky in reply.

Well, yeah, she thought. Okay, not a supergenius. That was fine. Gia didn't judge. She was glad he approved.

"Come here," he said, lifting her off her heels to bring her lips to his. She had to wrap her legs around his hips to stay up there. *Here we go,* thought Gia. Twenty minutes from club entry to hookup. This might be a record, even for her.

"Bitch, get away from him!" pealed a shrill voice from behind.

Bony fingers grabbed Gia's shoulder and yanked her out of Rocky's arms. She hit the floor on her heels like a cat, but then stumbled and landed on her ass embarrassingly. A few guys stared, jaws unhinged, at her sprawled on the dance floor. One started drooling.

"Oops," she said, realizing her dress was pushed up around her waist. Full-frontal thong exposure.

Bella and Bender were on her in a flash, helping her to her feet, yanking down her dress.

Gia met the eyes of the seething blond bimbo who'd thrown her to the floor. The girl's arms were in battle position, ready to go. Rocky stood behind her, grinning as innocently as a choirboy.

The blonde lowered her arms suddenly. "Gia friggin' Spumanti."

"Oh my freakin' God," said Gia. "Linda Patterson."

One of the girls from the Toms River High School cheerleading team. Gia and Linda were co-captains. Both high-energy and petite, they were the blond and brunette bookends on the squad, and besties. At the start of senior year, though, Linda turned on her. Gia couldn't remember exactly what happened. It was a blurry year.

"You look exactly the same," said Gia. True. Linda was, then and now, a cute blonde, head-to-toe in Juicy. She was uptight and snotty, which gave her a hard, brittle edge. And she was painfully thin. Linda made Lady Gaga look like a hippo.

"You know this girl?" Rocky asked. "Cool."

"Shut up, idiot," said Linda to him. Glaring at Gia, she said, "Once a whore, always a whore. Zeroing in on other girls' boyfriends."

"Don't blame me," said Gia. "You should keep him on a tighter leash. And I'm not a whore. I'm a slut. There's a difference."

Rocky laughed. "She's funny. Let's invite her over for dinner."

"Idiot!" shrieked Linda, who went at him with her fresh manicure.

Gia cringed. She hated to see anyone break a nail.

"Don't you ever . . . look . . . at . . . another . . . girl . . . again!" ranted Linda, bitch-slapping and kicking her boyfriend. Rocky put up his arms to defend himself, but Linda got in some solid punches.

"That's what he deserves," said Bella.

"Karma's a bitch," said Gia.

Bender said, "Is this awkward? Should we go?"

"What? Leave *now*?" asked Gia. "*Before* it gets ugly? Are you crazy?"

They wandered back to the bar for another drink and to watch round two on the dance floor.

Chapter Two

Make Me Beg

Bella was up bright and early for her already scheduled job interview. She'd love to chill at the beach until her hangover was gone. But until she got summer employment settled, Bella just couldn't relax.

She drove the Honda to the Toms River 24 Hour Fitness gym. Inside, Bella went up to the biggest, buffest guy in sight and said, "I'm looking for Tony."

"In his office, back that way, up a flight of stairs," he said.

"Thanks." Bella turned on her Nikes and headed for gym director Tony "Trouble" Troublino's office. She'd set up the interview before she left Brooklyn. Although her only reference was Gia pretending to be a devoted client, Tony asked her to come by when she got to town and he'd consider hooking her up.

She wasn't sure if she liked the sound of that.

Bella needed a job, not a pimp. Her hope was to teach a class or to try personal training. She didn't have any teaching or training experience, but, as a step-class fan, she'd climbed to the moon and back. As for training, how hard could it be? You put an out-of-shape pud on the treadmill, make him sweat and cry in the weight room. Bella had a fantasy of herself as a kick-ass dominatrix trainer, humiliating her clients into the workout of their lives.

The truth: Bella rarely yelled. She hated to raise her voice. She liked to think she could stop a raging bull with her icy glare. But screaming? Not her style. Gia thought Bella should yell more often. "You're repressed," her cousin told her, especially when Bella didn't fight back hard with Bobby.

All that was going to change. Her goal of the month in Jersey was to give her Brooklyn persona a rest. She'd been too good for too long, meeting her parents' expectations and putting her own dreams on hold. Out of the city, Bella could reinvent herself and be whomever or whatever she wanted, aka a dominatrix trainer, for starters.

As she searched for the right office, Bella thought about last night. Gia was still sleeping off their marathon bar crawl. After leaving Karma, Bella and Gia—and Bender—went on a sightseeing tour of the bottom of a dozen shot glasses. They hit nearly every bar on the boardwalk. At four in the morning, when they stumbled back to the beach house, Bella was glad Bender stuck by them like sand on wet skin. She needed help getting up the stairs to her room. Bender didn't try anything when he tucked her in, which Bella found both endearing and insulting. She didn't know if she'd see him again. They exchanged numbers. Maybe he'd call. Or not.

Bella noticed a door with Tony Troublino's name on it; also a sign that read ENTER AT YOUR OWN FREAKIN' RISK. THIS MEANS *YOU*. Gulping, she knocked.

"*What?*" barked a voice from inside.

Everyone in Jersey was so damn *loud,* she thought. Bella peeked inside and said, "Mr. Troublino? I'm Isabella Rizzoli. I called you a few weeks ago about working here this summer."

"Who?"

Bella stepped all the way into the office so he could see her better. "I filled out an application on-line. And sent photos." Front and rear views, just to be sure he got the point: she'd worked hard for this body, for a long time. Rome wasn't built in a day, after all.

Tony looked up from his computer. "Oh, yeah. Girl with angel tattoo. Brown belt, marathoner. I remember." *Now* he was friendly, she thought, once he got a look at her. A realist, Bella knew how lucky she was to have been born tall, with a decent face and thick hair. But she also knew that her good looks only opened doors. She still had to walk through them.

Tony probably stopped traffic himself. In his late twenties, the gym director was obviously well acquainted with the Nautilus machines. In contrast to his strong cheekbones and sharp jaw, he had green eyes, thick lashes like a girl, and dimples. Both cheeks. And they got deeper when he smiled at her.

A quick glance. No wedding ring. Bella heard warning bells clanging in her head. Unlike Gia, who would fuck on a dare, Bella moved more slowly. She'd been with only one man in her life. Since they broke up, she'd tried to get him out of her mind and soul via meaningless hookups. Bella just couldn't go through with it. Bad case of the chickenshits. She blamed her parents and her Catholic-school childhood.

Getting over that hump (as it were), and having fun, casual sex with at least a couple of guys was also on her list of summer goals.

Which got back to the problem of the gym director with the mad sexy eyes. How could any girl have casual sex with him—with his *body*—and not fall head over heels? *Trouble shouldn't be his nickname,* thought Bells. It should be tattooed on his forehead.

If she knew what was good for her, Bella would say, "Thanks, but I've changed my mind. I'm out of here."

Instead, she said, "Nice office."

"It's a shoebox," he said, apologizing for the cramped, windowless space with industrial carpeting, a desk, computer, file cabinet, and a few chairs. "This is where I facebook. My real office is in the weight room."

"So you're a trainer, too?"

"Sit." He jumped up from his chair to offer her a seat. He was tall, at least six-two, with thighs as strong as oak. "I used to be a trainer, right out of college. I still work with some of my regulars, but I can't take on new clients anymore. No time. How much experience do you have training?"

Now she had to lie. "Tons." The honest answer: none.

"Wanna show me your chops? Put me through your paces."

"Like an audition?"

"A tryout," he said, eyes glinting. "One hour. Make me beg for mercy."

Oh, God. She swallowed a lump and nodded. "Now?"

"Let's go."

"Okay, take me to the nearest treadmill."

Trouble gave her a quick tour of the facility, then she did her best to turn him into a rubber-armed, whimpering ball of sweat. She started with a treadmill interval run that would have made Eli Manning sob. Tony kept going, and going. He was like the Energizer Gorilla. Three miles into it, he said, "Should I be tired yet?"

After twenty minutes of squats and lunges, he asked, "Should I feel a burn?"

Finally, she put him on his back on a bench, pressing hundreds of pounds. A glimmer of hope: his hands got slippery, so he took off his tank top to wipe them dry.

His chest, she couldn't help but notice, looked like a marble statue (but tan). Beads of sweat trickled between the muscles, and Bella felt a smug satisfaction for putting them there. She cooled him down with some stretches, and the hour was up.

Tony said, "I enjoyed that, Isabella."

She smiled. "Glad to hear it."

"I should have hated it. You weren't tough enough."

Oh, crap. Exactly what she feared. "I can be mean. Look at me! I've got tattoos."

He laughed. "The biggest sweetheart I know is covered with ink."

"Your girlfriend?"

"My grandfather," said Tony, smiling.

Her guard crumbled. A man who bragged about his grandfather? It was irresistibly dorky.

"What about the job?" she asked.

"You're in sick shape, and you know what you're doing, but I breezed through that workout."

"You live here."

He laughed. "It feels like I do! Look around, Isabella." Tony swept his arms toward the gym's main floor. The place was packed with one perfect body after another. *Gia has got to get over here*, thought Bella. *She'd be like a kid in a pickle store.*

"They'd all breeze through your workout," he said. "As a trainer, you have to ask, 'What can I do for my client that he can't do for himself?'"

Bella smiled sexy, raising one eyebrow seductively. She could think of a few things, yeah.

Tony read her mind, and both his eyebrows went up. The air between them crackled, but just for a second.

"I'll tell you what," he said. "I'll give you a chance to prove yourself. Two weeks. Find someone to work with. Anyone. I'll pay you a freelance rate. If I see fast improvement, you're hired."

"I never back down from a challenge."

"I was hoping you'd say that."

————

"Gia, come *on*," pleaded Bella.

The two stood at the kitchen island. Gia was mixing a "morning after" smoothie—cranberry juice and bananas.

"It just doesn't taste right without the vodka," said Gia, adding a healthy slug of it to the blender. "Why do you want this job so badly, anyway? You could work somewhere else."

Tony's dimple smile flashed in Bella's head. "I just like the place, and I'd get paid to work out."

"I can't be your client! I have to get my own job. Besides, I hate the gym. I'd rather die than torture myself."

"I tried all afternoon to convince the regulars to work with me," said Bella. "It was horrible. No one took me seriously."

"You need just one client?"

"Or else I'm back on the boardwalk, begging some homy sleazebag to let me sell fried clams in a box." Bella watched, annoyed, as Gia started laughing. "What's so friggin' funny?"

"Give me your phone. If you can turn this puppy into a gorilla, you'll get Employee of the Week."

Bella handed over her cell. Her cousin started pushing buttons and said, "Aha!" Then she dialed a number.

"Who are you calling?"

"Your boy!" Then Gia said into the phone, "Hello, Bender? This is Gia, from last night. Thanks for getting us home safe. . . . Yeah. . . . What's up today? . . . You wanna come over? . . . Cool. . . . See you in a few."

Bella said, "Bender? This banana is tougher than he is. He's barely strong enough to lift my *mood*, for God's sake."

"Any other ideas? . . . No? Then shut up." Gia downed her drink and announced, "I'm going out now, and I'm not coming back until I have a job. Any job. And, by the way, selling fried clams for a horny sleazebag sounds kind of fun."

"Good luck with that."

"I don't need luck. I've got skills!"

Chapter Three

Hurricane Gia

You don't know how to use a computerized cash register, you've never been a waitress before, can't set a table or push a mop, but you have great people skills?" asked Mr. Lupo, the manager at E.J.'s, a burger-and-wings place a few blocks from the beach house.

"And great boobs!" she added. They sat at a front table inside the restaurant for the interview.

"I can see that," he said, chomping on an unlit cigar.

"You have waitresses and busboys already. But you don't have someone to lure the customers in from the boardwalk. Like a stewardess."

"A hostess."

"Whatever you call it. I'll double your business. Just clear some space for me, play some music, give me a tray of shot glasses and a bottle of whatever, and let me do my thing."

"What exactly is your thing?"

"I draw a crowd. Check this out."

Gia stood up and started dancing on the spot to music that, like dolphins and small dogs, only she could hear. Sure enough, every busboy, waiter, and customer was transfixed. She nodded at Mr. Lupo. "You see? Hurricane Gia. I'll *destroy* this place, I swear."

"Destroy my restaurant?"

"I guarantee it!"

Mr. Lupo looked at her as if she'd just landed in Roswell. The cigar hung on the corner of his lip. He didn't speak for, like, ever. It was starting to freak her out. "You know Spicy?" he asked finally.

"The Mexican restaurant down the boardwalk?"

"Yeah, the competition. Go destroy that place."

Then he kicked her out.

Gia had been kicked out of several bars and restaurants so far. And a few stores. If she weren't an optimist, she might feel a little discouraged. Fifty bosses could reject her, didn't matter. All she needed was just one open-minded person to notice her true potential and give her a shot.

Gia said as much at the Lucky Lady clubwear/guidette-jewelry boutique next door. "I'm telling you," she said to the owner. "I'm a gold mind!"

The woman replied, "Gold *mine*."

"Fine, it's yours! You don't have to be greedy."

Screw her. And Mr. Lupo, and all the negative pricks with limited imaginations. They would not ruin her afternoon. If you didn't care what other people thought about you, then you couldn't get discouraged when they turned you down.

"Get your head *up*," she told herself out loud, and made a mental attitude adjustment. Gia lifted her chin, stuck her chest out, and walked with purpose and determination. Okay, next place, an arcade with coin-operated games. Maybe she could be a Skee-Ball instructor.

Just as she was about to walk in, she spotted a couple heading toward her on the boardwalk. They were arguing. She ducked into a photo booth and watched them in secret.

"I told you before. That girl scooped on *me*," said blue-eyed Rocky, who, in the harsh glare of sober daylight was . . . just as hot, if not even hotter, than he seemed last night at Karma.

At his side, Linda was as pale and skinny as over-cooked spaghetti. "Even if that's true, and I'm not necessarily buying it, you didn't have to put your hands all over Gia Spumanti's fat ass! God, I hate that whore! Just the thought of her makes me want to kick something."

As Gia watched, Linda Patterson, former perky blond cheerleader, kicked over a trash can. The garbage spilled out. And then she just walked on. Gia covered her mouth in shock.

Go ahead, call me a fat whore, she thought, *but for God's sake, don't litter!*

What had she ever done to this girl? Gia hadn't a clue. How totally fucked up, to learn she was enemies with someone she'd practically forgotten existed.

Under the circumstances, Gia thought it wise to get off the boardwalk and avoid any chance run-in with crazy Linda and rocks-for-brains Rocky (honestly? he'd have to be stupid to be with that bitch).

Backing down a side street, Gia noticed a HELP WANTED sign in a storefront window. The awning read TANTASTIC SALON.

"Dang," whispered Gia to herself. The day's luck was turning good.

Entering the salon was like passing through a portal to heaven. She'd seen fancier tanning salons in the city, for sure, full of snobs and prissy bronzed bitches. But the vibe at Tantastic made her feel instantly at home. Who wouldn't warm to the wall mural of a rising sun with pretty pinks, oranges, and yellows? Gia loved pink! It was her favorite color. If she could wear yellow and not look like a lemon, she'd do it every day. Orange? Meh. That was too close to her skin tone to pull off.

The front desk was unmanned, so Gia took a quick look around the place. A few private rooms had tanning beds and Mystic tanning booths, much like the ones she knew from home. An entire wall held shelves of product—every tanning spray, cream, or lotion on the market was for sale, at reasonable prices, too.

At the sound of a toilet flushing, Gia called out, "Hello? I'm here!"

A puff of cigarette smoke exited the bathroom door before the woman did. When she appeared in the hallway, Gia broke out into a grin. She recognized (and adored) the species—cougar in a zebra-print, strapless dress, Candies mules, and a jet-black, teased-up pouf with a platinum skunk streak (totally cool). Strands of rhinestones and faux pearls dripped from her neck, which was kind of saggy. But otherwise, apart from some loose skin and wrinkles, the woman was hot. She must have been scorching in her day.

"Look at you!" she said to Gia, her voice scratchy. "You're cuter than a Princess Pony!"

"I'm your new assistant," announced Gia. "I belong here. It's my destiny. Can't you feel it?"

Up close, the woman was anywhere between forty and fifty—hard to tell with all the years of sun/tanning-bed worship under her hat. She put a cigarette between frosted-pink lips. "Well, it's obvious you work on your own tan," she said, blowing smoke.

"*Work* on my tan? It's not work! I *play* at my tan. Tanning is my second-favorite thing to do with my clothes off."

The woman laughed like a donkey. "I love the enthusiasm. What's your name, princess?"

"Gia Spumanti."

"I'm Mary Agatha Pugliani. Everyone calls me Maria. You're hired."

"I am?"

"Who am I to deny destiny?"

They worked out the boring details: hours, salary, responsibilities. Until Gia got trained on the machines—as if she didn't know how to operate a tanning bed!—she'd take calls, make appointments, clean up, sell product, and keep the customers happy while they waited for their turn. The job at Tantastic wouldn't make her rich, but the perks were friggin' unbeatable. Maria would let her use any of the tanning beds and/or the Mystic booths for free! That was a savings of a hundred bucks a week right there.

Honestly? Gia had dialed back on tanning lately. Purely a financial decision. There was the new 10 percent tax on it (do *not* get her started) and the problem of the deadly UVA and UVB rays that might give her cancer. She'd been using spray tan instead, but it made her palms and the bottoms of her feet bright orange. She left little orange footprints all over the floor of the bathroom, as if a melting Oompa-Loompa had padded through.

"Mind the store for me while I go on a cigarette run, okay?" asked Maria. "A few clients are coming in later, but it should be slow until then. If we get a walk-in, call my cell and I'll come right back."

As soon as her boss left, Gia did a victory lap dance on the arm of the sofa. A sweet job! With a cool cougar boss! If only her mom could see her now. Alicia wrung her hands to the bone, worrying that Gia would be lost away from her for a whole month. Gia did rely heavily on her mom. Alicia still did Gia's laundry. Most of their meals came from Uncle Charlie's deli, which was (way too) conveniently located on the street level of their apartment building. Gia could eat meatball heroes for breakfast, lunch, and dinner, and often did.

As comfortable as the Rizzoli/Spumanti brownstone was, Gia felt cramped sometimes, living and breathing family 24/7/365. When Gia talked about moving, Alicia got weepy and took to her bed. Loyal daughter that she was, Gia promised she'd never leave. The two were overly dependent on each other. They both knew it. But it was one thing to know a problem existed, and another to change it.

The salon door jingled open. Gia stopped humping the sofa. A guy walked in. Midtwenties and pale as flounder, he appeared to be what Gia called a cowboy. Irish or German descent? Definitely not Italian.

He smiled at her and said, "Hi."

She asked, "First day on the beach?"

"It's that obvious?"

"Like waving a white flag. I need a pair of sunglasses." She pretended to shield her eyes from the glare of his vampire skin.

"A tanning salon two blocks from the beach," he said, shaking his head. "Ironic, isn't it?"

Er, yes? No? Sort of? Gia wasn't sure, so she said, "Not necessarily."

"You have to admit, it's kind of ridiculous to pay for a tan when the sun is for free."

"A whole day in the sun versus ten minutes in a tanning bed," said Gia, weighing the options with her hands. "Even tanning time is money."

He laughed. "Here's my problem. I'm having a big party at my share house on July Fourth, two days from now. If I don't do something about this"—he touched his bare arm—"I'll glow in the dark. I'll ruin the fireworks. I need a base, right? I can get that here?"

"Don't worry. I can solve your problem. Come this way."

She led him to the room with the ultimate tanning bed, a Matrix 5000, twenty-eight high-density UVA and UVB lamps, 360-degree exposure, super-strong and effective. With the black casing and neon-blue lights, it looked futuristic. When Maria had given Gia the tour earlier, she'd called it the Spaceship.

"What'd you say your name was?" Gia asked.

"Neil Connor."

"I'm Gia. I had to know your name before I asked you to take off your clothes. A rule of mine."

He blushed, which was only too freakin' obvious. He started to undress. His bod was better than she thought. It was cute, how he folded his clothes. Gia decided to go for it. Why not? Landing a job and a date inside of fifteen minutes? *Definitely* a record.

"These, too?" he asked of his Calvins.

Gia, personally, was against tan lines. When she used a bed, she left her bra and panties on the chair. "When you're naked, do you want it to look like you're wearing a pair of flesh-colored shorts?"

"God no."

"Then take 'em off!"

"Is it safe? The tanning lights on my dick?"

"Skin is skin."

"You're the professional," he said, stepping out of his briefs.

Well, technically, she wasn't really. Gia thought

to call Maria back, but then decided against it. She'd used this tanning bed before.

While he undressed, Gia snuck a peek. Shrimpy. But she cut the guy some slack. He was nervous and the air-conditioning was cranked.

Neil climbed into the bed. Gia closed the clamshell top part and set the timer to . . . hmm . . . when she used a similar bed, she tanned for ten minutes. This guy didn't have a base. She set it to nine minutes and left the room.

When he came out, he seemed relieved. "That wasn't so bad. I'm still pale, though."

"It shows up later," she said. "By tonight, you'll look great."

He handed over his Visa. She ran it through the machine the way Maria had showed her. "So, you have a share house?" she asked.

"Yup," he said. "Close to the beach. It's awesome."

"And you're having a big party, huh?"

"Kick off the summer right."

"I'm new in town, too," she said, tearing off the receipt.

He looked at the slip, signed it. "Yeah?"

Gia sighed. The cowboy just wasn't picking up what she was throwing down. "My cousin and I don't have any plans yet for the Fourth. And I love a big house party."

Neil nodded. "Thanks a lot."

Oh, well. She tried. Rejection was an unfortunate and unavoidable part of life. Gia didn't take it personally when she struck out. Not every guy she liked felt the same way about her, and vice versa. Her face was pretty, she was confident about that. Her Smurf shortness? What she lacked in height, Gia made up for with enthusiasm. What could she do about it, anyway? This was her one and only body. She made the most of what she had. If Neil wasn't into her? It was his loss.

She said, "Stay cool out there."

He was halfway out the door, but then he turned around. "Listen, Gena . . ."

"Gia."

"Would you like to come to the party?"

"Will your girlfriend be there?" Smooth.

"She would be—if I had one."

Yay! A date! A single boy who she'd already seen naked wanted her at his party. "I hope I recognize you with a tan."

"You'll find me, don't worry," he said, writing down his address. "Just look for the keg."

Score!

Chapter Four

That New-Guy Smell

Stop twitching," said Bella impatiently.

"I can't help it," said Bender, a bit pained.

She was kneeling in front of him, wrapping a tape measure around his upper thigh. She had to take "before" measurements to compare to next week's. If Bella worked him hard, she'd bet he'd grow at least five inches of muscle in that time. Tony would have to hire her officially.

Unfortunately, measuring Bender's thigh had already made him get several inches in the groin area. Bella might've gotten poked if it weren't for his sweatpants.

"Ouch," complained Bender when she pulled the tape tighter. "Much as I want to help you, Bella, I'm having second thoughts. This gym thing. I'm more of a long-walk-on-the-beach-at-sunset kind of guy."

"We can take long walks on the beach," she said, moving down to measure his calves.

"We can?"

"After we finish running." He grumbled. "Come on, Bender. You've chased girls before, right?"

"Believe it or not, Bella, I'm used to girls chasing me."

Bella could believe it. She'd learned a few facts about Bender Newberry today: (1) He was seriously loaded. He pulled into the gym parking lot in a brand-new Beemer and paid for a month's membership as if he were buying a pack of gum. (2) He was one-eighth Italian. His great-grandmother was from Milan. (3) Although Bender was on the small side, he had an okay body. Not fat at all. And naturally toned abs. She could pour a shot of tequila down his belly and slurp it out of his navel without getting splashed in the face. The cumulative affect— cute smile, general niceness, hot wheels, and obvious attraction to her—forced Bella to see him in a sexier light. She tried to psych herself up to have meaningless casual sex with Bender. But she kept hitting a wall in her mind. And that wall had Tony Troublino's face painted on it.

"This him?" asked Tony himself, appearing suddenly in the stretching room. He looked slick in a red tank top that showed off his arms and chest, gray PUMA track pants, and black PUMA sneakers. The room was lined with mirrors, and they filled up with her boss from every angle—all of them good. Bella felt awkward suddenly, realizing she was on her knees in a compromising position in front of Bender.

"Tony, hey." She stood up and handed her boss the chart with Bender's measurements. "Here's the day-one assessment. By day fourteen, I'm sure we'll see some major improvement."

Tony barely glanced at the chart. "You from around here?" he asked the new client.

Bender said, "Got a summer house in Barnegat Light."

Tony nodded. "Nice."

"You live here year-round?"

"Yup," said Tony.

"Yeah," said Bender.

The two men stared at each other. Both were nodding and smiling, arms folded across their chests, feet planted hip-width apart. They mirrored each other's body language right down to the tilt of their chins—up and cocky.

Men. Always clashing antlers. "Wanna watch me warm him up?" Bella asked Tony.

"No, I'm going. Sorry to interrupt. Good to meet you . . . Benjamin Newberry," Tony read the name on the chart, handed it back to Bella, and retreated out of the room, almost as if he didn't want to turn his back on them. The gesture came off as rude.

"Is it me, or is your boss a prick?"

Bella shrugged. "Hard to say at this early stage. But, yeah, it's a possibility. You won't have to deal with him at all."

"That's a relief. He could kick my ass!"

She patted Bender on the shoulder. "Not once I'm done with you." Standing close to him, she picked up the scent of deodorant, soap, and BMW leather seats. *Mmmm,* Bella loved that new-guy smell. "I really appreciate you helping me out, Bender. You won't regret it."

"After, let's reward ourselves with a drink. I'm buying. Or we can take a spin. Drive down to Long Beach Island and have dinner at a great lobster place I know."

"Can I drive?" she asked, instantly seeing herself behind the wheel of his BMW.

He hesitated, but only for a second. "Sure."

"Awesome."

"Here's a thought. Let's skip the workout and go straight to the drive."

First thought: *Yeah, baby!*

Second thought: *No way.* She couldn't blow off work, not on her very first day. Her parents didn't raise her to be irresponsible. When she did a shift at Rizzoli's Deli, Bella was always on time. When Dad asked her to take inventory or log a delivery or stuff sausage, Bella did as she was told. The family business was her business, too. As her parents had been telling her since her birth.

"Actually, that's not such a good idea," she said.

Bender nodded. "Yeah, if I make you ditch, your boss might track me down and kill me."

"Can we go later?"

"Now that I think about it, tomorrow night is better for me."

"Great." Bella was surprised to feel a little annoyed. What was wrong with tonight? Did he suddenly remember he had plans to let some other girl drive around in his car, yanking his stick shift?

"We should get started. This way to the weight room," she said, taking his hand.

Chapter Five

The Rule of Ten

Benjamin Newberry limped to his car after his torture session with Isabella. His shoulder and chest muscles were screaming, and the pain would get worse as the night wore on. Tomorrow, she promised to move on to a different muscle group. If only she meant what was in his boxers! If he had a choice, he'd never step foot into the gym again. But he'd committed to this strategy, which had been handed to him on a silver platter when her ditzy cousin Gia had called him.

Speeding out of the parking lot, Bender winced from the effort of turning the steering wheel. The lengths he'd go to win a bet.

Smiling, he pictured Bella's face when he told her he changed his mind about tonight. He nearly burst out laughing at how easy she was to read and how well he'd played her. By this time tomorrow night, he'd have her right where he wanted her.

His cell rang. The car's automatic Bluetooth picked up the call and put it on speaker.

"Dude," he said, seeing the caller ID for Edward Caldwell. They were college roommates since freshman year and partners in crime.

"If you're answering your car phone, she's not with you," said Ed.

"No rush. I've got six days left."

"Five. Your week started the second we spotted her at Karma."

"Five and a half days then, you shithead," Bender said. "You're still pissed off I get first shot at her."

"We flipped for it. I accept the whims of fate. Unless you cheated."

"I guess you'll never know," said Bender, who had, point of fact, flipped the quarter fairly.

"What're you doing now?"

"Nothing."

"Meet at the driving range?" Ed loved to whack golf balls.

Bender wasn't sure he had the strength to pick up a club, much less swing it. "I'm going home for a Jacuzzi and shower, but I'll call you later."

He hung up, turned the corner toward Route 37 and the Garden State Parkway. Toms River was exit 81. Barnegat Light, on Long Beach Island, was exit 63. The two towns were twenty-five minutes—and light-years—apart. His place was on the *other* Jersey shore. The part that wasn't crawling with trash, human and otherwise.

As he drove, he flashed back to other summers

with Ed. Their tradition: On the first night of summer, they'd go slumming in Seaside Heights. Go to a club, get drinks, find a good spot to watch the door. Then they'd play the Rule of Ten. How it worked: They counted off each girl who came in. Fat chicks, grenades, bitter bitches, and quivering virgins were excluded. The tenth sufficiently easy bimbo who walked in the door became their target.

As fate would have it, this summer, that girl was Isabella Rizzoli.

And now, the fun part: After flipping a coin, the winner would get seven days to beg, seduce, bribe, trick, or trade that woman into bed. He could use any means necessary, except telling her about the bet. If he failed, then it was the other's turn to switch on the charm. If he *also* failed, then the game busted wide open. They could both go for it, a real sword fight, until the end of the summer. In the meantime, they'd pound other girls, too, of course.

At stake: bragging rights for the *entire year*. A satisfying prize, which Bender had won for two of the four summers they'd played the game. This year was the rubber match. It'd been a couple years now since he graduated college, and Bender's parents were starting to pressure him to get a job. They threatened to cut him off. Ed's parents were riding his sorry ass, too, to do something with his life. No doubt about it. This would be their last summer at the Shore.

The Rule of Ten winner this year would win bragging rights *for life*.

The sticking point (much debated over the years): proof. Ed insisted on either being in the room to witness Bender's seduction, or to have a time-stamped video recording of the event. Since having another guy in the room was too homo for Bender, they set up cameras all over the Barnegat Lighthouse. If he nailed Bella someplace else, he'd have to improvise.

The car alone was enough to seduce some girls. Others were talked into bed or swayed by champagne and a lobster dinner. Jersey girls were ridiculously easy. They might as well walk around with mattresses strapped to their backs. Bender got the sense that Bella would be a bit of a challenge.

Good, he thought. His victory would be that much sweeter.

Chapter Six

No Hug

You have to come with me!" pleaded Gia, seated at her mirror in her bedroom, getting ready for the night out.

"You go to parties by yourself all the time in the city," said Bella from Gia's bed. Only a few days here, and they already felt at home in their beach shack. That was a great sign of the fun to come.

"But I know people in Brooklyn. This is some random kid's party. I can't walk in alone. Please, Bells. I need a wingwoman."

"I have a date with Bender."

"Bring him to the party with us. Give me an hour to settle in, and then you can go have your romantic hump."

"We're driving to Belmar to go to his favorite ice cream shop."

"What, are you twelve? This party's going to be a blast."

Bella sighed. "I'll call Bender and ask if he's into it."

"Cool!" said Gia, jumping up and down in her fuzzy slippers and bathrobe. "I love you, Hell's Bells!"

"What's the big deal, anyway?"

"It's a holiday! I'm not staying home alone. And I really liked Neil when we met."

Pulling on her tightest jeans, Bella put her foot through a hole in the thigh. "You met this guy for—what?—ten minutes?"

Gia secured her pouf. "He's hot, single, he invited me to his house. We were vibing like crazy."

"Do you really like him, or are you convincing yourself?"

"Don't hate on my parade."

"I'm just saying."

Gia asked, "Do *you* really like Bender, or his hot car?"

Bella adjusted her new boobs in a ruffled red top. "You're right. What am I talking about? This summer isn't about falling in love. I'm single. Bobby is in the past. I can, and will, get with whoever I choose. Bender is as good a choice as any other kid."

Gia smudged her eye shadow and had to start over. "I'm with you. Just have fun and see what happens. When I'm old and desperate and no one will come near me with a ten-foot pole, that's when I'll be very picky."

"You should do red, white, and blue eye shadow."

"Cool idea."

"I do like Ben. He's been really trying at the gym. He pulled my boss Tony aside to tell him I was breaking his balls—in a good way."

"What about your boss?" asked Gia, trying out the patriotic-makeup idea, feeling it, and going for it. She hadn't met Tony—yet—but she loved what she'd heard so far.

"He doesn't even look at me."

"He must be blind."

"It is kind of insulting."

"First case of a female employee filing a complaint because her boss *didn't* sexually harass her!" Gia said. "Okay, I'm done. Wha'd'ya think?" She'd chosen a white-and-black ensemble for her sort of date with Neil, including her white satin halter top (no bra). It might strike some people as wearing your lingerie in public, but Gia didn't care. She thought she was a sexy bitch, and that was what mattered.

Plus, after two days at Tantastic, Gia (and Bella) had taken full advantage of the free Mystic tanning. She and Bella also went to Maria's favorite nail salon and got new French tips. Considering how gloriously bronzed and polished Gia was, it'd be a crime not to show as much skin as possible without getting arrested for indecency. Maria told Gia, "You're a living, breathing advertisement for the salon! Take flyers. Pass them out on the boardwalk." Gia was happy to. It was a great way to meet guys.

Bender pulled up in his Beemer, with the convertible top down.

"I can't ride in that!" said Gia. Her hands went up to preemptively protect her pouf.

Bender muttered something under his breath. She couldn't hear it, but she thought it was "So walk."

"What did you just say to me?"

He completely ignored her (!!). He didn't look at her or talk until Bella joined them at the car. "I took the top down," he said, "so we could feel the ocean air on our skin."

Romantic idea. And, God knows, Gia was a sucker for romance. Rose petals on the bed. A gift of a teddy bear with a heart that said I LUV YOU. Card with sappy handwritten messages like "You know you're my girl." Walk on the beach? Great. Moonlight swim? Awesome. But the way Bender said "skin" make Gia's flesh crawl. He still hadn't made eye contact with her or asked, "Sup?" or told her she looked hot. That was just plain obnoxious.

Bella said, "I really appreciate your coming along to this party. I promise, we don't have to say long."

"Happy to!" said Bender. "You think I'd pass up the chance to walk into a party with two beautiful women? Never."

Oh, so now he acts sweet, thought Gia. *Only in front of Bella.*

He helped Bella into the shotgun seat. Gia didn't

get a hand up to climb into the backseat. She told Bender the address and he typed it into his GPS.

"I'm serious, you guys," said Gia. "My hair won't stand a chance with the top down."

"I'll drive slow," said Bender, turning the ignition, then gunning it.

Jerkoff! Gia had to lie down on the backseat, then move to the floor of the back, to protect her pouf.

Meanwhile, Bender was talking to Bella as if she were a mentally challenged five-year-old: "So, what's your favorite color?" . . . "Favorite ice cream flavor?" Favorite movie, song, TV show? For each of Bella's answers, he said, "I love Rihanna! We have so much in common!"

If Gia weren't on the verge of puking from listening to him (and lying on the floor), she'd have told him to shut his big freakin' mouth and stop lying his ass off. Gia was willing to bet every penny she had that magenta was not Bender's favorite color. She doubted he even knew who Kendra Wilkinson was.

Why was Bella falling for it? It was one thing to be down for casual sex. But a girl still had to have standards. And she had to be careful, too. Gia's mom had told her countless times, "You can never tell with some guys. They seem normal, and then they get weird, or violent or obsessed." Even rich, cute, and seemingly sweet guys could fool you.

Tonight, Gia was picking up powerful bad vibes from Bender. She needed to have a serious talk with

Bella about him. Gia wasn't the smartest girl on earth, but she knew people. Her instincts told her Bender's ego was ten times the size of his kohl black heart.

"We're here," he said, pulling to a stop outside a house on the far north side of town. The lights were out; it was suspiciously quiet.

"Are you sure this is the right place?" asked Bella.

"Maybe the guy gave you a fake address," said Bender.

Gia said, "Fuck you."

But Bender might be right. Gia'd practically begged Neil for an invite. He might've felt as if he had to give her some address or come off like a jerk. "Let me double-check." Gia reread the address Neil had written down and realized she'd gotten it wrong. "Did I say First Street? I think it's actually I Street. Like the letter *I*. I got the number and the letter confused. Sorry!"

Bender punched the correct address into his GPS. "It's on the south side of town! It'll take half an hour to get there."

"Not that long," said Bella, trying to calm him down.

"Fucktard," he muttered.

"What'd you call me?" asked Gia.

"Nothing," said Bender, and peeled out of the parking spot, back in the direction they'd come.

Gia steamed the whole way. So she had a brain fart. Albert Einstein probably misread sloppy handwriting, too. It was an honest mistake! She was nervous about seeing Neil again, and she read the address too fast. *So freakin' sue me,* she thought. The only reason she didn't mouth off to Bender: he'd probably kick her out and leave her stranded on the road in heels, with miles to walk. That was his last chance, she thought. Next time Bender pissed her off, she'd say whatever popped into her head, regardless of the ride and Bella's feelings about him, whatever they were.

Bella's patience might be stretched, too. First Gia nudged her way into Bella's date. And now she'd messed up the details. This exact scenario had happened before, back in Brooklyn, Gia's dragging Bobby and Bells to a party the night after the event took place, or showing up an hour late for a double date and coming off like a stuck-up bitch when she'd just gotten the time wrong.

Gia decided to just shut up and hope the second address was right. It was, thank God. They found the right house—hip-hop music blasting, the people laughing, a party in full swing. And the house was only six blocks from Bella and Gia's beach shack.

"After all that," said Gia, "we could have walked."

Bender was so mad, he started to shake.

Heh, thought Gia. She checked her hair in the rearview mirror—it'd survived, miraculously. Aqua Net to the rescue, again.

They walked to the door and rang the bell. A woman opened it. She was wasted and shouted, "Happy birthday, America!"

"Does Neil Connor live here?" asked Gia.

"He's upstairs, poor guy."

Poor guy? What was that about?

The woman said, "Come on in!"

They entered the house. Gia took in the atmosphere. Girls in tight dresses or jeans, glittering tops, lots of big gold hoop earrings and bangles, iron-straight hair. Guys in Ed Hardy T-shirts, jeans, chains, gelled spikes, and basketball sneakers. Everywhere, people were grinding, kronking, holding plastic cups of beer. On the couches, couples were making out, visible tongues.

Gia's heart beat faster. Her first big house party of the summer, and it *rocked*. To her companions, she said, "Ya see?"

Bella, grinning and nodding to the beat, said, "Let's find some beers."

The keg was in the backyard in a bathtub full of ice. Cans and bottles of Budweiser and Amstel Light lay around it, as if the keg had given birth to dozens of baby beers. Gia scanned the crowd for Neil.

Gia grabbed a bottle and told Bella, "I'm going to find Neil."

Bella said, "We'll be around."

Gia searched for him in the living room, kitchen, and front and back porches. She found the stairs and checked the second-floor bedrooms, interrupting couples (and a threesome). Neil wasn't mixed up in any of those tangles of limbs. He might be up on the roof deck.

She noticed another door. Knocking first, Gia cracked the door. "Hello? Neil?"

A voice warbled, "Who's there?"

Opening the door all the way, she entered a small bedroom, sparsely decorated. A giant mutant lobster monster, bright red, with short light brown hair, sat up in the bed.

She screamed.

"It's okay! Calm down!"

Taking a second look, she realized the creature was a human dude. Bright red and naked with a washcloth draped across his groin.

A Fourth of July paint job? Were other naked guys painted blue and white running around somewhere?

"Gena? Is that you?"

"It's Gia." Her brain clicked. It *was* Neil. Except for oval white patches around his eyes, his face and body were as red as tomato soup. She stepped closer and sat on the edge of the bed. The movement of the mattress made him wince.

"What happened to you?" she asked.

"What happened to me? *You* happened to me!"

"A few minutes in the tanning bed did this?" she asked, horrified. "I am so so sosososo sorry!"

Gia was an animal lover. She'd rather get run over herself than hit a squirrel or a chipmunk with the Honda. Harming another person? Especially one she sort of had a date with, who'd given her a tip and invited her to a party? No friggin' way.

"I want to kill myself," she gasped. He looked as if he'd been to hell and back. As if he went hiking on the surface of the sun. "I swear, this has never happened before." Granted, she'd been a professional Mystician for only two days. But still.

Neil frowned. "It's not your fault. I left the tanning salon, and my skin was white as paper. I know you told me the effect was delayed. But I was impatient. So I came back here, put on some oil, and laid out on the roof."

"For how long?"

"All day."

"Naked?" Gia had to ask.

"Unfortunately."

"Roasted nuts?"

"Not yet seeing the humor," he said with a grimace. "One day, I'll laugh. When it's not physical agony to do it."

"I really am sorry."

"The whole point was to look good for my party. And for you," he added bashfully.

"So you blame me, not because I did this to you, but because you did it to yourself *for* me?"

He nodded. "I don't really blame you, but, yeah."

Whew. She exhaled. "I wasn't sure you liked me. I practically got on my knees to get an invite to your party."

"I know. When I thought about the conversation later, I realized. But at the time, I just wasn't getting it. It was like my brain was frozen. Does that ever happen to you?"

"Yes! All the time."

"I thought you were mad sexy as soon as I walked in. And then, when I undressed in front of you, I got nervous."

Flattered, Gia said, "I totally understand. I liked you, too."

She moved closer to him on the bed and opened her arms to give him a hug.

"No hug!" he squealed.

Backing off, Gia said, "Um, one question. Why are you lying here naked?"

"Clothes hurt too much."

"Should you be in a hospital or something?"

"There and back. Nothing they can do for me, except give me drugs and aloe."

"We should hang out, as soon as you're better. Have lunch or something."

Neil shook his head. "I can't go outside during daylight hours."

"So we can go out at night. Have a drink or go to the club."

"The ER doctor said the burn could take two weeks to heal. My pain meds rule out alcohol and I can't dance in my condition."

"Does it really hurt?"

He nodded. "It's pretty bad. Even with the pills."

Gia put her hand over his belly and could feel the heat from an inch away. "What can I do?"

"I don't think there's anything you can do."

Oh, really? Gia had an idea. "Relax, and close your eyes."

"Be careful."

Gia put her palm flat on his belly. Apart from the color, his stomach looked yummy. She moved her hand over it. Heat moved up her fingers and into the length of her arm. She glided her hand lower, over her favorite boy body part—the band of muscles right below the belly button. His were flat and taut and . . .

The white washcloth over his privates started to move. She gently glided her hand lower. The fabric made a tent. Dying to sneak a peak, Gia gently lifted the washcloth.

Some of the skin was pale, and some burnt. He must have laid out limp, and now, when he got hard, the stretching caused red and white stripes. Gia couldn't help herself. She started laughing. "It looks like a perverted candy cane. But thicker. Much thicker."

"I was thinking barbershop pole," he said grimly.

"Dr. Seuss hat."

His face was contorted. If she didn't know better, she might've thought he was in pain.

"This is probably the first time in history—and the last—I kick a hot girl out of my bed."

"I understand." Gia felt terrible for him. And disappointed. They couldn't even snuggle. "We can still be friends."

"I'm leaving town. I found someone to take my room. No point paying for the share if I can't drink, dance, fool around, go to the beach, or even walk. My parents are coming to drive me back to Connecticut tomorrow."

"So tonight's your last night."

He nodded. "My roommates are sick of taking care of me."

"I'll take care of you!"

"But you'll miss the fireworks. Please, go downstairs and have a good time at the party."

Gia shook her head. "I couldn't possibly have fun knowing you're up here alone."

"You're so cool. I wish we could get to know each other. But I'm, er, *responding* to you just sitting next to me. And it really kills to have a hard-on. Don't take it personally, but you have to go."

Gia believed in destiny. He was suffering now, but Neil was a sweetie, and he had some good fortune coming his way. Maybe this happened so he'd be forced to leave the Shore and would soon meet his soul mate back in Connecticut. By the same token, obviously, Neil was not meant to be her next boyfriend. Oh, well.

She went in to kiss him good-bye. "No kiss!" he said.

Waving farewell instead, Gia slipped off the bed and out the door. She went back downstairs. Where were Bella and Bender? Did they leave her? Bella would never. Bender? The second he got the chance. Gia decided to check if Bender's car was still parked on the street in front.

She went through the front door. Someone pushed her from behind.

"Move! I gotta get out!"

Gia gave the "Happy birthday, America!" drunk girl some room.

"'Scuse me," slurred the girl, stumbling forward.

She tripped and reeled across the driveway, coming to stop by the curb. She leaned on Bender's BMW. Gia smiled, glad to see it was still parked out front.

Bella came out of the house and said, "Gia? I thought I saw you leave."

Bender was behind her. He noticed the girl by the curb. He yelled, "Yo, get away from my car."

The girl looked up and waved as Bender ran toward her. Then she leaned forward and, in a silent gush, emptied her stomach onto the front seat.

"What the fuck!" Bender yelled.

The girl burped, wiped her lip, and said, "Sorry." She weaved back toward the front door, aiming her puke breath at Gia and said, "I feel much better now."

"This is your fault!" Bender ranted, pointing at Gia.

More instant karma. She giggled, which made Bender furious.

"What's so funny?" he roared.

"I *told* you to put the top up!"

Chapter Seven

Take a Deep Brain Breath

Bella threw all her dirties on her bed. The pile was as tall as she was. Between the gym and the clubs, she went through a lot of clothes in a week.

Gia hovered in the doorway of Bella's room. "Haven't I said 'I'm sorry' enough?"

The first fifty times were more than enough. It'd been two days since the Pukemobile incident. Bella was over it already. She appreciated Gia's apology, but it was unnecessary. True, if Gia hadn't made her go to Neil's party, that girl wouldn't have hurled into Bender's car. He wouldn't have freaked out and abandoned them to take the Beemer to a twenty-four-hour car wash.

Bella couldn't expect him to be *happy* about his leather seat covered in vomit. But, if you thought about it, drunks hurled into convertibles all over town. Maybe on every block. It was bad luck Bender's car got hit. But he couldn't realistically blame Gia, or Bella. Shit happened. Even to BMWs.

"Is Bender still mad mad?" asked Gia.

"He's cooled down to just mad," said Bella.

Gia hesitated, but then said, "He called me a 'fucktard' about getting the address wrong."

Bella stopped stuffing her laundry bag. "I didn't hear that."

"It was low, under this breath. But I'm pretty sure."

"If you were sure, I'd be pissed at him. But if you're not sure, what do you want from me?"

"He's a jerkoff and a fake. You should dump him."

"Because of something you think you might've heard?" said Bella, her voice taking on an edge.

"Chill, Bells. Take a brain breath."

When someone told her to chill, the opposite effect kicked in. Bella felt her blood start to boil. She loved her cousin to death, but Gia was working her last nerve. In Brooklyn, they had the buffer of their parents. With just the two of them in the house together, conflicts kept coming up. Gia wanted to go out *every single night*. She barely cleaned up after herself. Or remembered to lock the door behind her. Or do the shopping. Granted, Gia ate out a lot. But it'd be nice to see her contribute something (anything) to the fridge besides a giant jar of pickles and vodka mixers.

"Please don't take this the wrong way," said Gia. "I think your judgment is out of whack. You know, from Bobby."

"My judgment is fine."

Bobby had done a number on Bella, though, and she knew it. They started going out in high school when they were sixteen. Bobby was from the neighborhood; their families were old friends. Bella and Bobby were a great couple, as long as she agreed with him. If she dared to disagree—about anything, plans, politics, sports, if the pasta was al dente, if Leonardo DiCaprio was half- or full-blood Italian—he'd come down on her like a ton of brownstone. When Bella meekly declared that she wanted to enroll at New York University in September (she'd deferred twice already), Bobby hit the roof. A construction worker, he didn't go to college, and he didn't see the point of Bella's going either.

"It's a waste!" he told her. "Four years and thousands in student loans? You're going to wind up working at Rizzoli's anyway."

"If I don't know what I'm going to do, how do you have such a clear picture?" she countered.

Bobby snorted. "I know exactly what you're going to do because I'm telling you."

Six years of his telling her what to do was more than enough. On the college issue, Bella dug her heels in. "NYU is a great school, and, by some miracle, I got in. I've waited long enough. I'm going."

"When you're my wife, your debt will become my debt. And I'm not paying it."

"I'm *not* going to be your wife," she said, amazing herself.

According to Bobby, the breakup came out of nowhere. From Bella's perspective, it'd been building slowly for years. She'd rehearsed a breakup speech for months. When she finally got it out, it was like an actor replaying a scene she'd played a thousand times in her head.

Bobby refused to accept it. He called her constantly. He buzzed her building at all hours. He'd show up at the deli, demanding that she take him back, scaring away the customers. He followed her around the neighborhood. The two families called an emergency meeting to decide what to do. Bella made it easy for everyone, announcing the plan to leave Brooklyn for July and go to Jersey with Gia. Bella's offer to leave Brooklyn clicked in Bobby's head. He finally felt ashamed of his behavior and backed off.

Bella's nerves were still raw from the ordeal. She interpreted meeting Bender the first night in Seaside Heights as a good sign. He was the anti-Bobby. A cute guy who was nice to her, tried to help her, didn't tell her what to do, how to act or feel. Why shouldn't she like him? Okay, yes, he was oddly neg about going to a hot party. And he overreacted about his precious car. But Bella knew guys loved their wheels. She could forgive him for that.

The last thing Bella needed or wanted was Gia's advice about men or anything. She was sick and tired of people telling her what to do.

"I don't care if you like him or not," Bella announced to her cousin. "I like him, and I'm making the decisions for me." She gathered her dirty clothes in her bedsheets (also in need of a wash), slung the bundle over her shoulder like Santa, and said, "I'm going out."

"Wait, Bella."

She paused. "What now?"

Gia batted her two sets of lashes. "Can you take some of my laundry, too?"

Sighing heavily, Bella said, "Hurry up."

Gia moved fast when she wanted to. She had her pink laundry bag ready and in the Honda's trunk in two minutes flat. "Also," said Gia, "can you pick up some food on the way home?"

By the time Bella pulled into the Laundromat, she was furious at the world, her cousin, her ex, her dad (who'd asked her too many times if she was sure about college), and her mom (who asked her too many times if she was sure about Bobby). The only person she wasn't mad at . . . was Bender.

The Honda chugged to a stop. She hoisted the heavy bags and lugged them into the Tumble Wash 'N' Dry.

And nearly crashed into Tony Troublino.

"There she is," he said cheerfully, as if he expected to see her.

"Tony, hey," said Bella, surprised to find her boss at the Tumble. Seeing him anywhere but the gym was weird, out of context. It was especially strange to see him with a bottle of Downy instead of a medicine ball.

"Come here often?" he asked, smiling.

"My first time, actually."

"Welcome! The Tumble is my second home! I go through three outfits every day at the gym."

"Yo, T!" called someone from across the room.

Bella turned to see a scary-looking dude—bald head covered with ink, mustache, nose ring, massive arm and chest muscles bursting out of his black leather vest—lumber toward them.

Tony said, "What up, G?" They pounded fists.

"Spare some softener?" ask the biker.

"Strip or liquid?"

"Liquid, of course," said G.

Tony could spare some liquid. The biker thanked him and went back to his machine.

Seeing her reaction, Tony said, "Don't be fooled, Isabella. Even tough guys like Downy softness. One cupful of this"—he held up his bottle—"can make the difference between a good day and a bad day. Life is tough enough. Might as well do the easy stuff to make yourself feel better."

Bella nodded, frankly amazed. She'd never heard Tony speak more than a sentence or two at a time at the gym, but here he was rhapsodizing about philosophy.

She said, "I wish I had a fabric softener for my life."

"That's what I'm telling you. Try it! You'll see. Soft fabric can soothe a savage beast. That's me!"

She laughed. The way he grinned and pointed his thumbs at himself, it was too dorky. He seemed to like her reaction, which made him smile more (the dimples!).

"I think the quote is 'soothe a savage breast,'" she said.

"Then that's you!" he said, looking embarrassed for a second. "*Savage* is a compliment. I didn't mean to imply anything about your . . . bras."

"I know," she said, dumping dirty sports bras out of the laundry bag.

So he'd noticed Bella's boobs after all.

Before she knew it, they were grinning at each other and giggling for no apparent reason.

The anger she drove in with? Gone.

"Nice work at the gym, by the way," said Tony. "A few of the regulars asked me about you. They noticed you training that kid and liked what they saw. You learn quick. I'm impressed."

"Thanks. It feels right, you know?"

"When you're doing what you're supposed to, life just flows," he said, all Zen again.

"I really appreciate you giving me a chance."

"Can I ask you a question?" he asked suddenly, filling a dryer and pushing in his quarters.

"Go ahead," she said, examining the machine dials and feeling a little lost. Despite being twenty-one, Bella had never done her own laundry. Her mom insisted on doing it for her. If Bella tried to wash her own, her mom would say, "You don't need me anymore," and get a sad expression on her face. The thought of it made Bella miss her, badly.

Fumbling around, not sure how much detergent to use, what water temperature to set the machine, all she knew for sure was to separate the colors and the whites. But what about black? Did that count as a color? Most of her laundry—including the panties—was black.

Tony noticed her confusion. "Need help?"

"No." She put the whites, including Gia's favorite pair of short shorts, into the machine and set the temperature on COLD.

Tony, ever so subtly, shook his head. Bella changed the setting to HOT. He nodded.

Bella asked, "You wanted to ask something?"

"That guy you train, Benjamin Newberry. Is he your boyfriend?"

"No." At least, not yet. She was thinking about it, though.

"Don't," Tony said, reading her mind. "He's a weenie."

She barked a laugh. "How would you know?"

"Oh, I can tell. I've lived in Seaside Heights my whole life, and I can smell a summer slummer from a mile away. Funny his name is Benjamin. We call out of towners *bennies*. They come to the Shore every July, act like they own the place, and then leave the locals to clean up the mess. They get no respect from me."

Bella frowned. So now her boss and her cousin were singing the same cranky tune about Bender. "It's none of your business who I hang out with. You don't know anything about him, or me."

"Oh, I got the weenie down for sure. As for you, I'd guess, off the bat, you're running away from something, or someone, back home. You're in a holding pattern right now, trying to sort through some shit, and you thought the beach is as good a place as any to hide from your real life while you figure out your next move."

She blinked at Tony, hating him for calling it right on the first try. "You're way off." Was she that easy to read?

He looked at her with sweet sincerity. His eyes were emerald green, deep as a well, and a little sad, too. She could imagine Tony hugging a baby, or cuddling a cat, crying at a sad movie when the lovers died at the end.

"My read on you is that you think you know everything, and that you'd be smart to keep your opinions to yourself," she said.

"Not gonna happen."

"I haven't spoken to my mom in a week," said Bella out of nowhere. "I miss her." The words came out before she could stop them. She was dumbfounded she'd confide in Tony at all, much less make a confession that made her sound like a big baby.

"You should call her," he said softly.

Bella shrugged. It was too soon. She'd vowed to go two weeks at least before she fell back on her family for support.

"How did you guess all that about me?"

He shrugged. "Being a trainer is kind of like being a bartender, or a shrink. Clients talk to me. When they're physically exhausted, their emotional and mental guard goes down. They reveal themselves. Their strengths and weaknesses. I've developed a sense of people. I call it the Sixth Sense. By the sixth workout, I've got their number."

"So your Sixth Sense about me is Little Lost Girl?" Bella asked, blinking up at him, afraid of what he'd say.

Tony smiled slyly. "Jury's still out. I need to spend more time with you. My gut sense is that you're cool, though."

Bella gulped. When she was with Tony, her gut felt full of butterflies—a swarm. "I'm not sure about you either."

"That's how I like it. Keep 'em guessing."

Chapter Eight

Buzz Kryptonite

Oh, God, you look sick! Totally mad creepy sick!" said Gia.

"Really? You're not just saying that to be sweet?" asked Viv, the last customer of the day. She'd just received a Mystic head-to-toe tan dialed to a nutty brown.

"I wish I was that tan. I'm hitting the booth as soon as we lock up."

Viv tipped Gia ten bucks and was beaming as she left. Gia gladly accepted the money. Her conscience was clear. Viv did look like a million bucks. Gia felt like a million bucks, too, for bringing the joy, hard, to their customers. Since that first day with Neil, Gia'd become a master tanner. She'd helped customers into every bed and booth in the place and had done several spray-gun tans (the most expensive treatment they offered, at $100). Her tips had been good, and Maria seemed happy with her work—and the company.

"Is it locked?" asked Maria.

"Yup."

"Thirsty?"

Gia watched Maria put two shot glasses on the front desk at Tantastic and fill them with Hornitos tequila. Maria hoisted her glass and said, "Good work today, Princess. *Salute!*"

"*Salute.*" Gia gulped down the clear liquid.

"Another?"

Gia paused to think. She had to be careful. Too much tequila made her clothes feel small. Also, did she want to get drunk? Seeing as how Bella was pissed off at her, she might as well. Besides the Beemer incident (so not her fault), and having asked Bella to do her laundry (honestly? If it were such a big deal, Bella should have said no), Gia was supposed to meet Bella for lunch today and wound up (accidentally) blowing her off. She lost her phone and couldn't call Bella to ask her when they were supposed to be meeting. Bella found her at Tantastic later on and was furious. Apparently, she sat at Spicy for an hour—noon to one—waiting for Gia.

"That explains it," said Gia. "I did go by there looking for you, at one fifteen."

"We were supposed to meet at noon!" said Bella.

"I forgot, okay?"

It wasn't. Bella was starting to get annoyed over the smallest things. Sheesh. Gia was afraid to call

Bella at the beach shack to ask about going out tonight.

But here was Maria, with a bottle of tequila, ready to go.

"Set it up," said Gia.

During their breaks between customers, Maria had been telling Gia her marriage history. First, there was Otto, her high school boyfriend, who she eloped with against her parents' wishes and wound up divorcing five years later after he ran off to Atlantic City to be a professional poker player, aka a "broke, homeless-bum, alcoholic, cheating, loser asshole" as Maria described him.

Husband number two had been Vic, a guy she met at a pizza stand on the boardwalk about ten years ago. "A slice held up to his mouth, like this. When he saw me walk by, he dropped the slice on his lap and chased after me, sauce and cheese running down his leg" was Maria's "meet cute" story about him. That marriage ended badly, too. Maria discovered him in bed with her bestie at the time—a hairdresser named Bruce.

"Which brings me to Stanley, husband number three. We met right here, in this room," said Maria after pounding her shot and pouring another. "He's my landlord. He was after me for years until I finally gave in out of desperation. By the time you get to be my age, you can't just prop your boobs on the bar at Karma and expect ten men to give you their phone number. When you're young, all you have to do is stand there and look cute. But when you're older, you have fewer options. Most of them crappy." Maria held up her shot glass. "Here's to enjoying it while it lasts! *Alla salute!*"

Gia drank. It was hard not to feel bad for Maria, with her pile of failed marriages behind her. That wouldn't happen to Gia. She'd have her fun for a while, and then she'd find a sweet, romantic gorilla juicehead to marry. The wedding would have a kick-ass hip-hop band and a pickle buffet. She'd wear a skintight white satin wedding dress with a train that dragged all the way down the aisle. Her wedding cake? In the shape of a heart, with sprinkles, and cream inside.

"Where's Stanley now?" asked Gia.

Maria said, "He's asleep in my apartment across the street."

"I thought you were divorced."

"We are. But he's my landlord there, too. He owns half the run-down rentals on the boardwalk. But would he fix one up and move there with his bride? No way! Not if he can live like a bum in a crappy one-bedroom apartment. I still live there. When we split, he moved into his own crappy one-bedroom in the building next door.

"If he put us in a nice house," Maria continued, "or just once bought me a piece of jewelry or a car, we'd probably still be together. He never gave me any gifts. He made me sign a prenup, too. And now he raises my rent on the salon and the apartment. I paid rent for the salon *even when we were married!* Stanley Crumbi is the cheapest bastard in the state. *And* a fat shit. *And* a pervert. And he's always letting himself into my apartment when I'm in the shower."

"Maybe he still loves you."

Marie laughed donkey-style. "Oh, you are priceless."

Gia had had enough of Maria's crawl down Bad Memory Lane. "It's Sex on the Beach night at Bamboo," she suggested. "Wanna hit the club?"

Maria crunched up her face. "Bamboo? I haven't been there since I was . . . a bit younger than I am now. Everyone will be half my age! It'll make me feel even worse."

"I was there a few nights ago, and most of the guys at the bar were old enough to be my father."

"It must have been seniors' night," whined Maria.

"Come on. First round is on me. But let's get dressed first."

Over the last week, Gia had learned to bring her going-out clothes to work for a quick change. It saved her the twenty minutes walking time, and Maria was an expert with makeup and accessorizing. A lot of Gia's closet had migrated to the back room at Tantastic. They fixed their makeup, poufed their hair. Maria urged Gia to wear a red, sequined tank dress of hers. "It's a little too tight on me," said Maria.

It was tight on Gia, who was much smaller than Maria. "I love it!" she said, hoping Maria would give it to her.

"Just have it cleaned before you give it back," said the boss.

Maria slipped into a black spandex minidress and go-go boots. Gia put on her gold platform heels. They covered the four blocks to the club on foot. The trip took a bit longer than it should have, but walking on heels after doing shots wasn't easy.

The bouncer waved Gia and Maria through the VIP entrance. The older woman seemed to get an ego boost from skipping the line to get it. At Bamboo, though, *everyone* got in. No velvet ropes here. No paranoia about overcrowding. If the club was packed, good. Great! Made it easier to meet boys when they were crushed against you.

The decor at Bamboo was under-the-sea jungle, as if the Amazon rain forest were submerged in the Pacific Ocean. The wallpaper had water plants and fish swimming around, but the carpet was leopard print, as were the bars and seat covers.

It was tacky and gaudy and made no sense. Gia loved it, of course. She felt at home in the jungle.

It was early yet, only around nine. The real crowd wouldn't show up for hours. Gia decided to go slow. Honestly? She wasn't in much of a party mood. Story after story of Maria's romantic train wrecks bummed her out. The thought of Gia following in Maria's cougar paw-steps was Kryptonite to her buzz. Meanwhile, Maria was already weaving.

At the bar, Gia tapped a couple of guys on the shoulder. "Can you give us your seats?" She pointed at her feet, which, in those heels, needed a rest.

"Check it: she's pointing at her crotch!" said the guy—rhinestone studs in both ears—to his friend. "I *told* you about Jersey girls. They throw it at you! If you can't get laid in Seaside Heights, you might as well turn in your dick."

"Jerkoff," said Gia.

But RStud offered his seat to Gia as if it were a throne. Maria took it. Seated, she wriggled to the beat.

"How's it going?" RStud asked.

Gia said, "Go away." Ordinarily, she'd talk to anyone. But tonight, she wasn't into it. She didn't like being called a slut, either. Even if she was.

"Wanna do a body shot?" he asked, lifting his shirt.

"Eww, disgusting."

"I'll do it!" said Maria.

"You?" The guy laughed out loud. But then he decided, "Yeah, why not? It's dark enough in here."

Maria got on her knees in front of him with her lips at his navel. He took off his shirt and dribbled a shot of tequila between his pecs. Maria thirstily slurped it out of his belly button. Clearly, she'd done this before.

RStud's friend, a guido with a fauxhawk, said, "Got MILF?"

Fauxhawk, too, took off his shirt and poured his drink down his torso. Maria, lips open, was right there to catch it.

Gia had a rule: never torpedo someone else's fun. But Maria was, like, an elderly person. She shouldn't be cleaning a stranger's stomach with her tongue. Gia averted her eyes and glanced down the bar, only to notice a woman staring at her from a few stools away.

Shit! Another flashback to the Toms River High School cafeteria. The bleached blonde, cut from the same glacial rock as frenemy Linda Patterson, leaned forward and yelled over the music, "Giovanna Spumanti, is that *you*?"

"Janey Gordon, wow. Small freakin' world."

"I heard you were back in town," said Janey, coming over to give Gia a girl hug (double kiss, and clash of collarbone). Janey put a hand on either side of Gia's waist. "Good to see you. A lot *more* of you."

Bitch. "You look exactly the same. How do you stay so thin?"

But Gia knew only too well. Janey was a notorious bulimic back in high school. She bragged about it and carried around a photo of Lindsay Lohan (in coked-head fire-crotch mode) for "thinspiration." Gia and Janey were never good friends. If memory served (it didn't), Gia thought of Janey as a hanger-on, the type of girl who moved in after two other girls had a big fight.

"When I last saw you," said Janey, "you were passed out in a bathtub at Richie Paz's house. Remember that party? You probably don't."

The last year of high school was a bleak blur for Gia. Her parents' split was bitter and ugly. Not their finest hour; both her mom and dad failed to comfort their only daughter. Gia felt split down the middle by the separation and used alcohol to hold herself together. Didn't work. Neither did boys.

"Last time I saw you, Janey, you were talking about moving to New York to find a modeling agent. How'd that go?" After participating in a cheesy fashion show at the Toms River mall, Janey claimed to be an official teen model. Her dream? Strut the runways of the world.

"I got an agent," said Janey. "I met some great people and had some amazing experiences. But I decided that the modeling life wasn't for me. Too many scumbag photographers and methhead bookers. Paris, London, and Milan are great and all. But I'm a Jersey girl at heart."

Riiight. Gia almost made a snide comment about how hard it must have been for Janey to turn her back on *this* for fame, fortune, and travel. Obviously, Janey was full of shit. Gia doubted she'd ever modeled or seen Paris. But, then again, Gia felt the urge to come back to Jersey, too, to the one place on earth she thought of as home.

"So what are you doing now?" asked Gia.

"I live with my folks. And I'm the hostess at Lorenzo's. You should come by."

Lorenzo's. One of the restaurants that Gia couldn't get a job at. "I will, totally." Although Janey was a two-faced bitch in school—it was starting to come back to Gia—she seemed nicer now. "It really is good to see you. You look great. As always."

"Yeah, I know."

Gia waited for Janey to return the compliment. She might as well have waited for the second coming of Christ.

Janey pointed over Gia's shoulder. "Um, your friend?"

Gia turned around to see Maria heading for the club stage, where a bunch of girls were lining up for Jell-O shots. Maria was the oldest woman up there, by far. The other girls were whispering and laughing at her. The DJ shook a big can of whipped cream and got the crowd to count down from three. Then the women onstage started slurping shots. The DJ went up the line, randomly telling a contestant to open her mouth wide for a squirt of whipped cream. Or to lick it off his palm, lips, or chest. One girl lifted up her shirt and took a squirt on her boobs.

When the DJ got to Maria, he shook the can extra hard and shot a steam of whipped cream all over Maria's face and her pouf.

"Uh, God," said Gia. "I better go get her before she . . ."

"Embarrasses herself?" asked Janey snidely. "Too late."

"Excuse me." Fighting through the crowd, Gia reached the stage and got Maria's attention. The older woman grabbed a few Jell-O shots for the road and tripped down the stairs. Gia dragged her boss out of the club, up the block, and onto a bench on the boardwalk.

"Fresh ocean air. Inhale," said Gia.

"Smells like pot," slurred her boss.

Now that she mentioned it, Gia could smell it, too. She leaned over the boardwalk railing and saw a circle of hippies on the beach. They were huddled together like a family of Ellis Island immigrants just off the *Mayflower*.

Instinctively, Gia glanced up and down the boardwalk. She spotted a uniformed policeman heading this way.

"Yo!" she shouted at the hippies.

One of the guys looked up at her and smiled so big you could see it from China.

Gia couldn't help but smile back. The hippie had cute curly hair like Andy Samberg, who Gia had always crushed on. He was a skinny kid. A real lean cuisine.

"Yo, yourself," he said. "Come on down here."

"You come up here."

"Okay." He left his crew and jogged up the ramp from the beach to the boardwalk. In bare feet, he held out his hand. "I'm Pete, and you're gorgeous." He was even cuter up close, but the red-and-yellow-striped Baja pullover and drawstring pants (made from hemp fabric, probably) had to go.

Maria said, "That's what I'm talking about. All you have to do is stand there."

Pete asked, "Um, why does your friend have whipped cream all over her hair?"

"Never mind about her. Look that way." Gia discreetly pointed in the direction of the cop.

"Uh-oh," Pete said, seeing the man uniform. "Pardon me one second."

He leaned over the railing and said, "Dudes! Five-O!"

Gia watched as his friends buried the joint in the sand.

By now, the policeman—burly and bald with a mustache—was upon them. "You kids have beach badges?" he asked when he saw Pete's friends.

"We don't need no stinking badges," said one of the kids in an exaggerated Spanish accent. The others cracked up.

Gia didn't see what was so funny.

Pete said, "Sorry, sir. We were unaware that badges were required to enjoy this beautiful beach."

"I'll be back in twenty minutes," said the poli, close enough to smell the pot on Pete's clothes. "You better be long gone."

Once the cop was out of hearing range, Pete and his buds groaned. They knew not to push it, thank God, thought Gia. If they had, the whole Seaside Heights police force would have descended like locusts. Especially during the tourist season, they had a zero-tolerance drug policy.

The hippies climbed the ramp. "I guess we're taking off," said Pete. "Thanks for the warning."

"Where are you going?" asked Gia, suddenly hating to see them leave her alone with drunk, depressed Maria.

Pete shrugged. "No clue. We just got off the bus from New York this afternoon. My man Carl—dude, wave—had the inspired idea to get out of the city and sleep on the beach, under the moon and stars."

"You live in New York?"

"Yup. We're all art students at Cooper Union."

If Gia was supposed to know what that was and be impressed, she didn't, and wasn't. But she said,

"It's cool how you got the idea and just went with it. I love being spontaneous. It's my life philosophy. No planning, just action."

"Only problem with spontaneity, sometimes you wind up sleeping at the bus station. Anyway, nice to meet you. See you around."

He turned back to his crew, now huddled to sort out their next move. Gia half listened. They'd have no luck finding a place to sleep on the beach for miles in both directions, not with the summer crackdowns. A hotel room? That'd be a challenge, too, in prime season, on a weekend, without a reservation.

It might be destiny, meeting Pete. How else to explain how she left the club, sat on this bench, noticed the cop just in time to warn him? Granted, Pete wasn't anything like her usual type. No muscles. He wore clown clothes. No tan. But he did have one major thing going for him. He was *here*. She was not ready to go home to an empty house on a Saturday night. And she felt a little scared for him and his friends, having nowhere to go. The Jersey Shore could be dangerous.

Maria, sloshed, said, "You kids can hang out at my place for a bit."

"Yes! Great idea," seconded Gia.

Pete jumped on the offer. "Lead the way."

———

Gia gave Pete a tour of Tantastic. "How does this work?" asked Pete, picking up a spray-tan gun.

Gia turned on the appliance. "You pull the trigger, and a fine spray comes out the nozzle. We use this to do tanscaping."

He tried the gun, spraying his arm. "What's tanscaping?"

"It's for guys who want more ab definition. We spray lines and shading to create the illusion of a six-pack."

Pete was fascinated. "That's awesome! It's trompe l'oeil for the body!"

Huh? Gia said, "Okay." Who the hell was Trump Louie? Donald's Italian relative?

"How long does it last?"

"A week."

"Spray something on me," he said, patting his stomach. "Anything."

Gia thought about it for a second, then pulled the trigger. When she was done, he looked in the wall mirror and said, "A peace sign! Righteous!"

She'd figured he'd like it. That, or a pot leaf. Pete ran out of the private room to show the peace sign to his pals.

Carl said, "I want one!"

Gia sprayed a yin-yang symbol on his chest.

One of the hippie chicks wanted a dove on her back.

Another requested a pot leaf (so predictable). Gia had to ask her to draw it on paper first.

Meanwhile, Maria was at the front desk, a fat joint burning in her fingers. As each kid came out, she went nuts for the designs. "This could be a big new thing for us," said Maria. "Like body graffiti, but with tanning spray."

Gia nodded. "We can call 'em tan-tags."

The room fell silent for a minute, except for the hippie music from the salon's speakers—aka, not music to fist-pump by.

"Oh my freakin' God," gasped Maria. "Tan-tags!! I love that so much, I think I just wet myself. We're gonna get *rich*!"

Pete said, "You're a genius."

"Will I love this when I'm sober?" asked Maria.

"Hells yeah!" said Pete, who grabbed Gia, picked her up, and swung her around the salon. "Sexy *and* brilliant!"

Maria spent the next hour blowing huge clouds of cigarette and pot smoke with Pete's crew, rambling about the marketing potential of "Tan-tags by Tantastic." She said, "Think of the bridal business!"

Gia didn't see the connection. But whatevs. Maria was happy, which was a relief for Gia, considering her boss's dismal mood before. Carl and the other art students had a blast tan-tagging little flowers and birds and designs on each other's legs and arms, smoking joint after joint.

In the back, Gia and Pete stretched out on the Matrix 5000 together. Up close, he smelled grungy yet fresh, like a parking lot after a rainstorm.

"Do you really think I'm a genius?" asked Gia.

"You bet your ass!" he said, grabbing a big handful of it.

"We call this machine the Spaceship, by the way."

"Take a ride to the other side," he said, and started kissing her.

While making out, Gia wondered if he was using the old trick of telling a pretty girl she was smart (or a smart girl she was pretty) to get her to smush with him. But Gia was already down for it, so she decided to take him at face value.

As a kisser, she thought, Pete was lazy and mechanical. He just rolled his tongue around and around inside her mouth like a windup slug. It was boring and gross. The combo of bad technique and clown clothes added up to zero sexual chemistry. Oh, well. Gia came to the Shore to learn about herself. And tonight, she confirmed what she already knew: she liked her boys big, tan, Italian, with powerful sexual mojo. Pothead hippies with windup slug tongues just didn't cut it.

Only problem: how to end their ride on the Spaceship without crashing and burning? Gia hated to hurt Pete's feelings.

"I must be really stoned," he said. "I hear sirens."

She listened. "Yeah, I hear them, too."

The sirens got louder, and louder. And then lights flashed through the storefront windows.

Cops! Right on the street in front of the salon.

Coordinated like bats, the pothead hippies flew out the back door. Pete, closest to the exit, was the first one out. He moved pretty fast for a stoned hippie. Before Gia and Maria know what was going on, they were the only people left in the salon. Maria was smart enough to run to the bathroom, dump the ashtray, and flush.

From outside the salon, Gia heard shouting. Without warning, the front door slammed open, snapping off the hinges.

Through the dust and smoke, Gia could make out the silhouette of a man. A *big* man, holding a big ax.

Maria screamed, "Whatthefuckareyoudoing???"

But the fireman was already barreling toward them. He tucked Gia under one arm. Maria went under the other. Then he carried them out of the salon.

Granted, Gia was small. She was only five feet, around a hundred pounds. But still! He lifted her like a kitty. The fireman was mad strong. And not the kind of muscle you got from lifting at the gym. He'd earned his guns by splintering doors, turning over cars, saving lives and shit. Even though her teeth shook as he ran, she felt safe under his arm.

"Are you all right?" he asked after he'd put her down by the fire truck.

"Do it again!" she said, jumping up and down, clapping.

He squinted at her, then crashed back into the salon, followed by a couple other firemen.

Meanwhile, Maria was screaming, "Don'tfuckingbreakanything!"

The firemen came out again. "All clear," said Gia's hero. "False alarm. No fire. Plenty of smoke, though."

A police car pulled up and skidded to a stop. The same poli from the boardwalk—Officer Mustache—

hitched his belt up under his chubby belly and approached the scene.

"Smells like 1969," he said, sniffing the air.

"Just cigarettes!" said Maria nervously.

Another man arrived on the scene. He wore a cheap suit and had a ridiculous comb-over. "Maria! Are you okay?"

"Stanley, you asshole!" said Maria.

Was this *the* Stanley, ex-husband number three?

"Did you call in a friggin' fire?" asked Maria. "Have you lost your *mind*?"

"I saw smoke," said Stanley. "It's my building! If I think it's burning to the ground, I'm calling it in."

"Bullshit! You saw me having a good time with those younger guys, and you just *had* to ruin it. Like you weren't watching me with your binoculars." To Gia, Maria said, "He sits on his roof with the binoculars and looks at girls in bikinis on the beach."

Stanley said, "I'm watching for sharks!"

"Just as long as they have tits and ass," said Maria.

"I hate to interrupt," said the cop. "How you doing, Mr. Crumbi?"

"Been better, Sean," said Stanley, not taking his eyes off Maria.

"I'm going to take a look around inside," said the cop. Gia could see the name tag on his shirt: CAPTAIN SEAN MORGAN.

"Be my guest," said Stanley.

Maria whispered in Gia's ear, "This could be bad. I've been busted for possession twice. Third strike, I could get locked up." Gia prayed the hippies hadn't left behind a roach.

The big fireman, meanwhile, shrugged off his coat, hat, mask, and gloves. His forearms were tanned and bulging, with a fine dusting of dark hair. Gia liked a smooth chest on a man (not to mention back, sack, and crack). But some fur on the arms made her feel soft and girly in comparison. He held a clipboard and a pen. With his hat and mask off, she got a better look at his face. Rugged, clean-shaven, with a slightly crooked nose, stellar cheekbones, and full red lips—and yummy olive skin, as if he'd been baking under the Tuscan sun for generations. A guido, guaranteed.

Smiling, he asked her, "Can I get some information for my report?"

"Nothing to report. We were chain-smoking Camels."

"Name?"

"Giovanna Spumanti."

"I'm Frank Rossi. Nice to meet you."

"You, too." She showed him her most lethal smile.

"Address?"

She gave him her Smith Street, Brooklyn, address.

He said, "What's that?" and leaned way down to make sure he could hear. She repeated it right into his ear. He turned suddenly, his nose only half an inch from her lips. If she wanted to, she could bite if off.

"Your breath smells like lime. And tequila. And . . . pickles? No trace of cigarettes. Or anything else you might smoke."

For a guy who put out fires, he had super smelling. And he was dead right. Gia didn't smoke pot or do any drugs. Generally, she didn't like druggies. She liked drunks, though. Big difference.

But if she admitted that she didn't smoke, all the blame would be on Maria, and that could land her in serious trouble. Or not. The poli on the scene had been through the salon twice and obviously found nothing suspicious.

"You can't arrest us for smoking," Gia said to the poli anyway, in case he thought otherwise.

"If I were you, I'd shut up," said Captain Morgan. To Stanley he said, "No evidence of wrongdoing, Mr. Crumbi. Or any damage. Except, you know, the door."

"That's a relief, Sean."

"Anything else I can do for you?"

Gia whispered to Maria, "Why is he kissing your ex's ass?"

"Stanley is connec—he's got a lot of friends."

Her ex conferred with the cop and the firemen. After, her ex came over to Maria and Gia and asked, "Who's the kid?"

"My assistant, Gia Spumanti."

"Hello, Gia." To Maria, he said, "Since you're responsible for the smoke, you can pay to get the door fixed." Then he turned around and walked back across the street.

Maria yelled after him, "Cheap bastard!"

"You two," said the cop. "We all know what went on here tonight. On behalf of the Seaside Heights police and fire departments, we expect some compensation for our efforts. Your choice. You can either pay a fine for creating a public disturbance, or you can volunteer to do community service."

Gia asked, "How much is the fine?"

The cop replied, "Five hundred dollars. Each."

That would eat up her entire summer savings.

Maria said, "Send me a bill," and stormed back into the salon, slamming the pieces of the broken door behind her.

"What about you?" he asked.

"I don't have to scrub toilets, do I?" Gia asked.

The fireman gave her a sympathetic smile.

Morgan just smiled. Asshole.

Chapter Nine

You've Got Some Shell on Your Boob

Bella tried to breathe through her mouth on the drive to Crabby Dan's in Barnegat Light. The leather seat of the BMW had been cleaned, but the smell lingered.

Bender pulled up at the curb in front of the restaurant. A kid ran over to valet the car. Ben took the ticket and threw his keys at the valet. They bounced off his chest and fell on the sidewalk. The kid frowned, and Bella felt embarrassed on Bender's behalf. She would have bent down and picked up the keys, but Bender said, "This way, Bella," and held the door open for her.

Inside, the restaurant was dimly lit, with green glass sconces on the ivory stucco walls. Bender put his hand on her lower back to guide her toward the reservation desk. "Newberry, party of two. And make it a good table," Bender told the tuxedoed maître d'.

Bella thought she saw Bender press a $100 bill into the man's palm.

Bella felt instantly uncomfortable. The place was a lot classier than she was used to—or dressed for. The maître d' brought them to a table and held out a chair for her. She sat down. Her low-cut, backless minidress rode all the way up her thighs.

"I'm way underdressed," she said, glancing around anxiously.

"You look beautiful," said Bender, in a sports jacket straight out of Abercrombie.

"Shut up," she said, irritated he'd missed the point.

"I mean it," he said, moving aside a candle to hold her hand. "Did you notice how all the women in here are staring at you?"

Glaring, more like it. "Burning holes in my back."

"They're jealous. Every guy would be staring, too, if they could get away with it."

The waiter came over. Bella started to order a shot of Patrón to settle her nerves, but Bender said, "Bottle of Cristal."

"You don't have to do that," said Bella, even more uncomfortable about spending another $200 on the champagne.

He waved the waiter away and said, "I insist. It's my pleasure."

What was with him? He'd been piling it on thick all week, but tonight, he'd upgraded from a shovel to a bulldozer.

"Did you get the roses I sent this afternoon?"

"Yes, thank you."

They were dyed purple, big as her fist, and breath-taking. She'd never received flowers before, not even from Bobby. His idea of a romantic Valentine's Day gift was a Snickers bar.

"It's really nice to be with you, alone," he said. "Not to say I don't enjoy Gia's company."

"I know."

"She's a sweet girl, but when she's around, things just seem to go wrong."

"It's not her fault," Bella said, happy to steer the conversation away from Bender's lavish seduction efforts. "Gia's just accident-prone. She doesn't mean to cause trouble. Or give bad directions. Or break things. Or lose her phone and keys."

"Maybe that's why she's single. Too hard to deal with."

"Back home, with my ex, she was the third wheel a lot. We'd bring her out with us or try to fix her up, but it's always a hassle. She gets the time wrong or the place wrong. Like how she gave you the wrong address for the Fourth of July party. Or she gets really drunk and insults the guys over nothing. I love Gia. She's family. But family can make you crazy sometimes."

"I feel the same way. We have so much in common! I'm honored you feel comfortable enough to confide in me."

"No big thing," she said, suddenly wishing she hadn't. He sounded hyper and weird tonight. The expensive dinner and roses reeked of overkill. *What is going on?* she wondered.

"There is something I want to tell you," he said, getting serious.

"Okay," she said, a bit wary.

He cleared his throat.

The waiter brought the champagne. He made a show of popping the cork and pouring it into tall, skinny glasses. After wiping the neck with a linen napkin, he left the bottle in a silver ice bucket on a stand next to their table.

Bender raised his glass and said, "To us."

She lifted hers, too, clinked, and drank. Ordinarily, Bella preferred beer to champagne, but the bubbly hit her throat tonight in just the right way, sweet and cold. She drained her glass and let Bender refill it.

"You were saying?" she asked.

"I've been meaning to tell you how much I like you."

Gawd, what a creep. "Thanks."

"Do you like me, too?"

She took another swallow. Bella did like him, as a friend. When she lay in bed and fantasized about casual, meaningless sex with Bender, she got as far as picturing herself kissing him, then felt queasy and had to stop.

No matter how hard she'd tried, Bella couldn't convince herself to have sex with Bender. But if she told him that, she'd hurt his feelings. And probably make him angry, considering how much he'd spent on her. Bella already felt guilty about it.

Why did this always happen to her? Why couldn't

she speak up, say how she *really* felt? Gia was right about her. She repressed her feelings. Here she was, repeating her mistakes, possibly getting sucked into another relationship that was wrong for her. No, it would not happen. Bella had to grow some balls. Right now.

"Yeah, I like you. But only—"

He held up his hand. "Good! You mean so much to me. Over the last week, we've grown so close. That's why I don't want to lie to you anymore. There's something I haven't told you. Something very important. You see, Isabella, I'm sick. Very very sick." He frowned and was suddenly hit by a coughing fit.

"Are you all right?" she asked, getting up to whack him on the back.

He waved her off, took a sip of champagne, and got the coughing under control. "I'm sorry about that. I wanted tonight to be perfect."

Sitting back down, Bella noticed that the entire restaurant was looking at their table. Leaning forward, she said, "You seem totally healthy. Working out, partying."

"It's a rare blood disease, genetic. Not contagious, so don't worry. My doctor back in Westchester gave me two months to live. I decided to come down to the Shore and have one last great summer. And then, like an answer to my prayers, I met you. The second I saw those angel-wing tattoos on your back, I knew you were sent down from heaven to give me warmth and comfort before . . . I die."

Flagging down the waiter, Bella said, "I need a shot of SoCo, ASAP."

"And bring a couple of lobsters," said Bender. "Basket of bread. Baked potatoes. You want a salad?"

His rare disease didn't affect his appetite. "Caesar?" she suggested.

The waiter nodded and scurried off.

Silence. Bella didn't know what to say. "Are you in pain?"

"No pain. No loss of appetite—or sex drive. No symptoms at all. I'll just drop dead in a month or so. But until then, I'm a hundred percent fine. No limits on what I can do. I can work out, eat whatever. I can go all night long." He winked.

She cringed inside. "What's the disease called?"

He paused, the glass halfway to his lips. "Er, hemotitis."

"Never heard of it."

"It's rare."

"A genetic blood disease gives you coughing fits?"

"Circulation to the lungs. I'd rather not talk about it anymore. It's a very sensitive subject, as you can imagine. In fact, I've only told a few people about it. My family, of course. And now you. That's how much I trust you, Bella." Touching her hand again, stroking her middle finger, he said, "Enough depressing talk. Let's have a good time. Make tonight special."

Bella nodded, smiling warily. For half a second, she wondered if he was lying about the "hemotitis" to make her feel sorry for him and have sex with him. But that would be like spitting on the evil eye, basically begging God to strike you down for taunting fate.

But Benjamin Newberry wasn't Italian. He didn't know about the evil eye. He was rich, cute. He had no reason to lie his way into her pants.

She thought about Tony's theory that personal trainers were like shrinks. She'd had six sessions with Bender by now. She fixed on his hazel eyes and tried to get a Sixth Sense about him. While he guzzled the champagne and plowed into his lobster, cracking the shell with gusto, she saw only lust for life. He was making the most of the time he had left.

"You've got some shell on your boob," he said, reaching across the table to flick it off, his fingers lingering on her skin for a second too long.

"Thanks," she said, sensing his desire, his need to override sadness with passion. It was admirable, really.

Bella said, "I do like you, Bender."

"How much? Will you come to my place after dinner?"

The invitation wasn't only to his house, but into his bed. She said, "Yeah, okay. I'll do it."

"Check, please!" shouted Bender.

Chapter Ten

Smile, You're on Hidden Camera

Edward Caldwell was killing time, gunning down hos on *Grand Theft Auto: Las Vegas*, waiting for his boy Bender to text. On the one hand (currently holding the joystick), Ed hoped Ben would convince this bimbo to come back to the house. It'd be the trial run for their new video surveillance system. Four cameras in total. C1 in the bedroom. C2 in the kitchen. C3 in the living room, and C4 on the roof deck, overlooking the hot tub.

On the other hand (the one holding a beer), Ed desperately wanted his buddy to fail miserably.

In Ed's ideal world, they'd test the equipment *and* Ben would flame out with Bella. His boy was probably on his hands and knees right now, begging her to fuck him. That brought up a memory, a legend of the Rule of Ten game. Ed once asked a girl to marry him to get her to have sex. Then he dis-engaged her an hour later. That was an ugly scene. But Ed won the game that summer.

His phone vibrated in his pocket. A text alert from Ben: C4.

"Showtime," said Ed, swiveling away from the video-game monitor to switch on the streaming video feed for C4. From the command center in the basement, Ed could control any of the house cameras and see a live picture on his monitor. And there it was, a picture-perfect image of the roof hot tub. The camera was attached with duct tape to the lip of the satellite dish. It blended perfectly, just another piece of the equipment, easily explained if anyone asked. But who would? Ben's parents were hardly ever around. The girls the two men brought up there were too stupid or wasted to notice.

The image focused, Ed was ready to start recording as soon as Ben and the bimbo arrived. Ben was probably giving her a quick tour of the rest of the house before they went up to the roof deck. It was several long minutes before they did, and Ed got restless. He ran to the basement fridge to get another beer. By the time he was back in his chair, Ben and the girl had walked into the picture.

"Here we go," said Ed to himself. He hit the record button on the computer.

The only flaw in their system: no audio. From Ed's perspective, it was frustrating to watch their lips move but have no idea what they were saying. Ben would give him the running dialogue later when they watched the footage, complete with a falsetto imitation of the girl. But for now, Ed would have to fill in the dialogue for himself.

He smiled when, on-screen, Ben wasted no time and kissed the girl before she had a chance to put down her purse. She seemed into it. But then she pulled back and walked to the other side of the hot tub.

Ed was impressed by how sexy the bitch was. When she'd walked in the door of Karma a week ago, he hadn't gotten that close a look at her, just a general impression of hotness. Nice tits and hair. Good legs. Ben assured him that she could crush walnuts with her ass cheeks. Ed dearly wished he'd won the coin toss and got first shot at her. He had to settle for sloppy seconds. If Ben hooked up with her to-night, Ed would have until by the end of next week to nail her, too, or endure taunts from Ben for the rest of his life.

On-screen, Ben switched on the LED lights in the hot tub. He kicked off his shoes, took off his sports jacket and the rest of his clothes. In just boxers, he slipped into the water. It began to steam slightly, which didn't obscure the image at all, thanks to the moisture-resistant lens. Ben was, apparently, trying to talk the girl into joining him. She kept shaking her head.

What a cock tease. Why go home with a guy if she wasn't going to bang him?

Ben waded over to get closer to her. Then he grabbed her wrist and pulled her toward him. She resisted, tried to jerk her arm free. But Ben held on tight, talking the whole time. He got hold of her other wrist.

Oh, yes! As Ed watched, Ben pulled the girl right into the hot tub, in her clothes! She went under the water and sputtered to the surface. Ben didn't give her a chance to breathe. He was all over her, hands everywhere.

Once he got a girl in the hot tub, it was over. Done. Ben would pound her for sure, whether she liked it or not.

Whoa, a lot of splashing! This girl was putting up a fight. Most whores would just give in at this point and accept the situation they were in. If she ate the dinner, took the gifts, came home with you, she was obliged to put out. If she changed her mind and didn't want to? Too bad. Things might get a little rough. She deserved what happened. Whores didn't respect themselves. So why should Ed and Bender respect them?

Ed tried the zoom function on the camera, adjusting the focus to sharpen the picture. He moved in for a close-up and could see the girl's face a lot better. When things got heated, most girls looked scared. But this one was pissed! Ed smiled. He liked the fighters.

Ben tore her dress. Her tits popped out.

"Holy cow! Look at those udders!" said Ed to himself, momentarily stunned by the splendor.

Bender was distracted, too. On the monitor, he froze for a few seconds to admire the view. It was long enough. The bitch knit her fingers together to make a double fist and punched Ben in the face. Even though Ed couldn't hear the wallop, he could imagine the crunch sound and the splash of the water as Ben fell back into it.

The girl was out of the hot tub in seconds. Ed widened the lens to watch her pick up a plastic chair and throw it in the tub. Ben had to duck to avoid getting hit. She grabbed his clothes and shoes and heaved them at him. Whatever wasn't nailed down—a beach umbrella, a few potted plants, deck furniture—the bitch rained it down on Ben, apparently screaming like a maniac the whole time.

Ed couldn't help laughing at the sight of his boy Ben, cowering in the hot tub in his wet boxers, arms over his head.

The rain of furniture stopped when she ran out of shit to throw. She grabbed her purse and exited the monitor picture. Ed watched as Ben unfolded his arms and surveyed the damage. Ed didn't have to be a lip-reader to see what Ben was saying: "Fuckfuckfuckfuck!"

Ben looked right at the camera, as if into Ed's eyes, and repeated the sentiment again.

The roof deck looked as if a tornado hit. Furniture upended and all over the place. Dirt from the planters turned the hot-tub water to mud. Ben looked like a shipwreck survivor, just washed up on the beach.

Ed zoomed in for a close shot of Ben's face, his nose bloody and swollen from her double-fisted haymaker to the face. Already, Ed could see bruises darkening the area around Bender's eyes.

Ed switched the camera off and took a long pull of beer. His boy Bender's epic fail was recorded for posterity. He'd enjoy watching it over and over, until he was an old man. And now, it was his turn. Grinning to himself, Ed envisioned his game plan. He knew just how to play it. And he couldn't wait.

Chapter Eleven

Vin Diesel Is Hotter Than Jesus

Walking down a dark street, Bella cried into her phone, "Gia, where the hell are you? I need you! If you're screening me, I'm going to kill you!"

She'd called ten times in the last ten minutes, and it kept going to voice mail.

God damn it, thought Bella. *Where is she?*

Bella wiped her cheeks. Alone and scared and angry, she teared up despite herself. If Gia was screening just because they had a little fight . . . not possible. Gia wouldn't do that to her. Her battery was probably dead. Or, more likely, she'd lost her phone. Bella could picture it now, ringing like crazy under the red velvet cushions of the couch at the beach house.

She hoped she was walking in the right direction, along a dark street, barefoot in a barely there, ripped and soaking wet dress. She carried her heels and her purse. The adrenaline that had rocketed her away from Ben's house and a mile down the road had worn off, and now she was exhausted, upset, alone, and angry with herself. Gia and Tony had seen Bender for the weenie he was from the start. Why hadn't she?

Tony! Bella could call him. He knew the area. He could at least tell her where the hell she was. But it was midnight. Would he be awake?

Most likely, his night was just getting started.

She scrolled to his number in her contacts list. But she paused before hitting SEND.

She'd have to explain herself and admit that his Sixth Sense about Bender was right. And hers was pathetically wrong.

Oh, well. Bella might've been blind to Bender's true character—she'd bet her car that "hemotitis" didn't really exist—but she was smart enough to ask for help if she needed it. Her parents had hammered that message into her brain since she was five years old. She could hear her mom's voice saying, "If you ever, ever need a ride home, no matter what time, no matter where you are, call and I'll come get you."

Thinking about Mom made Bella's heart clench supertight. She missed home, her parents, the familiarity of Brooklyn. She could parachute anywhere into the city and know her way home. But she was completely lost and helpless here.

Maybe the lesson of this disaster night was that Bella couldn't survive outside her own territory. It could be a sign to go back to the city, marry Bobby, work in the deli, push out a few kids, and give up on her dreams before she'd had a chance to figure out what they were.

"No freakin' way," she said to herself out loud. "I'm not giving up after one friggin' week."

She made the call, hit the send button.

"There she is," said Tony Troublino when he answered (second ring), as if he'd been expecting her call.

"You were right."

"About what? The weenie? Did that little shithead hurt you?" asked Tony, heated.

"No. I hurt him, though. Look, I need a lift."

"I'm in my car right now. Where are you?"

"I don't know." She looked around for a street sign or a landmark. "Somewhere on Long Beach Island. Oh, wait, here's a gas station." She got the address from the attendant.

"Okay, I know the place," said Tony. "I'll be there in twenty minutes."

Bella sat down on the curb, ignored the leering gas-station attendant, and waited. Bella had broken a few of her parents' safety rules tonight: (1) She got in a car alone with a guy she barely knew—which, according to Mom, was any boy she hadn't grown up with or whose family she hadn't met. (2) She went alone to his house, knowing his parents wouldn't be there. (3) She didn't have her own ride home, either the Honda or access to a taxi. In hindsight, she'd obviously walked right into a trap without a means of escape (not counting her own two feet).

Bella could take pride in two things: (1) She hadn't gotten too drunk to be impaired or helpless. And, (2) she'd defended herself. As she'd been taught by senseis and health teachers, the most effective way to stop a date rape was to fight back. Playing to a rapist's sympathy or trying to talk him out of it would fail. Bella had been tested. In a bad situation, she had kept her wits. She didn't panic or freeze. Ten years of karate training came in handy.

But she was still shaken up. If she'd had another shot of SoCo, or if Ben were stronger, things might've gone differently in that hot tub.

Mom's voice in her head again. "Most men are sweethearts and will treat you well," Marissa told ten-year-old Bella. "But some men are scumbags who'll try to force you to do something you don't want to do. You can't always tell which is which from the way they talk or dress. You have to go with your gut."

Bella should have listened to her gut instead of her brain about Ben. "Next time," she promised herself.

A car turned into the gas station, a red Mustang with black racing stripes and a spoiler on the back. Another scumbag?

Not even close. In the passenger seat sat an old lady, gray hair and thick glasses. "Is that her?" she said, staring at Bella. "She looks like a drowned cat."

The driver's-side door opened, and Tony stepped out. He leaned over the roof, got a load of Bella on the curb, and shook his head. "When I see that kid, I'm going to tear his freakin' head off."

The sight of a friendly, familiar face flooded Bella with relief. She hadn't realized how scared she was until she knew she was safe.

"Don't just stand there, Anthony," said the old woman. "Help her."

"Yes, Gram," he said, and rushed over to Bella. He lifted her to her feet (filthy from walking on the street) and brought her to the Mustang passenger side. "Isabella, this is my Grandma Tina. We were on the way home from the movies when you called."

Bella smiled at Tina. "Nice to meet you." Bella then asked Tony, "Is this your typical Saturday night?"

"Oh, I made him take me. Whenever a new Vin Diesel movie comes out, we go on opening weekend."

"That's fun," said Bella. She walked around to the other side and slipped into the backseat. Tony got behind the wheel and put the car in gear.

He felt the need to explain himself. "It's a tradition, right, Gram?" To Bella he said, "She doesn't get out as much anymore besides Grampa's body shop. Just to the movies, and church."

"Vin Diesel is a lot hotter than Jesus," Tina said.

"He's hotter than just about everyone," Bella agreed. "Thanks for coming to get me. I know it's out of your way."

"Forget about it," said Tony.

"Anthony always helps his friends," said Tina. "When he was little, he got in more trouble getting his friends out of it. I'd get calls from the cops in the middle of the night. Anthony was always breaking up fights, returning stolen cars, dragging his friends out of bars."

Tony made eye contact with Bella in the rearview mirror. The look said it all: he got into plenty of trouble on his own.

Grandma Tina said she took the cop calls? "You all live together?" asked Bella. "We have three generations under one roof at my house in Brooklyn."

"Gram and Gramp raised me after my parents died," said Tony. "Boating accident. Don't look so horrified. It was a long time ago, twenty years this summer."

"You were so young," said Bella.

"Five," he said.

"A baby," said Tina. "But he never wanted for love and attention in my house."

"Or chicken parm," said Tony. "Or linguini diavolo."

"Now he cooks better than I do." Tina pinched Tony's cheek. Bella felt the love as if Tina had pinched her. The warmth in the front seat spread to the back, and she felt comforted and cozy. After the night she had had, Bella needed that, badly.

"Where am I going?" asked Tony.

Bella gave him the directions to the beach house on Kearney Avenue. "I don't think Bender is going to show up for his next training session," she said, fearing she'd lose her job now, too.

"Don't worry about it," said Tony. "I'm glad he's not coming back. I was thinking about setting you up with some classes anyway."

"You've been thinking about me?" she asked, trying to catch his eye in the mirror.

This time, though, he kept his eyes on the road.

Chapter Twelve

Swimming with Sharks

Gia and Bella padded along the beach, early Tuesday morning, to meet up with the lifeguard for her first of three hours of community service.

"You don't have to do this," said Gia. "If a guy got date-rapey on me, I'd hide in bed for three days."

"Ben should be cowering in bed," said Bella. "He got his ass beat by a girl."

"You're my hero," said Gia for the hundredth time. "I'm so impressed how you fought back. I don't know what I would have done."

"You would have screamed your lungs out. Half of Long Beach Island would have run to your rescue."

"Okay, I'm sold. Tomorrow, I'm going to the gym. I need to build some muscles." Gia held up her arm and flexed her biceps. Nothing. "Or not. I'll get a French manicure instead. Scratch his eyes out."

Gia was trying to joke about Bella's nightmare date. Bella wasn't laughing. She should feel great about knocking the douche bag's block off. He deserved it! Gia had been in fights before, but with girls. Hair-pulling and slapping got her out of the locker rooms unscathed. But landing a punch on a man's nose? She couldn't reach that far.

Her mom had drilled it into Gia's head that 90 percent of personal safety was avoiding dangerous situations. Don't get in a spot that might lead to serious trouble. That was why Gia had earned a bit of a reputation in high school and in Brooklyn for public displays of affection of the "Get a room" variety. When she made out with a new boy, it was usually at a party or a bar. She liked to have friends within screaming distance. When she was ready to go home with a kid, it was always to *her* home—with her mom's blessing. "You're doing it anyway, and I'd rather know you were safe," said Alicia Spumanti. "That means under my roof, and with a condom!"

Gia felt a black pit in her stomach, knowing that Bella had been with a strange boy, in a strange place, with no way to get home. "It kills me that I wasn't there for you," Gia said. When Bella arrived home that night—the same night Gia and Maria almost got busted—she seemed okay, emotionally. She gave Gia the story, but her voice sounded numb. Gia suspected Bella was tamping down her feelings because that was what she did. Gia knew that it was healthier to let it all out. But Bella was stubborn. Every time Gia tried to talk to her about what had happened, though, Bella shut her down. Physically, Bella was fine. She'd lost a few nail tips in the fight, which Gia took her to fix the next day. Since then, they'd gone to Karma one night, and the Beachcomber Grill the next. Bella danced and drank, but her heart wasn't in it. Gia made her leave early. She found it strange how Bella refused to admit she was rocked by what had happened.

"Change of subject, please," said Bella, sticking with her plan of denial. "I like your T-shirt."

Gia sighed. Okay, she wouldn't push it. Change of subject. Her T-shirt. She'd designed the logo herself, and Maria had shirts printed up at the Shore Store. The shirt was pink, with a black, swirly tribal design and the words TAN-TAGS BY TANTASTIC. Under that, the salon's phone number.

"Maria wants to use me for marketing. The girls, I mean," Gia said, plumping out her chest.

They kept walking. Gia had a lot she wanted to say, but was afraid to. About how she'd been right about Bender, and that she worried about Bella's judgment of character in guys, after what she'd been through with Bobby. She'd express her thoughts, eventually. For now, Gia would do what Bella wanted and keep it light. "Making out with Pete the other night was pitiful. No sparks at all. My nipples didn't even get hard," she said. "Strike one was Lobster Boy Neil. Strike two was Pothead Pete. The best-looking guy I've seen all week was the fireman, but he didn't see me at my best when I was getting slapped with community service! I'm starting to feel frustrated.

It's been over a week already. I thought we'd be waist-deep in guido juicehead gorillas by now. Where *are* they?"

Ten seconds later, the cousins stopped in their sand tracks and saw what had to be a hallucination. "Gia, look!" whispered Bella.

Dead ahead, the cousins gaped at a dozen half-naked, bulging, glistening, tanned monster men, one guy bigger and harder than the next. They were together, a pack, lifting enormous barbells that, apparently, they took with them wherever they went. One guy, shirtless in baggy shorts, was doing push-ups in the sand, his back muscles rippling, skin shimmering, in the morning sun.

Gia felt faint. She grabbed her cousin's arm for support. "Bella? Is this heaven?"

Bella said, "I don't remember dying. But, yeah, this is pretty much what I pictured."

The push-up guy finished his set, and then, with a heroic grunt (the sound made Gia's knees buckle), he stood upright, shoulders back, chest out, legs squared off.

"He's a Roman god," gasped Gia, "like Hercules."

The gorilla noticed the cousins gawking at him. He gave them an eyeful of his bod, turning slowly, striking poses, finishing with a dramatic *grrrrr,* arms bent, muscles twitching, neck bulging like the Incredible Hulk after he turned green.

Bella said, "Oh my God."

Gia said, "I just came." Waving, she yelled, "Hey! You from around here???"

"No, Gia. Don't talk to them while they're working out. It's sacred time for juiceheads, like church. Creeping would be disrespectful."

"Let's wait until they finish." Gia crossed her ankles to plop down on the sand Indian-style.

"Come on. Community service, remember?"

"I hate you," Gia grumbled.

They continued down the beach to the white lifeguard stand. Rick Shapiro, a surf boy with sun-bleached blond hair, a puka-shell necklace, board shorts, and a red T-shirt with the letters SHBP on the chest, was seated on top. He would be in charge of signing off on Gia's hours and telling her what to do.

"Dudettes!" he said in greeting, then jumped down to the sand.

"I'm not a dudette," said Gia. "I'm a guidette. I'm Gia, and this is Bella."

"Do guidettes like to surf?"

"Not really," said Gia.

"Swim?"

"Meh."

"'Cause you guys have some sick built-in floatation devices right there." Rick grinned at their boobs. "You'll never drown with those things." Then he started giggling.

Bella and Gia blinked at each other. This was a representative of the Seaside Heights Beach Patrol? He protected the safety of children and the elderly? Jersey standards had hit a new low.

"So what do you want me to do?" asked Gia.

"Does your baseball cap say, 'I heart head'?" he asked.

"It *is* a hat," Gia replied.

Rick dissolved into giggles again. "Okay, guidettes. Here's the deal. It's pretty slow this time of day. I usually kick off my shift combing the beach for garbage." He handed each girl a big black plastic bag.

"You want me to pick up other people's trash?"

"I know it sounds gross, but you'll see. It's kind of cool to make the beach clean and pure, like it was before humans came along and destroyed the environment, you know, global warming and pollution."

Gia said, "I like global warming. Longer summers, less clothes."

"Can't argue with that," Rick said. "I know it's a dirty job. Just do it for, like, twenty minutes, and I'll put you down for a full hour."

"Cool," said Gia. "Thanks."

The cousins got busy, picking up soda cans, empty cigarette packs, and sticky food wrappers now covered with sand and bugs. Gia couldn't believe people left so much crap behind. Pigs. She wished she had gloves or a germ mask.

Gia asked, "Twenty minutes yet?"

"Try three," said Bella.

"What is *that*?" asked Gia, pointing down the beach at an enormous black thing on the water's edge. From the distance of a hundred feet, it looked like a washed-up log.

They headed toward it, got about fifteen feet away, then they realized . . . *"Shark!"* they screamed.

Every beachgoer in hearing range immediately sprinted over. A mom with three kids. A couple of female joggers. An old man with a metal detector. Some early-morning sunbathers. Around a dozen people surrounded the giant fish—it had to be eight feet long—and watched it flail in the sand, desperate to get back in the ocean. Its tail swished from side to side. The gills opened and closed, struggling to breathe. The movements only dug it deeper into a hole on the shoreline.

"It's a sand shark," said the metal-detector guy.

"Keep back," said someone else.

The three kids started throwing rocks and shells at the shark, and one poked it on the head with a long piece of driftwood.

"Hey!" said Gia. "Stop that! What's wrong with you?"

The brat laughed at her and started hitting the helpless creature with the stick. Gia put herself between the kid and the fish and yelled, "How'd you like it if someone hit you on the head when you were helpless and suffocating? This shark might be a mother. Or a daughter. This shark might have a boyfriend who really cares about her and doesn't want her to die surrounded by asshole brats. Back off, kid. I mean it!"

Gia had taken a few steps back, as the waves carried her into the water, closer to the shark. She felt something hard and scratchy brush against the back of her leg. One of the joggers screamed.

Bella said, "Gia! Watch out!"

Before she knew what was happening, Gia fell backward into the surf, her head underwater. Gasping, she found her feet and stood—right next to the shark. She realized with a gasp that she'd fallen over it.

By now, lifeguard Rick and the pack of gorillas had arrived. They shouted and waved at Gia to run back to safety. Bella's face was red from screaming.

Yeah, it was scary to stand next to a shark with, like, thousands of rows of needle-sharp teeth. But at that moment, it was just a helpless, vulnerable creature that probably felt scared and lonely. Gia knew in her heart that the shark would not harm her.

Just to be sure, she said, "Don't eat me, bitch."

The shark rolled to look at her. Gia could see her eyes. They were black, flat, and sad, too. A wave came. The ocean rose to Gia's knees and lifted the shark high enough off the sand to move. One swish of its powerful tail propelled the fish to deeper water. For about ten hushed seconds, its dorsal fin zipped horizontally along the shoreline, then it disappeared.

Gia felt herself being picked up and carried out of the water. Her arms wound around a thick bull neck, her hands splayed on bulging shoulder muscles. She looked up into the face of the Incredible Hulk.

To get in his arms, she'd go swimming with sharks every day of the week.

Rick, meanwhile, was bouncing all over the place, keeping people out of the water, frantic on the walkie-talkie to beach-patrol headquarters to report a shark sighting.

Gia's arms stayed locked around the Hulk's neck, even though he'd put her down on the sand. "You can let go now," he said.

"Not so fast," she said.

Bella was next to her suddenly, hugging her. "You just battled a shark, *and won!*"

"I was protecting her," said Gia. "From that obnoxious kid." *Where is that little shit?* she wondered, searching the growing crowd of people around her.

"You okay? Can I get you something?" asked Hulk, who'd peeled her hands off him.

"A vodka cranberry with lime?" said Gia.

He grinned. "You got it."

Yay! A date!

Rick bent down over her. "That was beautiful, guidette! I could see the energy pass between you and the shark, like a wavy purple light. I've been trying to talk to animals my whole life! What did it tell you? Does it want humans to stop poisoning the ocean with oil spills and runoff?"

"It's a freakin' fish," Gia said. "We didn't have a heart-to-heart over cocktails. I just saw she needed help and tried to do something about it."

The metal-detector guy, who was pointing his

iPhone at her, said, "I hope you like attention. You're about to become famous." He lowered his device and said, "Uploaded to YouTube."

In a panic, Gia turned to Bella. "My hair?"

"Poppin' fresh," said her cousin.

"Cool."

Chapter Thirteen

Penises Look Bigger Underwater

Frank Rossi stood in jeans and nothing else at the kitchen counter of his apartment, rubbing garlic and oregano into a raw New York strip. Frankie craved downtime, which, for him, meant a juicy steak, a cold bottle of beer, and the Mets game on TV. It'd been a long week of car explosions, restaurant fires, a firecracker Dumpster blaze.

And that false-alarm tanning-salon incident. Stanley Crumbi calling in a fire because his ex-wife was smoking out the window. Dumbass.

That girl he "rescued" was something, though. She kept popping into his head at inappropriate moments. "Do it again!" she'd said, jumping up and down, clapping her hands. He'd have sworn she was stoned out of her mind. But when he bent down to look at her pupils and smell her breath, she was clean. And cute. *Huge* eyes, great lips.

Grabbing a Corona from the fridge, Frank took a long draw. "That's better," he said out loud. No one answered. When he was on duty, he lived at the firehouse with nine other guys. Lots of trash talk and one-upmanship. Before his ex moved out, he'd come home to more of the same from her. She'd start an argument with him the second he walked through the door.

But now he had peace. He had quiet. He could eat what he wanted, drink as many beers as he liked. Watch sports all day and night. He was happy in his cave.

But he was lonely, too. It'd been six months since his ex moved out. At first, he loved the alone time. He needed it, to recover from the blow of his breakup. But Frankie's sex drive had started to wake up. His long hibernation was coming to an end. And he was hungry.

Very hungry. Frankie's stomach growled. He focused on chopping the peppers and onions. For company, he turned on the local news.

"Another shark sighting today on the Jersey Shore," said the anchorwoman. "The third so far this season. An eight-foot sand shark was spotted this morning in Seaside Heights. It'd drifted into shallow water and was partially beached when a brave young woman made a dramatic rescue."

Frank watched the shaky-cam footage of the shark struggling on the sand. Some girl in a baseball cap splashed into the water and tripped over it! Then she talked to it, and it swam away. In-fucking-credible.

The image changed to a reporter on the beach. He said, "I'm standing on Muscle Beach in Seaside Heights with Giovanna Spumanti, who residents are now calling . . . the Shark Whisperer."

"Hey," she said, smiling and waving at the camera.

"Holy shit," said Frank, the knife in his hand falling onto the counter with a clatter. "It's her!"

The reporter asked, "Tell me, Giovanna, when you first saw the shark, were you scared?" He put the mike under her luscious lips.

She said, "Honestly? I didn't really think. I just reacted."

"Did you realize that the shark was eight feet long and outweighed you by hundreds of pounds?"

"Well, you know how everything looks bigger underwater? I had this boyfriend, and we went skinny-dipping together. When we got on dry land, I was amazed by how much smaller he was—all over, if you know what I mean. So, from the beach, I thought the shark was a lot smaller than it actually was. But when I tripped over it, I knew it was pretty freakin' huge."

The reporter seemed confused, but then said, "Do you consider yourself an animal lover?"

"I love gorillas," she said, and someone off camera—a girl—hooted loudly. "Until today, I can't say I had any feelings one way or the other about sharks. I did have a goldfish when I was ten and was really sad when it died."

"On the YouTube video of your daring rescue,

you seemed to be talking to the shark. What did you tell it?"

"I said, 'Don't eat me, bitch!'"

Frank burst out laughing.

Giovanna continued, "I want to look yummy, but not *that* yummy."

The reporter nodded and said, "Words to live by, from the Shark Whisperer of Muscle Beach. Back to you, Sue."

The anchorwoman appeared again on the screen. Frank padded out of the kitchen and into the living room. He turned on his computer, did a search for *shark whisperer seaside heights,* and found the link. He clicked on it. The YouTube video had already received over one hundred thousand hits.

The audio: People screaming. Some splashing sounds, lots of random *Oh my God*s and *Jesus Christ*s.

The image: A shark flailing on the shoreline. A stick, poking the fish. Then Giovanna in the water between the stick and the shark, stepping up and back as the waves ebbed and flowed, yelling at someone, pointing her finger. Getting closer to the shark, falling backward over it.

The shark rose on a wave and swam away. The camera stayed on the dorsal fin until it disappeared. Then the camera was back on Giovanna, in the arms of some sun-damaged steroid junkie who Frank was suddenly insanely jealous of.

Frank couldn't help staring at how the wet T-shirt clung to her chest. He could see *everything.*

She must have been cold.

His dick sprang to life in his jeans.

Frank would love to carry her from the beach directly into his bedroom. If he wanted to, he could call the fire station and get her address from the incident report he filed. But didn't she tell him she lived in Brooklyn?

Just as well. It'd be weird to set out to find her. He'd like to see her again, of course, but only under the right circumstances, such as if they ran into each other on the boardwalk or at a bar. That way, he'd know they were fated to meet again. It was unlikely at best. Seaside Heights was a small town, only around three thousand residents during the slow months. But in July and August? The population swelled to over thirty thousand. His chances of seeing her again were practically nil.

He'd have to settle for the virtual version. Frank hit the refresh button on his computer to watch the video again, in particular the part when she rose out of the water, dripping.

The phone rang. Caller ID: Dina. Shit, not *again*. He picked up anyway.

"I know you're not working tonight," she said. "Wanna go out?"

Not with you, he thought. "I'm busy."

"When are you going to forgive me? Please, Frankie. I'm sorry! I've said I'm sorry a hundred times."

Which would never be enough. Didn't matter if she threw herself off a bridge over how sorry she was. He'd given his heart to her, and she'd stomped on it.

"Frankie, you can't go through life with so much anger. You have to learn to forgive."

"I know how to forgive, but I don't forget. Stop calling me." He hung up.

Then he watched the video again.

Chapter Fourteen

Life Isn't Fair

Linda Patterson punched some numbers into her calorie-counter app. Five pieces of grilled shrimp were 120 calories, 25 grams protein, 0 grams carbohydrate, and 1 gram fat. Ten spears of grilled asparagus were 30 calories, 3 grams protein, 5 grams carbs, 0 grams fat. If she sliced a peach in half for desert, then her dinner total would keep her under 1,000 for the day.

She arranged the shrimp and asparagus into a decorative pattern on her plate. Rocky came into the kitchen and put his arms around her, nuzzled her neck. *Hmmm.* Linda closed her eyes. When she opened them, she realized he'd stolen three of her shrimp and was chewing them.

"Moron!" she said, slapping him. "That's my dinner!"

The idiot had already crammed a whole pizza

down his piehole. He could eat thousands of calories and never put on an ounce. It wasn't friggin' fair! This was God's cosmic joke, that a man could eat an entire cow and still look sexy. But if Linda so much as nibbled on a corn chip, her thighs would get as fat as an elephant's.

Rocky licked his fingers. "Just eat something else."

"Idiot! You don't get it," she ranted. "I can't 'just eat something else.' Those shrimp were carefully prepared and weighed. Now I have to go through the whole process again, and I'm hungry *now*."

He groaned, threw up his hands, and left her in the kitchen with barely enough to feed a cockroach.

Trying to talk to Rocky was a waste of time. The greasy ball of wool that was his brain could not comprehend half of what she said. He'd stare at her, nod, eyes unfocused. If she'd ask him what she'd just been talking about, he'd say, "Your tits look good in that shirt."

Hello, did he speak American?

Why do I put up with him? she asked herself fifteen times a day.

Linda knew why, of course. He was sexy, hot in bed, and he loved to fight. When Rocky pounded down some kid because she asked him to, Linda felt loved and treasured.

On the other hand, when he flirted with other women, which he did, often, she felt worthless and ugly. He was impulsive, like a toddler. She'd look away for a second and turn back to see his hands on some whore's ass, again. Last time they went to Karma, Rocky had kissed the one girl in the world Linda hated most. And she hated, like, hundreds.

Gia Fucking Spumanti.

The girl who made Linda's last year in high school a living hell. It all started when she and Gia were co-cheerleading captains. They had their customary pregame SoCo shots. Gia thought it'd be funny to go out there—last football game of the season, senior year—with only skimpy thongs under their skirts, no bloomers. Linda agreed. Gia made a big show of peeling off her bloomers and throwing them on top of the row of lockers. Linda took hers off, but then replaced them. In secret, she convinced the others to put their bloomers back on, too. Gia would be the only one with her ass hanging out.

Just a little prank between friends. Linda didn't feel the smallest twinge of guilt about playing a trick on Gia. That girl had it coming. The first girl to grow boobs, Gia had long had her pick of boys. Linda had played second banana to Gia since seventh grade. It wasn't fair, and she was sick of it. A little humiliation would be good for Gia, thought Linda. She needed to be knocked down a peg or two.

The squad took their places on the field at halftime. Gia counted down the first routine, which required the six cheerleaders to do cartwheels into back handsprings, one after the other. Gia went first. Her dental-floss thong was so minimal, she might as well have been naked. The crowd's collective jaws dropped. Then the next girl went. Linda was surprised to see that she, too, wore just a thong. Then the next, and the next. The whole team had double-crossed her and taken off their bloomers, too. After the third girl, the crowd got over the shock and started laughing, applauding, stomping the bleachers—way into it. Really, it *was* pretty funny. Linda realized her mistake, but it was too late to kick off her bloomers. She did her cartwheel last. She should have been the grand finale—the crowd was probably expecting no thong at all—but instead, she wore these big blue bloomers.

The crowd booed. Linda got the nickname Granny Panty or Granpan and it stuck to her like glue. Her friends in the hallway at school: "Sup, Granpan?" Her boyfriend, when he dumped her: "It's not you, Granpan, it's me." Even her own mother: "Those other girls are sluts! You're a nice girl. I'm proud of you, Granpan!" Linda never lived it down. She was downgraded to uncool from that day forward.

And it was all Gia's fault.

Linda's only friend had been Janey Gordon, a coldhearted bitch from birth. Linda and Janey bonded over their hatred for Gia, and their shared interests in fashion, dieting, calorie counting, and trolling for guys on the boardwalk. When Gia moved away from Toms River, they had a party to celebrate. They drank many SoCo shots, and each ate *three* cookies. *What a night that was,* thought Linda fondly.

But now, like a chronic STD, Gia was back.

Linda sighed and went to the freezer to get three

more shrimp. It'd take at least fifteen minutes to thaw, marinate in lemon juice, and grill them on the coil burners on her stovetop.

Her phone rang. It was Janey. "Turn on the TV, now!"

"I'm weighing my protein."

"Channel seven! Hurry up."

"Is it another Kate Moss paparazzi video?" asked Linda as she walked to the living room. "She's getting so fat, don't you think?"

Linda took the remote out of Rocky's hammy hand and flipped to Channel 7.

"Hey, it's that girl from Karma," he said.

Linda's blood ran cold. She watched the news with her mouth hanging open and the phone pressed to her ear. When the segment was over, Linda said into the phone, "Well, she's a water buffalo, for starters."

Rocky said, "No way! She looks *hot*. You could totally see her tits."

"Shut up, idiot!"

Linda's blood sugar was dangerously low. She hung up on Janey, ran into the kitchen, grabbed the carton of Rocky's Breyers Neapolitan ice cream, and started shoveling.

Once again, Gia had dumb-lucked herself into being the coolest girl in town. But this time, Linda wouldn't tolerate it. Gia Spumanti needed to be taken down a few notches—now *more* than ever— shoved back into the Dumpster where she belonged. And this time, Linda would not fail.

Chapter Fifteen

Shouldn't Have Had
So Many Oysters

Hulk was waiting for Gia, literally bending a stool, at the boardwalk raw-food booth. When he saw her coming toward him, he stood up too fast, knocking a nearby teenager off his feet.

"Sorry, kid," he said, and picked him up like a toy. Spooked, the kid ran away.

Gia smiled nervously. If he bumped into her by accident, she'd go flying ten feet. "Keep your distance," she said, hoping he wouldn't.

"I know, bull in a china shop. I'm still not used to being this big. You look awesome."

She felt awesome. She'd decided to wear Maria's red, sequined tank dress again, and her gold stilettos. They really made her stand out in a crowd. Hot date, hot dress.

Hulk offered her his seat at the counter. Four guys behind it were shucking oysters and clams, serving the quivering shellfish on beds of ice chips. They ordered a dozen of each.

Dinnertime, the place was packed. The boardwalk was bustling, too. It was a hot night in midsummer. Gia felt that she was at the right place, at the right time, with the right guy.

"I'm not used to the stares yet, either," he said.

Gia realized she'd been transfixed by Hulk's biceps. "Sorry," she said. "I can't help it!"

"Neither can I. When I go by a mirror, I lose twenty minutes, flexing."

Was he kidding? She wasn't sure, so she laughed. Honestly? If she were a guy and had a body like that, she'd probably spend a lot of time flexing in mirrors, too.

"People are staring at you, too, Gia. You're famous!"

A small cluster of kids pointed at her as they went by. One said, "Yo, Shark Whisperer!"

It'd been two days since Gia's shark "rescue" (which sounded way overstated, even to her). The metal-detector guy was right about her getting a lot of attention. Strangers called her Shark Girl, high-fived her, and fist-pumped as she walked by. She got free drinks in bars. Bella was way into it and had appointed herself Gia's official "one-woman entourage" at Bamboo both nights. Maria was *ecstatic* about the YouTube video, now viewed over a half million times. Tantastic's phone number was stretched across Gia's boobs. The phone at the salon hadn't stopped ringing. The most popular tan-tag? A shark. Gia had sprayed it on, like, a hundred people since yesterday. The Shore Store was selling T-shirts that read DON'T EAT ME, BITCH!

Gia had noticed two of the shirts go by in the last minute. "I'm not famous," she said bashfully, "I'm viral."

Hulk smiled, slurped an oyster. She waited for him to say something.

Crickets.

The guy could probably lift a car, but could he move his lips? Not so much. Okay, conversation was her responsibility. Gia brought up the one subject they had in common: a deep admiration for his bod.

"So, you got big recently?"

He nodded. "Around six months ago. I started working out with a trainer. I got serious about it and changed my life."

Gia was impressed. The guy set a goal for himself and reached it. "I totally respect that."

"Thanks," said Hulk.

His real name was Johnny Campano. She'd have to be careful about using the nickname she and Bella had given him. If she called out "Hulk!" later in bed, he might think she meant someone else.

"I thought we could go to Casino Pier, check out some rides," he said. "There's a roller coaster on the end of the pier that seems to plunge right into the ocean. You like that stuff?"

"Scarier the better."

He smiled. "We shouldn't eat too much now."

"Why not? I'm still starving." They'd polished off the shellfish already.

"Some people get sick from all that spinning and jerking around."

"Not me," said Gia, patting her stomach. "Iron."

Johnny Hulk smiled, patting his own. "Mine's a steel trap."

"Should we get another dozen? Oysters make you horny, by the way."

"I don't need them for that."

Almost like a battle on the dance floor, Gia matched Johnny Hulk bite for bite. Oyster for oyster. Clam for clam. Beer for beer.

"On the house, Shark Girl," said the shucker when they asked for the bill.

They went to another booth and got fried Oreos and a crazy thing called a Snooki Sandwich—Nutella and peanut butter between two chocolate chip cookies, deep-fried. Gia thought that one was a little too sweet. But just a little. When the cashier rang up their total, Johnny said, "You can't charge us! This is Shark Girl!"

The cashier said, "Who?"

"YouTube star! Come on, dude! She rescued a shark on the beach a couple days ago."

The cashier shrugged. People on line behind them were waiting. She felt awkward. "Johnny, just pay the kid," said Gia. "It's ten bucks."

He did, but wasn't happy about it.

They walked down the boardwalk toward the Casino Pier. Only problem with dinner ending? Their mouths were empty, and they'd have to talk. She waited for him to ask a question about her life. And waited. And waited.

Jiminy.

"You sure you won't turn green on the rides?" she asked. He was the Hulk, after all.

"Worry about yourself, kid." Hand in hand (hers disappeared in his), they entered the boardwalk amusement park.

It'd been years since she'd been on the Casino Pier, not since high school. When she was a little girl, she and Dad used to come every opening and closing summer weekend. It was one of their traditions, to be first on line for the first roller-coaster ride of the season, and then to take the last ride of the last day at summer's end. Incredible, considering how close they used to be, that Gia hadn't spoken to her father in months. He moved away from Toms River, too, about a year after Gia and Mom left for Brooklyn. Gia had never visited his house in Philly, where he lived with his new wife. She missed him badly. Or, more accurately, she missed how they used to be together, before it all fell apart. She hoped Johnny didn't notice her sudden emotional shift. That kind of downer conversation would torpedo a hot date.

Johnny Hulk was oblivious to her feelings. He was too busy laying claim to Gia as his girl. Holding her hand, rubbing her shoulders, and steering her with a hand on her back. She liked the touchiness and felt flattered of how proud he seemed of her. A group of tourists with cameras blocked a narrow passageway between rides. Johnny took advantage of the foot traffic and pulled Gia into a sexy smooch.

Yum. Johnny Hulk tasted like fresh gorilla. He let her down, and she realized a small circle of people, including the tourists, were watching them and taking pictures.

Gia instinctually smoothed down her hair. Hulk started flexing for the cameras. He said, "You like *this*?" and lifted his shirt to show off his abs.

"Come on," said Gia, pulling him up to the Centrifuge ride. She climbed onto the platform and strapped herself into the cage backing. He strapped in next to her. When the giant wheel started to spin around in a circle, it spun faster and faster, then tilted nearly vertical. House music blared, and the lights flickered on and off.

Gia laughed and screamed. She turned toward Johnny, to check if he was having fun. Where Hulk's face should be, Gia thought she saw Frank Rossi's. The fireman's.

She blinked, and there was Johnny Hulk, right where he should be.

Whoa, Gia thought. *Shouldn't have had so many oysters.*

As they stumbled, dizzy, off the ride, Johnny Hulk said, "That was *hot*. How do you feel?"

She was a little confused to be hallucinating firemen. But her stomach was steady. "Good."

"What next? Skyscraper?" The ride was a giant slingshot that flung you hundreds of feet around in a circle, while you spun round and round in a two-person capsule. "Can you handle it?" he asked, challenging her.

"Can you?"

"If not, you'll be the first to know."

"Back in high school, this kid I know went on the Skyscraper after drinking a giant blue Slurpee. When he was at the top and spinning, he got sick. The whole pier got sprayed with cold, blue puke."

"Impressive," he said.

"Your stomach is lurching right now, admit it."

"Not even close. Now I want a Slurpee."

"I dare you."

"Right over there." He pointed to a concession stand.

He sucked down a large as they walked to the Skyscraper. It was the scariest ride, and therefore the most popular. Gia went to the end of the long line. But Hulk tugged her to the front.

"What are you doing?" she asked.

"The Shark Whisperer of Muscle Beach doesn't wait on line," he shouted.

Gia was embarrassed and tried to hide behind the Hulk. But he pulled her in front of him and insisted they pose for some photos.

"You're famous, Gia. Soak it up," he told her, his arm clamped around her shoulder. He was soaking it up more than she was. And it didn't feel right, cutting the line. But what could she do?

The ride operator strapped them into the Skyscraper car. Gia felt uneasy on the ride, not only because she was hundreds of feet in the air. Hulk was acting like a famewhore. As celebrities went, Gia was a pretty sorry example. A viral video was one thing. But it wasn't as if Gia were a reality-TV star or anything. Lauren Conrad, she wasn't.

"Hold on," said Hulk.

"I'm holding," she said, gripping the bars.

"I meant, hold on to me!"

Well, *okay*. She put her arms around him, which thrilled her as much as the ride.

When they stumbled off, Hulk said, "How's the iron stomach now?"

"I'm okay."

He lifted up his T-shirt and slapped his bulging abs. "I'm a *rock*."

A few girls stopped dead in their tracks at the sight of his bod.

"Keep your shirt on," said Gia. As jaw-dropping as his body was, she had seen enough of it—in public. Was he an exhibitionist?

"Check it out, Gia. The peeps love me!" Hulk pulled his shirt higher and turned in full circle to flash his abs in every direction.

"It's an amusement park, not a nude beach."

"Like you don't want to be seen with me."

"We've been seen, okay? Now give it a rest." Gia had to wonder if Hulk wanted to be *with* her or just *seen* with her. Or just seen at all.

"Let's go in there." She pointed out another classic ride. "Stillwalk Manor. House of horrors."

"But it's dark in there."

"You scared?" she asked, smiling.

"People can't see us." Then, catching her reaction, he said, "I'm kidding, Gia."

"Not laughing."

The line was just as long as the Skyscraper's. He wanted to cut again but Gia insisted they wait like everyone else. So they stood there. Awkwardly. Not speaking a word.

Falling back—again—on his body (as a conversation topic), she asked, "So what made you decide to change your life?"

"You mean my body?"

Duh. "Yeah."

"A girl. I was really into her, but she rejected me. 'I like bigger guys,' she said."

"Ouch."

"The next day, I hit the gym for the first time. It was an instant addiction, you know? I got into supplements, vitamins, the juice. And now, that girl who shot me down? She's eating her heart out."

"Did you guys ever hook up?"

"No way. She's a skank! I can't believe I ever wanted that whore."

O-kay. Gia wasn't sure she liked the sound of *that.* But she tried to give him a break. Johnny got his feelings hurt, and that was how he reacted. Some people held on to grudges until they were old and crusty and smelled like rotten cheese. Gia's natural tendency was to forgive. Which was easy for her, because she usually forgot what made her mad in the first place.

Their turn. They got into a car for two and it

moved along the track into the dark tunnel. Within seconds, a skeleton sailed overhead, and a zombie popped out of the wall. Gia was a screamer. And a crier, and a laugher. She had a loud mouth, on all occasions. The haunted house was no exception. When a demon head crashed into the car, she howled.

"Protect me!" she said, and climbed onto the Hulk's lap.

His thighs were harder than the seat. She wished she could say the same for another part. Even after she put her arms around his neck and snuggled against his chest, she didn't feel anything.

When an alien appeared on the wall, its guts oozing out, Gia wriggled on his groin like a professional lap dancer. She knew this for a fact. She'd taken a stripper dance class and got a certificate at the end.

Still, not a hint of wood.

All her wriggling did have an effect. He started sweating. His skin felt sticky, even drippy, to the touch. Although he could handle the Skyscraper with a stomach full of oysters and a Slurpee, when a girl sat on his lap, he freaked.

What was *that* about?

Meanwhile, Gia was starting to wonder if he even *had* a braciola (in another context, a braciola was an Italian dish that looked like a nice, thick, er, piece of meat). Johnny Hulk of the Ken-doll crotch? Naturally curious, Gia had to find out what the hell was going on (or wasn't, more like it) in his baggy shorts. She pulled his waistband out and slipped her hand in. Groping between his legs, Gia found a couple of marbles in a tea bag and a mushy worm. When she touched the worm, it twitched.

Gia screamed.

A headless body flashed on the wall.

She screamed again. A real bloodcurdler. The kids in the car behind started screaming, too. And then everyone in the entire ride, up and down the track.

A moment later, the car crashed through a pair of double doors into bright daylight. As soon as it stopped moving, Gia jumped out and ran, hand over her mouth, to the nearest trash can. She emptied her iron stomach into it. Total *Exorcist* mode.

Hulk held her hair back, which was sweet. He wasn't a bad person. Just a bad date. She might've forgiven the famewhoring exhibitionism, freebie grabbing, and zero conversation. But the marble balls and worm dick? She'd been worried about calling out his nickname in bed while in the heat of the moment. Ha! She'd more likely say, "Is it in yet? I can't feel anything. It's like masturbating with a toothpick."

"Johnny, I really like you," she said. "Please don't take this personally. But I think we should break up."

Heated instantly, he said, "What the *fuck*, Gia? We're having a good time. You just said you liked me."

She took a deep breath and said, "I like bigger guys."

"So you're a skank whore, too?" he said, furious.

"Yes, I guess I am."

Chapter Sixteen

Just Because One Guy Is an Asshole Doesn't Mean They All Stink

Bella unpacked her groceries on the left side of the kitchen counter of the Kearney Avenue beach house. On the right side, Tony Trouble unpacked his bag. They eyed each other's choices carefully.

"You bought pregrated Parmesan," she said, showing him her brick. "I grate my own."

Tony said, "I bet you do."

Gia sat on a stool watching them, sipping a margarita through a crazy straw out of a long, red plastic glass. She wore a yellow T-shirt, orange boy shorts, a sparkly tiara (to cheer her up), and fuzzy pink slippers. "It was so small, you can't even call it a penis," said Gia, who'd been telling them about her bad date with Hulk.

"So call it a *peen*?" asked Bella.

"Juiceheads," said Tony, shaking his head.

"You mean to tell me that every gorilla on Muscle Beach has a worm dick?" asked Gia.

"Not *all* of them," he said. "Generally speaking, the bigger the guy, the smaller the package. Depends how much they use, and how long they've been doing it. You wanna know the gory details?"

Bella and Gia said in unison, "Yeah."

Tony put down his knife. "As you know," he said, in professor mode, "the cojones are little factories that make what you high-class ladies call 'spermilla cream.' They also churn out hormones, like testosterone. The more they make, the bigger the balls. Juiceheads are drinking or shooting steroids that, to the body, are just like testosterone. The balls don't need to make it anymore, and so they shrivel in the sac."

"Ewwww," said the cousins.

"Hey, you asked! Hulk must have been born in the Year of the Worm," said Tony. "Any juicehead will get *some* nut shrinkage. And bacne. They fly into a 'roid rage. In traffic, it is a 'road 'roid rage.'"

Bella and Gia laughed.

"Anabolic steroids aren't grape juice," Tony continued. "That shit will mess with your body chemistry. I can see why serious athletes use it, for a competitive edge. But guys like Johnny? Just to get muscles on top of muscles like a cartoon? It doesn't even look good!"

"I respectfully disagree with you there," said Gia.

"I'd never do anything to mess with my boys," he said, cupping himself.

"Not for a million dollars?" asked Bella.

"You don't need money to be happy."

"Maybe *you* don't," said Gia.

"I don't. Well, a little bit." He checked his receipt. "Twenty-three dollars and eighty-four cents. That's what I need to make me—and you, and you—cry with joy."

"I need only twenty-two even," said Bella, looking at her receipt. "And we'll see who's crying at the end."

The chicken-parm-off (the guido version of a bake-off) was Tony's idea. When Bella found out he cooked for his grandparents, she told him about Rizzoli's Deli on Smith Street, how people came from all over Brooklyn for her dad's chicken parm on ciabatta sandwiches. Bella had been making the sauce for years and knew all her dad's secrets. Tony was impressed and, like all men, felt compelled to turn their cooking chops into a competition. Bella never backed down from a challenge. They set the rules ($25 on ingredients, same kitchen). The winner would get bragging rights. The loser had to clean up. Game on.

Gia would judge. She offered to help slice onions or bread cutlets, but Bella made it a rule that she and Tony had to do all the cooking. That made the contest fair, and also, Bella would rather not put a knife in Gia's hand. Having worked at Rizzoli's with her, Bella knew Gia was a disaster in the kitchen. The famous tbsp. versus tsp. sugar in the marinara-sauce incident ruined their business for days after someone spat out their eggplant-parm hero and said, "Tastes like ketchup!"

So Gia's job was to leave the cooks to their own dishes and decide which one had the best flavor, texture, and soul. Italians didn't cook with ingredients and kitchenware only. They cooked with heart. They ate with passion. Cooking was love. Eating was sex. And chicken parm was the ultimate Italian classic. Bella was sure she'd win. Gia knew and loved Bella's dad's recipe. Tony seemed confident, too.

"Now I know why juiceheads wear baggy shorts," said Gia after a long sip.

Tony said, "You'll notice, girls, that I wear track pants that hang snugly across my hips. I've got nothing to hide."

"He's got nothing," said Gia. "He admits it!"

"Wanna see how much nothing I got?" Tony asked, grinning. "I'll show you nothing." He threatened to pull down his pants.

"Do it!" said Gia.

"I will, if you will," he said, daring Bella.

"Dream on," she said.

Gia said, "There's got to be a way to tell the difference between a big guy with normal balls from a big guy who's shriveled."

Tony shrugged. "You know how wine experts learn the difference between good and great vintages? They uncork a lot of bottles. You, Gia, are just going to have to uncork a lot of boys."

They all laughed. *Tony's cool to hang out with*, thought Bella. And he obviously had a lot of experience peeling garlic. Bella wasn't intimidated by his flashy knife skills. She knew her flavors.

"Sorry about the equipment," she said, holding up a plastic spatula and hard plastic plates. "But this is what came with the house."

Tony shrugged, slicing an onion. "Doesn't bother me. Only a poor craftsman blames his tools."

"You are such a dork," said Bella.

On her side of the counter, she laid her chicken cutlets on Saran wrap, folded it over, and started pounding with the back of the frying pan. When they were flat enough, she brushed her cutlets with egg, then dredged them in fresh Italian bread crumbs before frying them in canola oil with a few crushed (not chopped) garlic cloves.

Gia said, "Smells amazing."

Tony, on his side, dipped his cutlets in milk and dredged them in white flour, before frying them in vegetable oil with shaved garlic and chopped oregano.

"What if I can't decide? Can there be two winners?" asked Gia.

Bella and Tony said, "No."

"It's all about the sauce," said Bella, stirring her stewed tomatoes with red wine and red pepper flakes.

"She's right," Tony agreed, tasting his sauce. "I've got a secret ingredient. Which means you're gonna get your ass beat."

"What is it?" asked Gia.

"I'd tell you, but I'd have to get you shitfaced first."

Bella stirred her sauce and let it simmer. She

grated fresh moozadell and parm into a bowl and added more bread crumbs to the cheese mixture along with fresh-chopped basil, oregano, and thyme. When the cutlets were crispy on the outside and juicy on the inside, she placed the pieces on a paper towel to drain. On the bottom of a casserole dish, Bella swirled a few ladles of sauce, placed the cutlets on top, then more sauce, a thick layer of the cheese mixture, then a last finishing sprinkle of bread crumbs on top. A drizzle of olive oil, a dusting of crushed sea-salt crystals, and fresh-ground black pepper.

"Into the oven," said Bella, wiping her hands clean.

Tony said, "Right behind you," and inserted his dish into the rack alongside hers. They agreed on the bake temperature.

Gia whined, "I'm starving."

"Forty minutes," said Tony.

Bella asked, "What should we do while we wait? Oh, sorry. Stupid question," and poured herself a big glass of the Chianti she used in the sauce. Gia stuck with her margarita. Tony opened a beer. The three went to the boardwalk and watched the parade of people go by.

"Hey, it's Shark Girl!" said a kid. His crew of half a dozen fist-pumped in her direction.

Gia waved and shouted, "Save the whales!"

They cheered.

Another cluster of kids went by and recognized Gia (they would've noticed her anyway in that tiara). "Save the dolphins!" she shouted in greeting.

Tony said, "What next? Save the grouper?"

Gia giggled. "It's crazy, right? I could say anything."

Tony laughed along. Bella sipped her wine.

Even though Bella knew her cousin and boss weren't vibing on each other, she felt a pang of jealousy. She'd originally considered Tony, as her boss, off-limits. A friend—a good friend—he didn't fit her "casual flings only" qualifications. That said, Bella was starting to feel she couldn't keep Tony at arm's length. He'd been so cool since the hot-tub incident. Picking her up at the gas station. Setting her up teaching classes at the gym, which paid more. He made her laugh. Watching a man cook? Supersexy.

What held Bella back from jumping his bones right this second? Self-doubt. The night with Bender was still fresh in her mind. She'd consciously decided to forget it—no harm done. But the feelings weren't going away. Before Bella threw her punch, she'd felt genuine fear. Her body reacted to the threat as it'd been trained to do. But mentally? Emotionally? The aftermath was hard to add up. Talking about it? Even with Gia? Bella found it impossible to discuss. She was repressed! But knowing that didn't mean Bella could magically open up.

If she hadn't thrown hundreds of combos at the gym . . . if she hadn't been able to reach Tony on his cell . . . *Stop thinking like that*, she reminded herself. When Bobby went nuts and started five-degree stalking her, Bella sank into an all-men-are-assholes hole.

She'd come to the Shore to have fun with new guys, not to swear off them again.

"Just because one guy is an asshole doesn't mean they all stink," Bella repeated her mantra.

"You got that right," said Gia.

Bella put her hand over her mouth. "Did I say that out loud? Oops."

A strained silence. The scent of garlic wafted out onto the boardwalk.

Tony inhaled deeply and said, "That smell always reminds me of my mom."

Bella and Gia made eye contact. She'd told her cousin the tragic story about Tony's parents, that they'd died when he was five years old and he was raised by his grandparents.

"Practically every memory I have of her is in the kitchen, at the counter, cooking dinner," he said. "Always with her back to me, elbows out, a knife or a spoon in one hand. When I was little, right after the accident, I remember trying to change the movie in my mind. To make her put down the knife, turn around, and look at me so I could see her face."

"You must have photos," said Bella.

"Hell, yeah. Videos, too. And I can always just look in the mirror. The eyes. And the lashes."

Tony's lashes were long, curled, thick, and dark, like a set of Gia's falsies. His eyes were emerald green. Bella thought she could look into them for miles. He returned her gaze now, smiling at her. His lips were as soft and sweet as his eyes. Bella wanted to kiss him so badly, her lips burned.

Gia said, "The smell is killing me. Dinner's got to be done by now."

"Don't be in such a hurry to eat raw chicken," said Tony.

"Guidettes!" called out lifeguard Rick, ambling up the boardwalk in checkerboard pattern Vans, the red SHBP T-shirt, board shorts, and his puka-shell necklace.

"Dude!" said the cousins.

"How's it hanging?" he said when he reached them.

"Perky," said Gia, demonstrating with a pose.

Rick said, "Loving life as a YouTube sensation?"

Gia stood up on the bench, waited for someone to recognize her, which took all of fifteen seconds. "Save the cuddlefish!" she yelled. A bunch of passersby cheered.

"It's *cuttlefish*," said Rick.

"You knew what I meant. And *cuddlefish* is sexier."

"Can't argue with that," agreed Rick. "I come bearing good news. The SHBP and the SHPD, in our collective wisdom, are absolving you of further community-service duty, in gratitude for your brave act of animal kindness and preservation."

"What the fuck?" asked Gia.

"You're off the hook."

"Oh, thank God," she said, genuinely relieved. "So no more early mornings at the beach?"

"Afraid of seeing another shark?" asked Rick.

"Not that." Gia shook her head. "It's . . . someone else."

Bella and Tony laughed. "You're going to avoid the beach for the rest of the summer?" Bella asked.

"Totally!" said Gia.

Rick seemed confused. "Is it me?"

Bella shook her head. "We love you, dude. Come in for dinner and I'll explain Gia's terrifying encounter with a sandworm."

Tony said, "Good. Two judges. Now Gia can't play favorites."

"Dinner?" asked Rick. "Excellent! Smells like . . . chicken parm?"

"Best ever," said Bella. "I hope you're hungry."

———

Bella and Tony sprawled on the red velvet couch. "I have never eaten so much in my life," she said, her hand resting on her extended stomach. "I wonder if my food baby is a boy or a girl."

"You think it's okay to let Gia clean up?" said Tony, hearing a crash from the kitchen.

"First time for everything," said Bella.

After the official judging, Rick left to meet some friends. Gia volunteered to clean up and "let you guys chill," she said (not subtle, at all). Bella said, "Is your secret ingredient love? Because, if it is, I should have won."

"I do cook with love, but the secret ingredient is . . ."

He leaned close to whisper in her ear, but kissed it instead.

The vibe was suddenly sizzling.

"Do that again," she said.

Tony was built for speed. He was on her in a heartbeat, arms around her, lips on hers. He tasted like garlic and sauce. Which, to Bella, reminded her of home, cooking, love, passion.

Just as he bragged, Tony's thin track pants didn't hide a healthy, happy hard-on. No shrivel here!

After a few delicious minutes of making out, Tony went for her boobs. Only several months old, Bella's new breasts were truly virgin territory. She was eager for Tony to touch them, curious if it'd feel sexy, despite a slight postsurgical loss of sensation. Not a problem, she was relieved to learn. As Tony's hand tightened around her flesh, Bella felt an electric current career from her nipple straight to her crotch.

Tony seemed as turned on as she was. He unzipped her sweatshirt. "Mmmm," he mumbled, his face between her boobs, motorboating. When he came up for air, he said, "Sorry. I just had to do that once."

Bella was breathless from the attention. "Let's go upstairs."

Tony leaned back a bit. "Are you sure?"

"I'm sure," she said, irritated he'd hesitate.

"Or we can stay down here . . ."

"What? *Why?*"

"I'm just saying there's no rush."

"What's your problem?"

He frowned. "I like you a lot, Bella."

"Is there a girlfriend I don't know about?"

Tony shook his head. "I just thought we could go slow."

She was floored—literally sliding to the floor, in speechless shock.

"If I didn't respect you, I'd be all over you," he said. "I'd rip your clothes off."

Like Bender. Tony knew he'd torn her dress. But this was totally different! "I want you to rip my clothes off!"

He gulped. "I gotta go."

"If you leave now, you're never coming back," she said, icing over, finding her voice, and surprised by how angry she sounded.

"I don't want this to be just another summer hookup. I've had more of those than I can remember."

"Oh, I get it," said Bella.

"I can tell you don't."

"You'd rather hook up with girls you *don't* care about, don't like, and don't respect."

"Bella . . ."

"The girls you *do* like and respect? You make them feel like garbage. Get out of here. Go find some drunk slut on the boardwalk." Listening to herself, Bella was impressed. She was seriously pissed off and sounded it.

"This is exactly what I wanted to avoid. I know you think I'm an asshole right now. But I'm one of the good guys. I'm looking out for both of us."

What was he trying to say, exactly? That he'd serve her chicken parm on a plate, but not his heart? Or his braciola?

"I can look out for myself," she said. "If you're not gone in sixty seconds, I'm throwing you out."

Gia shuffled into the room as Tony walked toward the back door. "Where you going, champ?" she asked. He didn't reply, just slipped out the door and closed it behind him.

"You heard?" asked Bella, deflated on the couch. "He said he liked me too much to get with me."

"Not such big balls on Tony after all. And people say girls make no sense."

"You have to hate him with me."

"If you say, 'Hate him,' I'll hate him. Done. No matter how much I loved his chicken parm, I hate his fucking guts. You have to admit, the sentiment was sweet. But he read the situation wrong. I mean, you're not looking for a boyfriend, right?" Gia paused. "I have to say also, Bella—not that I spied on your conversation on purpose—that was the first time I ever heard you really stand up for yourself. I'm proud of you. How'd it feel?"

Surprised to find her eyes tearing, Bella said, "It sucked."

"Really?" Gia sat next to her and wiped her tears. "Didn't it feel good?"

"A little."

"I happen to have a lot of experience with this. The best thing to do if a guy turns you down? You find another guy."

"You're right. Let's go out. Tonight, we're all about the three D's. *Dance* until we're soaked. *Drink* until closing. And, *Duh*, find two boys who've got their priorities straight." Bella sniffed the air. "Hey, do you smell something burning?"

Gia took a whiff. "Yeah."

The two got off the couch and followed their noses.

"Motherfucker," said Bella. "The oven's on fire!"

Chapter Seventeen

Bumper Cars of Destiny

Gia put her fuzzy slippers on her hands and batted at the fire. It seemed to be contained to just the oven, but the flames were licking the countertop. They could jump to the curtains and cabinets, and that would be it.

"Call 911!" Gia hollered.

"Already did," said Bella, who'd found a fire extinguisher under the sink (at least someone knew her way around the kitchen) and started spraying white foam all over the oven and the room.

The next sound Gia heard was a fire truck pulling into the driveway. The back door splintered open, making her jump. A fireman—decked out head to toe in his gear—stomped into the kitchen.

"Under control," said Bella.

The fireman seemed to freeze midstomp. Through his smoke mask, he asked, "What's going on here?"

"It's not my fault!" whined Gia, dropping her slipper-covered hands to her sides. "Well, maybe it is." To Bella, she explained, "The oven had a setting on the dial that said AUTO CLEAN. So I figured, if I put the dishes in there and set the oven to clean itself, the dishes would get clean, too. But now I'm thinking that wasn't such a smart idea?"

Bella groaned, slapped her palm on her forehead. "The oven self-cleans at like a thousand degrees! You put the spatula in there? No wonder I smell burned rubber."

"I'm such an idiot," said Gia, feeling like one. But also hoping Bella and the fireman would assure her that she wasn't.

Friggin' crickets.

Squawk. The fireman turned on a walkie-talkie and gave the all clear to his partners. "Can I see you outside?" he asked politely. "I have to get some information and seal the room."

"Seal the room?" asked Gia.

"It's a hazard. Right this way," he said, pointing to the back door.

"Can we stay here, though?" asked Gia.

He asked, "Would you want to?"

"I'm calling the landlord," said Bella.

Gia followed the fireman outside. A white cop car pulled up and parked outside. The same poli who'd forced her into community service stepped out of the vehicle. *I'm cursed,* thought Gia.

The cop—Captain Morgan, she remembered—and the three firemen were staring at her, eyes and mouths wide-open. Looking down, she realized she wasn't wearing anything but a fire-extinguisher-foam-covered T-shirt, boy shorts, fuzzy slippers on her hands, and a tiara.

"I can explain," she said.

A crowd gathered, yet again. Gia wondered if she could do anything at this point without a crowd gathering.

Weakly she waved and said, "Save the guppies."

The cop frowned and said, "This girl is a walking disaster area. We should wrap her up in yellow tape and send her back to New York."

Aware of the built-in tension between locals and summer residents, Gia asked, "How do you know I'm not from Seaside Heights?"

The cop just rolled his eyes. "Considering your path of destruction, if you lived here, I'd know you by now."

The fireman laughed (but cutely) and removed his hat, and his mask. She knew that face. It'd been popping into her head at the weirdest moments. "Frank Rossi. Of course, it's you."

He seemed surprised to hear her say his name. "You remember me." His dark eyes glowed as if he'd just been struck by a thought, possibly the same one as Gia: although this fire was a terrible mistake, it was no accident. Well, it *was* an accident, technically. But it wasn't a karmic accident. It happened for a reason— you know, other than Gia's putting plastic in a six-hundred-degree oven. Fate had brought Gia and Frank together again. They were like bumper cars of destiny.

Or it could be that destiny meant for Gia and Captain Morgan to keep bumping into each other. But if that was true, fate was a total bitch.

Bella hung up her phone. "The landlord's coming. He's a block away and seriously pissed off."

Morgan asked, "Are you girls drinking?"

"Not yet!" said Gia.

"Not really," said Bella. "There's no major damage, no one got hurt. You don't have to make this into more than it is."

Whoa, thought Gia. Bella had had one taste of speaking her mind, and now she was on a mad roll.

"Let me through," said the man in cheap trousers, a Hawaiian shirt, and a comb-over. "This is my building."

Gia felt as if she'd lived this scene before, like DJ view. "Stanley Crumbi, hey. Remember me? Maria's assistant at Tantastic."

Her boss's ex-husband number three/landlord, aka the binocular peeper, blinked at Gia and then said, "Shark Girl?"

"Holla!"

He looked her up and down, three times. She curtsied.

"What are you doing here?" he asked.

"I live here. This is Bella, my cousin. We're your tenants. I didn't make the connection either. Until, like, now."

"You set my house on fire?"

"I wouldn't put it like that. You could say I turned up the heat a little."

Stanley gaped at her. Then he turned to the cop. "We meet again, Sean. Thanks for coming down."

The cop said, "Twice in one week."

"I need an official report for insurance," said Stanley. "Wanna walk through with me?"

The two of them entered the house and emerged about three minutes later. Morgan got in the cruiser and drove away.

That was quick, thought Gia.

Stanley put his hand on Frank's shoulder. "How's your mother, Frankie?"

"She's good."

"Your brother?"

Frank's eyes hardened for a minute. "He's fine."

"Sean's gonna make his report," said Stanley. "You boys don't need to hang around."

"Doesn't work that way," said Frank. "We came down here. We have to file a report, too."

"So file your report! You responded to a call, but the situation was under control when you got here."

The fireman didn't want to leave. "I need to do an assessment."

"Go ahead," said the landlord. "But it's hardly singed. You'll be wasting your time."

Gia could see Frank struggling with a decision. She hoped he was hesitating because he didn't want to leave her without getting her number. Again.

The walkie-talkie came to life on Frankie's belt. Something about a car wreck on Route 35. The firefighter waited a beat and gave Gia an apologetic look. He said, "Okay. We're out of here." His colleagues jumped on the truck. Frank got in the front seat (very sexy) and drove away.

Stanley raked back his comb-over, which had flopped to one side, and rushed back into the beach house. He groaned at the sight of the kitchen. "The ceiling needs to be repainted. The oven has to be replaced. The whole room has to be professionally cleaned top to bottom. Who's going to pay for all that?"

"You must have insurance," said Bella.

"Yeah, with a two-grand deductible."

"You can afford it," said Gia. "Maria told me you own half the buildings on the boardwalk."

"So?"

"She also told me you have a nasty habit of letting yourself into her place when she's in the shower."

"Maria has no right to talk shit about me behind my—"

"You're still in love with her, right?" asked Gia. "You want her back. I can help. I know exactly what to do. Trust me."

"Trust *you*? You set my house on fire! Your T-shirt says ORGASM DONOR. Besides," he said softly, "Maria hates me."

Gia knew she had him. "There's a thin line between love and hate, Stanley. You just need someone to help shove her back over. I'm your girl. Maria listens to me. I'm pushy as hell. All you have to do is sit back and do whatever I say. Oh, and forgive us the cost of kitchen repairs. Which, excuse me for saying, with respect, were desperately needed anyway."

Stanley stared at Gia and shook his head. "You're either incredibly stupid or insanely sincere."

Huh? "First thing you do is, call Maria and apologize for being a cheap bastard and not buying her a car and jewelry during your marriage. Say, 'if you give me a chance, I'll make it up to you.'"

"That's all she wants? For me to promise her a car and jewelry?"

"That's stage-one advice. Stage two comes after you put us up in a hotel while the kitchen gets fixed up."

He nodded, thinking about it. "Actually, the owner of the Inca Hotel on the boardwalk owes me a favor."

"You rock," said Gia.

"Just drive down there," he said, flipping open his phone. "The guy's name is Al 'Fresco' Testaverde. He'll be waiting for you."

Bella said, "The Honda won't start."

"We can't walk with all our stuff." Gia turned to Stanley. "Can you give a us a ride?"

"Jesus friggin' Christ," he said, shaking his head and chuckling. "Your plan better freakin' work, kid. And if you tell her about it, you're dead. You get it? Dead. Now, go pack. And make it quick. I don't have all night."

Chapter Eighteen

Does It Come in Pink?

Frankie almost died on the spot. The call came into the fire station, as usual. His team suited up and got in the truck, check. They drove to the site, a weather-beaten bungalow near the boardwalk.

And then the situation got surreal. Like a sooty version of his fantasies, Gia Spumanti stood in the kitchen, charred slippers on her hands, covered in foam, bare legs and feet with cherry red toes, her eyes big and deep as the ocean. Just crazy cute.

And he'd wasted *another* opportunity to ask her out.

He could punch himself. Why didn't he say something? Frankie made excuses for blowing it. Too many people who didn't need to know his business were around. And she had just put out a kitchen fire. She was probably upset. People thought of fire-fighters as protectors, not horny, opportunistic dogs. Imagine if he'd said, "Okay, you're safe. Fire's out. What're you doing later, baby?" She could've had him arrested.

Frankie had friends who wouldn't think twice about creeping on girls in dire straits, as in "Just got robbed? You could probably use a drink. How about a place I know around the corner." Not Frankie's style. His was . . . how would he describe it?

Rusty?

He'd barely talked to a girl romantically since he and Dina broke up. He was out of practice, to put it mildly. The question he had to ask himself: are you willing to go for it, even if you get shot down or make a fool of yourself over this girl?

Shit, yeah, he'd take a risk for Giovanna! Otherwise, he'd lose self-respect. That was not an option. Self-respect was how Frank ate breakfast, got dressed, did his job, and went to sleep at night. If you didn't have self-respect, you had nothing.

And he would know. At the moment, self-respect was all he had.

Tonight, or tomorrow, or sometime this century, Frank wanted to get in bed with a woman— specifically, Giovanna Spumanti—instead of just his self-respect.

Which brought him to where he was currently standing, on his day off, at Darling Divas, a lingerie store.

Frank was going to buy her a gift, something he knew she'd like. Generally, he could take or leave the frilly stuff. When his old girlfriends stepped out of the bathroom with the lace bras and silky thongs, he was grateful to them for making the effort. But then he rushed them out of their complicated underwear. A woman was sexiest completely naked. If she had to wear anything, he liked hoop earrings and a smile.

This will be a first, he thought, browsing in the aisles. Everywhere he looked were lacy, shiny, silky things with straps and bows and buttons. He was embarrassed, confused, and excited at the same time. Out of habit, his eyes swept entrances and exits, space between the circular racks of garments. The boutique would pass a fire-safety inspection, he was glad to say.

What a jerk he'd be if he bought Gia a see-through bra before he'd even asked her out! Did other guys do this? Creeps. Frankie would never. He had an item in mind and thought he might find it here. But, from a quick look around, among the panties and baby dolls, he didn't see anything close.

"Can I help you?" a woman around his mom's age asked.

"I'm looking for a specific item," he said, handing her a drawing he'd done himself. "I hope you have it in pink."

The woman glanced curiously at the sketch. Then she turned to Frank and looked at him as if he hadn't showered in a week. "I'm sorry, we don't carry *that.*"

"Any idea what store might have it?"

She sniffed, "Try Walmart."

Chapter Nineteen

Sexiest Wenis in the World

Tony wandered into Bella's "Beat Up the Beat" dance class to observe. As gym director, he had to evaluate each instructor, keep the quality high, and make sure the clients liked the class.

Okay, yes, he also wanted to observe Bella. He'd nearly swallowed his tongue when he saw her come into the gym this morning in just a sports bra and jogging short shorts. Had she done it to torture him? To make his eyes pop out with longing and regret for the body he'd turned down?

She ignored him completely, even when he asked her why she was already sweating. One of the boys repeated the question, and she said, "My car's busted. I had to run to work."

The beach house was three miles away. "I would have picked you up," Tony said.

She flipped a towel over her shoulder and it slapped him across the face.

Clearly, Bella was still pissed at him. All this drama because he didn't think with his dick and treated her with respect. Tony was mystified. Apparently, she would have preferred to be humped on the first "date" like some drunk slag he scraped off the bathroom floor at Karma. If he lived to be a thousand years old, Tony would not understand women.

Quietly entering the studio, he leaned against the rear wall. Not that anyone would have heard him. Techno music blasted from a boom box in the front of the room. Bella stood next to it, facing her class—all female members—and Tony. He was surprised the studio wasn't packed with men who'd put up with a dance class just to stare at Bella for an hour.

Of the women present, Tony counted three he'd been with. None compared to Bella in any category.

He watched for a few minutes as Bella guided them on dance moves, including lots of squats ("Lower! Low enough to beat on the floor, beat the beat, hold it, hold it," shouted Bella. "And slowly come up, pump that fist!") into a few reps of alternating pumps and jumps ("Right, left, work those triceps and biceps!").

The music faded out, and Bella congratulated the class. "Mad work. You're ready for the club." She caught Tony's eye. "Let's finish with some jabs. Feet shoulder-width apart. Fists at your hips. When I count off, uppercut right, uppercut left. Put some power behind it." Looking directly at Tony, she added, "Pretend like you're beating on a guy who rejected you. Here we go. Wait for the music. . . . One. Two. Three. Four."

He forgot Bella had karate training. She looked fierce, which, *dang*, was sexy as hell. Tony was glad she was punching the air, not his actual body.

The class finished the punishing upper-body workout, then Bella announced their time was up.

"No cooldown?" asked one client.

"Not today. Today, we stay heated. Take no prisoners." Again, Bella looked right at Tony.

Message received.

The clients filed out, and Tony approached Bella. "Great class. How about throwing some combos with me?"

"You've got a death wish?" she asked, wiping herself with a towel.

"Square off." He put one foot in front of the other on the mat and waved her in. "Show me how you pounded Bender the weenie last week."

"You asked for it," she said, and knit her fingers together.

"Hold on. You did *that*? I'm surprised you didn't crack a knuckle."

"I hit his cheek, which was pretty soft. But it did hurt."

"A wild haymaker is easy to duck. A lightning jab is a higher-percentage move. Aim for the chin. He'll never see it coming."

She went for it. But Tony ducked right and avoided the punch. He said, "Faster." A few of the weight-room regulars were watching from the studio doorway.

Bella jabbed a few more times, but she wasn't fast enough to make contact. Tony was liquid silver, flashing and untouchable. He said, "Let me know when you're really trying."

In frustration, she reverted to her old style and threw a massive haymaker at him. He could have seen it coming from space.

Tony caught her hands in one of his and held on. "I'm sorry about last night, Bella. Things were moving fast, and I tapped the brakes. That's all. I didn't mean to upset you or hurt your feelings."

"Too late." She kneed him in the stomach.

Tony did not see that coming. The wind knocked out of him, he fell to the mat. The lifters at the door whistled and cheered.

Bella took a bow. "My next class is in a few minutes. You guys should come. You might learn something."

Those guys wouldn't fit in the room together.

"Wait," Tony wheezed.

She didn't. Bella stepped over him and left.

Still winded, limping, Tony went after her. "Did you know," he panted, "that the piece of skin on the underside of your elbow, right here, is called the wenis?"

"You're so full of shit."

"It's true! Look it up."

"Shut up," she said, suppressing a grin.

Tony took a deep breath and felt his soul relax.

A smile was nice. Making her laugh would be better. And a wide spectrum of other female sounds and noises were far superior still. But he'd take the grin. It was a start, anyway.

"I'll come over and cook for you tonight." Moving closer, he said, "No more tapping the brakes. I learned my lesson."

"I don't know, Tony. Do you think you can like and respect a girl and still have filthy sex with her?" she asked, doubtful.

"I can certainly try!" he said, smiling.

She laughed. "You really are the biggest dork in the world, seriously."

"Does that mean yes?"

She shook her head. "Gia and I had to move out of the beach house last night."

Tony was dumbfounded by the kitchen-fire story. "Where are you staying?"

"The Inca. The manager went nuts over Gia. He took her picture for the website and is letting us stay for free for a few nights if she makes an appearance in the hotel bar tonight at eight."

"Free drinks, too?"

She nodded. "For free drinks, Gia volunteered to appear at the bar all summer long."

"I'll swing by around nine."

Bella hesitated, and he thought she'd changed her mind about forgiving him. "You went to college, right?" she asked.

"State University of New Jersey. Rutgers, New Brunswick."

"Was it worth it?"

Tony tried to figure out where she was going with this. Bella had been doing some soul-searching, apparently. "You mean, was it worth it to put myself in the hole for twenty-five thousand dollars in student loans? If it weren't for my college degree, I'd be fixing cars in my grandfather's garage, or still training in the weight room. I wouldn't be the boss. Or know that this"—he tickled her elbow—"is the sexiest wenis I've ever seen."

She giggled. Tony knew he was 100 percent forgiven. She reached out and pulled him into a tight hug. "Thanks, Tony."

The hug went on for a lot longer than necessary, and she capped it off with a kiss. Just a quick one. But it took his breath away.

When she jogged off for her next class, he felt as if he'd been kicked in the stomach again. Flattened, brought to his knees. And, no, he didn't see that coming, either.

Chapter Twenty

Nothing Says "I Do"
Like a Spray-On Tan

Skunked pouf resplendent even after a full day at work, Maria clicked around Tantastic in her go-go boots and leopard-print dress, arranging a huge bridal party of ten bridesmaids, two flower girls, the bride, the mother, and the mother-in-law into an assembly line. They'd come to get matching daisy tan-tags on their shoulders.

The maid of honor quipped, "Nothing says 'I, like, *love* you' like a spray tan."

"Shut up, Tiffany," said the bride. To Maria, she said, "Can we get this moving a little faster? We've been waiting for an hour. Tomorrow is my once-in-a-lifetime special friggin' wedding day. I have a vision, okay? I paid in advance, and I want service, *now*."

"Bridezilla wants her tan-tags," said Maria to Gia. "For her once-in-a-lifetime—*ha!*—special friggin' wedding day." To the bridal party, she said, "Okay, women, take off your clothes."

Maria and Gia got the line moving. Station one: Gia applied the flower design with tan-blocking lotion across a woman's shoulder blades. After a shower, it'd show up as white against bronzed skin. Station two: the Mystic booth for a head-to-toe spray tan via automated nozzle. Station three: Maria's spray-gun touch-up, for the hard-to-reach places the booth often missed, such as inside the elbows, armpits, the butt crack, and the toes. Last, station four: the hallway and other rooms where the women had to stand still, arms out, legs slightly spread, to dry. From start to finish, the process took about fifteen minutes. Maria and Gia moved the women through at a brisk pace. Before long, the hallway and waiting area were full of naked women with their arms out.

Gia thought to lower the blinds.

"Next!" called Maria.

The mother of the bride was butt ugly and huge, well over two hundred pounds. When they were done spraying her, though, even she looked passably attractive.

After half an hour, the entire bridal party was drying. "We've done it again," said Maria. "Made the world a bronzer place."

Gia looked at the damp women in the small space, trying not to touch each other and smear the color. "What would an alien think about earthlings if it landed right here, right now, and saw this?" she asked.

"That everyone—*everyone*—looks better with a tan," said Maria. To the bridal party, she said, "Just a few more minutes."

Exhausted after a long day of tanning, Gia and Maria flopped on the waiting-area couch.

Maria sighed again, with extra drama.

"Okay, what's going on?" asked Gia.

"Stanley called me three times today," Maria whined.

"Really?" Gia asked, all innocent.

"He said he's sorry for being a cheap bastard. He wants to make it up to me."

Exactly what Gia had instructed him to say. Word for word. Nice work, Stanley! But (crap) Maria wasn't feeling it. "I'm sure he's sincere," said Gia. "He obviously cares about you. I can tell you still care about him. You wouldn't call him an asshole with so much passion if you didn't."

"I do care. But Stanley is so *old*. I look at him and I see my father, or my grandfather. I feel young. I want to be with a hot young guy. But the men I'm attracted to don't look at me anymore. I need some trick to get their attention." Brightening suddenly, Maria clutched Gia's hands. "Teach me something, Gia. With dark lighting, I can still pass for twenty-five if I had a signature move."

Maria could pass for twenty-five in a pitch-black mine shaft, thought Gia. "I have no idea what you're talking about."

"Like in *Legally Blonde*, when Reese Witherspoon taught Jennifer Coolidge the bend and snap." Maria demonstrated. She reminded Gia of a chipmunk on crack.

The bride called from the back room, "The bend and snap is bullshit."

True, thought Gia. "It's too cutesy, right? Might work for blond sorority girls. But we're Italian ball breakers. We're . . . lethally brunette. No self-respecting lethal brunette would bend and snap."

"What would we do?" asked Maria.

The maid of honor shouted, "Get on all fours and crawl around."

The bride said, "Real classy, Tiffany."

Gia considered. "How about tree branching? It's a dance move. You put your wrist on a guy's shoulder, like this, and then shake around in front of him. And, if it gets creepy, I might wrap one leg around him, like this."

A flower girl shouted, "Tree hugging."

Maria said, "The 'branch and hug'! I can do that."

"You need music," said Gia, turning on the store's stereo system. The salon filled with Madonna's "Express Yourself."

Maria and Gia practiced. "I got it. Now all I need is a man," said Maria.

On cue, the door opened and the UPS delivery guy in a brown uniform entered the salon. He must have been young enough because Maria beamed at him, and said, "Hello, doctor!"

"I've got a package for Giovanna Spumanti," he said.

"That's me." Gia signed for the box and read the sender's name on the slip. "From Frank Rossi?" The fireman? What could it be, flame-resistant hair gel? A new spatula? So cute!

"Where're you going?" Maria asked the UPS guy, gyrating over to him. He looked confused, if not terrified.

Maria put her wrist on his shoulder and gyrated. Then she tried to lift her leg and wrap it around him. The poor guy shied away. He looked downright hor-rified when he noticed fifteen naked women, aged ten to sixty-five, watching (now that Gia thought of it) like a forest of tan trees, or members of a weird pagan cult.

"What is this place?" he asked, backing away, making the sign of the cross.

"Come back here," asked Maria as he ran out the door and into his truck. "I wasn't finished! Oh, balls. He doesn't know what he's missing."

"Practice," said Gia. "And give the guy a few shots of tequila first."

"Are you going to open it?" asked Maria, point-ing at the package.

Gia tore open the box and found a card. "It says, 'I thought you might need these. Fondly, Frank.' Fondly? What am I, his aunt or something?" She opened the smaller box inside.

Under pink tissue paper, Gia found a pair of fuzzy pink slippers, just like the ones that were ru-ined in the fire. Size child large.

Gia screamed with excitement. She kicked off her

sandals to put them on. She felt genuinely touched, almost as if she could cry. It was just so thoughtful. Plus, he was right. She did need them! She'd been missing her slippers. Frankie's phone number was on the card. "I'm calling him," she said. "Uh, can I borrow someone's phone? I lost mine again."

The maid of honor said, "I want a guy who sends me pink slippers!"

"If I were you, Tiffany," said the bride, "I'd hold out for a diamond."

Chapter Twenty-one

Party's Here

Bella waited alone at the Inca Bar, nursing her second beer. The space was okay. Stone-tile floor, U-shaped oak bar, a wall of windows behind the bar facing the boardwalk and the ocean. A lot of people filled the single room. No one Bella knew, unfortunately. She checked her cell phone again. Where was everyone?

Al Fresco, the manager, an owl-faced, bald schlub with glasses, shuffled over to Bella. She looked annoyed. "Giovanna was supposed to be here an hour ago," he complained. "I promoted the hell out of this. All these people are here to meet her."

"I tried her cell, but . . ." It rang and rang and went to voice mail because Gia either lost it, didn't answer it, or let the battery die. Last time Bella checked, Gia wasn't in the room either. "She'll be here," Bella promised.

"If she doesn't show up in ten minutes, you're paying for the room. Peak summer rates. Including tax. And tell Stanley Crumbi I said so."

Bella repeated, "She'll be here."

The boy next to her at the bar asked, "You know Shark Girl?"

Bella ignored him. No point talking to a random creepy guy. Tony was on his way.

"She's amazing," he said. "It must be hard for you, hanging out with her. She's supercute, and you're . . . okay, I guess."

Uh, *what*? Bella turned to look at the jerkoff who'd just insulted her. Ordinarily, with a line like that, she'd assume he was baiting her to get a reaction. But this kid's face was blank. No smirk or shit-eating grin. The expression seemed genuine, even earnest.

"Gia is an incredible person," she agreed. "When she gets here, I'll introduce you."

"Thanks." That was it. He didn't say another word.

His silence threw Bella off-balance. Most boys would jump at the slightest opening. She found herself wanting to get him into a conversation. "You from around here?" she asked, using Gia's favorite icebreaker.

"Up north."

Dead stop. No follow-up question or further explanation. Okay, this was bizarre. Since she was fourteen years old, men had been vying for her attention. One of Gia's theories about why Bella stuck with

Bobby so long: he was her protection from constant male creepage.

Was the kid at the bar just a quiet type? Or gay? Or actually repulsed by her?

Bella's top had a plunging V-neckline in front. Maybe he hadn't noticed her million-dollar boobs. She put one arm on the back of her chair to open up the view. A guy walking by stopped in his tracks. The guy behind him, jaw unhinged at the sight, crashed into him, and the two fell on the floor at her feet.

But "up north" at the bar? Barely glanced at her.

Was he gay? Then he'd be fawning all over her. Gay men adored Bella. And she loved them right back. Plus, Up North said he thought Gia was cute.

She took a closer look at him. He was in decent shape, neat profile, with a straight nose, light brown lashes. The natural-sun golden tan was a bit darker on the back of his neck from an outdoors "hat" sport such as golf or tennis. Unlike most of the other guys here, Up North wore a fancy watch, but no bling. His light brown, wavy hair was surfer long and product-free. The chinos and Ralph Lauren polo shirt finished the preppy picture.

He was beyond not her type. Yet, Bella found herself asking in her breathy, sexy voice, "Are you staying at the hotel?"

"Couple of nights." He yawned.

Un-frickin'-believable! She'd basically requested a tour of his bed, and he responded by flashing his dental work.

Now it was a challenge. Which Bella, as a rule,

could not back down from. She just had to turn this kid's head. Picking up her beer, she started licking the bottle. Not subtle at all. She kept at it for a full thirty seconds.

A circle of drooling boys formed around her.

But Yawnie checked his watch. Then he did turn his head, toward a commotion at the bar entrance.

"Party's here!" sang out a voice Bella had known her whole life. Gia had arrived. Behind the bar, Al Fresco looked only slightly less annoyed. A bunch of people surged toward the entrance.

Standing on tippytoes, Bella could only see the top of her cousin's pouf. Bella could try to penetrate that circle of fans, or she could just wait here for Gia. She'd get to the bar eventually.

"Um, Gia's here," Bella said to Yawnie. "Wanna meet her?"

"Sure."

"I'm Bella Rizzoli, by the way." She waited for him to acknowledge it. . . . Nothing! "What's your name?"

"Ed Caldwell." He held out his hand.

———

An hour later, Gia sat on the bar, her legs dangling over the side, feet kicking in Bebe six-inch, black patent leather pumps, as she greeted her public. Bella watched in awe as her cousin lorded over her admirers.

A line formed to meet Gia. She had it down to a routine. The fan would get an autograph, take a photo, and buy a round of shots. Gia raised her glass, said, *"Salute!"* They'd clink glasses and drink, the fans loving it.

Bella noticed Al Fresco watching Gia's every move, literally rubbing his hands together over how much paper was getting dropped at his establishment tonight. Favor to Stanley or not, Gia had brought in enough money to justify a free room all week.

"Bella," said Gia. "Dance on the bar with me. Al! Turn up that music. I wanna dance."

The manager said, "Shoes off! No scuff marks on the bar." He gave the bartender the signal. The volume rose from deafening to earsplitting. Before Bella knew it, Gia had climbed up on the bar. Bella joined her, if only to make sure her drunk cousin didn't fall off.

After a few minutes, though, the music took over. When Bella danced, she felt the beat in every cell of her body. Gia was an awesome dancer, too. She let the music flow through her and did whatever it wanted to do. Usually, a lot of grinding and shaking. Tonight, though, Gia was a few shots past twisted and couldn't stay balanced. Bella had to cut her off, whatever the consequences from the manager.

Bella glanced down to see if Ed Caldwell was watching her dance. Twenty men at the bar were transfixed, but Ed continued to ignore her. Bella was glad to see he wasn't watching Gia either.

Her cousin said, "Whoops," and knocked over some dude's scotch. Then she slipped on the wet bar and nearly flew off. Bella caught her seconds before Gia took a header.

"You're sloppy," Bella said. "It's a bad look on you."

"I love you, Bella," said Gia, pulling her into a tight hug.

Oh, great. We're in I-love-you mode, thought Bella. "Come on down, Gia. Time for a few shots of water."

"Did I tell you? I have a date tomorrow night with a yummy guido fireman! Is there anything sexier than a friggin' fireman? Hey, people!" she shouted to the fans. "What's sexier than a fireman?"

"Porn star!" someone shouted back.

Gia noticed Ed at the bar. He being the nearest cute male, she grabbed his sleeve and said, "Come dance with me."

He shrugged her off. "I don't dance."

Bella frowned. *That is kind of abrupt. He must be shy.*

"You don't dance?" asked Gia.

"Never."

"How embarrassing for you," said Gia.

"Gia, this is Ed," Bella said. "He's a big fan."

He smiled and held out his hand to shake.

"Wait a minute. You look familiar," said Gia, not taking his hand. "I've seen you before."

"Oh, I would've remembered meeting you," he said, shaking his head.

Gia got in his face and slurred, " 'Nothing much'! I remember now. You're the shithead at Karma from a couple of weeks ago. I said, 'What're you looking at?' and you said, 'Nothing much.' Fuck off, Abercrombie! Go back to Connecticut."

Ed looked horrified. "You have me confused with someone else."

Bella was beyond embarrassed and said to Ed, "She's wasted."

"You believe me over him?" asked Gia. "He's lying."

"You're a little impaired," said Bella.

"Where's Tony?" asked Gia. "You should get with him. He's hot. And smart. And Italian."

Ed said, "I don't want to cause a fight. It's a case of mistaken identity. If you'd prefer, I'll leave."

"Yes, I fucking prefer it," said Gia.

"Stop, seriously," said Bella. Ed had been nothing but polite. If anything, he'd been *too* respectful. "Don't leave."

"It's okay. I really enjoyed meeting you, Bella. I was wrong before, by the way. You're prettier than her."

He did notice her! He'd been pretending not to out of shyness and politeness.

"Let me give you my number," she said.

"You don't have to just to be nice."

"Please take it." Bella grabbed the phone out of his hand and added her to his contact list, and vice versa. "I want you to call me, okay?"

He nodded, smiled briefly, and made his way out.

"Thank *God* he's gone," said Gia. Then she accepted the offer from a fan to double-team a beer bong.

Bella steamed at the bar. What was wrong with Gia, insulting a stranger like that? That was a dangerous idea anyway. He might've hauled off and punched Gia in the face!

Meanwhile, what was wrong with Bella that Ed found her only marginally attractive? Was it her clothes? Her face? Bella knew her body was slamming. But she was insecure about her nose. It was on the large side. A legit Roman nose. Bobby used to kiss it, which made her feel self-conscious, as if he couldn't reach her lips under that big honker.

"There she is," said Tony, maneuvering skillfully through the crowd and appearing at her side. He bent to kiss her cheek. Gia saw him and grabbed him to dance.

Now, Tony was not shy. Not surprisingly, considering his physical prowess, he was a great dancer, fist-pumping higher and harder than anyone else. He was over a foot taller than Gia, so they looked funny (in a cute way) shaking it together. Bella was relieved they didn't start grinding. Her benevolence went only so far.

Bella joined them on the dance floor, and she got cozy with Tony. Up close, nose to nose.

He asked, "What up, funny face?"

"Funny face?" She stopped moving. "Are you saying I'm ugly? That I have a big nose?"

Tony stopped, too. "No! I'm just saying hello."

"You're an hour late. Gia's out of control, my car's busted, I'm almost broke, my nose is freakin' hideous, my parents think all I'm good for is making meatballs for the rest of my life, and I haven't gotten laid in months—no thanks to you, Brake Tapper. Also, men think I'm disgusting."

"They do not!"

"You rejected me last night! One kiss, and you're running for the door! A kid was sitting next to me for an hour tonight and acted like I was invisible."

Tony's eyes darkened. "The kid who was just here?"

"You saw him?"

"I saw him leave. Good thing. My Sixth Sense gave me a bad feeling."

"Just by looking at him? That's ridiculous."

"Let me guess how he played you. First, he insulted you," said Tony, counting off on his fingers. "Then he spoke in monosyllables. Then he acted like he had the hots for a friend of yours. Next, he ignored you. And last, he refused to take your number, even after you begged him to."

Bella glared at him. "You were spying on me?"

"I just walked in the door, saw you talking to him, and knew his game on sight. It's textbook."

"You think I don't know a player when I see one?"

Tony shrugged. "You were sitting next to one just now and didn't see it."

"Screw this," she said, anger taking over again. "You're just another version of my ex-boyfriend, telling me what to do and how to feel. And you're wrong about Ed. I have a Sixth Sense, too."

"With respect, Bella, you also thought Bender was cool."

Bella was getting better at expressing her feelings. But sometimes in life, there were not words.

And this was one of them.

She grabbed her beer from the bar and threw it in Tony's face. Bottle and all.

"I guess I deserved that," he said.

Chapter Twenty-two

The Fine Art of Bullshit

Ed Caldwell unlocked his hotel-room door and lay on one of the two queen-size beds. His head was splitting from listening to that god-awful techno music for an hour at the bar. Just the same beat, over and over, like a hammer to his skull. Why those stupid guidos loved it so much, he would never understand.

Bender Newberry came out of the bathroom and asked, "Well? Did she tear your head off yet?"

"By the end of the week she'll be eating out of my hand."

"Bullshit."

Bender, Ed's main man, was 100 percent correct. Ed was a bullshitter. No, scratch that. He was, in his mind, a bullshit *artist*. He created legendary land-scapes of bullshit, inspiring works that should be studied at college.

"You, Bender, made a common, fatal error," said Ed, reaching for his bottle of scotch on the night table. "You thought the road to Bella's pussy ran straight through her heart. A girl like that? She has no heart, for one thing. She's been chewing up and spitting out dipshits like you since she was old enough to speak her first lie. The road to Isabella Rizzoli's pussy runs straight through her ego."

"I played her ego like a Stradivarius. I must have told her a hundred times how hot she was."

"Which, as I just said, she's heard from every dude she's ever met."

"So how'd you play it?" asked Ben. "Tell her she's smart?"

They both laughed hysterically at that. Ed, wiping tears, said, "That's page one of the beginner's manual, dog. I'm in the advanced class. I don't tell a pretty girl she's smart. I don't tell her anything."

Ben seemed confused. "I don't get it. You sat there and said *nothing* for an hour?"

Ed chugged his scotch and reached for another bottle. "Exactly."

"And she talked to you?"

"She talked. She showed me her tits. She flashed her crotch at me when she danced on the bar. I'd be playing Evil Gynecologist with her right now if it weren't for that cock-blocking friend of hers."

"Cousin," corrected Bender. "God, I hate that girl. Even Bella bitched about Gia."

"That's interesting. Bella complained to you about Gia?"

"Little bit, yeah."

"Divide and conquer," said Ed after a few beats. "When Gia finds out her cousin's talking behind her back, it's war. Some Italian code-of-loyalty *omertà* thing. They'll declare each other 'dead to me.' Bella will be alone and unprotected. And vulnerable. That's when I'll move in."

Ben nodded, clearly impressed, as he should have been.

Ed found a notepad in the hotel room and started writing a letter.

"'Dear Bella,'" he wrote, and read out loud for Ben's benefit. "'I'm so sorry about what happened between us. I was just so in love with you, I couldn't control myself.'"

"Whoa, dude, you're writing a letter *from me*?"

"Of course."

"I don't get it."

"Listen and learn," said Ed, continuing to write. "'I was really touched when you shared your heart with me . . .'"

"I'd never say that!"

Ed laughed. "'. . . especially when you confided in me all the issues you have with your cousin Gia. I just hope you can forgive me one day and don't hate me too much. All the best, Ben.' There." Ed folded the note, found a hotel stationery envelope, and sealed it.

"I still don't get it. Bella reads the note, big deal."

Ed shook his head. "Bella won't read it." With different handwriting, he wrote *Shark Girl* on the envelope. "Gia will think it's for her. Her name's on it. She'll open it, read the letter. If those brainless twats even think that far, they'll probably assume the receptionist mislabeled the note when she put it in their hotel mailbox."

Ben shook his head in obvious awe. "You are the master."

"I know. I'm dangerous. I frighten myself."

Chapter Twenty-three

Just a Lot off the Top

Gia woke up in her queen-size bed at noon. Bella must have left early for a (shudder) run on the beach. Closing her eyes, Gia started to drift off again.

Then bolted upright in bed. She was supposed to be at Tantastic two hours ago. She grabbed the hotel phone—message light blinking, probably Maria calling to find out where the hell she was—and dialed the number at the salon.

A recorded message: "You have reached Tantastic, tanning salon to the stars. Open Monday through Saturday, ten to seven. Leave your name and number at the beep. Mystician Maria will get back to you. Thanks."

Gia hung up and fell back on the bed. That's right. It was Sunday. No salon hours today.

She so deserved a day off.

After the night she had.

Gia stretched and snuggled under the covers. It had really been a night to remember.

If only she could!

She knew she danced on the bar, sucked on a beer bong, and was scooped by, like, twenty hot guidos. She saved Bella from getting trapped into a conversation with that scrub Abercrombie. Had Tony been there? Gia thought she saw him. Easy to do, since he was a head taller than anyone else.

Then there was Frankie. Gia replayed the memory of opening his package, and the feeling that overwhelmed her when she saw the pink fuzzies inside. A pure, golden, mad rush of love. Like a double shot of espresso and sambuca, right to her heart.

She called him on the bride's cell phone. Maria and the bridal party listened in.

"The slippers rock," she said. "Thanks so much."

"I hate to think of you with cold feet," he said. "Nice red toenails, by the way."

"You noticed my pedicure?"

"I noticed everything. I couldn't tear my eyes away."

The maid of honor went, "Ahhhh."

"We should go out," said Gia.

"We *have to* go out," he said. "I'm working tonight. But how about tomorrow?"

They set the time and hung up. The bride said, "Congratulations. You're a goner."

When Gia got to the Inca Bar soon after, she felt great, and the good vibes just got better and better. Love came at her from every direction, and Gia soaked it up like a greedy sponge.

Suddenly ravenous, Gia checked the hotel phone for the room-service button. Couldn't find it. She called the front desk.

It rang. And rang. Usually, when she was hungover, she could barely stand the thought of food. But this morning, her head and stomach were fine. If Gia had had a hangover, she'd slept through it.

Finally, someone picked up. She said, "Hello? Yeah. Can I order some breakfast?"

She had to hold the phone away from her ear due to the barking laughing on the other side. "Oh, sorry, sweetie. You have us confused with the Ritz Carlton," said the receptionist.

"No room service?"

"Try the diner next door. They deliver."

The receptionist gave her the number. Gia called them next. "Hello? Can I get a delivery? . . . Inca Hotel, room 214. Do you know Al Fresco? . . . Right. It's on his account. We're cool? . . . Okay, I'll have one of everything on the breakfast menu. . . . Yup. French vanilla coffee. Thanks."

Hanging up, Gia wondered if anyone had ever felt as happy as she did at that second. She'd had a day from heaven yesterday, and another one coming up today. Just as she'd hoped, Gia had found her bliss at the Jersey Shore. She simply couldn't wait to see Frankie again. Only eight more hours.

The phone rang. "Hello?"

"Front desk. I forgot to tell you, there's a letter for you."

"From who?"

The receptionist said, "I don't know. It was dropped off, addressed to Shark Girl. Should I bring it over?"

"Sure!" Her first piece of fan mail. Should make good breakfast reading.

After a quick shower, Gia tried to settle on her outfit for *now*, and her outfit for *later*. Knock on the door. The delivery boy and the receptionist with the letter arrived at the same time. Gia welcomed them both into the room. She dropped the letter on the dresser and fished in her purse for a tip for the delivery boy. She had only a twenty.

"Here," she said, taking the bags (and bags) from him.

The kid, all of fifteen, took the bill without taking his eyes off her. She looked down, realized she was wearing a towel. "Show's over," she said, and shut the door on him.

Gia ate one bite of every dish. She was starving, but she didn't want to eat her way to China, either.

Full and happy as a cat, Gia turned on the TV and caught the second half of *8 Mile*, staring her favorite actress, Brittany Murphy, may she rest in peace, and yummy Eminem. Gia settled back under the covers to watch.

Phone, again. "Hello?"

"It's Stanley. I'm in the lobby."

Oh my God! She knew she forgot something. Not work after all, but her shopping date with Stanley for his guido makeover. A faint memory from last night surfaced in her mind. Stanley appearing at the

Inca Bar at, like, three in the morning and raging that Gia's advice sucked. She filled him in on what Maria told her about feeling young, wanting a hot young boyfriend, and that Stanley looked like her grandfather.

Yes, now it was all coming back. Gia promised to take Stanley to the mall and shave off a few decades. Since his style dated back to *Godfather I*, updating his look shouldn't be too hard.

"Give me ten minutes," she said into phone.

"Make it five."

In twenty minutes, Gia sailed into the lobby in her "flats"—three-inch platform sandals. She tried not to wince when she saw Stanley scratch his scalp and then flick a piece of dandruff onto the floor.

Taking her landlord by the sleeve of his faded gray jacket, she said, "You need some jeans, a few new shirts, a few tank tops, some bling-bling. Cool shades. We could get your ear pierced and definitely hit the tanning salon at the mall, which I hate to do, but whatever. Can't take you to Tantastic." She thought about it for a second, then an idea struck her. "But first, a quick stop at a place I know."

She directed Stanley—he drove a Cutlass—to Devito's barbershop in Toms River where Gia used to watch her dad get his hair cut. Twice a month, they'd pile into the Buick and drive over for his rit- ual "shave and a shear," he called it. Gia loved the time alone with her dad, and the barbershop itself. Devito's smelled like worn leather and menthol shave cream. She'd play in the old-fashioned chairs and ramble about her seven-year-old problems to Yuri, the Russian barber who owned the place. The two men would listen to her as if her problems really mattered, and Gia felt loved and cherished.

A wave of sadness broke over her. She'd always been such a daddy's girl, and now she and Joe hardly ever spoke.

"Park here," she said when they neared Devito's.

Seeing the barbershop awning, Stanley said, "No fucking way, Gia. The hair stays."

"Relax, Stanley. You're not Sampson."

"Who?"

"The guy from the Bible? His girlfriend cut his hair in the middle of the night. He bitched, but Fabio isn't a good look on anyone, even a hundred years ago. Delia did Sampson a favor. And that's what I'm gonna do for you."

Stanley shook his head. "I must be crazy, trusting you. I'm either desperate, or an idiot or . . ."

"You're a desperate idiot in love. Get out of the car."

They walked into the shop. A middle-aged man with gray hair, a ruddy, thick-featured face, barrel chest, and big, hairy forearms read the paper in one of the chairs, black shoes propped on the metal footrest. He lowered the paper and asked, "Can I help you?"

"Yuri? Do you remember me?"

"Giovanna? Is that you? Oh my God! Come here! Give me kiss!"

Giggling, Gia ran into the barber's arms, and he

twirled her around, just as he used to when she was little(r). "I haven't seen you in years, Giovanna. What happen? You move away?"

His Russian accent was heavy, despite his having lived in Jersey for decades. She said, "My mom and I moved to Brooklyn three years ago."

"Welcome home." Yuri hugged her again. "Tell me about Joe. How is your father? He moved to Philadelphia two years ago? Such a good man. Best tipper in twenty-five years of business. I miss him."

Gia blushed. She was embarrassed not to know what was going on in her dad's life. She resolved to call him, as soon as she found her cell phone. "He's good," she said vaguely.

"He came to see me last month. A baby sister or brother for Giovanna on the way. I'm so happy for you! Congratulations!"

What??? "Yeah, thanks."

Dad's wife was pregnant? This was the first she'd heard of it. All the old emotions rushed over her. The guilt and pain of the divorce. The awkward loneliness of Joe's second wedding, which Gia got through by drinking heavily and making out with the caterer.

Stanley reached out a hand and introduced himself. "I'm Gia's landlord, Stanley Crumbi. How you doing?"

Yuri shook hands and guided Stanley into a chair. He put his meaty hands on his customer's head to see what he was working with. Unwinding the spiral of Stanley's comb-over hair(s), Yuri held it up and up, ten inches straight up, and revealed Stanley's shiny bald skull underneath.

"A little off the top?" asked Yuri.

Despite her sudden onset of sadness and guilt, Gia giggled.

"Just some light shaping," said Stanley.

"Don't listen to him. Close-crop the whole head," Gia instructed Yuri. To her landlord and makeover subject, she said, "Bald is beautiful. Look at every guy who walks down the street. Close-crop, buzz cuts, and tape-ups, if not clean-shaved. Am I right, Yuri?"

"Gia has beautiful taste," said Yuri. "From the time she was eight years old."

"My comb-over is older than that! Oh, shit. Just do it."

Yuri didn't hesitate. The scissors flashed, the razor hummed. It was all over in just a few minutes. After the trauma of losing his hair, Stanley needed a relaxing professional shave. It always had a calming effect on Joe. He could growl into the shop a bear, but he always came out a lamb.

From under his hot towel, Stanley said, "Gia, your father was Joe Spumanti?"

"He ran a construction company in Toms River."

"Yeah, I knew him. His company did a few renovation jobs for me. Joe never jacked up his prices and always finished on time. He did what he said he was gonna do. That's a man you can trust and respect."

A wellspring of pride lifted Gia's heart. Stanley's and Yuri's stories reinforced what Gia already knew: her dad was a good man. Despite everything that'd happened, she shouldn't forget that, even if he made her mom cry every night for a year, and basically stopped talking to Gia, too, as the marriage unraveled. Despite pleading with both parents for answers, Gia never knew the real story of what went wrong between them. Their family was fine, until one random day. Then Mom started crying, and Dad stopped talking.

Gia had stuffed those feelings into a black hole in her heart for years. She hadn't intended to let them out again, ever. Definitely not now! The whole point of coming to the Shore was to have fun, hook up, the three D's.

But it occurred to her suddenly that maybe her subconscious had led her back to the Shore to force her to deal with the problems and emotions she'd left behind.

With the slap of aftershave, Yuri said, "Okay, you're beautiful. All finished."

Gia thought, *And I'm just getting started.*

"You really do look hot, Stanley," she said, returning her attention to the man in front of her. "Now let's get you some items on the guido shopping list. By the end of this afternoon, I'll have you looking like a supercreepy OG." The original guido.

Yuri laughed. "Good luck."

"Budget OG," said Stanley. "Only fake bling, Gia. And sale items. I am not paying more than twenty bucks for a T-shirt. Do you hear me?"

Chapter Twenty-four

I Just Want to Be Right

Drenched in sweat, Bella slowed to a walk. She'd run five miles in only forty minutes—on the beach. FYI: no sharks on the shoreline, and she was looking for them. Bella did have to avoid stepping on slimy piles of seaweed and some empty crab shells. Seagulls dogged her. Otherwise, the beach was practically deserted that early on a Sunday. The Atlantic Ocean, calm and blue, stretched out as far as the eye could see. It was almost like being alone on the edge of the world.

She put her hands on her knees and took a few deep breaths. She stretched out, holding on to Rick's lifeguard stand for balance. Then, she took her time, strolling where the waves broke on the sand, back toward the hotel. Gia was probably still passed out. Bella had checked the TV clock when her cousin came in—4:40 a.m. Bella cringed, imagining the hangover.

After Bella threw her beer at Tony last night, she left the bar and crawled under the covers of the bumpy hotel bed. Had she overreacted? He'd essentially called her a stupid bitch. Not in those words, but he might as well have used them. Bella would put up with a lot from her friends and family. Case in point: Gia's being such a hater to Ed last night. Bella was mortified, thinking how rude her cousin was to a total stranger. Gia was too wasted to know if they'd met before.

Up ahead, Bella spotted a crew of early risers like herself. They appeared large on the horizon. As she got closer, she realized the circle of half a dozen men didn't just appear large, they *were* large. Freakin' huge.

It was the gorilla juicehead breakfast club. Bella noticed Johnny Hulk among them and stifled a laugh, imagining the tiny package inside his XXL black shorts.

Keeping a respectful distance, Bella sat on a nearby dune and watched the gorillas go through their routine. They worked out in respectful silence, not wanting to interrupt the sanctity of morning, or each other from his private thoughts.

Like any Sunday in church.

Bella had been raised Catholic, like most of her friends and all of her family. She went to church every Sunday growing up. Her grandma Gloria made sure of that for all her grandchildren, although Gia escaped the worst of Gloria's religiosity because Aunt Alicia and Uncle Joe lived in Jersey. Bella, who lived in the same house as Gloria, was raised to fear and respect a living, loving God. Her own parents went through the motions to keep Gloria from threatening them with hell and the devil and burning in a river of fire for a thousand years, etc. But Bella knew her parents weren't devout, or even strong believers. When Grammy died a few years ago, her funeral was the last time Bella went to church.

The sight of the ocean, the minidrama of the seagulls diving for fish, the sun burning in the bluer-than-blue sky, the marvelous male form in all its glory—what Bella saw before her eyes was evidence enough that God existed and did fine work. This dune, she decided, before nature and beauty, was her pew. The sky was her church ceiling.

Bella closed her eyes, and she prayed. "Thanks, God, for making me strong and healthy, for giving me love and family. I'm blessed and grateful for the food I eat, and a safe place to sleep."

Pausing, she always felt a little greedy when she asked God for a favor. But this morning, she had nothing to lose. "Here's the thing," she said, closing her eyes again. "I've been good my whole freakin' life. I've done what was expected of me, at home, in school. Whatever my parents wanted. Whatever Bobby wanted, which included some seriously kinky shit. But I guess you already know that. Not that I'm accusing you of peeping from heaven. I know you're not a sick perv, God."

Bella was getting off track. "I'm twenty-one. Time to call the shots how I see them. I'm doing my best,

God. I know I got it wrong about Ben Newberry. I had him pegged as a nice kid. It pisses me off that Gia realized he was a dipshit before I did. I should know better. Now there's Ed Caldwell. He seems okay to me. Gia says no. Tony says no. God, I just want to be right this time. Can you do that for me? I'm praying that I'm right about Ed, and that Gia and Tony don't know their ass from their wenis."

It might seem silly, even demented. But around mile three, Bella made a bargain with herself. If she was right, that Ed Caldwell was a quiet, shy decent person, she'd have enough faith in her judgment to enroll in college this fall. Deep in her gut, she believed that putting herself in debt for an education would pay off in the end. But if she was wrong about Ed, if he turned out to be a mind-gaming player, why should she believe in her gut about anything?

"Except for boobs, I've never asked for anything, God," she said, "but now I'm asking for a sign."

The gorilla pack broke up and left. Bella waded into the ocean to cool off her feet, then went back to the hotel. She was starving, as if she might faint from hunger. The spontaneous prayer session made her feel emotionally empty, too.

She ran back to the hotel to shower, dress, get some food. Using the key she'd tied to her sneaker, Bella entered the room quietly in case Gia was asleep.

But Gia was gone. Bella dropped the key on the dresser, next to an envelope addressed to Shark Girl. Then, the smells hit her.

Looking closer, Bella noticed the plastic trays

of food on the table, the desk, and all over her bed. Eggs and home fries. Bacon and toast. Pancakes, fruit salad. Orange juice and coffee. Danishes, bagels, muffins, waffles. Corned beef hash, sausages. It was like a breakfast bomb had gone off.

Bella dove in, scarfing the still-hot food until she had to lie down among the empty plates.

She pointed with both hands at the ceiling. "I asked. You answered. Thanks!"

She was hungry; a buffet appeared. It had to be a sign.

Rolling to one side, Bella grabbed her cell phone and called Ed.

Chapter Twenty-five

Take My Breath Away

The mall trip turned out to be a blast. Gia and Stanley shopped all afternoon. His cheap-bastard tendencies did get in the way. At Ed Hardy, Stanley almost refused to buy a mad cool black T-shirt with gold tribal designs all over it.

"It's forty bucks!" he complained.

"Jeez, I need a crowbar to get you to open your friggin' wallet!"

At Bedazzled, a great source for all things bling, Stanley picked up a gold chain with a cross on the end. Well, not real gold. Gold-plated. It'd turn his neck green. But it was only $20.

At Alaskan Tanning, Gia convinced Stanley to do a facial, since he refused to get naked. He complained the whole time his head was under the lights. At Crissy's Nails, he submitted to a mani/pedi, with buffing. Gia nearly gagged at the sight of his toenails.

"Maria should thank *me* for this," said Gia. "And give that poor woman a *huge* tip." She meant the pedicurist, who'd broken out the hedge clippers kept in the back for big jobs. Kidding. But not really.

When he came out of the changing room at Lucky with ink-washed blue jeans, his new shirt, the haircut, and the hint of the tanned cheeks to come, old Stanley was gone. Fly Stanley had emerged. He looked twenty years younger. Gia thought he looked, like, a gazillion times better. Just one more thing, thought Gia. She took him to Claire's to get his ear pierced. He refused, though. Pussy.

Gia touched up her tips at Crissy's and picked up a few items for herself, including a cheetah-print bra-and-thong set that got her hot and bothered just carrying the bag. Guys thought girls wore lingerie to turn them on. Wrong! Gia wore lacy, silky sexy things to get herself in the mood.

Time check: one hour until Frankie. Bella must have come and gone. The maid service had come and gone, too, and cleared away all the breakfast garbage and even folded Gia's dirties from the night before. Gia would leave the housekeeper a gigantic tip when she checked out, on behalf of Al Fresco.

Gia tried Bella's cell. It went to voice mail, so she left a message. "I'm out with Frankie tonight. I'll see you later. Or not. Wish me luck! Peace."

Tonight, she'd pull out all the stops. She started with makeup, including her trick of using a dark stroke of blush on her cleavage to make her boobies look even bigger. Next, hair and makeup. She went with two rows of lashes tonight, black liquid eyeliner, and heavy mascara. No reason to dial back the drama. Natural lips, which took three layers of foundation and gloss. For hair, Gia decided against a pouf. Frankie had already seen that. Instead, she teased up the top, for a bit more height, used a flat iron for smooth hair over the top, and a curling iron to make waves in her extensions.

Gia tugged on a stretchy, tight, silver, sequined dress from BCBG and climbed into brand-new rhinestone-studded high-heeled sandals that tied around her ankle with a black satin ribbon.

With the shoes and the lingerie, big eyes and hot dress, Gia had never felt sexier. She examined herself in the full-length mirror, adjusted her hair, and tugged her dress up an inch, to the very top of her thighs. She puckered and kissed at her reflection.

"I should feel this way every day," she said to herself out loud. "Every girl should feel this way."

The TV clock said it was just eight o'clock. Frankie should be waiting in the lobby already. She finished herself with a misting of her signature scent, Britney Spears's Fantasy, and exited the room.

She saw him first. He stood by the reception desk, reading brochures for local attractions. Gia realized she'd never seen him without his fireman gear on. This was the first time she could really see his body, displayed nicely in jeans and the same T-shirt she'd made Stanley buy today at Ed Hardy.

Did Frank go shopping for their date, too? she wondered. If he had, thank God he hadn't seen her out with Stanley. That would've been weird.

He noticed her. Everyone in the lobby noticed her. He watched her walk toward him. At one point, he put his hand over his heart.

"You look . . . you take my breath away," he said, leaning down to kiss her on both cheeks.

"You look hot, too," she said, her heart beating so loud, she thought he'd hear it.

"You okay to walk on the boardwalk in those shoes?"

"I could walk on molten lava in these." Being a Smurf, Gia had learned to walk on any terrain in heels. She could probably run a marathon in six-inch stilettos. If she could run a marathon, which she couldn't, obviously. And, honestly? Why the hell would any sane person want to?

Frankie took her hand, and they left the lobby's sliding glass door straight onto the boardwalk. The sun was starting to drop over the horizon, turning the sky pinky orangey. Flattering to any skin tone, especially Gia's. "When I get home," she said, "I'm painting my room that color."

"Where's home?"

"I live in Carroll Gardens, Brooklyn, in a brown-stone on Smith Street with my mom, my aunt, my uncle, my cousin Bella—you met her—our grandfa-ther, and four cats. The first floor of the building is Uncle Charlie's store."

"What kind of store?"

Frankie seemed genuinely interested, not just

making polite pre-smush small talk. "Rizzoli's Deli," she said. "A real traditional Italian deli. Cured meats, homemade moozadell. Everyone in the house works at the store. Cooking, making sandwiches, deliveries."

"What do you do?"

Gia shrugged. "Whatever Uncle Charlie lets me. Mainly staying out of the way for everyone else. I had a couple of accidents early on. Nothing life-threatening. I messed up the recipe for marinara sauce, and they threw me out of the kitchen. I was put on roasting-coffee-bean duty, but I broke an antique brass grinder. Uncle Charlie moved me to the stockroom, and I spilled a twenty-pound bag of elbow macaroni. Then I worked the cash register, but I always gave out the wrong change. I tried, but I don't really fit in at the deli."

Frankie nodded. "What about college?"

"I loved college. Only a few more credits, and I'll have my degree. I had to take a year off, though. Recession-related tuition cash-flow issues."

"You seem to fit in at the tanning salon."

She smiled. "It's going great, actually. It's the first job I ever had that makes me happy. I make the customers happy. My boss, Maria, loves me."

Frankie squeezed her hand. "So you found your place."

"I guess. By accident, as usual." Gia didn't want to tell him that it was all for nothing. She was leaving town at the end of the month, back to treading water in Brooklyn.

"Have you ever had saltwater taffy?" Frank asked. They stopped in front of a candy store. "Taffy's pulled right here. It's great stuff. You should try it."

Gia let him buy her a few pieces. "I love that smell," she said, inhaling the sweet-shop aroma. "Takes me back to childhood. I grew up here, you know. In Toms River. My mom and I moved to the city after I graduated high school. So, yeah, I've had taffy before, boatloads of it." She popped a piece in her mouth, the chewy candy sticking to her teeth.

"I knew it! You *are* a Jersey girl."

Gia sang, " 'Nothing matters in this whole wide world . . .' "

" '. . . when you're in love with a Jersey girl,' " said Frank. "Springsteen."

"My baby blanket had the cover of *Born to Run* on it."

Frankie laughed. "I was raised on it, too. My dad still plays *Greetings from Asbury Park* in the truck."

They walked farther down the boardwalk. He held her hand tight. They passed a few booths with games. Break the Plate, Frog Bog, Balloon Darts.

"This one's near impossible," said Frankie, stopping her at a booth with the game of lobbing softballs into a basket. When Gia tried it, the balls always bounced out.

The kid behind the bench said, "Five dollars for three throws. You land one ball, choose from these prizes." Crap, cheap plastic junk. "Land two, you get this row." Small stuffed animals, some cute dogs and bears. "Land three in a row, you get to choose one of the mirrors on the back wall"—lots of Bon Jovi—"or the hanging prizes." He meant the giant pandas and teddies that hung from the booth's wire-mesh-lined ceiling.

Frankie and Gia watched as a couple of tourists tried their luck. The guy threw three balls, and all of them bounced out of the baskets. His girl said, "I told you it's rigged. You just wasted five bucks."

The loser said, "It's my friggin' money."

The couple walked away, bickering. "They need a drink," said Gia.

Frankie peeled five singles off his cash wad and gave them to the kid behind the counter. Frankie took the three balls, grinned at Gia, and asked, "Will you be embarrassed if I miss?"

"Totally."

"I better not then."

Frankie lobbed the first ball. It landed with a thunk in the back of the basket, rolled forward, but then settled at the bottom.

"Winner," said the kid.

Frankie threw the second ball and hit the sweet spot again. The ball stayed put.

"Winner again."

Third ball, same thing. The kid said, "We got a ringer here! I mean, a *winner*. Choose your prize."

Frankie turned to her. "All yours, Gia."

She clapped and jumped up and down. Yay! She loved prizes. "Oh, God, I want all of them." Her eyes went immediately to the giant gorilla doll. *But I don't need a stuffed gorilla,* Gia thought, hugging Frankie's huge arm. She had the real thing right here.

"That one." She pointed at the giraffe. The kid used a pole to unhook it. The doll was almost as tall as she was.

When they were a few steps away, out of earshot of the game booth, she said, "So now you can tell me how you did that."

He laughed. "I worked the basket booth for three summers when I was in high school."

"How old are you?" Gia asked. Maybe they'd met before and didn't know it.

"I'm twenty-seven."

"Six years older than me. That's hot."

"You like older guys?"

"I like you," she said.

Their paths probably hadn't crossed. When he was sixteen, working the booth, she was only ten, playing with Barbies in her bedroom. But even then, Gia dreamed of a party-filled future. Her favorite thing in the entire world? Barbie's hot tub. She'd put brunette Barbie in it, naked, with, like, four Ken dolls. They all held little party cups in their plastic hands.

"Did you go to college?" she asked.

He led her to a bench on the boardwalk. She sat next to him, wishing she'd taken the spot on his lap. "Hang out on the boardwalk for long enough, you'll see every person you know," he said, and throngs of people walked by. "College. Not in the cards for me. I went straight into training for the fire department right out of high school. My dad's a firefighter. My brother, too. It's in my blood. I never wanted to do anything else."

"You're making me jealous. I wish I had a clue what I'm supposed to do with my life." Gia felt like the bouncing softballs, popping out of one basket after another. Frankie didn't bounce, though. He could stick.

A couple walked by, pushing a stroller. He said, "You could get married. Have kids."

"I do want that. I know my mom would be happy if I had someone else to take care of me, like a husband. She married my dad when she was my age and had me a couple of years later. Now she's single and depressed. Plus, can you imagine me with a baby right now? No friggin' way! I'm not ready."

"Your parents divorced?"

"That's why Mom and I moved in with her sister, my aunt, in Brooklyn. I guess I could have stayed in Jersey with Dad. But he never asked me to. Mom was crying all the time, totally messed up. And my dad just turned to stone. Before the drama, he was a total sweetheart. But then he became a stranger. I took it personally. Hard not to. One day, I was Daddy's little girl and went everywhere with him. Then, it was like he forgot I existed."

Gia felt another wave of memory crash over her. Joe and Alicia had a big fight. Gia buckled herself into the shotgun seat of his car so he couldn't leave without her. He stormed out of the house and forcibly pulled Gia out of car, got behind the wheel, and drove away. The whole incident, Joe didn't speak a word to her. Gravel flew as he sped away. A piece hit her on the back of her hand, leaving a mark.

She rubbed it; the tiny scar still hurt. "He got married again, like, two seconds later," she said suddenly. "Rhoda. A younger woman, of course. I just learned today from my dad's barber that my stepmother is pregnant. I didn't even know."

"That's rough."

"I haven't talked to anyone about this," she said, turning to Frankie, comforted by the sympathetic look in his eyes. "Not even Bella." Actually, she hadn't even seen Bella since last night. But whatevs. She was opening her heart to Frankie, and it felt right.

Frankie said, "Sometimes, it's easier to talk to a stranger."

"But we're not strangers. We're friends."

Frankie put his arm around her shoulder and pulled her in close. The sun had set. The multicolored lights on the boardwalk glowed. For a few minutes, they sat quietly, taking in the sights and plinking sounds, the laughter and endless stream of people going by.

Gia realized that in all this time no one recognized her as Shark Girl. Maybe it was because, with Frank, she put off a private energy, emitting vibes that warded off intrusion. Or maybe the two of them were in a pink, shiny bubble together. That was how she felt, anyway.

A couple walked by. Frankie flinched. He grabbed the giraffe and put it on his lap, hiding his face.

"They're gone," said Gia. "You should have put me on your lap."

He smiled, but clearly he wasn't happy.

"Who was that? The guy looked a lot like you."

Frankie sighed. "My brother. Forget about it."

"After I just poured my heart out to you? No way. Start talking."

"Can we walk?" They stood up, and Frank pointed down the ramp to the beach.

"Okay, even I can't do sand," she said, pausing to take off her heels.

He carried the giraffe. She toted her shoes. The sand was still warm on her feet.

Frankie said, "That was my brother, Lou, the firefighter. The girl he was with is Dina, my ex. She and I lived together for two years. We started fighting about my hours. It's hard, being a firefighter's girl. My schedule is two days on, one day off. When I'm working, I live at the station. She hated worrying about me, being alone so much. I was sympathetic, but after a while, it seemed like all I did was apologize for my job and listen to her complain. She knew what she was getting into with me. We fought more and more. Instead of making up like we used to, I started sleeping on the couch. She turned to Lou to talk about our problems. I don't need to go on, do I?"

Gia could only imagine how painful that must have been. The betrayal, by both his girl *and* his brother. Italian men had big egos, too, and being thrown over must have been a savage blow.

Gia said, "That sucks."

"The worst part is that Lou is a firefighter, too. In Belmar, which is twenty minutes away. So he spends even *less* time at home. Actually, I take it back. The worst part is that Lou and Dina are after me to forgive them. They want my blessing."

"Is he older or younger?"

"He's thirty. And Dina's twenty-eight."

At their ages, they probably wanted to get married and have kids as soon as possible. But they wouldn't take the next step unless the family approved. Frankie had the power to seriously screw with their lives if he wanted to.

"You're holding out?" asked Gia. "Why? For revenge?"

By now, they'd reached the shoreline. He skirted the water in his boots. In bare feet, Gia got her toes wet.

"What would you do?" he asked.

She shrugged. "I'd give them my blessing."

"I want to. It's been six months. I'm not even mad anymore. But I can't seem to get over it."

"Uh, I think that means you're still mad. More at your brother. He's been in your life for your whole life. He'd be harder to forgive."

"You're right."

"I was cheated on once. I was seeing this guy for three months, and he called me drunk one night and said, 'I just banged a girl at a party.' I went ballistic and told him to drop dead. He said, 'Why are you so mad? I'm just being honest with you.' As if admitting he cheated made it okay!"

"What'd you do?"

"I burned his house down."

Frankie looked shocked. Gia started laughing. "I'm only kidding! You should see your face. I didn't do anything to him. Just never spoke to him or saw him again. And if I ever do? It'll be too soon."

They'd strolled all the way down the beach. He said, "Is this where you saw the shark?"

"You know about that?"

"I saw you on TV."

"How'd I look?"

He stopped and put his hands on her shoulders. "Dangerously cute. I watched the video on YouTube a dozen times."

"Only a dozen?"

"That story, about my ex and Lou. Does it make you lose respect for me?"

"You're not letting my giraffe get wet, are you?"

"It's fine," he said, hiking it higher under his arm.

"It's humiliating to be cheated on. I've been there. It's embarrassing, but what can you do? Refusing to give your blessing? That's not a good look on you. Your brother is blood. With family, you have to forgive, forget, and find a way to be happy for them, no matter how much it hurts."

"Easy to say."

"I should take my own advice," she said, "about my dad."

Frankie's hands roamed up and down her back. She got goose bumps, and not from the ocean breeze.

"Thanks again for the slippers," she said. "That really was so friggin' sweet."

"You're welcome."

Gia peered at him through her two sets of lashes. "The best way to get over an ex-girlfriend?"

"Another girl."

"Not just *any* girl."

"Oh, don't worry. You're not. Not by a long shot." He pulled her closer. The giraffe got in the way. "I'm going to drop the giraffe in the sand now. It's gonna get wet."

"That makes two of us."

Frankie could take a hint and plunged down for a kiss. Her mouth opened to receive it and filled deliciously with his tongue. She grabbed hold of him with both arms and deepened the kiss.

Frankie moaned and pressed Gia's body hard against his. His chest felt like a brick wall against her softness. Gia imagined herself melting, turning to mush against his rock-hard muscles.

He was granite elsewhere, too. No steroid shrinkage here, *obviously*. "I could hang my entire summer wardrobe on that," she said.

"We have to lie down. Right now," he said, his eyes shining like black diamonds.

"On the beach? I'll get sand in my thong!"

"I'll get it out," he promised.

She considered it. "Well, then, okay."

They stretched out on the sand. Frankie's hands and lips were gloriously busy all over her body. Didn't take long until Gia forgot about sand, and everything else. Her heated blood, pounding heart, and bones turned to goo. Hands on his ass, Gia pulled his hips toward her, pressing her belly against his hard-on until she felt her skin bruise.

"Slow down, Gia," he growled into her neck.

"I can't." Honestly? She didn't want to take it slow. She wanted everything, right away, and then to do it again, as soon as possible. She'd waited a long time to feel a real man's arms around her, his hot lips at her throat, an urgent throb against her thighs.

A wave came up and almost reached their entwined bodies. Gia said, "It's like that old Frank Sinatra movie. *To Eternity, and Beyond.*"

"I think it's called *From Here to Eternity.*"

"What am I thinking of?"

"Buzz Lightyear?" he said, and then did a good impression. " 'To infinity, *and beyond!*'"

Gia giggled into his chest, burying her face against the smooth muscles, finding his perfect brown nipple and giving it a taste. Frankie put his hand at the back of her neck, stroking her hair. Propping himself up on one elbow, he kissed her gently and guided her down so she was looking up at the moon and the stars. Kissing her face, her neck, her collarbone, he kissed her over her dress, then under it.

"Nice bra," he said. "Take it off."

Gia gulped. She reached for the front fastener and set her girls free. Her nipples popped when exposed to the air, grew bigger as Frankie's lips found them.

"Oh my freakin' God," she said.

"Yes? You called?"

They laughed. Gia couldn't remember laughing so much while smushing with a new guy. This was fun, to feel sexy and giggly at the same time. Gia realized, with a bit of a shock, that she hadn't had a single shot or cocktail tonight.

Frankie looked down at her face. Gia smiled at him, brushing sand from his hair.

"Point of no return, Gia. Should we stay here, or go to your hotel room?"

Gia wasn't entirely sure she *could* leave this spot, since her bones had turned to butter. But she knew smushing with Frankie would be even more fabulous in a clean bed with crisp sheets and air-conditioning. The beach was cool, in theory. But in practice? She felt sand in her butt crack.

"Hotel," she said.

"Good call."

Frankie pulled Gia to her bare feet. She righted her clothes, brushed off as much sand as she could, and said, "I demand total nudity when we get inside."

"Me, too." He took her hand and pulled her along.

"What's your hurry?"

"Are you kidding?" he replied.

Gia heard a squishy sound. "What was that?"

"I stepped on . . ." Another squish. "What the . . . ?" He examined the bottom of his boots, then sounded panicked. "Gia! Don't move!"

Under her bare foot, Gia felt a slimy sensation, as if she'd stepped on a glob of hair gel. And then, a sting. A burning sensation on her ankle grew hotter, until it scorched. Gia fell over from the pain and felt another glob, and another sting in her thigh. Both her ankle and her leg were on friggin' *fire*.

"*Waaaa!*" she cried. "What's happening?!"

Frankie said, "Gia, listen to me, you'll be okay. You were stung by a jellyfish. This happened before, last month. Jellyfish washed ashore and covered the beach."

"It kills!" Gia had never felt such pain in her life. Not when she got her nose pierced or when she almost got a tattoo on her back and walked out after the artist made a single dot. Or when she stubbed her foot on her dresser and broke her pinkie toe. Take all those hurts, wrapped together, times a million, and that was what she felt now.

"Mother*fucker!*" she said. "Make it stop!"

"Gia, I'm sorry for what I'm about to do. But it's the only way."

He unzipped his jeans. "What the hell are you doing?" she screamed. Even through the cloudy vision of her pain, and the just plain freakiness of Frankie showing her his dick *now*, Gia was impressed. He had some super-fine-looking junk.

The fire burned up and down her leg, spreading. She closed her eyes and nearly passed out. Then Gia felt a sprinkling of warm liquid on her leg, followed by instant, blessed relief. The sudden absence of agony was as big a surprise as the explosion of it.

"You peed on me! You . . . you *peed* on me!"

"I'm so sorry," he apologized again. "The ammonia in urine deadens the sting."

"That was totally gross! And disgusting! But, under the right circumstances, I can see how it could be hot. And I do feel better. But now, I really need a shower."

Frankie laughed and picked her up. He threw her over his shoulder. "Fireman's carry," he said, placing a supportive hand on her tushie. After he gave her a reassuring squeeze, he added, "I got stung when I was a kid. I know it hurts like hell."

"My giraffe!"

He swooped down and grabbed the stuffed animal. He carried both all the way back to the boardwalk.

"You can put me down now," she said.

"I'm taking you all the way to the hotel."

And he did. It was only another few steps.

"Are you okay?" he asked.

She nodded, gazing into Frankie's face. He glowed, as if a neon light had turned on inside him. Helping people, saving them and relieving their suffering, was obviously his prime directive in life. "You are so fucking hot right now," said Gia. "Let's go to my room."

"I would love to, but I have to alert SHBP about the jellyfish. We've got to keep people off the beach until it's cleaned up."

Crushed, Gia said, "But . . . but . . . oh, shit. You better go. I'd hate for some kid to get stung."

He kissed her hard, handed over her shoes and her giraffe. "I'm working tomorrow, but Tuesday, just me and you."

"Even if the whole town is on fire?"

"I promise."

Chapter Twenty-six

More Than Enough

Bella sat at the palazzo bar at Karma in her sluttiest metallic-pink micro bikini top and a miniskirt that could pass for a belt. She might as well be naked. Why be modest? Bella had "it"; she was gonna flaunt it.

She was meeting Ed here tonight. While getting ready, Bella decided she'd sleep with him. In her mind, he'd become the dividing line between her past and her future. Bella would lose her post-Bobby virginity tonight and double the number of men she'd slept with.

So where was he?

When she'd called him earlier, he said, "Oh, yeah, the girl from last night. Beth? Beatrice? Bella?"

"You wanna go out with me tonight?"

"Er, well, I had plans. Meeting my boys at Karma."

"I could find you there."

He paused. "Yeah, okay."

"What time?"

Another pause. "I'll be there at ten."

Bella would arrive, she planned, at 10:30 p.m. She spent part of the evening back at the Kearney Avenue house, sneaking into the construction site to get the bikini top she'd left behind. She also hit a boutique on the boardwalk to buy the skirt.

She sipped her tequila. It was almost eleven, and Ed hadn't shown up. A dozen other boys had hit on her. She accepted a few shots. But she'd settled in her heart and mind on Ed, even though she was starting to feel royally pissed off.

Finally, at just after eleven, when Bella was about ready to leave, she saw Ed walking toward her. He ordered a beer at the bar, smiled, and said, "Bella. Hey."

"I've been waiting for you."

"And here I am. The waiting paid off."

A year ago, Bella would have bit her lip if someone was openly rude to her. But lately? The cork was off the bottle.

"You said you'd be here an hour ago. Lateness is disrespectful, okay? I don't like it."

"Hold that thought one minute. I have to go talk to a guy." Then Ed left her alone, again. She watched him go up to a kid down the bar. He kind of reminded her of Rick, the lifeguard. Surfer-style, with board shorts and Vans, too long hair, and a real suntan. Ed seemed a lot happier to see him than vice versa. Surf boy went through the motions, the ritual bumping, slapping, the *Yo, bro*'ing back and forth. The greeting ritual reminded Bella of the gangsta act Bobby and his friends put on. Like they were so tough! Half of them were mama's boys who lived at home, hung around the corner bodega, and quoted *Godfather* movies all day long. "Leave the gun, take the cannoli," etc.

Five minutes went by. Ed seemed to be pestering the kid. From her perspective, Vans couldn't wait to get away. Meanwhile, Bella might as well have been on another planet for all Ed seemed to care.

To gather her dignity, Bella fiddled with her phone. Ed chose that moment to return. Bella pretended Tony had just called. "What up, T?" she asked.

If he'd really been on the line, he'd've said, "There she is!" Bella suddenly wished she'd made a date with Tony, not Ed. He wouldn't treat her like the Invisible Hottie. She was new to Shore seduction tactics. Maybe this was how it worked, as Tony explained. If a guy insulted you, it was a compliment. If he ignored you, he was captivated. Bella didn't understand the mind games. She didn't appreciate them, either. If Ed liked her, he should show it. Reverse psychology might work on gullible, insecure girls. But Bella had too much self-respect to keep on playing.

The more she thought about it, the clearer her thoughts. The breakfast in the room? *Not* a sign from God, but a gift from Gia. The real test of her judgment wasn't being right, but openness to being wrong. There was no shame in making mistakes. Like Bender. But there *was* shame in repeating them.

Ed said, "I just saw another guy I know. Stay right here. I'll be back."

That was it. Bella's mind turned. Her stubbornness stripped away, she could see Ed for what he was—a mind-gaming player, or a rude bastard, or both. In any case, she didn't want anything to do with him. Tony and Gia were right. She was wrong. And she had the wisdom and confidence to admit it.

Bella downed her shot and placed the empty glass on the bar.

The bartender said, "Another?"

Bella said, "I've had more than enough, thanks," and left.

Chapter Twenty-seven

Mr. Cool

Bender Newberry was on his second plate of onion rings at the Whistlestop diner. He'd been instructed by Ed to wait here for his call. The greasy snack, as well as this summer's Rule of Ten game, left a bad taste in his mouth.

The girls from summers past were typical Jersey Shore whores. Or, as Bender and Ed called them, shwores. One expensive dinner, a ride in the BMW, and Bender was in. Ed came on sneaky and snide, but usually got a blow job in the bathroom, at least.

Bella Rizzoli should be over and done with, in sixteen degrading positions, by now. Ben gently touched his cheek and nose where she'd punched him. Tender to the touch. His eyes were still black-and-blue. Women, contrary to what he'd long believed, were not attracted to guys who looked as if they'd been in a fight. When Ben walked into a bar, girls shied away, repulsed. He hadn't seen a naked girl for two weeks—except for that actual whore in Atlantic City.

Ben's back ached from the bed at the Inca. They'd been sleeping there two nights now. When they heard (via gossip and the giant promo poster on the boardwalk) that Gia—and her cousin—had moved there, Ed decided it'd be smart to get a room at the hotel, too. It'd save driving time back and forth from Barnegat Light. But the place was a shambles. The rooms were tiny. And Ben longed for his own Tempur-Pedic mattress.

Early that afternoon, he suggested, "Let's go back to my parents' house and find some bitches in Barnegat Light to pound. Just call the Rule of Ten a draw this year."

"You're only saying that because you know I'm going to win," said Ed, egomaniacal prick.

"You won't win. Believe me, I would love to see her humbled after what she did to my face. But Bella isn't some dumb slag. She's a nice girl."

"Nice girls have pussies, too," said Ed. "The whole point of the game is to bang the tenth girl who walks through the door—even if she's hard to get. And I'm not convinced Bella is so innocent and sweet. She shot you down. But that only means she's got taste."

If Bella had taste, she wouldn't have tattoos or wear motorcycle boots. Or hang out with that Gia, the shark-whispering she-devil. Ben's BMW still stank like pukey corn dogs.

On the table, next to the greasy plastic basket of onion rings, Ben's cell phone vibrated. "Yo," he said into it.

"Dude, she left!" said Ed over the club din.

"Gave you the slip? You ready to call it a draw yet?"

"I do not give up."

"You've got tonight," said Ben. Technically, Ed's seven days had already passed. But Ed insisted on giving Bella some time to resurface after the hot-tub incident before his seven days of seduction officially started.

Ed's voice came in more clearly. He'd left the club and sounded as if he was on the street. "Change in strategy. I pushed it too far. She felt ignored. So now I apologize for playing her, tell her I'm a scum-sucking asswipe. I've taken it to this level before. As soon as I admit I was a jerk, she'll let me into her hotel room. Once I'm in, I am *in*, dog."

Ben shook his head. "No video in her room."

"Do you accept audio confirmation?"

"You'll have to get her to confirm fuckage out loud. As in, 'This is Bella Rizzoli, and I am having sex with Ed Caldwell at this very second.'"

"I'll call you back."

While he waited, Ben tried to get the attention of a couple of shwores in bikini tops and shorts so skimpy, the pocket lining hung down lower on their thighs than the hem.

Ben ambled over, Mr. Cool, and asked, "You sure

you're old enough to drink that?" pointing at their beers.

"Yuck, what's wrong with your face?" asked one.

"He got hit repeatedly with the ugly stick," said the other.

The phone vibrated in his pocket. "Excuse me. That must be my stockbroker. I wonder how much richer I am now?"

The girls rolled their eyes. "That line is so 2008," said red-bandanna top. "It's a recession, dumbass."

Ben frowned. He would have to update his patter. "Hello?" he asked into the phone.

No one spoke, but he could hear voices. It was a bit muffled. Ed called him and left the phone in his pocket? Ben returned to his corner table, cupped his hand over the other ear. He could hear well enough to make out the conversation.

Ed said, "You left the club! Why'd you go?"

"I'm surprised you noticed."

Pause. "I'm an idiot, Bella."

Got that right.

"Can I come in?"

"No."

"Please, Bella! I'm a moron. You should hate me. You should spit on me. Kick my ass, right now. I deserved it."

Ben heard a banging sound. Ed said, "Stupid, stupid, stupid." Was he hitting his head on the wall?

Bella said, "Stop that, seriously. You might crack the plaster and then I'll have to pay for it. Just . . . are you crying? Oh, shit. Get a grip, okay? You can come in for one minute. But then I'm going to bed. Alone."

"I'm so embarrassed!"

The sound of a door closing, some movement. Bella said, "Here."

"Water? Got any beer?"

"It's water or nothing."

Rustling, a squeak. "I hope you don't mind if I sit down on the bed for second," said Ed. "I think I hurt myself."

"Your forehead is all red. Let me get some ice."

A clacking sound, then another squeak. From what Bender could discern, Ed and Bella were sitting next to each other on her bed.

Jesus CHRIST, he's good, thought Bender, resigned to losing the Rule of Ten this summer. It was just a matter of time before Ed had her naked.

"I wasn't very nice at Karma just now," said Ed. "It's pathetic. I have no dignity at all. I read a book on how to pick up girls, and I'm stuck in this pattern. It's the only way I know how. I pretend to be a coldhearted prick, but I'm just an ordinary, average guy who has tremendous respect for women."

Ben was in awe. What a speech! She'd never buy it.

"You should just be yourself," she said. "Hold still, this is cold."

Ben had to cup his mouth or blurt, "Damn!" Bella was either the most gullible or the most trusting girl in Jersey. Either way, Ed would jump on that, literally *and* figuratively.

Ed said, "That's sweet of you to say, but I don't

need your pity. I'm a loser. No girls will ever want me for me. You, for example, would never kiss a guy like me. Admit it."

"I would, totally!"

"Prove it."

Ben braced for what he'd hear next. Kissing, undressing, moaning, groaning, sexy noise that would force him out of the corner and into the bathroom for privacy.

But the next sound he heard was not smooching. It was the door slamming open, and another voice screaming, "Bella! I just had the greatest . . . What's going on in here? You!"

Ed said, "Oh, shit."

Gia said, "Bella, you can't be serious. I won't let this happen. No. Just, *no*. Get out of here now."

Bella said, "Wait, Gia, he's upset."

"He's upset, all right—that I'm here now to save you from making a disgusting mistake."

"You're calling *me* disgusting?" asked Ed. "You're the one who stinks like"—deep sniffing sound—"fresh piss?"

"If you're not out of here in ten seconds, I'm going to scream."

"Go ahead."

The scream made the phone shake. Ben instinctively yanked it back, but his eardrum felt punctured. The screaming went on for ten seconds, until Ben heard Ed said, "Stop! Okay, I'm leaving."

The door slammed. Footsteps echoed in a hallway.

Ed came back on the phone. "Dude? You there?"

"I wish I had that epic fail on video," said Bender. "Your week is officially over."

Ed agreed. "Now she's up for grabs. First guy to bang Bella wins."

Chapter Twenty-eight

The Jell-O Shot Caper

Janey Gordon shook her vial of pills, not liking the paltry plinking one bit. She was down to just three 10 mg Ritalin, with no refills left. It was getting harder and harder to convince her doctor to dole out prescriptions for Ritalin—which, in her vast experience, was the finest appetite suppressant out there.

Just looking at the three lonely little white pills, Janey panicked. For her, panic manifested itself in an extreme craving for a bacon cheeseburger with extracrispy fries and a cherry Coke.

She had a few choices: (1) Fight the panic on her own, (2) take one of the pills to kill her appetite, or (3) leave her post at the reservation desk at Lorenzo's restaurant, sneak into the kitchen, and get Raul to build her a burger, then inhale it.

She remembered one of her shrinks telling her that craving food didn't necessarily mean she was bored, weak, fat, anxious, stressed, upset, insecure, or crazy. "Sometimes," said Dr. Hamilton, "craving a cheeseburger means you're hungry."

Ha! Janey could stare down any hunger monster. She'd trained herself to squash those hollow, empty feelings until she *almost* fainted. Then she'd eat a peanut or a grape or a hard-boiled egg. She kept a bowl of hard-boiled eggs in her fridge at home for emergencies. One bad night, when she slipped, Janey ate a dozen of them.

Fortunately, they didn't stay down for long.

That experience had been so unpleasant, she vowed not to let it happen again. Dr. Hamilton refused to prescribe her any kind of appetite suppressant or fen-phen since Janey was, officially, underweight. So she studied up on ADD symptoms, went to a different shrink, and got herself some Ritalin. Ten or 20 mg taken before mealtime pretty much killed her desire to have the meal at all.

Cheeseburgers flew in and out of her field of vision—both real, on plates carried by waiters, and imaginary. Janey slipped a pill between her lips, took a sip of her seltzer with lime, and waited for the hunger to stop.

She needed to stay alert. Tonight, after years of resentment during high school and a rebirth of hatred since the unwelcome return, Janey and Linda were going to get their revenge on Giovanna Spumanti.

———

Linda—along with her human pet, Rocky—arrived at Lorenzo's right on time, a few minutes before closing.

"Do you have the stuff?" asked Linda.

Janey frowned. She handed the vial to Linda, who looked inside. "What the hell, Janey? Only one?"

"I couldn't help myself. But don't worry! I have a better idea. Come with me."

She led Linda and Rocky through the tables and into the restaurant's kitchen. Unlike fancy new restaurant kitchens like you see on TV cooking shows, Lorenzo's kitchen was cramped and rusty with one huge grill for burgers (90 percent of what was served), a deep fryer, a double sink, dishwashing spray machine, and an oven with thirty years of hardened grease holding it together. The prep station was just a cutting board on a platform with two Mexicans behind it, chopping onions.

Yes, New Jersey's "America's Best Burgers, like grandma used to make," were actually made by Raul and Pedro, who barely spoke English. So, unless your grandma was from Tijuana, the slogan was a bit misleading.

Janey didn't care about that. Or the quality of the food, or pretty much anything except looking hot, meeting rich guys, and getting revenge on anyone, anytime, anywhere, who didn't show her the proper respect. Including orange midget Gia Spumanti.

"Keep going back." Janey led Linda and Rocky to the freezer room. "In here," she said, opening the door.

"This is where you'd hide a body," said Rocky. "Like in a movie."

"Shut up, idiot," said Linda. "Why are we here? The plan was to put a few Ritalin in Gia's drink, she'll go crazy, we get some footage of her looking like the fat, wasted slut she is, post it as a video reply on her YouTube page, humiliating her forever all over the world."

Janey had agreed to the plan, but she was loath to part with even one of her precious Righties (as she called her Ritalin). She pulled a tray of little plastic cups off a shelf. Usually, they were for ketchup or mayo. But Janey had prepared her own special cup concoction during a lull tonight.

"Jell-O shots?" asked Linda, poking at the blue, wiggly surface of the gelatin inside.

"Cool," said Rocky, reaching for one.

"Don't!" warned Janey. "Two of them were made special for Gia."

"What's in there?" asked Linda.

"Suspended in each shot of Jell-O are four Dulco-lax pills. They're so small, Gia won't see them. And if she does it the right way, basically shooting it down her throat in a gulp, which you know she will, she won't taste them either."

"Dulcolax," said Linda. "A laxative."

"The very best," said Janey. "Fastest, most thorough. I should know."

She should. Janey had been experimenting with laxatives since her days as a preteen bulimic.

Linda nodded, liking it. "Gia will expect us to do

the shots with her. What if one of us takes the spiked one by mistake?"

"Won't happen," said Janey.

"How can you be sure?"

"There are six shots total. Two are spiked. I marked them on the bottom. I will personally feed the marked shots directly into her mouth. She'd probably do all six shots if we give her the chance."

Linda laughed. "You are so right. Okay, I like the change of plan. We have to get her early in the night, so when the urge hits, the bar will be packed with an endless bathroom line. She'll poo herself—hopefully, in public! I'm picturing precious Gia buried under a mountain of her own shit!"

Janey nodded. "It'll stink, getting video."

"A small sacrifice," said Linda. "My only reservation is that Gia will crap out calories. I hate to help her lose weight. Although, God knows she needs it."

"No plan is perfect."

"Why are we doing this again?" asked Rocky.

"Shut up, idiot," said Linda. "This has nothing to do with you. Giovanna Spumanti was a total bitch in high school. She stole boyfriends, backstabbed her friends. She was oblivious to how mean she was. And now, she'd going to pay."

"You guys backstab your friends all the time," said Rocky.

Linda sighed. "Why do you bother opening your mouth to speak? Leave the talking and thinking to people who actually have brains."

Chapter Twenty-nine

Code Brown

Gia puckered and blotted her lip gloss. The lighting in the hotel room was pretty bad. She could only hope her eyeliner was even. "I'm going to the bar. You coming?" she asked Bella. Al Fresco had begged Gia to return for another "appearance" tonight at the Inca Bar. More free drinks, fans, and fun.

Only Bella was being a dud pud. She lay on her bed, motionless. She said she was exhausted from leading five classes at the gym today. But Gia suspected Bella wasn't run-down as much as beat down, emotionally.

"You can't possibly be upset about that jerkoff Ed," said Gia. "Did you really want him? Honestly? Seriously? Or were you taking pity on him? No pity fuck goes unpunished, Bella."

"That's not what happened. You don't know as much as you think you do."

Gia was pretty sure she had that situation sized up. "Where's Tony tonight?"

"I don't know. He's not talking to me," said Bella, face squashed on the pillow.

"You did throw a beer at his face. When the bottle hits your forehead? Ouch."

"The only men I attract are date rapers and douche bags," whined Bella. "Tony liked me, and what did I do? Scared him away. I'm sabotaging myself. Maybe this means I should get back with Bobby."

Gia groaned. "You can't mean that. You've been single for a few months, and you're ready to run back to a stalker? I've been single for years. Sorting through jerkoffs to find a decent man takes time. But you have to do it, or else become a lesbian. Don't think I haven't considered it myself." Gia had done more than think about switching teams. But when she'd made out with girls, something was always missing. Something hard, jabbing her in the leg.

What could she say? Gia loved penises. She couldn't go through life without them. If only penises weren't attached to their jerkoff hosts, the world would be a better place.

"One drink," said Gia.

"I'll meet you later. You don't need me, anyway. Your fans will keep your company."

Yeah, Gia was a YouTube sensation. True, she had fans. And a boyfriend, too. Frankie had called the salon three times today, and Gia screamed with joy each time, frightening the customers.

But Bella was family. "I'm not leaving you in this depressed state."

"Go. I want to be alone for a while."

"I'm checking on you in one hour. That's when alone time officially ends."

Bella nodded. One last spritz of Fantasy (okay, three) from her travel atomizer, and Gia left the room.

———

By the cold light of day, the Inca Bar looked grubby and faded, with a sticky coating of twenty years of spilled beer, sand, and salt. You wouldn't want to eat there. But at night? The place got better-looking with each drink.

Gia was just hitting the bar for her first vodka cranberry of the night when she heard her name.

"Giovanna! Hey! We've been waiting for you," said Linda Patterson. She was nicely dressed, Gia had to admit, in a gold lamé monokini, hip-hugger swing skirt, and white go-go boots.

Next to her at the bar stood superskinny Janey Gordon, in a slinky black tube dress. "You look amazing, Gia! You're so freakin' hot. I'm, like, a fat hog compared to you," said the former alleged teen model.

Accepting double-cheek air kisses from both girls, Gia said, "I thought you guys hated me."

Linda and Janey started babbling, talking over each other. "Why would you think that? . . . We love you! . . . That YouTube video was mad cool!"

What, now that Gia was famous, her sworn fren-emies wanted to make amends? *Meh, why not?* she thought. Gia would share the spotlight with Linda and Janey for a few minutes. She prided herself on being a forgiving, loving person. Basically, the nicest bitch on the block.

Gia said, "Thanks. I'm glad you came down to see me."

Linda said, "Can we buy you a shot?"

"At least one!"

Janey nodded to the bartender, who produced a tray of Jell-O shots. Gia wasn't such a big fan. She hated that slithery slide in the back of her throat. Sniffing the cup Linda held out for her, she asked, "What's in these?"

"SoCo," said Linda. "Used to be your favorite be-fore cheering big games."

Gia smiled. She remembered. "Down the hatch!" She made a face after the blob of booze and gelatin slid down her throat. It was icky, but the quickest way to get trashed.

"More?" asked Janey.

"Just one," said Gia, slurping down another cup. Linda and Janey watched her intensely, almost studying her. It was kind of weird. "These aren't all for me?" she asked of the remaining shots.

"I'll do one." Linda examined the shot closely be-fore downing it. Janey did, too.

Then the three women smiled blandly at each other. Not a lot to say. Gia's eyes wandered. "Is that Rocky over there?"

Linda looked to where Gia was pointing. Over by the DJ riser, danced Rocky. Gia remembered how good a dancer he was from the night they met. He was a good kisser, too.

"Dumb as a bucket of sand," said Linda. "But Rocky knows how to move."

Rocky was grinding with three girls, each of them rubbing against him fast enough to start a fire. "You're not jealous?" asked Gia. When she'd danced with Rocky at Karma, Linda threw her on the ground.

"He can dance with ten girls, I don't care. But when he's with just one? I see red."

Gia laughed. "I totally get that."

She and Linda shared a smile. Gia pulled her two former classmates into a spontaneous group hug. "I love you guys," she said. "I'm so sorry if we fought in high school. Honestly? I don't remember what I did to make you hate me so much, but that's no excuse. I was a brat, and out of it for most of senior year with my parents' divorce. I'm just glad we can put the past behind us."

Linda and Janey hugged back weakly. To Gia, it was like squeezing two bundles of dry kindling.

When that was done, the odd, awkward feeling came back. The vibe went from cool to frosty in two minutes. This was all too strange to deal with before the shots took effect.

Gia said, "Okay, see you around. The hotel manager likes it when I circulate. You guys should come to Tantastic. I'll spray you for free. Seriously."

"We'll run right over," said Linda.

Janey said, "First chance."

As Gia walked away, she wondered if she was hearing things. Was there a snicker in their voices at the end? Oh, well, she drank with them and apologized for whatever she might have done, not that she had any memory of it. *You try to be a good person,* thought Gia, *and sometimes you got kicked in the teeth for it.*

———

A few hours later, Gia and Bella were dancing on the DJ riser. The crowd below moved like a multilimbed beast, jumping up and down, beating up the beat, totally in sync with each other, the music, the moment. Gia was used to being on the dance floor, at eye level with hundreds of collarbones. Seeing the room from above was fresh to death.

Gia screamed over the thundering music to Bella, "Glad you came down?"

Bella, in her red, crocheted bikini top, nodded. "Beats moping in the room."

"Word." Gia would always rather go out. Even sick, or injured, or tired. For the last few minutes, she'd been getting some stomach cramps, though. What was that about? Bad sushi at lunch?

The volume came down, and the DJ spoke into the mike. "A minute of your time, people! My spin philosophy is 'crank, don't wank,' so I'll get right back to the music in a sec. I want to remind you all that the five-dollar drink special tonight is the Piranha Pulp—vodka, cranberry, grenadine, and crushed cherries. Also, if you get the munchies, the Shore Shack next door is open twenty-four-seven. One last thing: A special friend to the Inca is in the house tonight. Hey, Gia! Get your buns over here."

Yay! Gia clapped her hands together and ran over to the DJ. It was one of her fantasies, to get a shout-out at a club. "Hello, Seaside!" she yelled into the mike.

The crowd chanted, "Go, Shark Girl! Go, Shark Girl!"

Gia danced around a little, shaking her peaches for show. She shook it hard. Too hard. In the middle of a shimmy, her stomach cramped. A fart slipped out. A loud one. And stinky.

The DJ said, "Whoa, girl, what'd you eat?"

Oh, jeez. Another one threatened to escape. The devil had possessed her guts! Had the microphone picked up her fart? Gia was hit by another major gut twist. She glanced at Bella. Her eyes must have been desperate.

"Are you okay?" asked Bella.

Gia needed a bathroom, *now!!* She could see the ladies' room door all the way on the other side of the dance floor. It might as well be a million miles away through the tightly pressed crowd. Meanwhile, they were still chanting, "Go, Shark Girl."

Go, Shark Girl. They got that right. Any second, she was going to "go" all over the stage.

To Bella, she whispered, "What's the quickest way to get from here to the bathroom?"

"Flying?" suggested Bella.

Into the DJ's microphone, Gia said, "Get ready, people! Here I come!"

She backed up a few paces, then went for it. She ran in heels to the edge of the riser, then jumped off, arms out like Supergirl.

The crowd cheered and caught her, passing her along on the river of their hands. She kept screaming, "That way! That way!" pointing toward the bathrooms in the back, but no one could hear her.

Meanwhile, like ten guys grabbed her boobies. If she weren't about to paint the room brown, she would've loved it. A few grabbed at her butt, too. "Not the ass!" A too tight squeeze and she might explode.

About halfway across the dance floor, she was lowered to her heels. She pushed and shoved to gain an inch, but was stuck. Four or five hot, half-naked guidos surrounded her, fist-pumping and grinding into her.

"Waa!" she cried. Any other time in her life, she'd be in heaven. But this was her ultimate fantasy and worst nightmare rolled into one sweaty mess. Oh, God. She wasn't going to make it. . . .

Suddenly, she was lifted off her feet by . . . Rocky!

"Help!" she said. "Get me to the bathroom. Hurry!"

Like a cannonball, Rocky busted through the crowd, knocking people out of the way. "Emergency!" he shouted.

They got to the bathrooms not a second too

soon. He let her down by the line for the ladies' room—long, of course, with a dozen women holding in gallons of margaritas.

The men's room? No line at all. Gia said, "Rocky, cover me. I'm going in."

She punched open the men's room door. Five guys at the urinals barely had a chance to zip before Rocky yelled, "Move it or lose it!" Once the men's room was cleared out, Rocky locked the door from the inside.

Gia crashed into a stall, the door clattering on its hinges. The second she sat down, her insides turned themselves out. The relief, after holding it for all that time, made her scream, "Yes! Yes! Oh, God, that's good."

"You okay in there?"

"Thank God. Rocky, you're my hero. You're the best."

When she was done, Gia stood up, wobbly from the effort, and crashed out of the stall. Only then did Gia notice how gross the bathroom was. Stained porcelain urinals, rust on the mirror, paper towels balled up on the floor and sink. Ick. She quickly washed her hands, then gave Rocky the nod to open the door.

"Oh, wait!" she said, spritzing Fantasy around the room. "Don't want anyone to think someone died in here."

He unlocked the door and let her walk out first.

Two dozen guys backed away from the door as if they'd been eavesdropping on the action inside.

When Rocky emerged, they applauded and broke into a chant. "Go, Rocky! Go, Rocky!"

Rocky bowed and accepted high fives and chest bumps.

Bella rushed to Gia's side. "Did you just smush with Rocky in there?"

Gia blinked. "No!"

"You were screaming his name! Everyone heard."

So much for the new truce with Linda. "I just shit my brains out, I can't think." Her guts wrenched again. Grabbing her stomach, Gia said, "Oh, shit! Literally! Get me to the room!"

Chapter Thirty

Blame Sushi

Listening to someone's explosive diarrhea for five hours? Not on Bella's list of her favorite night-time activities. It was four in the morning. *Gia must have crapped her weight by now,* thought Bella.

The toilet flushed, again. Gia emerged, red cheeks under her tan. "This would be much worse, sober. Hand to God, I am never, ever, under threat of death, eating sushi again."

"Any chance we can go to sleep now?"

Gia picked up Bella's annoyance. "I'm sorry I got food poisoning. This is not my fault."

Bella had heard that before. Nothing was ever Gia's fault. Not getting sick. Not burning down the beach house. Not ruining her date with Ed, and her July Fourth date with Bender (although she was grateful in hindsight about that). Gia tripped through life blameless. Her parents' divorce? Nothing to do with her. Dropping out of college? It wasn't her fault school was expensive. Her lost phone? It must have crawled away on its own. Gia's constant costly accidents when she worked at Rizzoli's Deli? She couldn't be expected to operate machinery. She was born with butterfingers and was a magnet for disaster, a one-woman wrecking ball. Bella had heard too many excuses, too many times.

"You seem really pissed off at me," said Gia.

"Just go to sleep."

"If you have something to say, then say it." Gia was stripping out of her club clothes and rummaging in her drawers for a T-shirt to sleep in.

"Nothing. I'm just tired."

"Check this out," said Gia, finding the envelope addressed to Shark Girl on the dresser. "I forgot all about this. My first piece of fan mail."

Bella, facedown on the bed, said, "Yippee for you."

"Wanna hear it?"

"If we can go to sleep afterwards."

Gia opened the envelope and started reading. " 'Dear Bella' . . . hey, this isn't for me. It's to you. 'Dear Bella: I'm so sorry about what happened between us. I was just so in love with you, I couldn't control myself.'"

Bella sat up. "It's from Bender?"

Gia scanned down to the end. " 'All the best, Ben.' Why is it addressed to me? He probably gave it to the front desk and said, 'Send it to Shark Girl's room for Bella.'"

Snorting, Bella thought, *As usual, I'm the afterthought.*

Gia said, "Want me to keep reading?"

"I'll take it," said Bella, reaching for the letter.

But Gia kept going anyway " 'I was really touched when you shared your heart with me, especially when you confided in me all the issues you have with . . . your cousin Gia. I just hope you can forgive me one day and don't hate me too much.' "

Bella sat up as if a bucket of cold water were thrown on her.

Gia stared at her, crumpling the note in her tiny fist. "You talked shit about me to Bender?"

"No!" Had she? If so, it was nervous chatter. Filling the conversation void before drinks arrived.

"What did you tell him? What are your *issues* with me?"

Too many to count. Too horrible to mention. "Let's talk about it in the morning." They both needed sleep, badly.

Her pint-size cousin seemed to grow large before her eyes. "I've got a few issues with you, Bells. How you don't trust me or respect me. You accused me of lying about Bender and Ed, the mean things they said to me. And I can't believe you would talk shit about me to Bender! If you have something to say to me—to anyone!—then say it."

"Okay, you want to do this? Let's go. I do have some issues with you, Gia. You're blameless, about every shitty thing that happens to you. Okay, it's not your fault that Bender tried to rape me. But it is your fault, Gia, that you lost your friggin' phone. It's your fault I was soaking wet, stranded on the street after I'd just fought for my life, and I couldn't reach you! I was totally alone out there, and scared, and I couldn't reach you."

Gia watched Bella with round eyes and a tiny round *O* mouth. "I'm sorry, Bells. I felt horrible . . ."

"Not only are you blameless, you're helpless, too! It's like how you love to be scooped up and carried by big strong guys. You want people to carry you! Do you not see the metaphor there? You have to carry your own friggin' weight in life, Gia. You can't expect your mom, or your dad, or me, or your next boyfriend, to take care of you. Man up, Gia! You're twenty-one years old. A bona fide adult, no matter how short you are. Act like it."

Breathless, Bella looked at Gia and saw that she'd crossed a line. She regretted the "short" remark. But the blameless, helpless stuff? "Someone needed to say it. I'm sorry to lay it on you now, at four in the morning after you've been sick. But I'm glad it's out there."

"How long were you holding that in?"

"Awhile."

"Since we came down the Shore?"

"Longer."

"Since Mom and I moved to Brooklyn?"

Bella sighed. "I guess, yeah."

"You've been secretly pissed at me for three years?"

Bella nodded, realizing how pathetic that sounded.

"If you loved me, you would have said something sooner. When I have a problem with you, Bells, I tell you. The fact that you didn't? Further proof that you don't trust me. You don't respect me. And if that's the case," said Gia, getting angrier with each word, "we have nothing. We are done. You're not my family. Family doesn't kick you when you're down." Gia crawled under the covers of her bed. "I can't believe you said 'short.' Not cool, Bella. Don't talk to me, ever again." Then Gia pulled the blanket over her head.

Bella pulled the covers over her head, too. If she thought she'd feel better to unburden herself to Gia, she was dead wrong. Bella felt guilty, dirty, coated in grime, as if she'd slept in a Dumpster.

Airing your grievances was a selfish act, she decided. But what was done, was done. Some things couldn't be unsaid. Now, she'd have to deal with the new reality: Gia hated her. Her best, oldest friendship was over.

Chapter Thirty-one

Broken Dawn

Hello? Open up! Management! Hello?"

The knocking on the hotel room door was like a mosquito in her ear, annoying and persistent. "Okay, I'm coming," grumbled Gia.

She threw back the covers and got up. Glancing in the mirror, she got a fright. Ewww, hair matted, makeup smeared. Disturbing. Whoever woke her up was about to get the shock of his life.

"You asked for it," she said, turning the lock, pulling the door open.

Al Fresco had seen worse, apparently. He barely reacted to the sight of her. He was already upset. "You have one hour to pack your things and leave the hotel."

What? "It's dawn," said Gia.

"It's ten o'clock," he corrected.

Bella was awake now, too, and took charge, as usual. "Is there a problem?"

"Is there a . . . I'll tell you what the problem is," he said with a forced hush. Al stepped into the room and shut the door. Pointing at the floor, he said, "Complaints from the room downstairs about rattling plumbing all night long." He pointed to the side. "Complaints from the rooms on the left and on the right about screaming at four a.m." Index finger aimed at the ceiling, he added, "Complaints from the room above about banging. I won't stand for it. You're bothering my guests. I want you out."

"It's not my fault your plumbing sucks!" said Gia. Shamed, she remembered what Bella had said last night, about how she was always "blameless." But she was! In this case, loud pipes and bad sushi were not her fault! But she didn't dare defend herself further. That would just prove Bella right.

Al didn't want to hear it. "You know why I got into the hotel business? Because every time I traveled, there was always some rude, loud, obnoxious jerk in the room next to mine. I'd lie there all night, furious, and swore to myself that if I ever opened a hotel, it'd be a clean, pleasant, *quiet* place to sleep."

"You call this place clean?" asked Bella. "The mold in the bathroom has thicker hair than I do. The sand on the floor is absolutely pristine! The rusty radiator, the leaky shower, and peeling paint . . ."

Gia added, "Not to mention the fact that you have a loud bar and a DJ spinning right next door."

"The bar is separate!" ranted Al, but softly. "The DJ is separate! I've been gracious enough to allow you to stay in my hotel for free, as a special favor to

Stan Crumbi. But if you insult my hotel, you insult me. You're out of here. Now."

"You just said we had an hour," said Gia.

"I take it back," he huffed. "Five minutes, and then I'm calling the cops."

He left, closed the door with all the gentle hostility he could muster, as not to disturb his clean, quiet guests. Gia screamed at the top of her sleepy lungs, "*Fuck!*"

Bella said, "Enough. I'm going back to Brooklyn. I'll get the rest of my stuff at the beach house and drive back to the city."

"The Honda won't start," reminded Gia.

"I'll take the bus."

In a rush, Gia remembered every cruel comment Bella had made to her last night. The anger rose in her chest all over again, and she said, "Good riddance," and started cramming her clothes into her pink laundry bag to carry back to Kearney Avenue.

Obviously, Gia didn't need Bella to have fun at the Shore. She'd have *more* fun without that backstabber whining in bed all night long. Gia still had Maria. Linda and Janey were cool to her last night. And there was Frankie, of course. In fact, Bella's leaving was the *best* news she'd ever heard. Gia would have the whole beach house to herself.

Shouldering her laundry bag and giraffe, Gia left the hotel. Bella was behind her and kept fifty feet back. The walk was only four blocks, but it took half an hour. Gia had to stop and rest often. Her bag was heavy. And she wasn't used to hauling things. Bella plowed past her without even asking if Gia was okay. Bitch.

The outside of the house looks different, she thought when she finally got to the driveway. *Something's missing.* But what?

Bella was sitting on top of her suitcase by the back door, waiting for Gia. "The door's locked. Front door, too. You have a key, or did you lose that, too?"

Gia said, "Yes, I have a key."

"Well? Where is it?"

"It's right where it should be. On top of the . . . dresser. Inside."

Bella gave her a smug, shit-eating "My point, exactly" grin.

"Where's your key?" asked Gia.

Bella sighed. "I gave it to you, after you lost your original key."

"Oh. Yeah."

"Yeah."

Gia's blood pressure went up. "Call Stanley."

Fifteen minutes later, during which time the cousins sat on opposite sides of the driveway with their stuff, Stanley arrived in the Cutlass—wearing his usual baggy party shirt and faded, shiny gray trousers.

At least his comb-over hadn't grown back.

He got out of the car slowly, sorting through a ring with a hundred keys on it. "You two look like shit," he said, finding the right one and inserting it in the lock.

"What happened to your new clothes?" asked Gia. "Where's Stan the Man?"

"Stan the Man broke out in hives. I got a rash all over my entire body from the mall clothes. You wanna see?" He went to unzip his pants.

"No!" said Gia. "Keep your rash to yourself."

Bella said, "Can we go in now, please?"

Stan gave Gia a questioning look. "What's with her?"

"Forget about it," said Gia.

"You mean *fuggedaboutit*?"

As soon as he opened the door, Bella ran up to her room and slammed her door. Gia took a look around. The renovated kitchen was half-done. A new oven and stove sat in the middle of the room, not yet installed. The walls were primed white, with a few stripes of test colors, all shades of pale pink. Without curtains, the sunlight flooded in, the ocean twinkling in the distance. For a dump, the place sure felt like home.

"Stanley, have you seen Maria?" asked Gia. It'd been a couple of days since their shopping expedition.

"I showed up at her apartment . . ."

"When she was in the shower?"

"She lives in the friggin' shower!"

"What happened?"

"She laughed at my jeans and sneakers. Told me to act my age."

"I'm so sorry!"

He shook his head. "Not your fault. I know you meant well. Screw Maria. I cut my hair for her! If she doesn't want me, I don't want her."

Gia felt horrible. "I don't get it. Maria said she wanted a car, so you offer a car. Then she said she wanted a younger-looking man. And then tells you to act your age."

Stanley threw up his hands. "If you women don't understand each other, then we're all doomed."

"Aren't you pissed off?"

"You tried, kid. So what now, for you? Your rent is paid until the end of the month. If you don't mind living in a construction site with no kitchen, you can stay."

"Got any other ex-wives you want to get back in with? Maybe I can help with them."

He scoffed, sat down on the make-out couch, and started barking into his cell as if he owned the place. Which, actually, he did.

Gia dragged her laundry bag up the stairs to her room and dropped it on the floor. She found the key right where it was supposed to be.

Thinking it would make a point (not sure what), she grabbed it and stomped into Bella's room. "See?" Gia said, holding it up.

The sight of Bells packing the rest of her stuff, one bikini at a time, dulled Gia's anger. She fought a strong urge to beg Bella to stay.

"If by some miracle, the Honda starts," said Bella, zipping her suitcase, "I'll drive it to the bus station and leave it there for you. I don't need it in the city as much as you do down here."

"That's stupid. It's your car."

"Are *you* calling *me* stupid?"

Short, blameless, helpless, and now Bella was calling her stupid? This was how a best friendship dissolved faster than Alka-Seltzer. Gia was struck by the cynical epiphany that nearly any relationship, such as her parents', such as hers with Bella, was susceptible to sudden death. How freakin' sad was that?

Then she heard a bouncy beat.

Gia recognized that sound. It was her Deadmau5 ringtone. "My phone!" she sang. Following the sound, Gia found her cell in the bathroom medicine cabinet, right between her Paul Mitchell hair spray and her St. Tropez bronzer.

Like the keys, her phone wasn't really *lost,* per se. Just put somewhere she didn't remember. "Hello?" she answered.

"Gia, it's Frankie."

Yay! Someone who cared. "Hi! How's it going? I'm so glad you called. You don't even know."

"What happened with you and Rocky Gato last night? Ten people called me today, saying you hooked up with him in the men's room at the Inca."

"Not true, at all."

"Ten different people are lying to me?"

Gia couldn't believe this was happening. She found her phone only to be accused of a crime she didn't commit, by the first guy in forever she thought she could fall in love with. "I swear, Frankie."

"He didn't carry you into the men's room, kick everyone out, and lock the door?"

She stammered, "But . . . but . . ."

"And you didn't scream, 'Rocky, you're the best'?"

"It's not what you think." It was far more embarrassing than that. Gia didn't want to get into all the nasty details, especially to Frankie. They kind of shook the sexy off. "I'm asking you to trust me. Regardless of what you heard, nothing happened."

After a few beats, he said, "I don't own you, Gia. You have every right to do whatever you want, with whoever. After one date, I can't expect you to act like you're my girl. But I really opened up to you. I told you some sensitive stuff, about my brother and Dina. And then you get wasted and wind up in a men's room with another guy one night later? If that's the kind of girl you are, I'm not interested."

Then he hung up. She stared at the phone, stunned. The ground was crumbling beneath her feet.

"Gia! Come outside, quick!" It was Bella, calling her from the street, panic in her voice.

Taking the stairs two at a time, Gia found Bells standing in the driveway, next to her suitcases.

"What now?" asked Gia.

Bells's face was white. "Where's the Honda?"

Something clicked in Gia's brain, and she realized what she was missing when they'd first arrived. "It was right here!" she said, pointing at the grease spot on the pavement.

"It's gone," said Bella, stating the friggin' obvious.

Gia blinked at the place where Bella's car should be and started shaking all over. They were robbed! She felt sick to her stomach.

Drawn by the commotion, Stanley wandered outside. "Wassup?"

"Did you move the Honda?" Gia asked.

He seemed confused. "I thought you did. I noticed it was gone a couple of days ago."

Bells sat down on a suitcase. She looked as defeated as Gia felt.

But just when things were at their darkest, a pinpoint of light appeared.

A blue sedan cruised down the street and pulled into the driveway, right where the Honda should be. Two women stepped out of it, both squinting in the Jersey July sunshine. One of them smiled at Gia and waved.

"Mommy!" Gia cried, and ran into Alicia Spumanti's open arms.

Chapter Thirty-two

Welcome to New Jersey, the Olive Garden State

Not five minutes ago, Bella had been in her room, furiously packing, missing her mom so badly, her heart actually *hurt*. Now, as if she'd conjured Marissa Rizzoli out of thin air, she was here and walking toward Bella with her arms out.

Meanwhile, Gia and Aunt Alicia were hugging in the driveway as if it'd been two and a half years, not weeks, since they'd last seen each other.

Aunt Alicia was crying. Gia was crying. "Why didn't you return my calls?" asked Alicia.

Gia said, "I lost my phone!"

"You lose everything! Better be careful, or you might lose your virginity," said Alicia, which made them both snort with laughter.

Marissa gathered Bella into her arms and stroked her hair. Bella sank into her softness and said, "I missed you."

"I miss you, too," said Marissa, breaking the hug to hold her daughter at arm's length to get a look at her. "You lost weight. What are you eating?"

Bella said, "I want to come home. I've made my decision. You and Dad were right. College makes no sense. Why get into debt up to my armpits? I'm coming home and committing to Rizzoli's. Dad can rest easy. I'll take over the family business."

Bella assumed Mom would be thrilled to hear it. Marissa surprised her by saying, "Let's talk about this, Bella."

"Ahem. Aren't you gonna introduce me?" asked Stanley, rocking on his heels, hands in his pants pockets, creepy smile on his face. "These lovely ladies must be your older sisters."

"Stanley, you dog," Gia said, then made introductions. "Mom, Aunt Mari, this is our landlord, Stanley Crumbi. He's been supersweet to us, even when I burned his kitchen down."

Aunt Alicia's eyes got big, just like Gia's, and she looked like a slightly older, slightly taller version. "You *what*?"

"It wasn't my . . . it was an accident," said Gia, glaring at Bells.

Stanley shook Alicia's hand and said, "Welcome to Seaside Heights. Handsome-bachelor capital of New Jersey."

God help her, Aunt Alicia giggled.

Stanley turned to Marissa and said, "And you're Bella's mama?" The family resemblance was obvious, although Marissa was heavyset compared to Bella.

After decades in the deli's kitchen, Marissa's extra weight was inevitable. The roundness looked good on her, besides.

"I'm Marissa Rizzoli, hello," she said flatly to Stanley. No giggling and flirting from her. Alicia and Marissa were sisters, but they couldn't be more different. Sort of like Gia and Bella. Marissa was a classic older child, responsible, a planner. Alicia, like Gia, seemed blown through life by the winds of luck and fate.

"What brings you to the Shore?" he said.

"We haven't heard from our babies," replied Alicia. "So we decided to drive down for the day. Check on the girls, see the ocean."

"I rescued a shark," said Gia as if she'd gotten an A on a math test.

"You did?" said Alicia. "Tell me about it."

The two of them went into the house, arms around each other's shoulders.

Stanley shuffled on his feet. He clearly wanted to follow them inside, but knew it was inappropriate. "Anyway, business calls." He held up his phone, got in his Cutlass, and took off.

Which left Bella and her mom in the driveway, with the Camry rental, Bella's suitcases, and a weird vibe between them.

"You don't want me to come home?" asked Bella. "I thought you'd be happy."

Marissa frowned. "Let's take a drive."

"Where?"

"Give me a tour of Seaside Heights." Mom

glanced up the block. "Where's the Honda, by the way?"

———

That old impulse to earn Mom's approval had Bella steer the Camry toward the 24 Hour Fitness. She wanted to show her mom where she worked, how much everyone seemed to like her there.

Except Tony, who hadn't spoken to her in days.

"This is Studio A," she said, giving Marissa a quick look. "I teach a hip-hop dance class here."

One of Tony's clients, a gorilla juicehead named Thor, gave Bella a high five as he thundered by.

"That man is enormous," said Marissa, whispering.

"They grow 'em big in Jersey."

A few women waved at Bella from the treadmills. Bella waved back, feeling in her element. They wandered over to the stationary bikes and took seats.

"You've made a real life for yourself," said Marissa, pulling up her skirt a few inches to pedal.

"It's nothing compared to Brooklyn, though."

"Do you have a boyfriend?"

"Mom!"

"You're not afraid to date, are you? After the mess with Bobby?"

Bella shrugged. "I've met a few guys. Nothing worked out, though. But that's not why I've decided to come home and commit to the deli."

Marissa frowned. "Bella, I need to tell you something important. I didn't drive down here just to spy on you."

She looked grave. Bella got a bad feeling. "Is Dad okay?"

"He's fine. He's great." Marissa took a deep breath. "We got an offer on the deli. A few corporate men came by. They want to buy us out and open an Olive Garden restaurant in the space."

Bella laughed. It was ridiculous! Her parents *hated* Olive Garden. They literally spit whenever they saw an Olive Garden commercial on TV. To them, the chain represented the absolute *worst* of Italian food in America. "Did you spit on them?"

"It's a lot of money," said Marissa. "A lot, a lot."

"How much?"

"Enough for your father and me to retire."

"You're only fifty years old!"

Her mom's eyes flashed. "And we haven't taken a single day's rest in thirty years! We're tired, Bella." Her voice softening, she said, "We want to travel, go to Italy. I've never been. Your father hasn't seen Rome since he was a baby."

"So go on a vacation!" said Bella, her vision of a ready-made future slipping away.

"I understand why you're upset."

"For three years, you've been telling me not to go college so I can run the store. And now you're going to sell out to Olive Garden?"

"Your father thought your going to NYU—the most expensive college in the country, as you well know—was a bad business decision. He's a businessman. That's how he thinks. Now he's making a business decision for us. I'm sorry. I know it seems selfish."

"*Seems*? It is selfish, Mom. Dad sent you down here to do the dirty work? That takes some balls."

"Do *not* speak about your father that way!"

Instantly cowed, Bella muttered, "Sorry."

"We've worked hard, and now we want to enjoy ourselves. You should follow your heart, too. I was always secretly rooting for you to go to college, have a career that was separate from the family business."

"You say that now."

"It's the truth," said Marissa.

"What about Bobby? Until he went crazy, you urged me to stick with him."

"Oh, baby, I just didn't want you to feel alone. I was wrong about that, too."

"I can't believe I'm hearing all this now. Why didn't you tell me how you really felt years ago?" Despite her anger, Bella heard the echo from last night, when Gia accused her of withholding her true feelings. Now that the shoe was on the other foot, Bella understood why Gia was so enraged. "I've wasted three years of my life," said Bella, suddenly realizing the harsh fact.

"That's simply not true. You've grown up, and now you'll be a better student for it. Now, tell me the truth. You don't really want to come home. Something happened? You got scared?"

Bella nodded. "Gia and I had big fight. And I . . . made some stupid decisions. I don't think I have a clue what I really want, or who's good for me, or what's good for me. Life is coming at me in a blur."

"Drink less?"

"Mom."

"All I can say is that I love you. I'm sorry to spring my news on you when you're upset about something else. And that it's okay to feel confused, to make mistakes, and to be scared." Marissa got off the bike to give Bella a hug and stroke her hair. "No matter what happens with the deli, we're keeping the apartments above it. You'll always have a home. Grandpa, Aunt Alicia, and Gia will be there for you. The cats aren't going anywhere. And your father and I will stay close—even when we're in Europe."

Bella nodded numbly. Her emotions felt as if they'd been through the meat grinder at Rizzoli's.

Marissa said, "I saved the best for last, honey. Your father and I want to use some of the Olive Garden money to pay your tuition. Not all of it. You have to struggle in life to build character. But you won't struggle as much. Does that take the sting out of the news?"

"A little bit."

Marissa eyed Bella suspiciously.

"Okay, a lot," said Bella, the promise of financial help settling into her brain. "Suddenly, I love Olive Garden."

"And now you can tell me about the man over there who hasn't taken his eyes off you from the moment we walked in here," said Marissa, glancing over Bella's shoulder.

Bella didn't need to look. "Really tall, green eyes, dark hair?"

"Very handsome. And neat, as if he irons his sweatpants and tank tops."

"He does! He's a big fan of fabric softener, too."

"Is he one of the stupid decisions you talked about?"

"Yes," said Bella, remembering with shame how she behaved when Tony tapped the brakes on her. He'd treated her with respect and she reacted like a spoiled brat. Throwing the beer at his face? Kneeing him in the stomach? Unforgivable. He'd been 100 percent right about Bender and Ed. She should have listened and been nicer to him.

Marissa said, "From the way he's staring, I'd say you still have a shot at turning things around. He's much cuter than Bobby. Oh, he saw me looking at him. He's coming over."

Bella's blood heated. She felt Tony at her side before she dared look at him. When she glanced up and saw his profile, Bella realized how badly she wanted him. Not just as a casual meaningless-sex supplier. She desired Tony in her bed, at her side—just in the same room, smelling like Downy, chicken parm, and clean sweat.

"Mom, this is Tony Troublino. My boss. And friend. I hope."

She smiled at him and was relieved to see that he returned it. He turned his attention to Marissa and said simply, "It's nice to meet you."

They shook hands. Then Marissa leaned back

against the bike machine and took them in. "My gracious, you two are a gorgeous couple."

Bella flamed with embarrassment. But Tony put his arm around her shoulder and said, "Don't I know it!"

Chapter Thirty-three

Like a Friggin' Racehorse

Gia broke off a piece of her corn dog and threw it at a turkey-size seagull. The bird flapped once and snatched the food in its bill.

"Do it again!" said Alicia, clapping her hands.

Smiling, Gia felt so happy to be with her mom, just chilling together on the beach. "Watch this." Gia chucked a bit of corn dog as far as she could. Three seagulls battled it out, diving and dipping, until one snagged it midair.

"Gia!" squawked Rick into the bullhorn from the lifeguard stand nearby. "Don't feed the seagulls!"

"Okay!" She waved. To Mom she added, "You feed one, and a dozen surround you."

"They're like pigeons."

"But a lot bigger and tougher."

A good metaphor for life down the Shore compared to Brooklyn. Not only the birds were tougher down here. Getting a boyfriend, for one thing, had been damn near impossible. Back home, she could snap her fingers and get a date. Then again, Gia thought, it was one thing to make a man come. And another to make him stay.

Gia flashed back to an hour before, Frankie on the phone, telling her she wasn't his kind of girl.

"What's up, baby?" asked Mom. "You seem sad all of the sudden."

That did it. One note of sympathy from Mom, and Gia gushed. "I got dumped—again!" she said, the tears flowing. "I really thought this guy was the one. He was so nice to me. He saved me when I got stung by a jellyfish and bought me fuzzy slippers. When we kissed . . . I was like a stick of butter on a subway rail. I melted."

"What went wrong?"

"*I* went wrong! I'm cursed, Mommy! It just blew up on me. No reason, no rhyme. Just *bam*! Okay, there was a misunderstanding, but still. He should have trusted me. I'm starting to believe it's my destiny to be single forever."

"That's crazy," said Alicia.

"Even if I do strike gold and find a decent guy, it might blow up anyway. I'll wind up alone and miserable, and bitter." Gia bit her tongue before she said something she'd regret.

But Alicia saw where Gia was going. "You mean, like me?"

"No!" said Gia reflexively. "Okay, yes." After she'd accused Bells of holding back her feelings for years,

Gia would be a hypocrite if she didn't speak her mind—now or never. "Mommy, what happened with you and Dad? We never talked about it, and I have a right to know."

Alicia broke off a piece of her funnel cake and flung it at the flock. A dozen birds fought for it. "We intentionally kept you out of it, so it wouldn't affect you."

"It did affect me, though. I was screwed up the whole year. I didn't know what was happening, except that both of you were ignoring me and hating each other. Dad barely spoke. And you just cried and told me, 'It's not your fault.' But I had to wonder, 'Is she saying that because it *is* my fault?'"

Maybe that was part of why Gia was so quick to push blame off herself—because she was terrified that everything that went wrong, big or small, *was* her fault.

Whoa. Major aha moment! Which would be awesome, if she didn't have to pee, really bad. That would have to wait. She was on a roll and Gia didn't want to stop.

Alicia sighed. "First of all, I'm not bitter. I'm not miserable. And"—she smiled shyly at Gia—"I'm not alone. I met someone, baby. That's what I came down here to tell you."

"Who is he?"

"You know the guy who manages the movie theater on Court Street?"

"*That* old guy? I mean, that totally cool, mad banging hottie?"

Alicia laughed. "His name is Ted Katz. He's not old. Unless fifty is old. And, no, he's not Italian, or hot or cool, mad, barking, banging, whatever. But he is a sweetheart. We've been having a wonderful summer together."

"So my leaving town was actually a good thing for you," said Gia, remembering how Alicia practically begged Gia not to leave Brooklyn when she first mentioned the idea of going down the Shore with Bells.

Alicia said, a little guiltily, "I wish you were having as nice a summer as I am."

"I want to hear more about Ted and all the free movies and popcorn I'm going to get back in Brooklyn. But no more stalling, Mom. First you have to tell me why you and Daddy split up." Gia's bladder was screaming, but she was not going to move until she had her answer. It seemed really important to know the truth about her parents, for her own sake. Gia didn't understand why she believed that. But, as a general rule, Gia didn't like to ask, "Why?" She had more fun asking, "Why not?"

Alicia said, "I don't want you to think of me as a selfish person."

"Just tell me."

Mom took a deep breath. "You know Joe and I got married when we were kids. And then we had you when I was twenty-three. We were wrapped up in being parents, and our jobs, and paying the bills. You got older, and I had less to do taking care of you. It was like waking up from a seventeen-year nap and realizing that, somewhere along the way, I fell out of love with Joe. We hardly ever had sex by then. And when we did, it wasn't good for me, if you know what I mean."

"Mom, yuck."

"Sex is a huge part of marriage, Gia. Without sex, it's not a marriage. It's a friendship. At the end, that's what Joe and I had—a very close lifelong friendship. But it wasn't enough for me. I wasn't willing to close the door on passion at forty years old. I was—am— still young. And I need love and passion in my life."

Like curtains being drawn back, Gia suddenly remembered scenes of her blurry senior year. Joe accusing Alicia of putting her selfish desires before her family. Of Alicia begging for forgiveness, and swearing she still loved him. It was hard for Joe, who grew up in a strict Catholic family, to see divorce as anything but a huge personal failure.

"Did Daddy still feel passionately about you?"

"If he did, he would have touched me more than once a month."

"TMI, Mom, please," said Gia, cringing.

"Only he knows if he still loved me. He claimed he did. His emotional response was to shut down completely. He stopped talking. And my response was to let the guilt and loneliness pour out of me. So I cried a lot, which you remember."

"That's why I thought Daddy ended it. All this time, I blamed him. But it was you. I thought he rejected us and left us for Rhoda. But it was you."

"I knew you thought that about Joe, and I let

you. I'm so sorry, Gia. I know it was an important time for you—senior year. We were both so distracted by our own situation, we didn't pay enough attention to you. It was unfair. I really am sorry about that, and letting you think the worst of Joe. I just couldn't stand the idea of you hating me. You probably do now."

"Honestly? I don't. I feel bad for Dad, and for me. Every boyfriend I've had, I lived in fear he'd one day just cut me off. And, guess what? Most of them did. I was so worried about being left, it became a self-fulfilling prophecy. So, right now, I'm just glad to know that Daddy didn't leave me. This is big, Mom. I can feel the weight sliding off my shoulders."

"Well, if you don't hate me now, you'll probably hate me tomorrow."

Gia shook her head. "I'm not a hater. It's not in my nature. I'm like you, Mom. I just want love. That's all I care about. Money, success, none of that matters to me. All I want is love, giving it, getting it. So friggin' corny, but it's true."

"I understand completely, baby. I feel the same way. Except I care about one thing more."

"Really awesome hair extensions?" asked Gia.

"I meant *you*."

"I know, Mommy. Did you know Dad and Rhoda are pregnant?"

Alicia's jaw dropped. "I didn't. Good for them."

"Do you ever talk to him?"

"Every month or so. To do the Gia update."

"Why doesn't he call me himself? I've never even been to his house in Philly. He should invite me."

"Joe shuts down when he's upset. He probably wants to have you come, but gets nervous about asking. I'm sure he would love to see you. You should go to Philly and have a heart-to-heart. If anyone can get him to open up, it's you."

A strange city? Alone? To walk into an emotional minefield? That was *not* going to happen. But Gia nodded anyway and said, "I'll call him."

"So you feel better?"

"I still got dumped this morning."

"It's hard to wait for what you want," said Alicia. "Patience isn't my strong suit either. But when a relationship is right, it's worth all the pain and loneliness that came before."

"And that's how you feel about Ted Katz?"

Smiling, Alicia said, "I do."

"I'm happy for you, Mommy." Gia gave her a squeeze.

"Um, I hate to ruin the moment. But I've had to pee this whole time."

Gia laughed. "Me, too! Like a friggin' racehorse. It's four blocks back to our place. The public bathrooms on the boardwalk are about two blocks that way."

"I don't think I can make it."

"Only one option." Gia pointed toward the water. Standing up, Gia took off her denim skirt and her tank top. Her pink panties and bra looked like a bikini.

"Are you serious?" Mom glanced sneakily up and down the beach. "All these people."

"Like everyone doesn't do it? Chill, Mom. It's like leaving your personal mark on the ocean."

Alicia laughed. She stood up and stripped down to her underwear, an impressive matching set in neon blue. They walked into the waves. When they were waist deep in the ocean, Gia and Alicia moved a few yards apart.

"Ahhhh," said Gia.

"Ahhhh," said Alicia.

Squawk. "I see you, Gia!" said Rick on the bullhorn. "I know exactly what you're doing!"

The women burst out laughing. When a few moments passed (as well as a few waves), they reached for each other's hand and turned to face the horizon.

"I can't believe I've been here nearly three weeks and I haven't gone swimming yet," said Gia.

"The water's cold," said Alicia. "But it feels good."

It felt good to be with her, thought Gia. They bobbed in the waves for a while, then ventured back to dry land.

The seagulls had been busy, scarfing the remains of their funnel cake and corn dog. And trampling their clothes with their fat feet.

Looking down at the sandy pile, Alicia asked, "Any suggestions?"

"Let's go shopping," said Gia.

Chapter Thirty-four

Like You, Only Bronzer

Bella drove, while Marissa took in the sun from the shotgun seat. Her phone rang. "Hello?" Turning to Bella, she asked, "Do you know where Tantastic is?"

"That's the salon where Gia works."

"They're waiting for us there."

"No, Mom," complained Bella. "Gia and I are in a big fight, and I'm not in the mood to deal with her."

"You're going to have to talk to her eventually. Alicia and I fight constantly, but we love each other and always make up. I'm sure you and Gia will be fine. Alicia says there's a pitcher of margaritas waiting."

Oh, well, in that case . . . Bella made a hard right and headed for the salon. She wasn't convinced she and Gia would *ever* make up after the fight they had. But she could use a drink. And her tan needed a tune-up.

"I'll go to Tantastic, but I'm not talking to Gia."

"Thank you, sweetie," said Marissa.

As soon as Bells and her mom walked in the salon, Gia came over and put drinks in their hands.

"Aunt Marissa, don't take this the wrong way, but you desperately need ten minutes in the Spaceship," said Gia.

"It's a tanning bed, Mom," Bella explained.

Marissa touched her cheek. "I guess I am pretty pale."

Gia said, "Mom's in there now. She's getting the Bronze Star treatment."

Maria came out of the back room. "Alicia's all set. And you must be Marissa. I can see the resemblance."

"Hello," said Marissa, a bit taken aback at Maria's appearance. It wasn't a Brooklyn thing for a middle-aged woman to wear a skintight, bright yellow corset dress, with stiletto cage pumps and a black pouf with a skunk stripe, carrying a smoke and a drink, at noon, on a Wednesday.

"Right this way," said Maria, already clicking back down the hallway. "I've got the Spaceship warmed up for you."

"Is it safe?" Marissa asked Bella. "I won't come out looking like a different person?"

"You'll look like you," said Bella. "Only bronzer."

After her mom left the waiting area, Bella was alone with her cousin.

After an awkward beat, Gia said, "I'm sorry I called you a backstabbing, buzz-killing shit-talker."

Bella exhaled deeply and said, "I'm sorry I called you a cock-blocking, helpless disaster magnet."

"You were right, though. I was angry at the moment, but I get your point. I want to be a better person. Only a real friend would be that honest. Even if it took a while."

Bella felt like crying. So much had happened in so short a time. Right now, though, she was just relieved her best friend forgave her. "You were right, too. If I ever have anything to say about you again, it'll be right up in your grill. And I'm grateful you got me away from those jerkoffs."

"So we're cool?"

"Glad that's over," said Bells, smiling despite herself.

The cousins ran at each other and hugged. Gia's head fell right between Bella's boobs.

Gia and Bells toasted, "*Salute,*" and drank.

"My parents are selling the deli to Olive Garden," said Bella.

"I hate Olive Garden!" said Gia.

"That's what I said. They're going to use some of the money to pay my tuition."

"I love Olive Garden!"

"Also what I said."

"My mom's dating the manager of the movie theater on Court Street."

"That old guy?" asked Bella.

"Exactly what I said."

"Free movies and popcorn?"

"Also what I said," replied Gia.

The cousins raised their glasses to each other and drank. A somber feeling came over Bella, though. "We'll be going home to a much different world than the one we left."

"I know," said Gia. "Change is good, right? Does this mean you're staying until the end of July after all?"

"I wasn't really going to leave. Maybe. But I would have come back."

"We've got nine days left," said Gia. "We're both still single. Neither one of us has fallen in love, or smushed. We've barely snuggled! So what do we do now? I'm sick of the bars and the clubs."

"Me, too," said Bells, wincing at the idea of running into Bender or Ed at Karma or Bamboo.

"I'm not going back to Brooklyn without having hooked up with at least one guy," said Gia.

"Only one thing we can do at this point."

Gia nodded, smiling, her enormous eyes shining like klieg lights. "Exactly what I was thinking."

The cousins clinked their glasses again, sang in unison, "House party!"

Maria appeared in the hallway. "Did someone say 'house party'?"

"You bet your sweet ass," said Gia.

"When?" asked the cougar. "I need to plan my outfit."

"Tomorrow night," announced Gia. "We invite everyone, and tell them to bring cute boys."

Chapter Thirty-five

Love Is Loud

Hand me that socket wrench," said Giuseppe Troublino, his tat-and-engine-grease-covered arm appearing from underneath a car.

Tony handed him the tool. "How bad is it?"

Giuseppe rolled out from under the car on a flat mechanic's dolly. His craggy face was covered in grime from this car and the thousands of cars he'd fixed over forty years of owning the garage. Tony had learned, working summers and after school with the mechanics, that it can take months of scrubbing to rid your fingernails of motor oil and grease. Tony was a neat freak. He liked to be clean. Maybe he was a little compulsive about it. With good reason!

Girls *hated* dirty, greasy fingernails.

The life of a mechanic was not for him. Tony wasn't particularly good at it, besides. Tony preferred the machinery of the human body, how muscle, ligament, and bone could be fine-tuned to go faster, rev higher, pull more weight. Tony secretly compared his own body to a monster truck. Rally-ready.

Giuseppe might've been a little disappointed that his grandson went his own way, going to college and finding a job outside the garage. But as the old man said, "I'd be a lot more disappointed if you worked here for my sake. And I'd be stuck with you. I'd have to fire your ass, too. Ugly situation, to be avoided."

Wiping his hands on a filthy rag, Grandpa said, "I don't know, Tony."

"Too far gone?"

"What a pile of junk. I can make it start, and it'll probably hold together for another thousand miles. But no promises."

Tony smiled with relief. "That's awesome, Pops."

"Why am I doing this again?" asked Giuseppe, bending over the motor. "I do have paying work on my plate."

Tony shrugged. "Favor for a friend."

"A girlfriend?"

"A girl. Who happens to be a friend."

"Of course. If you'd banged her already, she'd be out of the picture. Favors only for the girls you haven't nailed yet."

"Hey, dude, not cool," said Tony. "I'd do favors for this girl—correction, *you'll* do the favor—even if I had banged her. I like her, Pops."

Giuseppe froze, midcrank. His wrinkles ironed out in surprise. He looked at Tony. "Did hell just freeze over?"

"I thought I heard a cracking sound," said Tony, laughing.

"You've never said you liked a girl before. You say girls are 'cute,' and 'sweet,' and 'down.'"

"I do like her."

Giuseppe pointed the wrench at his grandson accusingly. "Is she the reason I haven't seen girls sneaking out of the house in . . . has to be weeks?"

Tony had been off the market for the last few weeks, yeah. Since he met Bella Rizzoli, the girls he met in town and at the gym left him cold. "Her name is Bella, by the way."

"The same girl you and Tina picked up at the gas station after the movie?"

"We cooked together. Don't raise your eyebrows at me. I mean we actually cooked. Chicken parm." Tony smiled at the memory of Bella licking her sauce spoon. Frowning, he also remembered how angry she was when he left that night.

"Don't marry for food," warned Giuseppe. "Marry for sex."

"Stop. No one is talking about marriage! It'll never get that far. She's not exactly into me, Pops. She kicked me in the stomach once."

"Did you deserve it?"

"Probably. I met her mother yesterday. She looked good."

"Now you 'like' the mother?"

"It's a good sign. If you want to know how the daughter will turn out, look at the mother."

Giuseppe banged on the carburetor. "So you *do* want to marry her."

Tony groaned. "I'm just saying."

"Why would you care how she looks in twenty years if you're not going to be lying next to her every night?"

"I don't!"

Giuseppe glared at his grandson. "My opinion? Do not marry this girl. Look at the piece of shit she drives! A Honda? Find a girl with an American car. Better yet, don't marry anyone! You'd stop bringing girls into my house, and I will never forgive you. I've got so few thrills left! I need those half-naked girls sneaking out at dawn. They always carry their shoes. Why do they do that? It's so cute! Don't deprive an old man of half-naked girls, tiptoeing, carrying their shoes."

"You're a dirty old man," shouted Grandma Tina from the garage office's open window.

"Stay out of my business, woman!" Giuseppe screamed back.

"I like Isabella, Tony," said Tina. "And she likes Vin Diesel, which shows she has excellent taste in men."

"Vin friggin' Diesel," grumbled Giuseppe.

Tony rolled his eyes. They fought, his grandparents. But they also snuggled on the couch watching TV, laughed together at their lame sitcoms. They spent long afternoons in the kitchen, cooking side by side, feeding each other tastes. In his grandparents' house, love was loud. It was the wealth of his family. Without it, they'd have nothing.

"When does Honda girl want her car back?" asked Giuseppe.

"I don't know," said Tony. "She doesn't know I have it."

"You stole her car?" asked Grandma.

"I was going to tell her, but she threw a beer at me! A couple days went by, and I didn't get the chance to explain I towed it here. And now, I like the idea of surprising her, pulling into her driveway with it, clean and shiny, motor purring."

"She kicked you in the stomach and threw a beer at you?" asked Pops. "It must be love."

Crash!

"Oops," said Giuseppe.

Tony looked under the car. A football-size piece of greasy metal had fallen off the motor and hit the floor.

"Maybe it's a good thing she thinks it's stolen," said Giuseppe.

Grandma came out of the office and said, "Isabella seems like a nice Italian girl. Polite, respectful." Patting Tony's cheek, pinching it, then giving it a loving little slap, she said, "I know your parents would have liked her, too."

Oh, shit. Tony hated/loved when his grandma talked about his parents. He fought his emotions, battling to keep them under control.

Giuseppe shook his head. "Don't upset the boy, old woman."

"Shut your filthy mouth, old man!"

Tony smiled. Listening to them fight was the sound track of his childhood. They only played the hits.

Chapter Thirty-six

Come One, Come All

"You are *such* a ho!" said Gia.

"You're a much bigger ho than me," said Bella.

"I wish!"

The cousins stroked on mascara, liquid liner, and bright red lipstick in front of the mirror in Gia's room. As a general rule, Gia was against back-combing her hair. But for the Bros and Hos fiesta tonight at their place, she'd tease like there was no tomorrow.

When she was done, her hair was ratty enough for three generations of rodents to call home.

She'd bought the leather bustier top yesterday at the Lucky Lady boutique. Fishnet stockings, with black hot pants, her cherry red velvet heels, and a trucker hat with the words COUGAR IN TRAINING, completed the outfit. Gia looked like the cutest little ho in town.

But her cousin was a close runner-up. She had on a backless swing shirt, basically a drape of shiny metallic fabric that dipped from her shoulders to her navel, showing at least 60 percent of her gravity-defying breasts. Strips of double-stick tape on her boobies kept the fabric in place. Although they didn't want to be too matchy-matchy, Bells also wore black fishnets and scorching hot pants.

Along with the look, Gia also had a new outlook. The talk with Mom on the beach was like pushing the reset button in her mind. Before Mom and Aunt Marissa drove off this morning, Alicia pulled Gia into a hug and said, "From this day forward . . ."

"From this day forward . . . what?" asked Gia.

"What*ever*."

"A new mantra?"

"Do you like it?"

Gia thought about it and decided that she did. The mantra was optimistic and spontaneous, her two favorite big words. Plus, it made her feel as if she was in control. Destiny would always play a part in her life. But a girl shouldn't let destiny knock her around. Gia wasn't destiny's bitch. Destiny would bend to *her* will. From this day forward . . .

As soon as the moms drove off, Gia and Bells went to work, organizing beer and booze delivery, party favors, and snacks from Treasure Chest, the local sex-toy shop (cocksicles and boobpops for everyone). Maria volunteered to bring crucial party supplies: extra plastic cups, rolls of toilet paper, paper towels, and garbage bags.

Bells already had a few playlists she used for her "Beat Up the Beat" exercise class. Tony had agreed to let her use the gym's boom box. Dancing in the living room. Smushing (fingers crossed) in the bedrooms. Stanley's crew installed the new oven earlier, so the kitchen was safe to hang out in.

With a final all-over spritz of Fantasy, Gia checked her phone (not lost). Ten o'clock. People should be here soon.

"Is that everything?" asked Bella. "Beers in the fridge, vodka on ice. What else?"

"Oh my God! I forgot something!"

As a totem to the Party Gods, Gia propped Giraffe on the bed. She strapped a sexy bra across its chest, layered beads around the long neck, and slipped a thong over its legs. With some difficulty, she got four sets of lashes to stick on the plastic eyes.

Bella said, "I take it back. Giraffe is the biggest ho here."

Gia arranged it in a sexy pose on the make-out couch. "There. Now we're ready."

———

By midnight, the party was in full swing.

Everyone showed up. Rick the Lifeguard came with a few friends from the Seaside Heights Beach Patrol. Yuri the barber brought his sons, two dangerously sexy blue-eyed Russians. Pimped-out Tony, among the first to arrive, brought some of the heavyweights from the gym, all of them Bro'ed juicehead gorillas. Maria came with a date, a much younger guy who worked at the balloon-dart booth on the boardwalk. Some of Gia's regular tan-tag clients came, with friends. The girls from Bells's aerobics class showed up, looking deliciously slutty. Even Rocky Gato was around here somewhere.

No Linda and Janey, though. Gia was disappointed her old/new friends couldn't make it. But fewer girls meant more boys for her.

She'd considered inviting Frankie, just to say, "No hard feelings." But then she decided against it. Tonight was about having fun, meeting new guys. Ex-boyfriends at hookup parties usually caused problems. She didn't want to go near that with a ten-foot stripper pole. But, from now on, her new name was No Drama Giovanna.

The room filled, the drinks flowed, and the music made the beach house rock on its foundation. A few kids broke out a homemade party beer bong with *five* drinking tubes. That made the rounds.

Gia didn't stopped dancing. Her friends and their friends, and their friends, kept handing her drinks and refilling her cup.

At one point, Bells battled by with Tony, their limbs in motion, bodies shaking, faces close, grinning at each other. Bells shouted to Gia, "Why didn't we throw a party before?"

"Because we're friggin' idiots!" screamed Gia back.

Eventually, though, Gia had to take a break. She needed air and stepped out the front door. A group of kids were smoking on the boardwalk, and they quickly surrounded her. She didn't know any of them personally, but she accepted their thanks for having the party, and the compliments. What girl could hear "You look hot" enough?

"Gia, are you out here?" asked Maria, dressed like a ho in a black, shiny spandex catsuit, bondage cage heels, and faux pearls and diamond necklaces worn as a belt. Her pouf had reached new heights, too, with bling clips all over it.

"What's wrong?" asked Gia.

"Stanley just showed up. With a date!"

The two mysticians went back inside, and Maria pointed across the kitchen. Stanley—in his OG jeans, Ed Hardy T-shirt, and gold-cross necklace—was fixing a cocktail for a sexy woman Gia recognized. "It's the Lucky Lady lady. I bought this top at her place. I love that store!" Seeing Maria's reaction, she said, "But the clothes are cheap crap."

"Look at her!" said Maria. "She's horrible."

The woman was pretty, actually, with long dark hair, flat-ironed and neat, in a silver metallic tube dress with a cute pink cardigan, kitten heels. Sexy and sweet. She looked good.

"She's ancient!" said Maria.

Gia put the boutique owner at forty-five, around her mom's age. "How old are you, Maria?" asked Gia.

"None of your freakin' business!"

"Honestly? You have no right to be upset, Maria. You turned him down, repeatedly. Stanley came after you, and you told him to take off. Where's your date anyway?"

Maria reluctantly gestured to the dance floor. Balloon Dart bro was doing body shots with three tan-tagged hos.

"Oh," said Gia. "Yeah. Well. Like we didn't see that coming."

"Younger men," Maria cried. "It's an addiction! I can't help myself."

"Dart Boy would be young *for me*. I mean, is he out of high school?"

"Do you think I'm taking the cougar thing too far? Be honest."

"You know I love cougars." Gia tapped her CIT trucker hat.

"But?"

"But you have to ask yourself why seeing Stanley with another woman makes you so heated. It's possible, even if it burns you to admit it, that you still have feelings for the cheap-bastard, fat-shit, saggy old man you once loved enough to marry."

"I do like his haircut."

Gia swelled with pride. "I did that. It took some convincing. But he agreed to it, for you."

"That's so sweet."

"So what are you waiting for? Go get him."

"It's too late! He's with someone else."

Gia grabbed Maria's shoulders and gave her a pouf-rattling shake. "Mary Agatha Pugliani! Are you going to let some boutique bitch get between you and the man you love? You're a lethal brunette! You take no prisoners!"

Gia's boss seemed to gather strength. "You're

right." Maria drew herself up on her stilettos. "What do I do?"

"Put the moves on him!"

"Branch and hug?"

"Go, girl!"

Maria's black eyes flared, and she stomped through the kitchen. Gia watched her grab Stanley's arm and drag him to the dance floor. Stanley seemed confused and anxious, especially when Maria put her wrists around his neck and started writhing like a python on fire in front of him. She was so wriggly, people noticed and formed a circle around them.

When Maria wrapped one leg around Stanley's hip, the crowd cheered, "Go, Cougar! Go, Cougar!" Stanley got into it. He put his hairy hands on Maria's butt and started dancing, too.

As Gia watched, all the couples started mimicking their moves. The living room became a forest of tree branching and hugging. Gia grabbed the first guy she saw—Rocky Gato—and pulled him onto the dance floor.

"This is how we met, remember?" asked Gia, shaking her bacon in front of him. "My first night at Karma? Linda saw us dancing and you two got in a fight."

"We're still fighting," he said, his shoulders tensing under Gia's hands.

"Sorry to hear it."

"Gia, the other night, at the Inca?"

"Thanks again for helping me. You saved my life."

"Linda and Janey spiked the Jell-O shots with laxatives."

Gia froze midshimmy. "What?"

"They wanted to embarrass you. Don't ask me why. It's jealousy, or revenge, girl bullshit. Two guys would just pound each other bloody and be done with it."

"I can't believe it," said Gia, her party bubble instantly deflating. "I thought they were my friends."

"I'm only telling you because, once, when I was in junior high, during a football game, I got hit so hard by a linebacker, I shit myself. I swore on that day that if I could help anyone in the future not poop themselves, I would."

Gia blinked. "It's pretty amazing that you got the opportunity."

"Weird, right?"

She patted him on the chest. "You're a good person, Rocky."

"You're cool, too, Gia. And your tits look great in that top."

Chapter Thirty-seven

Rage On

Although you are devastatingly sexy in that outfit," said Tony, "I think you're even hotter in a sports bra and running shorts."

Bella smiled and sipped her margarita. The two were taking a break from dancing on the red velvet couch. Next to them, Giraffe Ho. Next to it, Rick and a girl from the gym were dry-humping to the beat.

"This is where we kissed," Bella said.

"The memory is burned into my brain," Tony said, leaning closer.

"I just noticed," said Bella, peering into his face. "You're wearing eyeliner and lip gloss."

"It takes a real man to wear what you girls call makeup."

"What do you boys call it?"

"Finishing touches."

When he said "touches," his eyes dropped to her

nearly naked boobs. He licked his shiny lips, a comic gesture with sound effects, as if he wanted to eat her alive.

She laughed. "You really are such a dork."

"Just as long as you like me," he said, coming in for a kiss.

When their lips touched, Bella's heart beat up the beat. It pounded louder and harder, until she thought it'd explode. Tony's pimp shirt was unbuttoned, exposing his smooth, ripped chest. Moving on their own, her hands reached for the exposed wall of muscle. She'd been itching to touch him from the second he arrived. She moaned into the kiss when she finally pressed her palms on him.

"Dang," he said into her mouth, and gathered her up, squeezing her body hard against him. Bella was locked inside the steel cage of his huge arms, and she didn't want to escape.

Tony broke the kiss to graze on her neck. "Your skin tastes like caramel."

"It's my vanilla body spray," she said.

"It's you." He nuzzled her in just the right spot, the supersensitive patch of skin at the base of her neck, right under the ear.

A bolt of electricity crackled all the way down to her crotch. "We have to go upstairs, right now," she said.

"Are you sure?"

"Yes, I'm sure! Enough tapping the brakes!"

"Let's go." Tony jumped to his feet, his hard-on painfully obvious in his jeans.

He held out a hand, which she needed. Her head was swimming from the kiss, and she was wearing six-inch heels, too.

Rick, meanwhile, had stopped snogging his girl and was loudly greeting a friend with a five-step. "Dude!" said the lifeguard. "Bella, wait, before you run off, I want to introduce you to my boy Jeff Spicoli. Dude, this is Bella, Shark Whisperer's cousin, and our host tonight."

Bella was not in the mood for introductions. She wanted to get upstairs, out of her clothes, and under Tony. "Hello," she said, barely looking at the guy, and pulled at Tony's sleeve.

"Yo, I know you," said Tony. "You're Shoot the Geek."

"You recognized me," said Jeff. "Bravo."

"I got you right between the eyes," said Tony. "Last week. I won a pocket protector."

Jeff laughed. "I remember that. Most people aim for my balls. So, thanks, man, for shooting my face."

Shoot the Geek? It took a second for Bella's hormone-clouded brain to sort it out. "The boardwalk booth? The human-target paintball game? That's you?"

"I wear a geek costume. Horn-rimmed glasses, white shirt, tie, pants belted up to here. This is me in my natural state."

Baja sweater, cargo shorts, long dirty-blond hair, and beaded necklace. A hippie. "I've seen you somewhere else," said Bella, placing it. "At Karma. You were talking to Ed Caldwell."

Jeff's face darkened. "Friend of yours?"

"Just a guy I met."

"Do yourself a favor. Stay away from that dude."

"Why?" asked Tony.

Jeff hesitated. Rick said, "They're cool."

"Like three years ago, I sold Ed some ecstasy. Every summer since then, he dogs me to buy drugs. I got out of the business a long time ago, mainly because I found out that Ed used what I sold him to drug some girl and do her while his friend watched. They have this competition to pound the same girl each summer, taking turns to get her in the sack. The Rule of Ten, some shit like that. It's disgusting, man. Totally disrespectful to women. I'm sorry to even mention it in mixed company."

Bella's skin went cold. "Is Ed's friend Bender Newberry?"

Jeff shrugged. "Sounds right, but I can't say for sure."

"That little shit!"

"You okay?" asked Jeff.

Bella said, "We're good. Enjoy the party."

Shoulder to shoulder, Bella and Tony headed toward the kitchen where they could talk. Going upstairs was forgotten. The sexy vibe was gone.

"That asshole Bender came to the gym looking for you this afternoon," said Tony. "I told him you weren't around, and that he was excluded from the premises. Shithead wouldn't leave. I had to throw him out. He kept shouting for you. Something about a note."

Bella nodded. "Ed called me a few times this week, too. I guess they stopped taking turns. They're both going for it. Race to the finish."

His breath fast and hot, Tony said, "I'm going to kill them. Track them down and dismember them."

"Not if I get there first."

"We can dismember together," said Tony, grinning.

"You mean, like a date?" she asked, smiling despite her anger.

Tony pulled her into a hug, more protective than sexy.

"We need a plan," she said. "Gia will want to help."

"She could mess it up. I'm just saying."

"She's the reason I never hooked up with Bender and Ed. If she hadn't put the doubt in my head about them, I might've done something awful."

"I never liked them either," said Tony. "Mainly because the idea of another guy touching you . . . of another guy *thinking* of touching you . . . Okay, we're gonna find those fuckers *right now*. Come on."

Bella let Tony push her through the crowd. She saw Gia on the dance floor with Rocky, having what looked like an intense conversation.

How many girls had Ed and Bender taken advantage of for their competition? Jeff said "three years ago." So Bella was at least their fourth target. The idea made her feel sick legit. She gagged a little. She felt violated, as if she *had* been raped. How could she have been fooled for a single second by their act? Gia hadn't been. She'd gone by her gut. Bella stopped Tony. "I have to listen to my gut."

"What's it telling you now?"

"To wait. Be smart. Make a plan."

He exhaled, struggling to regain emotional control. "It's your call. But they came after my girl. We take them down together."

"I'm your girl?" she asked, liking the sound of that.

He answered by kissing her again.

Each kiss with Tony had its own flavor and personality. The last one: pure heat. This one: still hot. But warm. Unmistakably loving.

Then another interruption: "Giovanna!"

Bella and Tony heard the booming voice over the music. So did everyone else. Fifty heads turned in the same direction, toward the boardwalk entrance of the house, where a giant struggled to fit through the doorframe to get inside.

"It's Hulk," said Bella, gaping at the man mountain. He was even bigger than last week, if that was humanly possible, as if he'd consumed nothing since then but steroids, protein powder, and raw meat.

"Geeeeeyahhhh," screamed Hulk, making the windows rattle, and the party guests quake.

He was so enormous, Hulk didn't notice that Gia had pushed her way through the guests and was standing right in front of him. "I'm right here, dumbass," said Gia, kicking Hulk in the shin. "Ow. That hurt my foot."

Hulk ranted, "I heard you were having a party. But I didn't believe it. Why didn't you invite me? Don't you love me?"

"We went on one bad date."

"You touched my dick!" he screamed.

Gia shuddered. "Don't remind me. It was gross enough the first time."

"But I love you!" he screamed, a 'roid rage contorting his face. "I made myself even bigger for you. I wanna marry you!"

"Honestly? You're delusional," said Gia. "And you're ruining my party."

"I'm not leaving! You can't make me leave."

He barreled into the kitchen, punching holes in the walls.

Stanley shouted, "My new walls!"

Tony rushed Hulk, along with Rocky, Rick, Jeff, and a handful of gym regulars. Six guys leaped on Hulk's back, but he brushed them off like flakes of dandruff.

One guy sailed through the window.

Stanley yelled, "My new window!"

Another smashed into the banister, splintering it.

"My stairs!"

Poor Stanley. The guy was pulling out the few hairs he had left. He was, by now, the only man in the house not actively trying to bring down Hulk. He threw them off, one by one. The place was getting trashed.

Gia found her way to Bella's side. "You can't

blame me for this. I purposefully didn't invite the exes. I'm No Drama Giovanna."

"Trouble finds you," said Bella, putting an arm around Gia's shoulder, watching the Hulk flick men off him like lint. "At least you're consistent."

"Waa."

"I know," said Bella, and gave her cuz a squeeze.

Flashing lights beamed through the (smashed) windows from outside. A squad of cops ran into the house. Using a bullhorn, one said, "Cease and desist!"

But Johnny Hulk's 'roid rage was blind, deaf, and incredibly *stupid.* He was in destructo mode, and nothing was going to bring him down.

The cops had him surrounded. A few stun guns came out. "Last warning!" said the one with the bullhorn.

The Hulk screamed primally, from a deep place, and lunged.

A set of Tasers hit him in the chest. And another.

But Hulk kept coming. He took another few steps before he went down.

"I can't watch," said Gia, turning away as Johnny finally toppled, convulsing on the floor.

The poli put plastic cuffs on him. The entire squad moved in and managed to herd him out of the house.

Stanley yelled after them, "I'm pressing charges! I want that idiot behind bars! I want his balls on a plate!"

Bella whispered, "Small plate."

"From my Barbie tea set," said Gia.

The partyers followed the police outside to watch the slapstick comedy of fitting Hulk bulk into the backseat of a squad car. After a few attempts, they radioed for a van.

Captain Morgan pulled up in his white cruiser. Shaking his head, he spotted the cousins waving him over.

Gia said, "Hey, you got my invite! I'm so glad you could make it."

"Can't I go a week without seeing you two?" But the captain was smiling. With his eyes. His lips were invisible under the mustache.

"I've been meaning to call you," said Bella to him. "I'd like to report a stolen car."

Chapter Thirty-eight

What's Italian for *Payback*?

The party broke up, no thanks to the cops and Stanley, who decided he'd seen enough destruction for one night. Gia, Bells, Tony, and Giraffe were the only ones left in the trashed house.

Gia passed around leftover cocksicles. Bella and Tony sat down on the red velvet couch next to Giraffe. Gia plopped down on the beanbag chair nearby. They licked their penis pops.

"You think Johnny Hulk will be okay? Three Tasers? That's more juice than he's used to," asked Bells.

Tony said, "I don't want to be in the same state when his brain unscrambles."

Gia asked, "Tony, you speak Italian, right?"

"*Prego.*"

"What's the Italian word for *revenge*?"

"*Vendetta,*" he said, his accent perfect.

"That was hot," said Bella. "Say it again."

Tony obliged, but he said it really slowly. "*Ven-det-ah.*"

The cousins pretended to swoon and die from the sound of his voice, so he kept saying it, over and over. Then: "How's this? *Amore.*"

The cousins shrugged. "Revenge is sexier than love, sorry," said Gia.

Bella said, "Let's focus on a plan. Two plans."

"One to show those Jell-O-shot-spiking, lying slags Linda and Janey the true meaning of being in deep shit," said Gia.

"And one to teach those women haters Bender and Ed a lesson in getting screwed," said Bells.

"Two hot girls, two dirty fights, and me," said Tony, rubbing his hands together. "I'm the luckiest guy on earth."

Gia got quiet. She wished Frankie were here, too. He'd love to be a part of this. But she wouldn't call him. If he'd believed her, she would've explained the night at Inca. But now? Even with the full truth out? Calling Frankie would feel like groveling. Gia would not lower herself like that. She'd happily lower herself in many other ways, of course. But she refused to grovel when she'd done nothing wrong in the first place.

Bella put her hand on Gia's shoulder. "You okay?"

"I'm fine," she said, realizing exactly how true it was. Gia might have her share of bad luck. But she had self-respect and good instincts. She'd been right on the money about Bender and Ed, those scumbags, after all. She'd seen from the start how cool Tony was. And she was right about Frankie, too, even if he was wrong about her.

"Actually, I take it back," said Gia. "Until I see our enemies on their backs—and not in a good way—I will not be okay."

Bells smiled. "Good. I've got a few ideas."

"Me, too," said Gia. "Nasty ones."

———

"Welcome to Tantastic," trilled Maria when the customers came in.

From down the hall, Gia whispered to Bella, "They're here. Yay!"

"We have tanning appointments with Giovanna," said Linda.

Janey added, "Comps. On the house. Free."

Maria smiled. "Yes, I know what *comp* means."

"So, uh, where is she?" asked Linda. "We don't have all day. Gia swore it wouldn't take longer than an hour."

That was Gia's cue. "I'm here," she sang, coming into the salon's waiting area. "Great to see you both! I was so sad you didn't come to my party a few days ago. I wanted to thank you personally for being so nice to me, giving me Jell-O shots, and just being excellent friends."

Linda shrugged. "Yeah. We're besties." She pointedly checked her phone for the time. "Uh, ticktock."

"How's Rocky?" asked Gia. "You're so lucky to have such a great boyfriend."

Linda frowned. "He's good. Can we get on with this?"

Gia had made them an offer they couldn't refuse. A full-body Bronze Star tanning treatment with custom color, no charge, as her way of showing her appreciation for her old friends.

Greedy bitches, they jumped on it.

Maria wanted to do the wet work along with Gia, but Bella insisted.

"I know how busy you are," said Gia. "First, let me introduce you to my assistant for today. This is mystician Rizzoli."

Gia didn't think Linda and Janey had ever met Bella, but just to be sure, she had had her cousin pull her hair into a severe ponytail and wear fake black glasses (borrowed from Jeff "Shoot the Geek" Spicoli).

Maria said, "If you ladies would sign right here, agreeing to receive services. It's just a standard form. All new clients have to sign."

The blondes scribbled their signatures without reading the waver, just as Gia knew they would. Now Maria and the salon were protected.

With a meatball Italian accent, Bella said, "Righta this-a way, gurls."

Linda and Janey were unimpressed, but they followed the cousins down the hall, into the spray-tanning room.

Mystician Rizzoli took Janey into room one. Gia took Linda into room two.

"You have to take off everything," Gia said.

"Just hang your dress here. And leave your undies on the chair. Wow! You have a slamming body, Linda. You're so skinny! I wish I were as skinny as you."

"Thanks. Are we going to talk, or tan?"

Gia grinned. Linda just couldn't wait for payback. "Have you ever done a spray tan before?"

"I tan naturally. I don't need to pay for it. Unlike some."

Bitch.

Gia stayed in character. Laughing lightly, she said, "I'll adjust the color setting, to make sure you turn a natural-looking caramel. Now, lie down on the table. . . . Good. The first step is to put some of this solution on your palms and the bottoms of your feet."

"What is it?"

"It's color-block gel."

"Okay," said the skinny bitch, closing her eyes, relaxing on the table. Right where Gia wanted her.

"Now I'll apply a special moisturizer to your skin."

Gia could feel Linda relaxing under her hands as Gia spread and massaged some lotion into her skin. She was so entitled and accustomed to pampering, Linda let her guard down. Perfect!

"Next, I'm going to apply a base coat to prepare the skin to absorb the color."

This was the tricky part. Gia squirted some color-block solution into her hands and started drawing on Linda's skin with it.

"Shouldn't you smear it on?" said Linda, her eyes closed.

"Trust me. My technique seems strange, but it works. And now, I'm going to spray on your color."

"Whatevs. Just hurry up."

Twenty mintues later, her enemy rose from the table, having been three-step treated front and back. She submitted to being dried with a handheld fan, then inspected herself in the full-length mirror.

"Huh," said Linda, turning to the side, checking herself from behind. "I gotta admit, the color is good. But look at this." She held up her palms and pointed at the bottoms of her feet, which were colored. "That blocker lotion didn't work at all."

Gia said, "It did. The blocked areas won't absorb the spray tan. The color will wash off clean in the shower. But wait an hour or two, or you might get streaks on the rest."

"How long will the color last?" asked Linda, examining herself, clearly loving the look.

"A week. A *whole* week."

"Cool," Linda said, her dress back on. "I hope you don't expect a tip. Free is free."

"Of course not. This way out."

Just as Linda and Gia emerged from room two, Janey and Bella exited room one.

The blondes used each other as a mirror. "You look amazing," gushed Janey.

"No, you!" squealed Linda.

Not a word of gratitude for Gia or Bella, of course. Ungrateful haters.

Maria smiled as they all came down the hall and into the waiting area. "You're both beautiful."

Janey said, "We know."

"You're welcome," said Gia, as they headed out the door.

"Oh, yeah," said Linda. "Thanks, Gia. It really does look good."

When they were safely gone, Gia asked Bella, "How'd it go?"

"She didn't speak one word to me! It was weird. As soon as she lay down, she fell into a pampering coma. I could have done anything to her."

"Same," said Gia, giddy now that the job was gone. "That was almost too easy."

"Famous last words," said Maria from behind the desk. "I hope they don't come back after you."

"Don't kryptonite my vendetta," said Gia.

Chapter Thirty-nine

The Return of Granny Panty

Linda felt supersexy. Much as she hated to admit that Giovanna Spumanti could be the source of anything good, Linda loved her spray tan. Walking along the boardwalk, she felt aglow. As if she were shimmering with each step.

If Rocky, aka the Idiot Traitor ex-boyfriend, could see her now, he'd be eating his heart out.

But her palms and feet, yuck. They were stained and slippery. Her flip-flops were ruined. She'd have to buy new ones and send Gia a bill.

After two hours, Linda decided she'd waited long enough. She climbed in a steamy shower and soaped up. She was surprised to see just how much of the color ran off her body. The shower water looked dirty as it swirled down the drain. But hadn't Gia warned her it was normal to lose a little color? She had to assume even a dimwit like

Gia knew what she was doing if she worked at the salon.

Stepping out of the shower, Linda checked her palms. They looked good, back to normal color. So were the bottoms of her feet. She dried herself with an old washcloth, not wanting any residual color to ruin her fluffy, white towels.

She needed to scrutinize herself much more closely, though. She hoped that the spray tan would make her look thinner. For that, she'd (1) put in her contacts, and (2) gone to the high-wattage-fluorescent-bulb-lined full-length bedroom mirror.

Lenses in place, Linda padded into her bedroom, switched on what she called her Mirror Mirror, and stood before it in her freshly showered, newly tanned one-thousand-calories-a-day skeletal nakedness.

"What the fuck?" she said at the sight.

At first, her brain couldn't compute the startling sight. Her tan must have streaked in the shower. It wasn't even, anywhere. Not on her arms, legs, chest, or her face. Taking a step closer to the mirror, Linda realized that, no, those weren't streaks. Just as the color had washed off her palms and feet bottoms, the shower had washed away other areas, revealing pictures and words all over her body, as if she were covered in graffiti.

Across the forehead, the word BITCH.

Up and down her arms and legs: HATER MEAN GIRL FAKE LIAR JELL-O SHOT SPIKER SAD LONELY RUDE SPITEFUL.

Across her chest: several graphic drawings of a smiling penis.

Across her back: her butt cheeks dimpled with white dots, as if she had a hideous case of cellulite. Wavy stink lines rising from her crack. And words with an arrow pointing down her spine: NEEDS GRANNY PANTIES.

Linda screamed. And screamed. And screamed some more. The sound waves reverberated through the Seaside Heights ozone.

Outside the house, a man walking his dog held his ears. The dog whimpered.

On the boardwalk, players froze mid-dart-toss.

On the beach, a flock of seagulls suddenly took flight.

Linda screamed so loud, and so long, she didn't hear the phone ringing at first. She grabbed her cell to call Janey, flipped it open, and found her friend already on the line, also screaming.

They screamed together.

Hoarse-voiced, fire in her eyes, Linda ranted, "I . . . will . . . kill . . . her!"

Janey was shrieking, "My forehead says USELESS."

"It could be worse."

"My chin says TWAT!" cried Linda's friend. "I didn't even know! People were looking at me funny on the walk to work, but I didn't know why."

"You didn't notice, after you showered?"

"I was running late," said Janey. "I just threw on my outfit and left."

"No makeup?"

"That was the whole point of the spray tan! The first customer came in to be seated, a hot guy who's been creeping on me for weeks. He took one look at me and said, 'Were you aware that the words USELESS TWAT are written on your face?'"

Linda gulped. "Janey, listen to me closely. Where are you now?"

"In the bathroom at Lorenzo's."

"And you're wearing a long-sleeved shirt?"

"My blazer. What I always wear to work."

"Have you, er, looked at your body?"

"You don't mean . . . hold on."

Linda could hear rustling, then the phone clunking on the counter next to the sink. Then she had to pull the phone away from her ear from the screams coming through.

Janey came back on the line. "On my chest . . . it's a . . . a smiling dick!"

Linda closed her eyes. "I know what it looks like. Listen closely, Janey. Meet me on the boardwalk outside Gia's house in five minutes."

"But I'm working . . ."

"With the words USELESS TWAT on your face?" Linda screamed. "It's war, Janey. Battle stations."

"Okay. I'll be there."

Chapter Forty

Four-Way Catfight

Frankie used his shoulder and plunged the shovel into the sandy dirt. The hole kept filling itself back in, though. He felt like a mythical creature, doomed to repeat the same task over and over, getting nowhere. Something had to change.

After his overnight shift, Frankie had come home. Showered. Made lunch. He'd been digging around in his backyard for an hour, trying to weed the garden that Dina had kept so well. It'd be helpful if he knew what was a weed and what was a real plant. But, then again, his goal wasn't a pretty garden. The goal was distraction. Frankie had been filling his nonworking hours, one by one, with activity—useless, pointless, backbreaking busywork.

It was a hard-fought battle, resisiting the desire to call Gia.

If he called her, he'd have to admit he was an

asshole and beg her to forgive him. But to do *that*, Frankie would have to admit he was wrong.

Thanks to his web of Seaside Heights friends and connections, Frankie learned that Rocky Gato swore nothing happened between him and Gia. The report came through reliable sources—more reliable that the gossips he'd picked up the story from in the first place. Frankie believed the second account to be accurate.

Word was, Rocky evoked the Guy Code. Tenet number one, as everyone knew: if your boy cheated, never let on to his girl about it. Tenet number two upheld the same spirit of loyalty: if you didn't touch a girl, never say you did. Only losers lied about their conquests. Only dickwads took credit for work they didn't do.

Rocky said nothing happened. The kid wasn't too bright—Frankie had gone to school with him— but Rocky wasn't a dickwad. Frankie believed him.

Why hadn't he given Gia a chance to explain what happened? Frankie let his wildfire emotions take over his good sense. The idea of Gia fooling around behind his back tore at his still-open wound. After four days of obsessing, Frankie saw that clearly. He'd taken out his anger at Dina on Gia, and now he was screwed. How could he apologize? He was too ashamed to try.

Frankie halfheartedly dug his shovel into the dirt again. It was useless. Nothing would grow here. Sandy soil, salty air, not enough rain.

Now he'd need another shower. As Frankie

walked into the back door of his house, through the kitchen, toward the bathroom, he had to pass through the living room, where his computer loomed on the coffee table. He slowed as he went by. It called to him, whispering urgently, "Turn me on."

"Oh, screw it," he said, sat on the couch, and booted up.

Within seconds, Frankie had navigated to You-Tube. He found the link to the video of Gia he'd watched about fifty times since they broke up.

"What's this?" He noticed a video response on the webpage, and a link to a new clip called "Four-Way Catfight."

Frankie edged forward on the couch, clicked on the new link, and watched.

The image: poor quality and shaky cam. Must have been taken with a phone camera. Frankie recognized the familiar corner on the boardwalk by Gia's rented bungalow. Two skinny blond girls yelling and banging on the door to the house. One picked up a rock and threw it through a window.

The audio: glass shattering. The video shooter's voice saying, "Damn!" Then the beach-house door crashed open. Gia and her cousin Bella emerged.

Gia looked furious. Her eyes round as quarters, she ran up to one of the blondes, finger in her face. "Stanley just fixed that window!" she yelled.

The other blonde went for Bella, manicured claws out. Bella got in a karate stance and knocked the blonde on her ass on the sidewalk in a flash.

Girl didn't know what hit her. Bella said, "Hey, the shit works! I never tried that move on a real person before!"

The shooter zoomed back to Gia and the skanky blonde, who had each other by the hair. The blonde yipped and grunted. Although she was taller than Gia, she was painfully thin. A strong fart would send her spinning. Gia could take her.

"Consider yourself tagged, bitch!" said Gia.

"I'll kill you," replied the blonde. Something about her face and her skin was funny. It looked as if she were covered in white graffiti. If there were actual words on her skin, she was moving too much for Frankie to read them.

By now, Gia and the Illustrated Bitch had thrown each other on the ground. The video shooter stayed with the action. A crowd formed a circle around them and cheered them on. At one point, Gia's skirt flipped up, and her bare bottom was caught on camera.

The shooter said, "Ass! Ass!" as if he'd never seen one before. Maybe he hadn't, the prick. If Frankie had been there, he'd have broken up the fight, not fanned the flames.

Then again, it was kinda hot.

The image froze there, on Gia's cute tush. Frankie checked the time stamp. It was uploaded only ten minutes ago. What happened next? He had to know if Gia was okay. Not sure what to do, he replayed the video.

When he refreshed the page, he noticed a video

response, a brand-new clip uploaded eight minutes ago, called "Shark Girl in the Tank."

Head reeling, Frankie clicked on it.

The image: Same stretch of the boardwalk, different angle. This one taken with the ocean in the background. The flashing lights of a police car. The shooter pushed forward, in time to catch footage of Gia, Bella, and the two blondes stepping through the double rear door of the police van. Their legs were visible, then the doors were slammed shut. The shooter stayed with the scene until the van siren bleated out a warning to move the crowd, then turned down a street access ramp and sped away.

He knew exactly where the van was headed. Like a shot, Frankie grabbed his car keys and tore out of the house.

Chapter Forty-one

Get In and Out of Jail Free

Gia had never before been in jail. It wasn't nearly as gritty and disgusting as she'd seen on TV prison shows. The Seaside Heights drunk tank—on a weekday afternoon—was clean and quiet as a church. After posing for mug shots against an ivory-painted cinder-block wall, and having their fingerprints taken, Gia, Bella, and the tan-tagged girls were taken to a windowless room. Nothing inside but a long bench, which was bolted to the gray linoleum floor. The room smelled faintly of ink and piss. One wall did have bars for that prison touch. Otherwise, as she sat, arms crossed, on the bench, Gia could have been waiting for a bus.

When they first arrived, Gia and Bella asked for Captain Morgan. Ironically, it was his day off.

"I hope you rot in here," said Linda, skin covered as much as possible in a hoodie.

"It's your fault, Linda! You did this! You! If you hadn't spiked those Jell-O shots, we wouldn't be here right now. Rocky told me what you did. Both of you."

"Look at what you did to me!" Linda unzipped her sweatshirt, to show the drawing on her chest.

Gia couldn't help admiring her artwork. Bella said, "The braciola looks really happy."

"I'm stuck with this for a week!" railed Linda.

"Big deal," said Gia. "What you did to me caused real physical pain, for hours. I had bruise marks on my thighs from riding the toilet all night."

Bella put up her hand, like swearing in at court. "It's true. I've seen them."

"The tan job is nothing compared to that," said Gia. "As far as we're concerned, you got off easy."

Janey, aka Useless Twat, who'd hit the boardwalk hard thanks to Bella, hadn't spoken much at all.

Linda said, "You're ugly! And stupid!"

Gia shook her head at Bella. "Can you believe this?"

A young cop, couldn't have been older than Gia, came into the tank with a plate of sandwiches. "Do any of you have peanut allergies?" he asked. None did. "Great. All we have to offer is PB and J. Hope that's okay. Also, I can make coffee, if anyone wants."

"Do you have French vanilla latte?" asked Gia.

He shook his head. "I can make a hazelnut cappuccino. Or an espresso. We chipped in last year and got a Krups."

"I'd love an espresso," said Bella.

"Twist of lemon rind?" asked the cop.

"Perfect," said Bella.

"Are you a friggin' waiter, or a cop? Christ!" sneered Linda.

"I apologize for her," said Gia. "She was raised by cockroaches. I'd love a hazelnut cappie. Two sugars, please."

He smiled and left.

Gia and Bella helped themselves to sammies and dug in. Gia was about halfway done when she noticed the other girls hadn't taken any.

"You're not hungry?" asked Gia, who was starved after the fight and the police station processing.

"I'm not eating that!" Linda snapped. "It's a thousand calories. You go ahead, shovel that into your fat face, and it'll land on your fat ass."

Janey didn't even look at the food, although she seemed to be swallowing back saliva.

It dawned on Gia, suddenly, that as much as her two enemies hated her, for God knew what reason, they hated themselves more. Denying themselves food? When they had to be ravenous? Gia was an extreme dieter herself in high school, briefly. She stopped after her first fainting spell. These kids had been starving themselves for years. No wonder they were so mean.

"Tell me why," said Gia. "What have I ever done to you? And don't give me that old story when we were cheerleaders, how you tried to prank me with the bloomers and the cartwheels, and you wound up pranking yourself."

"I hate you," said Linda coldly, "because the world is at your friggin' feet. You can just sit there, eating your food, not caring about how fat you are. In case you haven't noticed, we're arrested. In *jail*. Does that bother you? No. You flirt with the cop."

"Making the best of a bad situation is a crime?" said Gia. "I wasn't arrested for flirting."

"You just glide through life! You don't care!"

"I do care. And I'd say *stumble,* not *glide.*"

"That's not what I mean," said Linda, frustrated.

"Then what do you—"

Bubbling over, Linda yelled, "All my life, I've been trying to be perfect. That's what my parents wanted, and I did whatever I could to deliver. Instead of loving me for being perfect, people hate me for it!"

Bella said, "I wouldn't say *perfect*. But she's right about the other thing. People do hate her."

"But *you,* Gia," Linda spit. "You do whatever you want. You eat whatever you want. Make a fool of yourself. Act like an *idiot*! You don't care what people think, and they love you for it."

"Right again," said Bells. "You are lovable, Gia."

Janey finally spoke. "I'm not jealous like Linda. I'm just a hater in general. I enjoy it. Gives my life meaning."

Gia frowned. Janey really was a useless twat. But Linda? She was exploding with rage. "If you just ate like a normal person, you might be nicer, and people would like you more," Gia suggested. "You have to cut yourself some slack, Linda. No one's perfect. No one should try to be. Relax a little. Here. Have a bite. You'll feel better."

The blonde shrank from the sandwich like a vampire from garlic. "I'm not eating that."

The cop delivered their drinks. Gia took a sip and said, "You've spent too much of your life denying yourself and resenting people who don't. If you hate me because I don't worry about getting fat—"

"*Fatter*," said Linda.

"Do you even know what would make you happy?" asked Gia.

Linda thought about it. "I'd be happy if you were as miserable as I am."

"Well, that's not going to happen, Linda. I love food. I love drinking, boys, dancing until my feet swell. I love my family, my friends, my job, my boss. And I love my body, especially the badonk." Gia slapped her ass. "I'm not signing up for misery, no matter what happens to me. I'll always find a way to have fun and be happy."

"That's some jailhouse wisdom right there," said Bella.

"Bullshit," said Linda.

But it wasn't. Gia felt another sparkling wave of clarity wash over her. Maybe it was the sugar rush, but whatever. Life might knock her off her stilettos. She might lose more often than she won in the softball basket toss of life. But even in her bleakest hour, Gia could reach into her soul and pull out a nugget of joy. This was her special and unique talent. Having fun and raising the spirits of people around her just might be what she was born to do, how she could contribute to society in a meaningful way.

It was as if a thousand neon lights flickered on in her head.

Whew, she thought. How awesome to have figured out her life's real purpose. She thought her purpose was to fall in love with a hot guido. But Gia was already in love—with life itself. She made a vow to remind herself of that whenever she stressed over not having a boyfriend. Eventually, one would arrive. She was only twenty-one years old. Her years of passion and love were just beginning. True excitement was waiting, and the surprise when love arrived. And it surely would. Sooner rather than later. When it did, love would set her free. Freer than she was at the moment, you know, in jail.

"Giovanna Spumanti!" Another, older cop appeared at the bars, calling her name.

"Present."

"You've been released."

"I'm not leaving without Bella," Gia said, taking her cousin's hand.

"Isabella Rizzoli?" he asked. "You're sprung, too."

They jumped up and down, hugging. The cop opened the cage door for them. Gia grabbed a sammie for the road.

Janey bitched, "What about us?"

"As soon as the clerk gets back from her dinner break," he said.

"Why do they get to go?" asked Linda.

The cop closed the cage door and locked it again. "They've got friends in low places."

Gia paused, turned back to her old classmates, and said, "I forgive you both. I'm sorry for what we did. Sort of. I hope you can forgive us, too, and move on."

"Fuck off," said Linda.

"Happy to," Gia said. "Bye!"

———

Gia had to blink to make sure she wasn't hallucinating. Nope, it was definitely him, pacing the lobby of the police station, worrying his baseball cap to shreds. "Frankie!"

"You're out! That's a relief. You look . . . you look great, Gia. I'm so sorry," he spouted. "I was out of line on the phone. I shouldn't have said those things to you. It doesn't mean anything, but I've been in hell since we hung up."

"Slow down," she said, laughing. "How did you get us out?"

"I asked the chief of police to drop the charges."

Bella asked, "Just like that? He did?"

Frankie smiled. "*She* did. Old friend of the family."

"Anyone in this town who isn't?"

He thought about it for a second. "No."

"Can we go?" asked Bella. "They might change their minds."

The trio walked out of the station house onto Sherman Avenue, into the waning sunlight of evening. "Where are we?" asked Gia.

"Only a few blocks from the boardwalk," said Frankie, pointing toward the ocean. "I've got my truck, if you want a lift."

The three of them piled into the Ford pickup. Gia could barely see over the dashboard. Frank drove them back to the Kearney Avenue shack. Bella got out and waited for Gia to follow.

Gia said, "I'm going to take a ride with Frankie."

"Are you sure?" asked Bella. "No offense to you, Frankie, but you dumped my girl over something she didn't do."

"I was . . . wrong," he said. "Whoa, that wasn't as hard as I thought. I was wrong. Wrong, wrong, wrong."

Frankie's expression, the peaceful relief, was irresistible. He was the same beautiful gorilla Gia had fallen for at first, but now he was humble, too. Nothing was sexier than a man who owned up to his mistakes and tried to put things right.

A rush of heat hit her, as if she'd mainlined Spanish fly. "Oh, I'm sure," said Gia, grinning at Frankie.

"Got your phone?" asked Bella.

Gia flashed her cell. When Bella was gone, Gia said, "Let's go."

"Where to?"

"Your place."

"Not much to see there. My ex took most of the furniture."

"Do you have a bed?" Gia asked.

He gulped, then gunned the motor.

————

Three hours later, the pair lay naked on Frankie's bed, breathing hard, their clothes all over the floor.

Gia said, "That was all I hoped it would be. And I thought about it. Like, a lot."

"Me too," he said, lazily stroking her skin, up and down, giving her chills. "I thought about it pretty much constantly since the night we met."

"The nonfire at Tantastic? That was weeks ago."

"It was your breath. I couldn't get it out of my mind. I thought, 'Who is the girl, and why does she smell like pickles?'"

"Love at first sniff?"

He laughed. "What about you?"

She thought about it. "I loved it when you carried me out of the salon like a doll. And when you sent me the slippers. And when we smushed on the beach. Even when you peed on me."

"I felt really bad about that," he admitted, nuzzling her neck. "But if I had to do it again, I would."

"I'd want you to!" she said, feeling her insides turn gooey from his lips on her throat. "Okay, I know when I really fell for you. It was when you confided to me about your brother and your ex. I felt a real connection then."

Gia had to go there. If they were to have a real relationship, his grudge-holding issue had to be dealt with. He couldn't possibly be with her 100 percent if anger hovered over his head like a dark cloud.

Frankie started to kiss along her collarbone, and down between her boobs. When he took her nipple into his mouth, she gasped, "Okay, conversation over."

But then Gia's phone started Deadmau5-ing. "Not now!" she said, reaching for her cell and checking caller ID. "It's Bella. I have to take it. . . . Hello?"

Bella said, "Game on."

Gia sat up in bed.

"What?" asked Frankie.

"They were spotted at the Beachcomber Bar," said Bella.

"Okay, I'll be there."

Gia hung up and started getting dressed. "I have to go. Something's up. You shouldn't get involved."

Frankie groaned. "Am I going to have to get you out of jail again?"

She smiled. "Maybe?"

He laughed. "I'm coming with you."

Chapter Forty-two

To a Great Night

Ed Caldwell looked around the Beachcomber Bar and shook his head. "Nothing but zoo creatures here. That girl is a fox trap. I'd gnaw my own arm off to get away from her the morning after."

Bender Newberry pointed with his beer bottle at a couple of girls on the end of the bar. "What about those two besties?"

"More like *beasties*," said Ed, snorting. "Only dimes will do, bro."

Only tens. Only the sexiest girl in town would do. After the humiliation of being shot down by Isabella Rizzoli, Ed needed a major ego boost. The only way he could redeem himself was to pound a smoking-hot bitch, then leave her like trash as soon as he was done. That'd make him feel so much better.

His boy Bender startled, then swiveled on his

stool, ducking his face under his hand. "Dude, it's her."

"Who?"

"Bella," said Ben.

Looking toward the entrance, Ed saw her coming. Everyone in the place watched her with hungry eyes. No question, Bella was the hottest girl in the room, in any room. And she was alone. Unprotected. No cock-blocking cousins or guido, muscle-brained bodyguards. Ben had told Ed how her boss, Tony, had thrown him out of the gym a few days before.

"What's the play?" Ben asked.

Ed thought about it. "Be cool. If she sees us, she'll probably walk out."

But she didn't. The opposite. As Ben and Ed watched, Bella took a seat at the horseshoe-shaped bar directly opposite them. She ordered a shot of tequila, drank it, then looked up. Bella blinked when she saw them and seemed confused.

Ed smiled, raised his beer in salute to her. Bender, the little bitch, squirmed nervously, muttering, "Holy shit, holy shit . . ."

"She has no idea we know each other," said Ed. "Look at her trying to figure this out."

Bella appeared to be totally thrown off by the sight of them together. Curiousity got to her.

"She's coming!" squeaked Ben.

"Shut up," hissed Ed. "Let me do the talking."

Bella strutted over, the dress she was barely wearing—some low-cut, black mini-thing—hugging every miraculous curve of her body. *Not an ounce of lard on her,* thought Ed. A woman who knew how to maintain herself properly. The boys swiveled in their stools as she got closer, and closer. Standing right in front of them, she said, "I don't freakin' believe this. You guys are friends?"

"Actually, we just met," said Ed. "Just this minute."

"Really," she said, not convinced. "What are the odds?"

Ben got into it. "Wait, you two know each other?"

Ed smiled. Good boy. "I guess we're all friends now."

Bella said, "I wouldn't say that."

"Something between you two?" asked Ed, pointing with his beer at one, then the other.

Ben said, "We had a misunderstanding. All cleared up, though. I hope. You got my note, right?"

Bella nodded slowly. "Yeah. How are you feeling?"

Looking confused, Ben said, "I'm good."

"Last time I saw you, you said you had two months to live," she reminded him.

"Whoa! Dude! That's harsh," said Ed, keeping up the we-just-met act. "Can I buy you a drink?"

Ben said, "Uh, sure. Alcohol doesn't affect my condition."

"How about you?" Ed asked Bella.

"I don't know."

"Are you meeting someone?" asked Ben.

"No."

Ed's lips turned into his most seductive smile. "Then why not? Yo! Bartender. Shots all around."

The bartender set up three shot glasses and filled them to the top with tequila.

"Whatever's happened in the past, let's forgive and forget and focus on the future," said Ed. He raised his glass, as did Bella and Ben. "To a great night!"

They drank.

Chapter Forty-three

Fucking Out of Towners

Weaving on her heels, Bella slurred, "So this is my room."

Ed, wasted, asked, "Is your cousin here?"

"She's on a date," said Bella, stumbling around, knocking against the dresser. By all appearances, she was shitfaced-wasted, drunky drunk. Not so. She *was* buzzed. After five shots, anyone would be. But Bella could hold her tequila.

"Are you sure Gia's not around? I do *not* want to see that girl," said Bender, twisted beyond belief.

"We're all alone," said Bella. "Just the three of us."

She dimmed the lights and slowly took off her jewelry. The two guys stared in rapt amazement at the sight. She said, "What're you waiting for? Strip!"

Bender and Ed immediately fumbled to undress. Bella struggled to keep her face under control, and to act as if she were totally turned on by their bodies. Which, she grudgingly had to admit, weren't that bad.

"Sit on the bed," she said.

The guys sat down on her queen-size bed, naked, semihard, openmouthed, practically drooling. "Come 'ere," said Ed, reaching for her.

Swallowing her disgust, Bella let him guide her onto the bed and sat between them. Thank God she had her clothes on, or there was no way she could fake not being grossed out.

Ed said, "Yo, bro, this is a first. No verification needed tonight."

"Sweet!" said Ben, then they high-fived over her head.

Bella said, "I thought you guys didn't know each other."

"We don't," said Ed. "Shhh. Don't talk anymore, okay? Just relax, close your eyes, and let us do our thing."

It took every ounce of Bella's strength not to unleash a nose-crusher jab on him. But she bit her lip, hard, and started to lie down.

The bedroom door crashed open.

"What the fuck?" said the boys.

The lights came on. In the doorway, Tony Troublino was holding a rifle.

Aimed at Ed Caldwell's forehead.

"Who the hell are you?" asked Ed.

"I'm the badass mother who's going to splatter this room with your brains," Tony shouted. "And

then your guts. Intestines all over the freakin' walls!"
He cocked the rifle. "Fucking out of towners!"

Oh, Jesus H. friggin' Christ, Bella thought. She
couldn't help rolling her eyes. She knew he'd
overdo it.

"No, Tony!" she pleaded, playing her role far
more convincingly. "Don't hurt them!"

"I have to *kill* them, Bella! If I can't have you, no
one will. And after I blow their heads off, I'm going
to kill *you.* And then, I'm going to put this gun in my
mouth and blast my own brains across the room."

Ben started crying. "I just wanted to get laid."

"You can have her, man. She's all yours. We'll just
slip out of here," tried Ed.

Tony re-aimed the rifle and fired. Ed was hit in
the forehead. The impact flung him back on the bed.
Red splattered the walls and covered his face.

"Mommy!" cried Ben.

"Your mommy can't save you now," said Tony, recocking and firing, hitting Ben right over his heart.
Green splattered across his chest, and all over the
bed.

"I'm bleeding green!" sobbed Ben. "I'm an alien!"

"Or is it your hemotitis?" asked Bella.

Ben touched his green blood, smearing it all over
his chest.

Bella said, "Green, Tony? It's supposed to be red."
She looked down at herself. "And it's splattered on
my dress!"

"Yo, Jeff! Man, you fucked up," said Tony. "We
said red paintballs only."

Jeff "Shoot the Geek" Spicoli came into the room. "Sorry, man. I thought it was all red. Let me check."

The human target reloaded the rifle with red paintballs, pointed the rifle at Ed, who was still in shock. "This is for dogging me to sell you E. I'm not a dealer, dude. I told you a million times, but you don't listen!" Jeff fired, and a burst of red appeared on Ed's thigh, close to his balls.

"Damn," said Jeff. "So close."

Rick came into the room and said, "Let me try it." He shot off a round, hitting Ben in the stomach.

Frankie squeezed in and said, "I've always wanted to do this," and shot both Ed and Ben, in quick-fire succession, in the shoulders.

"Clear out, boys, it's my turn," said Gia.

Rick, Frankie, Jeff, and Tony made way for her. Gia took the rifle and said, "Okay, Bender. You deserve this for being rude and obnoxious and calling me 'fucktard.' And you, Ed. 'Nothing much'? I'll show you nothing much!" Gia tried to cock the rifle. "Um, how does this thing work? Point and shoot? Oops."

A splatter of red paint appeared on the ceiling. Gia said, "I got this. Let me try one more . . . yikes." A paintball hit the window. "Don't tell Stanley!"

Ben, meanwhile, was still whimpering, his hands covered in paint, not comprehending what was happening. Ed was back in control and seemed to understand the situation. "Stop, okay? Everyone, stop," he screamed.

"Will *you*?" asked Bella, taking the rifle from Gia.

Ed asked heatedly, "Will I what?"

"Stop your revolting Rule of Ten summer date-rape game? Stop drugging girls' drinks and perving on them when they're not even conscious of how disgusting you are?"

"Mind your own business, bitch," spat Ed.

Bam. Bella shot him in the balls.

He howled as if he'd been shot for real and curled into the fetal position.

Ben said, "We're done, okay? Never again. It was all Ed's idea. I just went along with him because—"

"Because you're a wimp and a follower who does whatever your master tells you?" asked Bella. "Including throwing me in your hot tub and ripping my dress?"

Bam. She clipped his nuts, too. He caved into himself, sobbing and sniveling like the prissy little bitch he was.

Recocking, Bella fired again. The rifle clicked.

Out of ammo.

Bella flipped the rifle around and took a step toward the bed to beat their heads in with it. But Tony grabbed the barrel on her upswing and said, "I think you got them, sweetheart."

"I'm not sure they understand," she said.

Tony said, "You boys get the message?"

Ed and Ben nodded, gasping, from the bed.

Just to make sure, Tony leaned in, real close. Softly, chillingly (it made Bella's neck hairs stand up), he said, "Stay out of Jersey."

"I took some money to clean the walls," said Gia, who'd found their wallets in their jeans. She threw the pile of their clothes on the floor. "Now get out."

Still hunched over, Ben and Ed fell off the bed, took their clothes, and slithered away.

Gia smiled. "That was fun!"

Jeff said, "Um, can I have my gun back now?"

He looked a little nervous when Bella handed it to him.

———

"Is it weird that I got really turned on firing the rifle?" asked Bella later, in her bed, naked, and not alone.

Tony lay next to her, on his back, arms folded behind his head. "Is it weirder that I got excited watching you shoot those bastards?"

"Meanwhile, your acting! 'I'm the badass mother who's gonna splatter your brains and guts and then bite your heads off, and grind your bones . . .' Where'd you get that?!"

Tony smiled. "I see a lot of Vin Diesel movies."

She laughed and decided she'd never been happier than she felt at this moment. One night with Tony erased six years with Bobby. Sex with Tony felt like a completely different experience, as if she were born the moment he took her into his arms. As if they were the only two people who'd ever done it.

Tickling his elbow, she said, "You have the sexiest wenis I've ever seen."

"You have the sexiest everything. I need to study

each part of you much more closely, though. It could take a while. Hope you're not going anywhere."

Oh, shit. The crash landing back to reality. "We're supposed to leave town in three days," she blurted. "I'm sorry. I should have told you sooner. I shouldn't have lied on my job application, either. The plan was always to come for a month and then go back to Brooklyn." Bella would start college in September. After years of campaigning for it, she finally had the blessing (and financial support) of her parents. She should be thrilled to begin her new life, free of Bobby, free from guilt, free from Rizzoli's.

Bella didn't want to be free of Tony.

"But that was before," he said.

"Do you believe in signs?"

"What, like stop signs, or yield signs?"

"Don't be a jerkoff," she said. "I'm serious. I've been waiting for a sign about my future. And I think I got a pretty clear one last week. You know, my car was stolen."

He seemed to tense up. "Oh?"

"If that's not a sign to go back to Brooklyn, then what is?"

"You should see that as a sign to stay. It's a message that you shouldn't go anywhere."

Bella hadn't considered that. "Maybe."

"I'm not going to tell you what to do. I know you don't like that. But I want you to stay. Work in the gym, move into my house."

"With your grandparents?"

"We'll get our own place. Stanley will rent us

some crappy dump. We'll have mad hot sex every night and every morning."

She liked the sound of that. "But I'm going to NYU in the fall. I've put off college for years already, Tony."

"You should go to college. Rutgers is just as good as NYU. Maybe you could get into Princeton. It isn't too far away."

"Yeah, right."

"I'm just saying. New Jersey has great colleges, too. I totally support your going back to school. I'll drive you, round-trip, every day. And then, you can do your homework while I cook you the best food you'll ever taste in your life. We'll eat. Make love, snuggle all night. It'll be heaven."

"But I can't enroll at Rutgers in September. I'd have to apply, get in, fill out all the forms . . ."

"I've got some friends. Just establish residence in New Jersey—which we can set up tomorrow if you want—and you're in. I'm telling you, Bells, it's a great school."

"Okay," she said, surprising herself. "Yes. I'll stay."

He sat up in bed, excited. "You will? Do you want to think about it?"

"Now you change your mind?"

Tony pulled her into a tight hug. "I don't want you to regret it later on. But I'm not changing my mind about you. I've never felt this way before, and— don't mean to brag—I've been with a lot of women."

"I get the point," she said, swatting him.

"I'm falling for you. I'm not letting you go."

Chapter Forty-four

Don't Beat Me, Bitch!

Gia couldn't stop smiling when she saw Frankie
waiting for her. He looked yummy in a suit. Not as
yummy as in his birthday suit, but close.

It was July 30, her last night in the beach house.
Frankie invited her to a dress-up fancy dinner at Luna
Rosa, a classy Italian restaurant next to Karma. She'd
never been, although she'd wanted to try it. Gia put off
going with Bella because she hoped to have a romantic
dinner there, just her and the man of her dreams.

And here he was, standing as she approached
their table.

"I got you a present," he said after kissing her.

"Another present?"

"Here."

A T-shirt, folded up. She unfurled it. It had the
DON'T EAT ME, BITCH! lettering, but with a big pink *B*
stuck in front of *eat*.

"Oh my God!" said Gia.

He said, "They started selling them at the Shore Store after your four-way catfight video appeared on YouTube."

"Thanks." She kissed him again. Any excuse to snuggle, not that she needed one.

"I have another surprise. They're coming this way."

Gia followed his eyes and saw a vaguely familiar couple heading to their table. She had seen them before, on the boardwalk. They were holding hands. The guy was smoking hot. But, of course, he would be.

"You must be Gia," said the woman.

"And you're Dina, and Lou," said Gia, smiling, shaking hands. "You guys could be twins," she added to Frankie's older brother.

"We were as inseparable as conjoined twins when we were kids," said Lou. He and Frankie smiled at each other. Dina exhaled with her whole body.

The older couple sat down to join Frankie and Gia for dinner. A double date, with family, at the best restaurant in town. Gia had been excited about a romantic dinner, just the two of them. But this was even better.

Dina and Lou talked excitedly about their wedding.

"We want you to come, Gia," said Dina, reaching to hold her hand across the table. "If it weren't for you, the wedding wouldn't be happening."

Dina had acknowledged the elephant at the

table, which had been reduced to a tick. Apparently, at some point in the last few days, Frankie had given his brother and ex-girlfriend his blessing. He'd forgiven them. He'd released his anger and let his heart fill again with joy. If Gia had anything to do with that, well, dang. She was honored.

Gia blushed. "Of course I'll be there! I'm so happy for you both." Smiling at Frankie, she said, "For all of us."

"*Salute!*" said Lou, toasting to their happiness.

He insisted on paying the bill, too. Frankie let him, which was another goodwill gesture between the brothers. After they left, Frankie and Gia lingered at the bar.

"Dina's right," he said. "If I hadn't fallen for you, I don't know if I could've gotten over it."

"I'm sure you would have eventually," she said.

He shifted on his seat. Taking her hands, he said, "I have to know where we stand."

Gia had been thinking about nothing else since Bella told her she'd decided to stay in Seaside Heights with Tony.

It'd be easy to stay here, too, with Frankie. Gia could move into his practically empty house, decorate it for them. She'd work at Tantastic with Maria. Learn to cook. Learn to clean. She'd find a comfortable place for herself in Frankie's family. Now that her mom had Ted Katz, Gia wasn't obliged to go back to Brooklyn and keep her company.

"I want to stay with you, Frankie. You are my dream come true."

"But?"

She nodded. "I know I said that we couldn't get serious unless you could find it in your heart to forgive your brother. I'm so proud of you for doing it, really. But seeing you tonight with Lou made me miss my father, badly. His wife is pregnant, I told you that. I couldn't live with myself if I didn't fix things between Dad and me now, before he becomes a father again. He deserves a clean slate. Otherwise, it wouldn't be fair to my future brother or sister. I'm going back to Brooklyn to pack up, and then I'm moving to Philly to be near Dad."

Frankie looked unbearably sad. "I guess I get it."

"It's not far. We'll talk every day."

"Twice a day."

"And we'll visit. As soon as Dad and I are cool, I'll come back here," she promised. "To you. You're still my boy. No matter where I am." Gia put his hand against her heart. "You feel me?"

"Yeah, I feel you. And I love you."

Gia's heart melted. "I love you, too."

And just like that, Gia got everything she'd ever wanted.

Chapter Forty-five

The Surprise Factor

A car honked in the driveway outside. Gia and Bella were both busy packing and ignored it.

But the horn toots didn't stop. In the city, you'd get fined for honking like that, thought Bella. Five minutes later, she'd had enough.

Throwing her underwear into the suitcase, she said, "I'm going to shut that guy up."

She jogged out to the driveway. Her Honda was parked there, shining in the sun, looking brand-new. And next to it stood Tony.

"My car! I can't believe it!"

She rushed over to touch it, amazed. This was a freakin' miracle. Her car found, in better shape than when it was stolen? How often did that happen? Like, never? It should be stripped down to the frame, on cinder blocks somewhere. Not souped up with the motor purring!

Then it hit Bella. Tony's sly, smug expression was the final clue. "You did this. You stole my wheels."

"You were jogging to work, so I towed your car to my grandfather's garage. The idea was to get it running and drive it back that day. But then you and I got in a fight before I could tell you. And it took a lot longer to fix the motor, which was held together with rubber bands and chewing gum, by the way. You should get your money back from the Brooklyn greaseballs you go to."

"It's been ten days! You could have told me."

"But then I was committed to surprising you." Meekly he added, "Surprise!"

Bella wasn't laughing.

"You'd rather I didn't fix it?" he asked, seeing her expression.

"Don't get me wrong. I'm grateful. Thanks so much for doing this for me, Tony."

"You're welcome?"

"You convinced me that the stolen car was a sign that I should stay. But you knew it wasn't stolen. You lied."

Gia came out to see what was going on. "Hey! The Honda! Is it running? Does this mean you'll drive me back to Brooklyn? Please? I hate the friggin' bus."

"We're both going back to the city," said Bella.

"*What?*" That was Tony.

"Gia, can you give us a minute?"

They waited for Gia to leave. Then he said, "You're overreacting. I lied because I wanted to surprise you. And I really want you to stay."

"I know," said Bella softly. "I really want to stay, too. These have been the best three days of my life, with you."

"And that made you change your mind?" he asked sharply.

"I'll never do better than you. You're the best boyfriend in the world and I love you. But my heart was set on NYU before we ever met. It's been my dream since I was a kid, to go to college in the city. I already had one boyfriend talk me out of it. And I don't want to look back five years from now and think of you as another Bobby."

"But Rutgers . . ."

"With respect, Rutgers isn't NYU. I have an amazing opportunity, financial backing. My parents would never pay my tuition if I lived down the Shore with you. They're old-fashioned that way. I've been in a relationship since I was sixteen years old. It makes no sense to say falling in love with you made me want to be by myself. But that's how I feel."

Tony opened his mouth to protest. But then he said, "I hate this. So we end here? I'm never fixing your car again."

"Can't we just, like, float? See each other when we see each other?"

"We can try that. The city's only eighty miles away. And now you've got reliable wheels."

"You'll visit me, too?"

"Damn straight. I love New York. I'll come up whenever you want. And if you tell me to take off, I'll go."

They smiled at each other. Bella got the sense that this was an ending, even if she and Tony did stay in touch and continued to see each other. It was an ending of a beginning. Bella felt sad, and proud of both of them, for doing the right thing. Whatever this moment was—a soft breakup—Bella fell deeper in love with Tony.

"It'll work out," she said.

"If not, we'll always have Seaside Heights."

"Don't say *that*," she said, suddenly terrified that they'd never see each other again.

"I'm kidding!"

She groaned and took a playful swing at his belly. Tony caught her fist in his hand and kissed her knuckes. She fell against him and tucked her head under his chin.

"We're not done," he said. "We're marinating."

Chapter Forty-six

Tramps Like Us

Maria, honestly? She was a big, bronzed baby. When she cried, mascara streamed down her face.

"The orange face and black stripes," noticed Gia. "It says tiger more than than cougar."

Stanley said, "I should be crying! This renovation is costing me a friggin' fortune."

"It's gonna be fantastic," said Maria. "So shut up, you cheap bastard. With love."

"You forgot *fat shit, with love*," whispered Gia.

Her former (as of today) boss said, "Who am I to talk?" and pinched her tiny paunch through the cheetah-print halter dress.

Stanley said, "Hey, squeezing you is my job." He grabbed his once and future wife and dipped her into a smooch. Considering the brand-new kitchen and soon-to-be-replaced banister, not to mention the new windows and freshly painted bedroom walls, the Kearney Avenue dump was now a palace, fit for the real estate king and Mystic queen of Seaside Heights.

Gia's pouf might as well have been ten feet tall. That's how proud she was of herself for reuniting her summer mom and dad, which was how she thought of Maria and Stanley. Hey, what she couldn't fix in her real life, she could manage down the Shore.

She wouldn't bet a fitty they'd be together this time next summer. But, then again, who knew what made love last? It was a game of chance, luck, *destiny*, experience—but not too much hard work, as far as Gia could tell. How hard could it be to show the person you loved that you cared? All you had to do was smush every chance you got and treat them with kindness and respect. Easy.

Bella came out the back door and loaded the last of their suitcases into the trunk of the Honda. "I think that's it," she said. "If you find anything . . ."

"You'll have to come back for it," said Maria. "I might've hidden a few things to make sure you do."

"I'll call you," promised Gia, giving Maria a hug. "Treat her right," Gia said to Stanley. "Make sure she gets plenty of fresh air, sunshine, and tequila."

Bella said her good-byes, and they were off.

———

One stop before they hit the road. Bella parked by a ramp leading to the beach. The cousins jumped out and ran toward the ocean. They waded into the surf up to their ankles. In a habit by now, Gia scanned the horizon for a telltale dorsal fin on the ocean surface. No sign, as usual. No sharks had been spotted in Seaside Heights since the "rescue" weeks ago. Gia hoped that her shark was safe, healthy, happy, and hooking up with a hot boy shark somewhere out there in the deep, wide ocean.

Bella said, "The water is much warmer than when we first arrived. By September, it'll be like a bathtub."

"But we won't be here to feel it," said Gia. "Tell me the truth. Are you sad to go?"

Bella drew a circle with her toe in the sand. "I was upset last night with Tony. I heard you waaing, too."

Gia's saying her good-byes to Frankie had been a soggy, ten-tissue scene. "It was sad. But this morning? Honestly? I feel kind of relieved to go. I love Frankie. He's the ultimate future husband. And if I stayed here, I could see us getting married one day."

"Same with Tony," said Bella. "I love that kid to death."

"But I don't want to get married," said Gia. "All my life I wanted to find a boyfriend. And now that I have a great one, a really great one, I want to be single."

"I totally get that. We're only twenty-one! Tony and Frankie, God bless 'em, they took us to the next level. But I agree with you. I think our future husbands are somewhere out there. Far out there. Men we haven't met yet."

"Men who haven't been born yet!" said Gia.

"You think there'll be a lot of cute boys at NYU?"

"Are you kidding? Dozens on every block. A lot

of them will be gay, but whatever," said Gia. "What about Philly?"

"Come on! Philly? A hardworking industrial town? It'll be crawling with guido juicehead gorillas."

Gia hugged Bella. "No matter where we go, or who we hook up with . . ."

"Or whatever happens with our parents . . ."

"We'll be cousins, besties, sisters, roomies."

A big wave came in and knocked them backward. Gia went down. "Help!" she said, giggling. Not really needing it.

Bella sighed heavily, then went in to fetch her. "Now my shorts are gonna get wet," she grumbled. "If I didn't love you so much, I'd let you drown!"

Gia pulled Bella under, and they came to the surface laughing. They walked barefoot back to the car, squeezed out their hair and changed into dry shorts and T-shirts. With one last look at the ocean, the cousins got back in the Honda—which smelled like evergreen air freshener now, and not week-old anchovy pizza the way it used to—and drove down Ocean Terrace, toward Route 37 and the Garden State Parkway.

"The car. It's reborn to run," said Bella in the driver's seat.

"What if it dies and we're stranded in the Pine Barrens?" asked Gia, opening her window to get a last whiff of the salty air.

"We use our phones, duh. I've got mine right . . . should be in my pocket . . . check my Chanel."

Gia searched through her cousin's handbag, but couldn't find her iPhone. "Well, my cell is right here," Gia said, displaying hers like a game-show prize. "At least *one* of us can keep track of her shit."

Shaking her head, Bella said, "I bet Maria really did hide it."

They got about two blocks before a white cruiser flashed its lights and pulled them over. "What now?" asked Bella.

The cop exited his car slowly and ambled over to the driver's-side window.

"I have a report this car's been stolen," said Captain Morgan.

"You shaved!" said Gia, not missing the mustache at all. "I love it. But you have a mustache tan line. Go to Tantastic. My girl Maria will hook you up with a facial mist."

"Is that a drug? A facial mist?"

Bella said, "The car wasn't actually stolen. It was borrowed. By a friend, and returned."

"The passenger in the backseat is not wearing her seat belt," he said. "I could give you a ticket for that."

The three of them turned to look at Giraffe, still in her bra, beads, and thong. Also accessorized with sunglasses and a hat that said ITALIAN AMERICAN PRINCESS.

"I'll do it," said Gia, reaching over to put on Giraffe's seat belt.

"All right then," said the cop. "You girls leaving town?"

"Fleeing the scene," said Bella.

He guffawed. "It'll be a lot quieter around here without you."

"Does that mean you'll miss us?" asked Gia.

"Are you coming back? I'll need some time to prepare."

"Hells, yeah!" said Gia. "We'll be back next summer for sure."

"Probably before," said Bella.

"I'll watch my back." He smiled, which was the first time they'd seen it. "Have a safe trip home." He thudded the Honda roof twice.

Bella peeled back onto the road. "I guess we have official clearance to leave."

They took a right. Big blue-and-white signs on either side of the highway-ramp exit to the town read THANKS FOR VISITING SEASIDE HEIGHTS! HURRY BACK!

Gia screamed out the window, "We will! Bye for now, Seaside. See you next year!"

"Stay cool!" added Bella. She slowed at the top of the ramp. "Can I merge?"

"Wait, a car's coming," said Gia, looking out the window.

"Tell me when."

"Now! Go, go, go!"